Candace Bushnell is the critically acclaimed and bestselling author of *Sex and the City*, *Four Blondes*, *Trading Up* and *Lipstick Jungle*. Her first book, *Sex and the City*, was the basis for the HBO hit television show and movie. Her fourth, *Lipstick Jungle*, is now a drama on NBC. She lives in New York City.

For more information, visit www.candacebushnell.com

'Bushnell's unparalleled ability to capture type borders on uncanny; the perceptiveness of David Attenborough studying a rare bird . . . Bushnell is clearly a master observer: no details evades, from the trapping of her protagonists' world to their hopes and dreams'
The Times

' this clued-up a   only gets the labels right, but tell   *Independent*

' s a shining examp   mentary . . . s has matured as   o expose the warped materialism that life in the fast lane breeds, turning decent people into twisted, label-obsessed caricatures. It's all served up with a dose of devilishly dark humour, which makes us blissfully unaware we re being preached to. A hugely entertaining yarn with fascinating, and at times repellent, characters'
Time Out

'Bushnell writes like a dream'   Book of the Week, *Daily Mirror*

'Bushnell reveals a world packed with feuds, friendships and inappropriate affairs in the stylish company of a bunch of engagingly shallow urbanites . . . Mercilessly observed interactions between all her very rich characters in all their bitchy, ditsy, self-serving glory'
Daily Mail

'Every so often a writer comes along who is so in tune with the times in which they are living that their creation becomes an emblem of their era . . . Bushnell has done it again. *One Fifth Avenue* manages to be slap-bang on the nose about current preoccupations'
Express

ALSO BY
Candace Bushnell

Sex and the City

Four Blondes

Trading Up

Lipstick Jungle

Candace Bushnell

One
Fifth
Avenue

ABACUS

First published in Great Britain in 2008 by Little, Brown
This edition published in 2009 by Abacus
Reprinted 2009 (three times), 2010

A CIP catalogue record for this book
is available from the British Library.

ISBN: 978-0-349-11954-0

Design by Chris Welch
Printed and bound in Great Britain by
Clays Ltd, St Ives plc

Papers used by Abacus are natural, renewable and
recyclable products sourced from well-managed forests and certified
in accordance with the rules of the Forest Stewardship Council.

Mixed Sources
Product group from well-managed
forests and other controlled sources
www.fsc.org Cert no. SGS-COC-004081
© 1996 Forest Stewardship Council
FSC

Abacus
An imprint of
Little, Brown Book Group
100 Victoria Embankment
London EC4Y 0DY

An Hachette UK Company
www.hachette.co.uk

www.littlebrown.co.uk

FOR HEATHER SCHRODER

Prologue

It was only a part in a TV series, and only a one-bedroom apartment in New York. But parts of any kind, much less decent ones, were hard to come by, and even in Los Angeles, everyone knew the value of a pied-à-terre in Manhattan. And the script arrived on the same day as the final divorce papers.

If real life were a script, a movie executive would have stricken this fact as "too coincidental." But Schiffer Diamond loved coincidences and signs. Loved the childlike magic of believing all things happened for a reason. She was an actress and had lived on magic nearly all her life. And so she took the part, which required moving back to New York City for six months, where she would stay in the one-bedroom apartment she owned on Fifth Avenue. Her initial plan was to stay in New York for the duration of the shoot and then return to L.A. and her house in Los Feliz.

Two days after she took the part, she went to the Ivy and ran into her most recent ex-husband, lunching with a young woman. He was seated at a table in the center of the room, reveling in his new status as the president of a network, and given the deference the staff showed the young woman, Schiffer understood the young woman to be his new girlfriend. She was rumored to be a concert pianist from a renowned family, but had the glossy appearance of an expensive prostitute. The relationship was a cliché, but twenty-five years in Hollywood had taught Schiffer that men never minded clichés, especially when the cliché concerned the penis. Shortly thereafter, when she handed her ticket to the valet and stood outside the restaurant in her sunglasses, she decided to sell the house in Los Feliz, make a clean break of it, and move back to One Fifth.

❦

"Schiffer Diamond has taken a part in a TV series," Enid Merle said to her nephew, Philip Oakland.

"She must be desperate," Philip said, half-jokingly.

Enid and Philip occupied two of the second best apartments in One Fifth, located on the thirteenth floor with adjoining terraces, separated by a charming white picket fence. It was across this fence that Enid now spoke to her nephew. "It may be a very good part," Enid countered, consulting the piece of paper she held in her hand. "She's going to play a mother superior who leaves the church to become the editor in chief of a magazine for teenagers."

"Now, there's a believable concept," Philip said, with the sarcasm he reserved for most matters Hollywood.

"About as believable as a giant reptile that terrorizes New York. I wish you'd quit screenplays and go back to writing serious novels," Enid said.

"Can't," Philip said with a smile. "*I'm* desperate."

"It may be based on a true story," Enid continued. "There *was* a woman—Sandra Miles—who was a mother superior and became an editor in chief. Back in the seventies. I had her to dinner once or twice. A thoroughly miserable woman, but that may have been due to her husband's cheating. Being a virgin for so long, it's possible she never got the sex part right. In any case," Enid added, "the series shoots in New York."

"Uh-huh," Philip said.

"I suppose we'll be seeing her around the building again," Enid said.

"Who?" Philip said, trying to appear uninterested. "Sandra Miles?"

"Schiffer Diamond," Enid said. "Sandra Miles left New York years ago. She may even be dead."

"Unless she stays in a hotel," Philip said, referring to Schiffer Diamond.

"Why on earth would she do that?" Enid said.

When his aunt had gone back in, Philip remained on his terrace, staring out at Washington Square Park, of which he had a superior view. It was July, and the park was lush with greenery, the dry August heat yet to come. But Philip wasn't thinking about foliage. He was miles away, standing on a dock on Catalina Island twenty-five years before.

"So you're the schoolboy genius," Schiffer Diamond said, coming up behind him.

"Huh?" he said, turning around.

"They tell me you're the writer of this lousy movie."

He bristled. "If you think it's so lousy—"

"Yes, schoolboy?" she asked.

"Then why are you in it?"

"All movies are lousy by definition. They're not art. But everyone needs money. Even geniuses."

"I'm not doing it for the money," he said.

"Why are you doing it?"

"To meet girls like you?" he asked.

She laughed. She was wearing white jeans and a navy blue T-shirt. She was braless and barefoot and tanned. "Good answer, schoolboy," she said, starting to walk away.

"Hey," he called after her. "Do you really think the movie is lousy?"

"What do you think?" she asked. "Besides, you can never really judge a man's work until you've been to bed with him."

"Are you planning to go to bed with me?" he said.

"I never plan anything. I like to see what happens. Life's much more interesting that way, don't you think?" And she went to do her scene.

A minute later, Enid's voice startled Philip out of his reverie. "I just talked to Roberto," she said, referring to the head doorman. "Schiffer Diamond is coming back today. A housekeeper was in her apartment this week, getting it ready. Roberto says she's moving back. Maybe permanently. Isn't that exciting?"

"I'm thrilled," Philip said.

"I wonder how she'll find New York," Enid said. "Having been away for so long."

"Exactly the same, Auntie," Philip said. "You know New York never changes. The characters are different, but the play remains the same."

Later that afternoon, Enid Merle was putting the finishing touches on her daily gossip column when a sudden gust of wind slammed shut the door to her terrace. Crossing the room to open it, Enid caught sight of the sky and stepped outside. A mountain of thunderclouds had built up on the other side of the Hudson River and was rapidly approaching the city. This was unusual, Enid thought, as the early July day hadn't been particularly hot. Gazing upward, Enid spotted her neighbor Mrs. Louise Houghton on her own terrace, wearing an old straw hat and holding a pair of gardening shears in her gloved hand. In the last five years, Louise Houghton, who was nearing one hundred, had slowed down, spending most of her time attending to her prizewinning roses. "Hallo," Enid called loudly to Mrs. Houghton, who was known to be slightly deaf. "Looks like we're in for a big thunderstorm."

"Thank you, dear," Mrs. Houghton said graciously, as if she were a queen addressing one of her loyal subjects. Enid would have been annoyed if not for the fact that this was Mrs. Houghton's standard response to just about everyone now.

"You might want to go inside," Enid said. Despite Mrs. Houghton's quaint grandeur, which was off-putting to some, Enid was fond of the old lady, the two having been neighbors for over sixty years.

"Thank you, dear," Mrs. Houghton said again, and might have gone inside but for a flock of pigeons that flew abruptly out of

Washington Square Park, diverting her attention. In the next second, the sky turned black, and rain the size of pellets began to pummel Fifth Avenue. Enid hurried inside, losing sight of Mrs. Houghton, who was struggling against the rain on her spindly old legs. Another strong gust of wind released a lattice screen from its moorings and knocked the elegant old lady to her knees. Lacking the strength to stand, Louise Houghton tipped sideways onto her hip, shattering the fragile bone and preventing further movement. For several minutes, she lay in the rain until one of her four maids, unable to locate Mrs. Houghton in the vast seven-thousand-square-foot apartment, ventured outside and discovered her under the lattice.

Meanwhile, on the street below, two Town Cars were slowly making their way down Fifth Avenue like a small cortege. When they reached One Fifth, the drivers got out and, hunched against the rain and shouting instructions and oaths, began pulling out the luggage. The first piece was an old-fashioned Louis Vuitton steamer trunk that required the efforts of two men to lift. Roberto, the doorman, hurried out, paused under the awning, and called for backup before waving the men inside. A porter came up from the basement, pushing a large cart with brass poles. The drivers heaved the trunk onto the cart, and then one after another, each piece of matching luggage was piled on top.

Down the street, a strong gust of wind ripped an umbrella out of the hands of a businessman, turning it inside out. It scuttled across the pavement like a witch's broom, coming to rest on the wheel of a shiny black SUV that had just pulled up to the entrance. Spotting the passenger in the backseat, Roberto decided to brave the rain. Picking up a green-and-white golf umbrella, he brandished it like a sword as he hurried out from under the awning. Reaching the SUV, he angled it expertly against the wind so as to protect the emerging passenger.

A blue-and-green brocade shoe with a kitten heel appeared, followed by the famous long legs, clad in narrow white jeans. Then a hand with the slim, elegant fingers of an artist; on the middle finger was a large aquamarine ring. At last Schiffer Diamond herself got out of the car. She hadn't changed at all, Roberto thought, taking her hand to help her out. "Hello, Roberto," she said, as easily as if she'd been gone for two weeks instead of twenty years. "Crap weather, isn't it?"

Act
One

I

Billy Litchfield strolled by One Fifth at least twice a day. He once had a dog, a Wheaten terrier, that had been given to him by Mrs. Houghton, who had raised Wheaten terriers on her estate on the Hudson. Wheaty had required two outings a day to the dog run in Washington Square Park, and Billy, who lived on Fifth Avenue just north of One Fifth, had developed the habit then of walking past One Fifth as part of his daily constitutional. One Fifth was one of his personal landmarks, a magnificent building constructed of a pale gray stone in the classic lines of the art deco era, and Billy, who had one foot in the new millennium and one foot in the café society of lore, had always admired it. "It shouldn't matter where you live as long as where you live is decent," he said to himself, but still, he aspired to live in One Fifth. He had aspired to live there for thirty-five years and had yet to make it.

For a short time, Billy had decided that aspiration was dead, or at least out of favor. This was just after 9/11, when the cynicism and shallowness that had beaten through the lifeblood of the city was interpreted as unnecessary cruelty, and it was all at once tacky to wish for anything other than world peace, and tacky not to appreciate what one had. But six years had passed, and like a racehorse,

New York couldn't be kept out of the gate, nor change its nature. While most of New York was in mourning, a secret society of bankers had brewed and stirred a giant cauldron of money, adding a dash of youth and computer technology, and voilà, a whole new class of the obscenely super-rich was born. This was perhaps bad for America, but it was good for Billy. Although a self-declared anachronism, lacking the appurtenances of what might be called a regular job, Billy acted as a sort of concierge to the very rich and successful, making introductions to decorators, art dealers, club impresarios, and members of the boards of both cultural establishments and apartment buildings. In addition to a nearly encyclopedic knowledge of art and antiquities, Billy was well versed in the finer points of jets and yachts, knew who owned what, where to go on vacation, and which restaurants to frequent.

Billy had very little money of his own, however. Possessing the fine nature of an aristocrat, Billy was a snob, especially when it came to money. He was happy to live among the rich and successful, to be witty at dinner and house parties, to advise what to say and how best to spend money, but he drew the line at soiling his own hands in the pursuit of filthy lucre.

And so, while he longed to live at One Fifth Avenue, he could never raise the desire in himself to make that pact with the devil to sell his soul for money. He was content in his rent-stabilized apartment for which he paid eleven hundred dollars a month. He often reminded himself that one didn't actually need money when one had very rich friends.

Upon returning from the park, Billy usually felt soothed by the morning air. But on this particular morning in July, Billy was despondent. While in the park he had sat down on a bench with *The New York Times* and discovered that his beloved Mrs. Houghton had passed away the night before. During the thunderstorm three days ago, Mrs. Houghton had been left out in the rain for no more than ten minutes, but it was still too late. A vicious pneumonia had set in, bringing her long life to a swift and speedy end and taking much of New York by surprise. Billy's only consolation was that her obituary had appeared on the front page of the *Times*, which meant there were still one or two editors who remembered the traditions of a more refined age, when art mattered more than money, when one's contribution to society was more important than showing off the toys of one's wealth.

Thinking about Mrs. Houghton, Billy found himself lingering in front of One Fifth, staring up at the imposing facade. For years, One Fifth had been an unofficial club for successful artists of all kinds—the painters and writers and composers and conductors and actors and directors who possessed the creative energy that kept the city alive. Although not an artist herself, Mrs. Houghton, who had lived in the building since 1947, had been the arts' biggest patron, founding organizations and donating millions to art institutions both large and small. There were those who'd called her a saint.

In the past hour, the paparazzi apparently had decided a photograph of the building in which Mrs. Houghton had lived might be worth money, and had gathered in front of the entrance. As Billy took in the small group of photographers, badly dressed in misshapen T-shirts and jeans, his sensibilities were offended. All the best people are dead, he thought mournfully.

And then, since he was a New Yorker, his thoughts inevitably turned to real estate. What would happen to Mrs. Houghton's apartment? he wondered. Her children were in their seventies. Her grandchildren, he supposed, would sell it and take the cash, having denuded most of the Houghton fortune over the years, a fortune, like so many old New York fortunes, that turned out to be not quite as impressive as it had been in the seventies and eighties. In the seventies, a million dollars could buy you just about anything you wanted. Now it barely paid for a birthday party.

How New York had changed, Billy thought.

"Money follows art, Billy," Mrs. Houghton always said. "Money wants what it can't buy. Class and talent. And remember that while there's a talent for making money, it takes real talent to know how to spend it. And that's what you do so well, Billy."

And now who would spend the money to buy the Houghton place? It hadn't been redecorated in at least twenty years, trapped in the chintz of the eighties. But the bones of the apartment were magnificent—and it was one of the grandest apartments in Manhattan, a proper triplex built for the original owner of One Fifth, which had once been a hotel. The apartment had twelve-foot ceilings and a ballroom with a marble fireplace, and wraparound terraces on all three floors.

Billy hoped it wouldn't be someone like the Brewers, although it probably would be. Despite the chintz, the apartment was worth at least twenty million dollars, and who could afford it except for one of the new hedge-funders? And considering some of those types, the Brewers weren't bad. At least the wife, Connie, was a former ballet dancer and friend. The Brewers lived uptown and owned a hideous new house in the Hamptons where Billy was going for the weekend. He would tell Connie about the apartment and how he could smooth their entry with the head of the board, the extremely unpleasant Mindy Gooch. Billy had known Mindy "forever"—meaning from the mid-eighties, when he'd met her at a party. She was Mindy Welch back then, fresh off the boat from Smith College. Full of brio, she was convinced she was about to become the next big thing in publishing. In the early nineties, she got herself engaged to James Gooch, who had just won a journalism award. Once again Mindy had had all kinds of grand schemes, picturing she and James as the city's next power couple. But none of it had worked out as planned, and now Mindy and James were a middle-aged, middle-class couple with creative pretensions who couldn't afford to buy their own apartment today. Billy often wondered how they'd been able to buy in One Fifth in the first place. The unexpected and tragic early death of a parent, he guessed.

He stood a moment longer, wondering what the photographers were waiting for. Mrs. Houghton was dead and had passed away in the hospital. No one related to her was likely to come walking out; there wouldn't even be the thrill of the body being taken away, zipped up in a body bag, as one sometimes saw in these buildings filled with old people. At that instant, however, none other than Mindy Gooch strolled out of the building. She was wearing jeans and those fuzzy slippers that people pretended were shoes and were in three years ago. She was shielding the face of a young teenaged boy as if afraid for his safety. The photographers ignored them.

"What is all this?" she asked, spotting Billy and approaching him for a chat.

"I imagine it's for Mrs. Houghton."

"Is she finally dead?" Mindy said.

"If you want to look at it that way," Billy said.

"How else can one look at it?" Mindy said.

"It's that word 'finally,'" Billy said. "It's not nice."

"Mom," the boy said.

"This is my son, Sam," Mindy said.

"Hello, Sam," Billy said, shaking the boy's hand. He was surprisingly attractive, with a mop of blond hair and dark eyes. "I didn't know you had a child," Billy remarked.

"He's thirteen," Mindy said. "We've had him quite a long time."

Sam pulled away from her.

"Will you kiss me goodbye, please?" Mindy said to her son.

"I'm going to see you in, like, forty-eight hours," Sam protested.

"Something could happen. I could get hit by a bus. And then your last memory will be of how you wouldn't kiss your mother goodbye before you went away for the weekend."

"Mom, please," Sam said. But he relented. He kissed her on the cheek.

Mindy gazed at him as he ran across the street. "He's that age," she said to Billy. "He doesn't want his mommy anymore. It's terrible."

Billy nodded cautiously. Mindy was one of those aggressive New York types, as tightly wound as two twisted pieces of rope. You never knew when the rope might unwind and hit you. That rope, Billy often thought, might even turn into a tornado. "I know exactly what you mean." He sighed.

"Do you?" she said, her eyes beaming in on him. There was a glassy look to *les yeux*, thought Billy. Perhaps she was on drugs. But in the next second, she calmed down and repeated, "So Mrs. Houghton's finally dead."

"Yes," Billy said, slightly relieved. "Don't you read the papers?"

"Something came up this morning." Mindy's eyes narrowed. "Should be interesting to see who tries to buy the apartment."

"A rich hedge-funder, I would imagine."

"I hate them, don't you?" Mindy said. And without saying good-bye, she turned on her heel and walked abruptly away.

Billy shook his head and went home.

Mindy went to the deli around the corner. When she returned, the photographers were still on the sidewalk in front of One Fifth. Mindy was suddenly enraged by their presence.

"Roberto," Mindy said, getting in the doorman's face. "I want you to call the police. We need to get rid of those photographers."

"Okay, Missus Mindy," Roberto said.

"I mean it, Roberto. Have you noticed that there are more and more of these paparazzi types on the street lately?"

"It's because of all the celebrities," Roberto said. "I can't do anything about them."

"Someone should do something," Mindy said. "I'm going to talk to the mayor about it. Next time I see him. If he can drum out smokers and trans fat, he can certainly do something about these hoodlum photographers."

"He'll be sure to listen to you," Roberto said.

"You know, James and I do know him," Mindy said. "The mayor. We've known him for years. From before he was the mayor."

"I'll try to shoo them away," Roberto said. "But it's a free country."

"Not anymore," Mindy said. She walked past the elevator and opened the door to her ground-floor apartment.

The Gooches' apartment was one of the oddest in the building, consisting of a string of rooms that had once been servants' quarters and storage rooms. The apartment was an unwieldy shape of boxlike spaces, dead-end rooms, and dark patches, reflecting the inner psychosis of James and Mindy Gooch and shaping the psychology of their little family. Which could be summed up in one word: dysfunctional.

In the summer, the low-ceilinged rooms were hot; in the winter, cold. The biggest room in the warren, the one they used as their living room, had a shallow fireplace. Mindy imagined it as a room once occupied by a majordomo, the head of all servants. Perhaps he had lured young female maids into his room and had sex with them. Perhaps he had been gay. And now, eighty years later, here she and James lived in those same quarters. It felt historically wrong. After years and years of pursuing the American dream, of aspirations and university educations and hard, hard work, all you got for your efforts these days were servants' quarters in Manhattan. And being told you were lucky to have them. While upstairs, one of the grandest apartments in Manhattan was empty, waiting to be filled by some wealthy banker type, probably a young man who cared only about money and nothing about the good of the country or its people, who would live like a little king. In an apartment that morally should have been hers and James's.

In a tiny room at the edge of the apartment, her husband, James, with his sweet balding head and messy blond comb-over, was pecking away mercilessly at his computer, working on his book, distracted and believing, as always, that he was on the edge of failure. Of all his feelings, this edge-of-failure feeling was the most prominent. It dwarfed all other feelings, crowding them out and pushing them to the edge of his consciousness, where they squatted like old packages in the corner of a room. Perhaps there were good things in those packages, useful things, but James hadn't the time to unwrap them.

James heard the soft thud of the door in the other part of the apartment as Mindy came in. Or perhaps he only sensed her presence. He'd been around Mindy for so long, he could feel the vibrations she set off in the air. They weren't particularly soothing vibrations, but they were familiar.

Mindy appeared before him, paused, then sat down in his old leather club chair, purchased at the fire sale in the Plaza when the venerable hotel was sold for condos for even more rich people. "James," she said.

"Yes," James said, barely looking up from his computer.

"Mrs. Houghton's dead."

James stared at her blankly.

"Did you know that?" Mindy asked.

"It was all over the Internet this morning."

"Why didn't you tell me?"

"I thought you knew."

"I'm the head of the board, and you didn't tell me," Mindy said. "I just ran into Billy Litchfield. *He* told me. It was embarrassing."

"Don't you have better things to worry about?" James asked.

"Yes, I do. And now I've got to worry about that apartment. And who's going to move into it. And what kind of people they're going to be. Why don't we live in that apartment?"

"Because it's worth about twenty million dollars, and we don't happen to have twenty million dollars lying around?" James said.

"And whose fault is that?" Mindy said.

"Mindy, please," James said. He scratched his head. "We've discussed this a million times. There is nothing *wrong* with our apartment."

❦

On the thirteenth floor, the floor below the three grand floors that had been Mrs. Houghton's apartment, Enid Merle stood on her terrace, thinking about Louise. The top of the building was tiered like a wedding cake, so the upper terraces were visible to those below. How shocking that only three days ago, she'd been standing in this very spot, conversing with Louise, her face shaded in that ubiquitous straw hat. Louise had never allowed the sun to touch her skin, and she'd rarely moved her face, believing that facial expressions caused wrinkles. She'd had at least two face-lifts, but nevertheless, even on the day of the storm, Enid remembered noting that Louise's skin had been astoundingly smooth. Enid was a different story. Even as a little girl, she'd hated all that female fussiness and overbearing attention to one's appearance. Nevertheless, due to the fact that she was a public persona, Enid had eventually succumbed to a face-lift by the famous Dr. Baker, whose society patients were known as "Baker's Girls." At eighty-two, Enid had the face of a sixty-five-year-old, although the rest of her was not only creased but as pleasantly speckled as a chicken.

For those who knew the history of the building and its occupants, Enid Merle was not only its second oldest resident—after Mrs. Houghton—but in the sixties and seventies, one of its most notorious. Enid, who had never married and had a degree in psychology from Columbia University (making her one of the college's first women to earn one), had taken a job as a secretary at the *New York Star* in 1948, and given her fascination with the antics of humanity, and possessing a sympathetic ear, had worked her way into the gossip department, eventually securing her own column. Having spent the early part of her life on a cotton farm in Texas, Enid always felt slightly the outsider and approached her work with the good Southern values of kindness and sympathy. Enid was known as the "nice" gossip columnist, and it had served her well: When actors and politicians were ready to tell their side of a story, they called Enid. In the early eighties, the column had been syndicated, and Enid had become a wealthy woman. She'd been trying to retire for ten years, but her name, argued her employers, was too valuable, and so Enid worked with a staff that gathered information and wrote the column, although under special circumstances, Enid would write the column herself. Louise Houghton's death was one such circumstance.

Thinking about the column she would have to write about Mrs. Houghton, Enid felt a sharp pang of loss. Louise had had a full and glamorous life—a life to be envied and admired—and had died without enemies, save perhaps for Flossie Davis, who was Enid's stepmother. Flossie lived across the street, having abandoned One

Fifth in the early sixties for the conveniences of a new high-rise. But Flossie was crazy and always had been, and Enid reminded herself that this pang of loss was a feeling she'd carried all her life—a longing for something that always seemed to be just out of reach. It was, Enid thought, simply the human condition. There were inherent questions in the very nature of being alive that couldn't be answered but only endured.

Usually, Enid did not find these thoughts depressing but, rather, exhilarating. In her experience, she'd found that most people did not manage to grow up. Their bodies got older, but this did not necessarily mean the mind matured in the proper way. Enid did not find this truth particularly bothersome, either. Her days of being upset about the unfairness of life and the inherent unrelia-bility of human beings to do the right thing were over. Having reached old age, she considered herself endlessly lucky. If you had a little bit of money and most of your health, if you lived in a place with lots of other people and interesting things going on all the time, it was very pleasant to be old. No one expected anything of you but to live. Indeed, they applauded you merely for getting out of bed in the morning.

Spotting the paparazzi below, Enid realized she ought to tell Philip about Mrs. Houghton's passing. Philip was not an early riser, but Enid considered the news important enough to wake him. She knocked on his door and waited for a minute, until she heard Philip's sleepy, annoyed voice call out, "Who is it?"

"It's me," Enid said.

Philip opened the door. He was wearing a pair of light blue boxer shorts. "Can I come in?" Enid asked. "Or do you have a young lady here?"

"Good morning to you, too, Nini," Philip said, holding the door so she could enter. "Nini" was Philip's pet name for Enid, having come up with it when he was one and was first learning to talk. Philip had been and was still, at forty-five, a precocious child, but this wasn't perhaps his fault, Enid thought. "And you know they're not young ladies anymore," he added. "There's nothing ladylike about them."

"But they're still young. Too young," Enid said. She followed Philip into the kitchen. "Louise Houghton died last night. I thought you might want to know."

"Poor Louise," Philip said. "The ancient mariner returns to the sea. Coffee?"

"Please," Enid said. "I wonder what will happen to her apartment. Maybe they'll split it up. You could buy the fourteenth floor. You've got plenty of money."

"Sure," Philip said.

"If you bought the fourteenth floor, you could get married. And have room for children," Enid said.

"I love you, Nini," Philip said. "But not that much."

Enid smiled. She found Philip's sense of humor charming. And Philip was so good-looking—endearingly handsome in that boyish way that women find endlessly pleasing—that she could never be angry with him. He wore his dark hair one length, clipped below the ears so it curled over his collar like a spaniel's, and when Enid looked at him, she still saw the sweet five-year-old boy who used to come to her apartment after kindergarten, dressed in his blue school uniform and cap. He was such a good boy, even then. "Mama's sleeping, and I don't want to wake her. She's tired again. You don't mind if I sit with you, do you, Nini?" he would ask. And she didn't mind. She never minded anything about Philip.

"Roberto told me that one of Louise's relatives tried to get into the apartment last night," Enid said, "but he wouldn't let them in."

"It's going to get ugly," Philip said. "All those antiques."

"Sotheby's will sell them," Enid said, "and that will be the end of it. The end of an era."

Philip handed her a mug of coffee.

"There are always deaths in this building," he said.

"Mrs. Houghton was old," Enid said and, quickly changing the subject, asked, "What are you going to do today?"

"I'm still interviewing researchers," Philip said.

A diversion, Enid thought, but decided not to delve into it. She could tell by Philip's attitude that his writing wasn't going well again. He was joyous when it was and miserable when it wasn't.

Enid went back to her apartment and attempted to work on her column about Mrs. Houghton, but found that Philip had distracted her more than usual. Philip was a complicated character. Technically, he wasn't her nephew but a sort of second cousin—his grandmother Flossie Davis was Enid's stepmother. Enid's own mother had died when she was a girl, and her father had met Flossie backstage at Radio City Music Hall during a business trip to New York. Flossie was a Rockette and, after a quick marriage, had tried to live with Enid and her father in Texas. She'd lasted six months, at which point Enid's father had moved the family to New York. When Enid was twenty, Flossie had had a daughter, Anna, who was Philip's mother. Like Flossie, Anna was very beautiful, but plagued by demons. When Philip was nineteen, she'd killed herself. It was a violent, messy death. She'd thrown herself off the top of One Fifth.

It was the kind of thing that people always assume they will never forget, but that wasn't true, Enid thought. Over time, the healthy mind had a way of erasing the most unpleasant details. So Enid didn't remember the exact circumstances of what had happened on the day Anna had died; nor did she recall exactly what had happened to Philip after his mother's death. She recalled the outlines—the drug addiction, the arrest, the fact that Philip had spent two weeks in jail, and the consequent months in rehab—but she was fuzzy on the specifics. Philip had taken his experiences and turned them into the novel *Summer Morning*, for which he'd won the Pulitzer Prize. But instead of pursuing an artistic career, Philip had become commercial, caught up in Hollywood glamour and money.

In the apartment next door, Philip was also sitting in front of his computer, determined to finish a scene in his new screenplay, *Bridesmaids Revisited*. He wrote two lines of dialogue and then, in frustration, shut down his computer. He got into the shower, wondering once more if he was losing his touch.

Ten years ago, when he was thirty-five, he'd had everything a man could want in his career: a Pulitzer Prize, an Oscar for screen-writing, money, and an unassailable reputation. And then the small fissures began to appear: movies that didn't make as much as they should have at the box office. Arguments with young executives. Being replaced on two projects. At the time, Philip told himself it was irrelevant: It was the business, after all. But the steady stream of money he'd enjoyed as a young man had lately been reduced to a trickle. He didn't have the heart to tell Nini, who would be dis-appointed and alarmed. Shampooing his hair, he again rationalized his situation, telling himself there was no need for worry—with the right project and a little bit of luck, he'd be on top of the world again.

※

A few minutes later, Philip stepped into the elevator and tousled his damp hair. Still thinking about his life, he was startled when the elevator doors opened on the ninth floor, and a familiar, musical voice chimed out, "Philip." A second later, Schiffer Diamond got on. "Schoolboy," she said, as if no time had passed at all, "I can't believe you still live in this lousy building."

Philip laughed. "Enid told me you were coming back." He smirked, immediately falling into their old familiar banter. "And here you are."

"Told you?" Schiffer said. "She wrote a whole column about it. The return of Schiffer Diamond. Made me sound like a middle-aged gunslinger."

"You could never be middle-aged," Philip said.

"Could be and am," Schiffer replied. She paused and looked him up and down. "You still married?"

"Not for seven years," Philip said, almost proudly.

"Isn't that some kind of record for you?" Schiffer asked. "I thought you never went more than four years without getting hitched."

"I've learned a lot since my two divorces," Philip said, "i.e.: Do not get married again. What about you? Where's your second husband?"

"Oh, I divorced him as well. Or he divorced me. I can't remember." She smiled at him in that particular way she had, making him feel like he was the only person in the world. For a moment, Philip was taken in, and then he reminded himself that he'd seen her use that smile on too many others.

The elevator doors opened, and Philip looked over her shoulder at the pack of paparazzi in front of the building. "Are those for you?" he asked, almost accusingly.

"No, silly. They're for Mrs. Houghton. I'm not that famous," she said. Hurrying across the lobby, she ran through the flashing cameras and jumped into the back of a white van.

Oh, yes, you are, Philip thought. You're still that famous and more. Dodging the photographers, he headed across Fifth Avenue and down Tenth Street to the little library on Sixth Avenue where he sometimes worked. He suddenly felt irritated. Why had she come back? She would torture him again and then leave. There was no telling what that woman might do. Twenty years ago, she'd surprised him and bought an apartment in One Fifth and tried to position it as proof that she would always be with him. She was an actress, and she was nuts. They were all nuts, and after that last time, when she'd run off and married that goddamned count, he'd sworn off actresses for good.

He entered the cool of the library, taking a seat in a battered armchair. He picked up the draft of *Bridesmaids Revisited*, and after reading through a few pages, put it down in disgust. How had he, Philip Oakland, Pulitzer Prize–winning author, ended up writing this crap? He could imagine Schiffer Diamond's reaction: "Why don't you do your own work, Oakland? At least find something you care about personally." And his own defense: "It's called show 'business.' Not show 'art.'"

"Bullshit," she'd say. "You're scared."

Well, she always prided herself on not being afraid of anything.

And that was her own bullshit defense: insisting she wasn't vulnerable. It was dishonest, he thought. But when it came to her feelings for him, she'd always thought he was a little bit better than even he thought he was.

He picked up the pages again but found he wasn't the least bit interested. *Bridesmaids Revisited* was exactly what it seemed—a story about what had happened in the lives of four women who'd met as bridesmaids at twenty-two. And what the hell did he know about twenty-two-year-old girls? His last girlfriend, Sondra, wasn't nearly as young as Enid had implied—she was, in fact, thirty-three—and was an up-and-coming executive at an independent movie company. But after nine months, she'd become fed up with him, assessing—correctly—that he was not ready to get married and have children anytime soon. A fact that was, at his age, "pathetic," according to Sondra and her friends. This reminded Philip that he hadn't had sex since their breakup two months ago. Not that the sex had been so great anyway. Sondra had performed all the standard moves, but the sex had not been inspiring, and he'd found himself going through the motions with a kind of weariness that had made him wonder if sex would ever be good again. This thought led him to memories of sex with Schiffer Diamond. Now, that, he thought, staring blankly at the pages of his screenplay, had been good sex.

At the tip of Manhattan, the white van containing Schiffer Diamond was crossing the Williamsburg Bridge to the Steiner Studios in Brooklyn. Schiffer was also attempting to study a script—the pilot episode for *Lady Superior*—for which she had a table read that morning. The part was especially good: A forty-five-year-old nun radically changes her life and discovers what it means to be a contemporary woman. The producers were billing the character as middle-aged, although Schiffer still had a hard time accepting the fact that forty-five was middle-aged. This made her smile, thinking of Philip trying not to act surprised to see her in the elevator. No doubt he, too, was having a hard time accepting that forty-five was middle-aged.

And then, like Philip, she also recalled their sex life. But for her, the memory of sex with Philip was laced with frustration. There were rules about sex: If the sex wasn't good the first time, it would probably get better. If it was great the first time, it would go downhill. But mostly, if the sex was really great, the best sex you'd had in your life, it meant the two people should be together. The rules were juvenile, of course, constructs concocted by young women in order to make sense of men. But sex with Philip had broken all the rules. It was great the first time and great every time thereafter, and they hadn't ended up together. This was one of the disappointments one learned about life—yes, men loved sex. But great sex didn't mean they wanted to marry you. Great sex held no larger implications for them. It was only that: great sex.

She looked out the window at the East River. The water was brown but somehow managed to be sparkling as well, like a grand old lady who won't give up her jewels. Why did she bother with Philip at all? He was a fool. When great sex wasn't enough for a man, he was hopeless.

This led her back to her only conclusion: Maybe the sex hadn't been as special for him as it had been for her. How did one define great sex, anyway? There were all the things one could do to stimulate the genitals—the kissing and licking and firm yet gentle touches, hands wrapped around the shaft of the penis and fingers exploring the inside of the vagina. For the woman, it was about opening up, spreading, accepting the penis not as a foreign object but as a means to pleasure. That was the defining moment of great sex—when the penis met the vagina. She could still remember that first moment of intercourse with Philip: their mutual surprise at how good it felt, then the sensation that their bodies were no longer relevant; then the world fell away and it seemed all of life itself was concentrated in this friction of molecules that led to an explosion. The sensation of completion, the closing of the circle— it had to mean something, right?

2

There were times now when Mindy Gooch wasn't sure what she was doing in her job, when she couldn't see the point of her job, or even exactly what her job was. Ten years ago, Mindy, who had been a cultural columnist for the magazine, who at thirty-three had been ambitious, smart, full of beans and fire, and even (she liked to think) ruthless, had managed to ratchet herself up to the head of the Internet division (which no one had really understood back then) to the tuneful salary of half a million dollars a year. At first she had flourished in this position (indeed, how could she not, as no one knew what she was doing or what she was supposed to do), and Mindy was considered one of the company's brightest stars. With her sleek, highlighted bob and her plain but attractive face, Mindy was trotted out at corporate events, she was honored by women's media organizations, and she spoke to college students about her "recipe" for getting ahead ("hard work, no job too small, no detail too unimportant," words no young person really wanted to hear, though they were true). Then there were rumors that Mindy was being groomed for a bigger position, an executive position with dominion over many minions—the equivalent, she'd liked to think, of being made a knight in the sixteenth century. At that time, in the beginning of the upswing of her career, Mindy was full of a magical hubris that allowed her to take on any aspect of life and succeed. She found the apartment in One Fifth, moved her family, got herself on the board, got her son, Sam, into a better private kindergarten, made Toll House cookies and decorated pumpkins with nontoxic finger paints, had sex with her husband once a week, and even took a class with her girlfriends on how to give a blow job (using bananas). She'd thought about where she might be in five years, in ten years, in fifteen. She did have fantasies of flying around the world in the corporate jet, of heading up meetings in foreign countries. She would be a noble star while being silently and secretly beleaguered by the pressure.

But the years had passed, and Mindy had not fulfilled her promise. It turned out there were no extra innings in which to make her dreams come true. Sam had had a brief bout with "socialization issues"; the experts at the school thought he'd benefit by spending more time with other children—not unusual in a household consisting of a single child and two adults—requiring subsequent layers of organization and the forcing of Sam into afterschool sports, playdates (the apartment filled with the bells and whistles of video games as "the boys" engaged in side-by-side playing), and the pricey ski weekends in Vermont (during one such jaunt, Mindy sprained her ankle and was on a crutch for a month). And then James, who had won the National Magazine Award in 1992, had decided to write fiction; after three years of what felt to him like hand-to-hand combat with the written word, he managed to publish a novel that sold seventy-five hundred copies. His depression and resentment permeated their lives, so in the end, Mindy saw that everyday life with its everyday disappointments had simply worn her down.

And yet she often thought, all this she could have overcome if it weren't for her personality. Anxious and awake in the middle of the night, Mindy often examined the details of her interactions with "corporate" and saw they were lacking. Back then, corporate had consisted of people like Derek Brumminger, the pockmarked perpetual teenager who seemed to be in a never-ending quest to find himself; who, when he discovered that Mindy had no knowledge of seventies rock and roll, tolerated her in meetings with only the barest acknowledgment. It was silently understood that in order to become corporate, in order to be one of them, one had to literally be one of them, since they hung out together, had dinner at each other's apartments, invited each other to endless nights of black-tie charity events, and all went to the same places on vacation, like lemmings. And Mindy and James most decidedly did not fit in. Mindy wasn't "fun." It wasn't in her nature to be sassy or witty or flirtatious; instead, she was smart and serious and disapproving, a bit of a downer. And while much of corporate was made up of Democrats, to James, they were the wrong kind of Democrats. Wealthy, privileged Democrats with excessive pay packages were unseemly, practically oxymorons, and after the third dinner party during which James expressed this opinion and Derek Brumminger countered that perhaps James was actually a Communist, they were never asked again. And that was that. Mindy's future was established: She was in her place and would go no further. Each subsequent yearly review was the same: She was doing a great job, and they were happy with her performance. They couldn't give her a raise but would give her more stock options. Mindy understood her position. She was trapped in a very glamorous form of indentured servitude. She could not get the money from those stock options until she retired or was let go. In the meantime, she had a family to support.

On the morning of Mrs. Houghton's death—on that same morning when Philip Oakland was wondering about his career and Schiffer Diamond was wondering about sex—Mindy Gooch went to her office and, as she did most days, conducted several meetings. She sat behind her long black desk in her cushy black leather swivel chair, one ankle resting on the other knee. Her shoes were black and pointy, with a practical one-and-a-half-inch heel. Her eleven o'clock meeting consisted of four women who sat on the nubby plaid couch and the two small club chairs, done up in the same ugly nubby plaid fabric. They drank coffee or bottled water. They talked about the article in *The New York Times* about the graying of the Internet. They talked about advertisers. Were the suits who controlled the advertising dollars finally coming around to the fact that the most important consumers were women like themselves, over thirty-five, with their own money to spend? The conversation turned to video games. Were they good or evil? Was it worth developing a video game on their website for women? What would it be? "Shoes," one of the women said. "Shopping," said another. "But it already exists. In online catalogs." "Why not put the best all in one place?" "And have high-end jewelry." "And baby clothes."

This was depressing, Mindy thought. "Is that all we're really interested in? Shopping?"

"We can't help ourselves," one woman said. "It's in our genes. Men are the hunters and women are the gatherers. Shopping is a form of gathering." All the women laughed.

"I wish we could do something provocative," Mindy said. "We should be as provocative as those gossip websites. Like Perez Hilton. Or Snarker."

"How could we do that?" one of the women asked politely.

"I don't know," Mindy said. "We should try to get at the truth. Talk about how terrible it is to face middle age. Or how lousy married sex is."

"Is married sex lousy?" one woman asked. "It's kind of a cliché, isn't it?" said another. "It's up to the woman to stay interested." "Yes, but who has time?" "It's the same thing over and over again. It's like having the same meal every day of your life." "Every day?" "Okay, maybe once a week. Or once a month."

"So what are we saying here, that women want variety?" Mindy asked.

"I don't. I'm too old to have a stranger see me naked." "We might want it, but we know we can't have it. We can't even talk about wanting it." "It's too dangerous. For men." "Women just don't want it the way men do. I mean, have you ever heard of a woman going to a male prostitute? It's disgusting." "But what if the male prostitute were Brad Pitt?" "I'd cheat on my husband in a second for Brad Pitt. Or George Clooney."

"So if the man is a movie star, it doesn't count," Mindy said.

"That's right."

"Isn't that hypocritical?" Mindy said.

"Yeah, but what's the likelihood of it happening?"

Everyone laughed nervously.

"We've got some interesting ideas here," Mindy said. "We'll meet again in two weeks and see where we are."

After the women left her office, Mindy stared blankly at her e-mails. She received at least 250 a day. Usually, she tried to keep up. But now she felt as if she were drowning in a sea of minutiae.

What was the point? she wondered. It only went on and on, with no end in sight. Tomorrow there would be another 250, and another 250 the day after, and the day after that into infinity. What would happen if one day she just stopped?

I want to be significant, Mindy thought. I want to be loved. Why is that so difficult?

She told her assistant she was going to a meeting and wouldn't be back until after lunch.

Leaving the suite of offices, she rode the elevator to the ground floor of the massive new office building—where the first three floors were an urban mall of restaurants and high-end shops that sold fifty-thousand-dollar watches to rich tourists—and then she rode an escalator down into the damp bowels of underground corridors and walked through a cement tunnel to the subway. She'd been riding the train ten times a week for twenty years, about a hundred thousand rides. Not what you thought when you were young and determined to make it. She arranged her face into a blank mask and took hold of the metal pole, hoping no male would rub up against her, rub his penis on her leg, the way men sometimes did, like dogs acting on instinct. It was the silent shame endured by every woman who rode the subway. No one did anything about it or talked about it because it was performed mostly by men who were more animal than human, and no one wanted to be reminded of the existence of these men or the disturbing baseness of the natural male human. "Don't take the train!" exclaimed Mindy's assistant after Mindy regaled her with yet another tale of one such incident. "You're entitled to a car." "I don't want to sit in traffic in Manhattan," Mindy replied. "But you could work in the car. And talk on the phone." "No," Mindy said. "I like to see the people." "You like to suffer, is what," the assistant said. "You like to be abused. You're a masochist." Ten years ago, this comment would have been insubordination. But not now. Not with the new democracy, where every young person was equal to every older person in this new culture where it was difficult to find young people who even cared to work, who could even tolerate discomfort.

Mindy exited the subway at Fourteenth Street, walking three blocks to her gym. By rote, she changed her clothes and got onto a treadmill. She increased the speed, forcing her legs into a run. A perfect metaphor for her life, she thought. She was running and running and going nowhere.

Back in the locker room, she took a quick shower after carefully tucking her blow-dried bob under a shower cap. She dried off, got dressed again, and thinking about the rest of her day—more meetings and e-mails that would only lead to more meetings and e-mails—felt exhausted. She sat down on the narrow wooden bench in the changing room and called James. "What are you doing?" she asked.

"Didn't we discuss this? I have that lunch," James said.

"I need you to do something for me."

"What?" James said.

"Get the keys to Mrs. Houghton's apartment from the super. I can't have those keys floating around. And I need to show the real estate agent the apartment. Mrs. Houghton's relatives want it sold quickly, and I don't want the place sitting empty for long. Real estate is at a high now. You never know when it might drop, and the price of that apartment needs to set a benchmark. So everyone's apartment is worth more."

As usual, James zoned out when Mindy talked real estate. "Can't you pick them up when you get home?" he asked.

Mindy was suddenly angry. She had excused much over the years with James. She had excused the fact that at times he would barely make conversation other than to respond with a two-syllable word. She'd excused his lack of hair. She'd excused his sagging muscles. She'd excused the fact that he wasn't romantic and never said "I love you" unless she said it first, and even then he only, when obligated, said it three or four times a year. She'd excused the reality that he was never going to make a lot of money and was probably never going to be a highly respected writer; she'd even excused the fact that with this second novel of his, he was probably going to become a bit of a joke. She was down to almost nothing now. "I can't do everything, James. I simply cannot go on like this."

"Maybe you should go to the doctor," James said. "Get yourself checked out."

"This has nothing to do with me," Mindy said. "It's about you doing your part. Why can't you help me, James, when I ask you to?"

James sighed. He'd been feeling up about his lunch, and now Mindy was spoiling it. Feminism, he thought. It had wrecked everything. When he was younger, equality meant sex. Lots of sex, as much as you could grab. But now it meant doing all kinds of things a man wasn't prepared to do. Plus, it took up a huge amount of time. The one thing feminism had done was to make a man appreciate what a bummer it was to be a woman in the first place. Of course, men knew that anyway, so maybe it wasn't much of a revelation.

"Mindy," he said, feeling kinder, "I can't be late for my lunch."

Mindy also tried a different approach. "Have they told you what they think of the draft of your book?" she asked.

"No," James said.

"Why not?"

"I don't know. Because they'll tell me at lunch. That's what the lunch is about," James said.

"Why can't they tell you on the phone? Or by e-mail?"

"Maybe they don't want to. Maybe they want to tell me in person," James said.

"So it's probably bad news," Mindy said. "They probably don't like it. Otherwise, they'd tell you how much they loved it in an e-mail."

Neither one said anything for a second, and then Mindy said, "I'll call you after your lunch. Will you be home? And can you please get the keys?"

"Yes," James said.

At one o'clock, James walked the two blocks to the restaurant Babbo. Redmon Richardly, his publisher, wasn't there, but James hadn't expected him to be. James sat at a table next to the window and watched the passersby. Mindy was probably right, he thought. His book probably did suck, and Redmon was going to tell him they weren't going to be able to publish it. And if they did publish it, what difference would it make? No one would read it. And after four years of working on the damn thing, he'd feel exactly the same way as he had before he started writing it, the only difference being that he'd feel a little bit more of a loser, a little bit more insignificant. That was what sucked about being middle-aged: It was harder and harder to lie to yourself.

Redmon Richardly showed up at one-twenty. James hadn't seen him in over a year and was shocked by his appearance. Redmon's hair was gray and sparse, reminding James of the head of a baby bird. Redmon looked seventy, James thought. And then James wondered if he looked seventy as well. But that was impossible. He was only forty-eight. And Redmon was fifty-five. But there was an aura about Redmon. Something was different about him. Why, he's *happy*, James thought in shock.

"Hey, buddy," Redmon said, patting James on the back. He sat down across from James and unfolded his napkin. "Should we drink? I gave up alcohol, but I can't resist a drink during the day. Especially when I can get out of the office. What is it about this business now? It's busy. You actually have to *work*."

James laughed sympathetically. "You seem okay."

"I am," Redmon said. "I just had a baby. You ever have a baby?"

"I've got a son," James said.

"Isn't it just amazing?" Redmon said.

"I didn't even know your wife was pregnant," James said. "How'd it happen?"

"It just happened. Two months before we got married. We weren't even trying. It's all that sperm I stored up over fifty years. It's powerful stuff," Redmon said. "Man, having a baby, it's the greatest thing. How come no one tells you?"

"Don't know," James said, suddenly annoyed. *Babies*. Nowadays, a man couldn't get away from babies. Not even at a business lunch. Half of James's friends were new fathers. Who knew middle age was going to be all about babies?

And then Redmon did the unthinkable. He pulled out his wallet. It was the kind of wallet teenaged girls used to have, with an insert of plastic sleeves for photographs. "Sidney at one month," he said, passing it over to James.

"Sidney," James repeated.

"Old family name."

James glanced at the photograph of a toothless, hairless baby with a crooked smile and what appeared to be a peculiarly large head.

"And there," Redmon said, turning the plastic sleeve. "Sidney at six months. With Catherine."

James assumed Catherine was Redmon's wife. She was a pretty little thing, not much bigger than Sidney. "He's big," James said, handing back the wallet.

"Doctors say he's in the ninety-ninth percentile. But all kids are big these days. How big is your son?"

"He's small," James said. "Like my wife."

"I'm sorry," Redmon said with genuine sympathy, as if smallness were a deformity. "But you never know. Maybe he'll grow up to be a movie star, like Tom Cruise. Or he'll run a studio. That would be even better."

"Doesn't Tom Cruise run a studio, too?" James smiled feebly and tried to change the subject. "So?"

"Oh yeah. You probably want to know what I think about the book," Redmon said. "I thought I'd let Jerry tell you."

James's stomach dropped. At least Redmon had the courtesy to look distracted. Or uncomfortable.

"Jerry?" James said. "Jerry the mega-asshole?"

"One and the same. I'm afraid he loves you now, so you may want to amend your assessment."

"Me?" James said. "Jerry Bockman loves *me*?"

"I'll let him explain when he comes by."

Jerry Bockman, coming to lunch? James didn't know what to think. Jerry Bockman was a gross man. He had crude features and bad skin and orange hair, and looked like he should be hiding under a bridge demanding tolls from unsuspecting passersby. Men like that shouldn't be in publishing, James had thought prudishly the one and only time he'd met Jerry.

But indeed, Jerry Bockman wasn't in publishing. He was in entertainment. A much vaster and more lucrative enterprise than publishing, which was selling about the same number of books it had sold fifty years ago, the difference being that now there were about fifty times as many books published each year. Publishers had increased the choices but not the demand. And so Redmon Richardly, who'd gone from bad-boy Southern writer to literary publisher with his own company that published Pulitzer Prize–winning authors, like Philip Oakland, and National Book Award winners, and authors who wrote for *The Atlantic* and *Harper's* and *Salon*, who were members of PEN, who did events at the public library, who lived in Brooklyn, and most of all, who *cared*—cared about words, words, words!—had had to sell his company to an entertainment conglomorate. Called, unimaginatively, EC.

Jerry Bockman wasn't the head of EC. That position was held by one of Jerry's friends. Jerry was the head of a division, maybe second in command, maybe next in line. Inevitably, someone would get fired, and Jerry would take his place. He'd get fired someday, too, but by then none of it would matter because he would have reached every goal he'd ever aspired to in life and would probably have half a billion dollars in the bank, or stock options, or something equivalent. Meanwhile, Redmon hadn't been able to make his important literary publishing house work and had had no choice but to be absorbed. Like an amoeba. Two years ago, when Redmon had informed James of the impeding "merger" (he'd called it a merger, but it was an absorption, like all mergers), Redmon said that it wouldn't make any difference. He wouldn't let Jerry Bockman or EC affect his books or his authors or his quality.

"Then why sell?" James had asked.

"Have to," Redmon said. "If I want to get married and have children and live in this city, I have to."

"Since when do you want to get married and have kids?" James asked.

"Since now. Life gets boring when you're middle-aged. You can't keep doing the same thing. You look like an asshole. You ever notice that?" Redmon had asked.

"Yeah," James had said. And now Jerry was coming to lunch.

"You saw the piece about the ayatollah and his nephew in *The Atlantic*?" Redmon asked. James nodded, knowing that a piece about Iran or Iraq or anything that had to do with the Middle East was of vast importance here on the little twelve-mile island known as Manhattan, and normally, James would have been able to concentrate on it. He had quite a few informed opinions on the subject, but all he could think about now was Jerry. Jerry coming to lunch? And Jerry loved him? What was that about? Mindy would be thrilled. But it put an unpleasant pressure on him. Now he was going to have to perform. For Jerry. You couldn't just sit there with a Jerry. You had to engage. Make yourself appear worthwhile.

"I've been thinking a lot about Updike lately," James said, to ease his tension.

"Yeah?" Redmon said, unimpressed. "He's overrated. Hasn't stood the test of time. Not like Roth."

"I just picked up *A Month of Sundays*. I thought the writing was pretty great," James said. "In any case, it was an event, that book. When it came out in 1975. A book coming out was an event. Now it's just like . . ."

"Britney Spears showing her vagina?" Redmon said.

James cringed as Jerry Bockman came in. Jerry wasn't wearing a suit, James noted; suits were for bankers only these days. Instead, Jerry wore khakis and a short-sleeved T-shirt. With a vest. And not just any old vest. A fishing vest. Jesus, James thought.

"Can't stay long," Jerry announced, shaking James's hand. "There's a thing going on in L.A."

"Right. That thing," Redmon said. "What's going on with that?"

"The usual," Jerry said. "Corky Pollack is an asshole. But he's my best friend. So what am I supposed to say?"

"Last man standing. That's what I always aim to be," Redmon said.

"The last man standing on his yacht. Except now it's got to be a mega-yacht. You ever seen one of those things?" Jerry asked James.

"No," James said primly.

"You tell James what I thought about his book?" Jerry asked Redmon.

"Not yet. I thought I'd let you do the honors. You're the boss."

"I'm the boss. Hear that, James? This genius says I'm the boss."

James nodded. He was terrified.

"Well, to put it mildly, I loved your book," Jerry said. "It's great commercial fiction. The kind of thing every businessman is going to want to read on a plane. And I'm not the only one who thinks so. There's already interest in Hollywood from a couple of my buddies. They'll definitely pay seven figures. So we're going to push the production. That's right, isn't it?" Jerry said, looking to Redmon for affirmation. "We're going to push the hell out of this thing and get it out there for spring. We were thinking next fall, but this book is too good. I say let's get it out there immediately and get you started on another book. I've got a great idea for you. Hedge-fund managers. What do you think?"

"Hedge-fund managers," James said. He could barely get the words out.

"It's a hot topic. Perfect for you," Jerry said. "I read your book and said to Redmon, 'We've got a gold mine here. A real commercial male writer. Like Crichton. Or Dan Brown.' And once you've got a market, you've got to keep giving them the product."

Jerry stood up. "Got to go," he said. "Got to deal with that thing." He turned to James and shook his hand. "Nice to meet you. We'll talk soon."

James and Redmon watched Jerry go, watched him walk out of the restaurant and get into a waiting SUV. "I told you you were going to want a drink," Redmon said.

"Yup," James said.

"So this is great news. For us," Redmon said. "We could make some real money here."

"Sounds like it," James said. He motioned to the waiter and ordered a Scotch and water, which was the only drink he could think of at the moment. He suddenly felt numb.

"You don't look so happy, man. Maybe you should try Prozac," Redmon said. "On the other hand, if this book takes off the way I think it will, you won't need it."

"Sure," James said. He got through the rest of the lunch on automatic pilot. Then he walked home to his apartment in One Fifth, didn't say hello to the doorman, didn't collect the mail. Didn't do anything except go into his little office in his weird apartment and sit in his little chair and stare out the little window in front of his little desk. The same window a hundred butlers and maids had probably stared out of years before, contemplating their fate.

Ugh. The irony, he thought. The last thirty years of his life had been made tolerable by one overriding idea. One secret, powerful idea that was, James had believed, more powerful even than Redmon Richardly's friggin' sperm. And that was this: James was an artist. He was, in truth, a great novelist, one of the giants, who had only to be discovered. All these years he had been thinking of himself as Tolstoy. Or Thomas Mann. Or even Flaubert.

And now, in the next six or eight or ten months, the truth would be revealed. He wasn't Tolstoy but just plain old James Gooch. Commercial writer. Destined to be of the moment and not to stand the test of time. And the worst thing about it was that he'd never be able to pretend to be Tolstoy again.

▽

Meanwhile, on a lower floor in Mindy's grand office building, Lola Fabrikant sat on the edge of a love seat done up in the same unattractive nubby brown fabric as the couch in Mindy's office. She swung one sandaled foot as she flipped through a bridal magazine, studiously ignoring two other young women who were waiting to be interviewed, and to whom Lola judged herself vastly superior. All three young women had long hair worn parted down the middle, with strands that appeared to have been forcibly straightened, although the color of the women's hair varied. Lola's was nearly black and shiny, while the other two girls were what Lola called "cheap blondes"; one even sported a half inch of dark roots. This would, Lola decided, briskly turning the pages of the magazine, make the girl ineligible for employment—not that there was an actual job available. In the two months since her graduation from Old Vic University in Virginia, where she'd gotten a degree in fashion marketing, Lola and her mother, Beetelle Fabrikant, had scoured the Internet, sent e-mails, and even made phone calls to prospective employers with no luck. In truth, Beetelle had done most of the actual scouring, with Lola advising, but even Beetelle's efforts weren't easily rewarded. It was a particularly difficult time to find a job in fashion in New York City, with most of the positions taken by interns who spent their summer vacations angling for these jobs. Lola, however, didn't like to work and had chosen instead to spend her summers sitting by her parents' pool, or the pools of her parents' friends, where she and a gaggle of girlfriends would gossip, text, and talk about their fantasy weddings. On inclement days, there was always Facebook or TiVo or the construction of elaborate playlists on her iPod, but mostly there were trips to the mall and endless shopping sprees paid for by a credit card provided by her father, who, when he occasionally complained, was silenced by her mother.

But as her mother pointed out, adolescence couldn't go on forever, and as Lola wasn't engaged, finding the boys in her hometown and at the university nowhere near good enough—an assessment with which her mother agreed—it was decided Lola should try her luck in New York. Here, she would not only find interesting employment but meet a much more suitable class of male. Indeed, Beetelle had met her husband, Cem, in New York City and had been happily married for twenty-three years.

Lola had watched every single episode of *Sex and the City* at least "a hundred times," and adored the idea of moving to the city and finding her own Mr. Big. If Mr. Big weren't available, she would happily take fame, ideally becoming the star of her own reality show. Either option was acceptable, the result, she figured, being much the same: a life of pleasurable leisure in which she might indulge in all the usual pamperings and shopping trips and vacations with girlfriends—the only real difference from her current life being the possible addition of a husband and child. But her mother insisted she at least make an effort to work, claiming it would be good for her. So far, her mother had been wrong; the experience was not good at all, merely irritating and annoying. It reminded her of being forced to visit her father's relatives, who were not as well off as her own family, and who were, as Lola commented to her mother, "frighteningly average."

Having been blessed with the pleasingly uniform features of a beauty contestant—made more regular and pleasing by the subtle shaving of the cartilage on her nose—Lola considered herself most definitely not average. Unfortunately, despite several interviews with the human resources departments at various fashion magazines, her superiority had failed to impress, and when she was asked "What do you want to do?" for the fifth or sixth time, Lola had finally answered with a curt "I could probably use a seaweed facial."

Now, putting down the magazine and looking around the small waiting room, Lola imagined her next interview would go very much like the last. An efficient middle-aged woman would explain what the requirements would be if a job were to become available and if she were to get it. She'd have to get to the office by nine and work until six P.M. or later; she'd be responsible for her own transportation and meals; and she might be subjected to the indignity of a drug test, although she had never touched a drug in her life, with the exception of several prescription drugs. And then what would be the point of this job? All her time would be taken up by this work business, and she couldn't imagine how the standard salary—thirty-five thousand dollars a year, or eighteen thousand after taxes, as her father pointed out, meaning under two thousand dollars a month—could possibly make it worthwhile. She glanced at her watch, which had a plastic band with tiny diamonds around the face, and saw that she'd already been waiting forty-five minutes. It was, she decided, too long. Addressing the girl seated across from her—the one with the inch-long roots—Lola said, "How long have *you* been waiting?"

"An hour," the girl replied.

"It isn't right," the other girl said, chiming in. "How can they treat us like this? I mean, is my time worth nothing?"

Lola reckoned it probably wasn't, but she kept this thought to herself. "We should do something," she said.

"What?" asked the first girl. "We need them more than they need us."

"Tell me about it," said the second. "I've been on twelve job interviews in the last two weeks, and there's nothing. I even interviewed to be a researcher for Philip Oakland. And I don't know anything about research. I only went because I loved *Summer Morning*. But even he didn't want me. The interview lasted like ten minutes, and then he said he'd call and never did."

At this information, Lola perked up. She, too, had read *Summer Morning* and listed it among her favorite books of all time. Trying not to appear too keen, she asked slyly, "What did he want you to do?"

"All you basically have to do is look things up on the Internet, which I do all the time anyway, right? And then sometimes you have to go to the library. But it's the best kind of job, because you don't have regular hours, and you don't have to go to an office. You work out of his apartment, which happens to be gorgeous. With a terrace. And it's on Fifth Avenue. And, by the way, he is still hot, I swear to God, even though I normally don't like older men. And when I was going in, I ran into an actual movie star."

"Who?" the second girl squealed.

"Schiffer Diamond. And she was in *Summer Morning*. So I thought it had to be a sign that I was going to get the job, but I didn't."

"How'd you find out about it?" Lola asked casually.

"One of my mother's friends' daughters heard about it. She's from New Jersey, like me, but she works in the city for a literary agent. After I didn't get the job, she had the nerve to tell her mother, who told my mother, that Philip Oakland only likes to hire pretty girls, so I guess I wasn't pretty enough. But that's the way it is in New York. It's all about your looks. There are some places where the women won't hire the pretty girls because they don't want the competition and they don't want the men to be distracted. And then there are other places where, if you're not a size zero, forget about it. So, basically, you can't win." She looked Lola up and down. "You should try for the Philip Oakland job," she said. "You're prettier than I am. Maybe you'll get it."

◆

Lola's mother, Mrs. Beetelle Fabrikant, was a woman to be admired.

She was robust without being heavy and had the kind of attractiveness that, given the right lighting, was close to beauty. She had short dark hair, brown eyes, and the type of lovely cherry-brown skin that never wrinkled. She was known in her community for her excellent taste, firm sensibility, and ability to get things done. Most recently, Beetelle had led a successful charge to have soda and candy vending machines removed from the public schools, an accomplishment made all the more remarkable by the fact that Beetelle's own daughter was no longer even in high school.

Beetelle was, in general, a wonderful person; if there was anything "wrong" with her, it was only the tiniest of flaws. She tended toward an upward trajectory in life and could occasionally be accused of being a tad too conscious of who was where on the social ladder. For the past ten years, Beetelle, Cem, and Lola had lived in a million-dollar McMansion in the Atlanta suburb of Windsor Pines; in an uncensored moment, Beetelle had let slip that one had to have at least six thousand square feet and five bathrooms to be anyone these days.

Naturally, Beetelle's desire for the best in life extended to her daughter; for this parental ambition, Beetelle forgave herself. "Life is the question and children are the answer" was one of her favorite mottoes, a homily she had picked up from a novel. It meant, she'd decided, that doing everything for your child was the most acceptable and unassailable position one could take.

To this end, Beetelle had now established her little family in two large adjoining rooms at the trendy Soho House hotel. Their first three days in New York had been spent in an intense search for an appropriate abode for Lola. Lola and Beetelle wanted a place in the West Village, both for its charms, which couldn't help but inspire a young person, and for the neighbors, who included, according to the celebrity magazines, several movie and television stars as well as fashion designers and musical artists. Although the ideal abode had yet to be found, Beetelle, always efficient, had already begun furnishing it. She'd ordered a bed and various other items, such as sheets and towels, from the vast warehouse of a store called ABC Carpet. The loot was piled up in the entryway of the hotel room, and in the middle of this, Beetelle lay exhausted on a narrow couch, thinking about her swollen feet and wondering if anything could be done about them.

The Fabrikants, after endless discussion, had decided the most they could pay in rent was three thousand dollars a month, which was, as Cem pointed out, more than most people's monthly mortgage payment. For this price, the Fabrikants imagined they'd find a spacious apartment with a terrace; instead, they'd been shown dirty little rooms that were reached by several flights of stairs. Beetelle imagined Lola living in such a space and being attacked at knifepoint in the stairwell. It wouldn't do. Lola had to be safe. Her apartment must be clean and at least a reasonable facsimile of what she had at home.

Across the room, Cem lay facedown on the bed. Beetelle put her hands over her face. "Cem," she asked, "did you get the reservations for Il Posto?"

There was a muffled groan into the pillow.

"You forgot, didn't you?" Beetelle said.

"I was just about to call."

"It's probably too late. The concierge said it can take a month to get a reservation at a Mario Batali restaurant."

"We could eat at the restaurant here," Cem said hopefully, despite the fact that he knew another dinner at the hotel would result in a very chilly evening with his wife and daughter.

"We've already eaten here twice," Beetelle scolded. "Lola so wanted to go to Il Posto. It's important. If she's going to succeed here, she needs to be exposed to the best. That's the whole point of New York. Exposure. I'm sure most of the people she meets will have gone to a Mario Batali restaurant. Or at least a Bobby Flay one."

Cem Fabrikant couldn't imagine that this was true—that recent college graduates regularly frequented two-hundred-and-fifty-dollar-a-person restaurants—but knew better than to argue. "I'll call the concierge," he said. And keep my fingers crossed, he added to himself.

Beetelle closed her eyes and folded her lips as if trapping in a sigh of frustration. This was the typical construct of their marriage: Cem would agree to do something and would then take so long to do it that Beetelle would have to take over.

An impatient ringing of the buzzer, which sounded like an angry wasp trying to get into the suite, broke the tension. "Lola's back," Beetelle said with relief, getting up and making her way to the door. She pulled it open, and Lola brushed past her, a large yellow shopping bag slung over her shoulder. She let the bag slip to the floor and held out her hands excitedly. "Look, Mom."

Beetelle examined her daughter's fingers. "Black?" she asked, commenting on Lola's choice of nail color.

"No one's forcing you to paint yours black. So it doesn't matter," Lola said. She knelt down and extracted a shoe box from the bag. "Aren't these amazing?" she asked, lifting the cover and tearing away the tissue paper. She held up a gold platformed boot with a heel at least five inches high.

"Oh, sweetheart," Beetelle said with dismay.

"What?"

"It's summer."

"So what?" Lola said. "I'm going to wear them to dinner tonight. We're going to Il Posto, right?"

The combination of the boot and the mention of Il Posto roused Cem from the bed. He was a short, round man who resembled a hazelnut and tended to blend into the background. "Why would you buy winter shoes in the summer?" he asked.

Lola ignored him, taking off her current shoes—black leather sandals with a Lucite heel—and slipping on the boots.

"Very nice," Cem said, trying to get into the spirit of things. After so many years of marriage, however, he knew better than to reveal any vestiges of male sexuality. He aimed to be neutral and enthusiastic, a delicate balance he had learned to attain years ago, shortly after Lola was born. If memory served him correctly, it was precisely at the moment of her birth that his sexuality had effectively been neutered, save for the four or five times a year his wife allowed him intercourse.

"I told you," Lola said, examining herself in the large round mirror above the couch. She didn't go on to explain the meaning of her comment, but it didn't matter. Standing up, Lola towered above her parents, and confronted with the sight of a creature so stunning that she had to remind herself that this girl was indeed the result of her very own genes, Beetelle immediately forgot her dismay over the black fingernails and the gold boots.

Having grown up in an era when young women pampered themselves as vigorously as Roman royalty, Lola was like a piece of granite that had been rubbed and polished until it nearly resembled marble. She stood five feet eight inches tall, had a surgically enhanced chest, wore Victoria's Secret lacy bras, and weighed 130 pounds. Her teeth were white and perfect, her eyes hazel with long mascaraed lashes, her skin buffed and moisturized. She'd decided her mouth wasn't wide enough, but the lips were plump, made more so by regular injections of collagen.

Satisfied with her appearance, Lola plopped down on the couch next to her mother. "Did you get those sheets I wanted?"

"Sheets and towels. But how was the interview? Did you get the job?"

"There was no job. As usual," Lola said, picking up the clicker for the television and turning it on. "And the woman who interviewed me was kind of hostile. So I was kind of hostile back."

"You must be nice to everyone," Beetelle said.

"That would make me a hypocrite," Lola said.

A muffled chortling came from Cem's vicinity.

"That's enough, you two," Beetelle said firmly. She turned once again to her daughter. "Darling, you have to find a job. Otherwise . . ."

Lola looked at her mother. Wishing her mother wouldn't hover so much, she decided to punish her by delaying the news about the possible job with Philip Oakland. She took her time changing the channels on the TV, and after she got to four hundred and decided there was nothing worth watching, finally said, "I did hear about something today. Working for Philip Oakland. The writer."

"Philip Oakland?" Beetelle repeated with fervent interest.

"He's looking for a researcher. I met a girl at the interview who e-mailed me his information. Then I e-mailed him myself, and he e-mailed me right back. I have an interview next week."

Beetelle was nearly speechless. "Darling, that's wonderful." She pulled her daughter into a smothering embrace. "Philip Oakland is exactly the kind of person you came to New York to meet. He's an A-list screenwriter. Think of the people he must know—and the people you'll meet through him." Gaining momentum, she added, "This is everything I always wanted for you. I just didn't expect it to happen so soon."

Lola wriggled out of her mother's grasp. "It hasn't happened yet," she said. "He still has to hire me."

"Oh, but he will," Beetelle insisted. She sprang up. "We'll have to get you a new outfit. Thank goodness Jeffrey is right around the corner."

Hearing the word "Jeffrey," Cem shuddered. Jeffrey was one of the most expensive stores in Manhattan. "Weren't we just there?" he asked cautiously.

"Oh, Cem," Beetelle scolded. "Don't be silly. Please, get up. We need to shop. And then we've got to meet Brenda Lish. She has two more apartments to show us. I'm so excited, I don't know what to do."

Fifteen minutes later, the threesome exited Soho House and came out on Ninth Avenue. Lola had decided to break in her new boots; in the gold platform heels she elicited gaping stares from passersby. After a few feet, they were forced to stop when Cem brought up a map on his iPhone. "We go straight. And then we veer to the left at the fork." He looked down at the iPhone again. "At least I think we do," he added. His few days in the West Village had been a continual exercise in navigational frustration.

"Oh, Daddy, come *on*," Lola said, and strode off ahead of them. She had officially outgrown her parents, she thought, teetering along a cobblestoned street. They were just too slow. The evening before, it had taken her father ten minutes to work up the confidence to flag down a cab.

The Fabrikants met the real estate agent, Brenda Lish, in front of a plain white brick building on West Tenth Street, one of many constructed all over the city in the sixties as middle-class housing.

Brenda would not normally have dealt with such small potatoes as the Fabrikants, who were only seeking a rental, but Cem was an acquaintance of one of Brenda's major clients, who had asked if she would help them out. Since the client was spending several million dollars on an apartment, Brenda was happy to be generous to these nice people with the beautiful daughter.

"I think this will be perfect for you," Brenda said in her happy, flighty voice. "It's a twenty-four-hour doorman building, and it's filled with young people. And you can't beat the West Village location."

The apartment was a studio with a separate kitchen and dressing area. The exposure was southern, which meant good light. The cost was thirty-five hundred a month.

"It's so small," Lola said.

"We like to call it cozy," Brenda said.

"My bed will be in the same room as my living room. What if I want to have people over? They'll see my bed," Lola protested.

"You could get a foldout couch," Brenda said cheerfully.

"That's awful," Lola said. "I don't want to sleep on a foldout couch."

Brenda had recently returned from a spiritual journey to India. There were people in the world who slept on thin mats made of plant materials, there were people who slept on cement slabs, there were people who had no beds at all. She kept a smile on her face.

Beetelle looked at Lola, gauging her mood. "Is there anything else?" Beetelle asked Brenda. "Anything bigger?"

"Honestly, I've shown you everything available in your price range," Brenda said. "If you want to look in another area, I'm sure you can find a one-bedroom for the same amount of money."

"I want to live in the West Village," Lola said.

"But why, honey?" Cem asked. "It's all Manhattan. It's all the same, isn't it?"

"Some people might look at it that way," Brenda said. She waited.

Lola crossed her arms and stood with her back to her parents, looking out at the street. "Carrie Bradshaw lived in the West Village," she said.

"Ah," Brenda said. "There is another apartment in this building. It's probably exactly what you're looking for. But it's much more expensive."

"How much more?" Cem asked.

"Six thousand a month."

Cem Fabrikant did not sleep well that night. He hadn't slept so badly for years, from around the time when he'd purchased the McMansion in Windsor Pines with an eight-hundred-thousand-dollar mortgage. Back then, Beetelle had convinced him that it had to be done for the future of the family in this highly competitive world where appearances were as important as reality. Where reality *was* appearance. The thought of owing so much money made Cem sweat, but he never expressed his fears to his wife or daughter.

Now, lying next to his soundly sleeping wife in the big bed with the starched hotel sheets, he reminded himself that the whole world, or rather, his whole world of decent, upwardly mobile and righteous people, ran on fear. Even his livelihood ran on it—the fear of a terrorist attack or a school shooting or a madman run amok. Cem was a tech man and for the past three years had been working on a system to alert people to these dangers via a text message, so they could at least avoid arriving needlessly into danger. But he sometimes wondered if these larger fears masked the smaller and less worthy fears that drove everyone in his world: the fear of not making it, of being left behind, of not utilizing one's skills or potential or advantages to the fullest. What everyone wanted, after all, was a happy, carefree life full of pleasant and wonderful things, a life in which no one was hurt or died needlessly, but most of all, a life in which no one was denied his dream.

And so, he realized, he was going to have to refinance his mortgage again to pay for Lola's dream of a big life in New York City.

Cem did not understand why she wanted this dream or even exactly what this dream was and why it was important, but he did know that if he did not support it, then for the rest of her life Lola might be unhappy, might have to wonder "what if?" and "if only." And even worse: Is this *all* there is?

3

"It is I, the prodigal nephew," Philip said the next morning, knocking on Enid's door.

"You're just in time," Enid said, jangling a set of keys. "Guess what I've got? Keys to Mrs. Houghton's apartment."

"How'd you get them?" Philip asked.

"As the board president emeritus, I still enjoy certain perks."

"The children are definitely selling?" Philip said.

"They want out fast. They think real estate prices can only go down." They went upstairs, and opening the door to Mrs. Houghton's apartment, were immediately assaulted by a riot of flowered chintz. "Society lady circa 1983," Enid remarked.

"You haven't been in here since?" Philip asked.

"Only a couple of times. Louise didn't want visitors toward the end."

There was a scratching at the door, and Mindy Gooch and the real estate agent Brenda Lish came in. "Well," Mindy said, staring at Philip and Enid. "It's like Grand Central Station in here."

"Hello, Mindy, dear," Enid said.

"Hello," Mindy said coldly. "So you do have the keys."

"Didn't Roberto tell you?" Enid asked innocently. "I picked them up yesterday afternoon."

Philip glanced at Mindy but didn't acknowledge her. He knew vaguely who Mindy was, knew vaguely that her husband was some kind of writer, but as he didn't know them, he never said hello. And so, as sometimes happened in these buildings, Mindy and James had decided that Philip Oakland, who was successful, was also smug and arrogant, too arrogant to even greet them politely, making him their sworn enemy.

"You're Philip Oakland," Mindy said, wanting to put herself in his face but not wanting to sink to his level of disregard.

"Yes," Philip said.

"I'm Mindy Gooch. You know who I am, Philip. I live here. With my husband, James Gooch. For God's sake, the two of you have the same publisher. Redmon Richardly?"

"Ah, yes," Philip said. "I didn't know that."

"You do now," Mindy said. "So the next time we see you, perhaps you'll say hello."

"Don't I say hello?" Philip said.

"No, you don't," Mindy said.

"The bones of this apartment are amazing," Brenda Lish interjected, wanting to defuse a spat between warring residents. With an apartment like this, there would undoubtedly be many skirmishes ahead.

The group trooped up the stairs, eventually reaching the top floor, which contained the ballroom. The ceiling was a dome, sixteen feet high; at one end was an enormous marble fireplace. Mindy's heart beat faster. She'd always dreamed of living in an apartment like this, with a room like this, an aerie with three-hundred-and-sixty-degree views of all of Manhattan. The light was astounding. Every New Yorker wanted light, and few had it. If she lived here, in this apartment, instead of in the half-basement warren of rooms her family now occupied, maybe for once in her life, she could be happy.

"I was thinking," Enid said, "we might want to split up the apartment. Sell off each floor."

Yes, Mindy thought. And maybe she and James could buy the top floor. "We'd need to have a special quorum of the board," she said.

"How long would that take?" Brenda asked.

Mindy looked at Enid. "It depends."

"Well, it would be a shame," Brenda said. "Apartments like this never come up in Manhattan. And especially not in this location. It's one of a kind. It should probably be on the National Register of Historic Places."

"The exterior of the building is on the register. The apartments are not. Residents are entitled to do anything they want with them," Enid said.

"That's too bad," Brenda said. "If the apartment were part of the national register, you'd attract the right kind of buyer, someone you'd probably want in the building. Someone who appreciates beauty and history. They wouldn't be able to destroy these deco moldings, for instance."

"We're not going to turn it into a museum," Mindy said.

"How much is it worth?" Enid asked.

"My guess? Intact, around twenty million. If you split it up, you'll hurt the value. Each floor will probably be worth three point five."

In a fluster, Mindy went down to her apartment. The still air was stifling; in the afternoon on a bright day, when the sun was angled just right, a strip of light illuminated the back of the rooms, which looked out onto a small cement patio. The patio was eight feet wide, and she and James were always thinking about fixing it up, but never got around to it. Any kind of construction had to be approved by the board, which wouldn't have been a problem, but it also required materials and workers to do the job, and the logistics of organizing such an event were too much on top of everything else she had to do. So, for the ten years she and James had lived there, the patio had remained the same—a cracked cement patch through which stubborn tufts of grass grew. A small Weber barbecue grill and three folding chairs completed the picture.

Mindy went into her office. Finding her latest bank statement, she added up their assets. They had two hundred and fifty-seven thousand in savings, four hundred thousand in a retirement account, thirty thousand dollars in checking, and maybe ten thousand dollars in stocks. A long time ago, James had wanted to invest in the stock market, and Mindy had said, "Do I look like someone who wants to throw away her money? The stock market is nothing more than legalized gambling, and you know how I feel about gambling. And the lotto, for that matter." Adding up all their cash, they had barely seven hundred thousand dollars. Mindy knew this sum was more than what most Americans had, but in their world, it wasn't much. It cost thirty-five thousand a year to send Sam to private school, and it would take at least a hundred and fifty thousand dollars to send him to college. On the plus side, their apartment—which they had bought slowly in pieces and put together during the real estate downturn in the mid-nineties—was worth at least a million dollars. And they'd paid only two hundred and fifty thousand. Altogether, their assets were close-ish to two million dollars. If they wanted to buy just one floor of the penthouse, they were still one and a half million short.

Maybe they should sell everything and move to the Caribbean, Mindy thought.

How much could a house in the Caribbean cost? A hundred, two hundred thousand dollars? She could swim and make salads and read. James could write pathetic novels about the local goings-on. They'd be giving up, but so what? The only glitch was Sam. He'd love it, but would it be good for him? He was a genius and such a nice boy. Not the least bit arrogant about his intelligence, unlike some of his friends. But if they left New York, it could throw Sam's whole educational career off track, meaning he might not get into an Ivy League school. No, Mindy thought, shaking her head. We will not give up. We will persevere. We will stay in New York with our fingernails digging into the cement, if only for Sam's sake.

The buzzer rang, and she jumped up, wondering who it might

be. Probably James, who was out buying overpriced food at Citarella and who'd probably forgotten his keys.

Instead, it was Enid Merle.

"Is Sam home?" Enid asked. "I need to install some new software, and I was wondering if he could help." Sam was the building's resident computer expert; whenever anyone had a problem, they called on Sam, who was a computer genius and had built up a cottage industry in the building.

"Sam isn't here," Mindy said. "He's away for a few days."

"How nice for him. Where?"

Mindy stood in her doorway, blocking Enid's entry. She didn't want Enid to see her apartment. She was private about her space, but also embarrassed. Plus, her hostility toward Philip often extended to Enid, as she was his aunt. "He's gone upstate with friends. I'll tell him to ring your buzzer when he gets back."

Enid didn't move away. "What do you think?" she asked.

"About what?" Mindy said.

"It might not be a bad idea to break up the apartment."

"I don't know why you're interested," Mindy said.

"I've lived in the building for over sixty years. Naturally, I'm interested in everything that goes on here."

"I appreciate that, Enid. But you're no longer on the board."

"Not technically," Enid said. "But I have a lot of friends."

"We all do," Mindy said, although in her case, she wasn't sure this was entirely true.

"If we split up the apartment, we could probably sell to people who already live in the building. It could save you a lot of headaches," Enid pointed out.

Ah, Mindy thought. Enid wanted the bottom floor for Philip. It made sense. Philip could break through from his own apartment. And he probably had the money. Not enough for the whole apartment but enough for one floor.

"I'll think about it," Mindy said. She closed the door firmly and went back to her accounts. No matter how she added them up, they were still short. That was that, then. There was no way she would allow Philip Oakland to get the bottom floor of that apartment. If she and James couldn't have a floor, why should he?

❦

"Check out *Sanderson* vs. *English*," Annalisa Rice said into the phone. "It's all very clear. And of course there's the moral element, which always sways juries. It's like an Aesop's fable."

"Damn, Rice," said the male voice at the other end. "Why'd you have to go and move to New York on me?"

"Change, Riley," Annalisa replied. "It's good, remember?"

"I know you," Riley said. "You're probably already on to the next big thing. Are you running someone's campaign? Or running for office yourself?"

"Neither." Annalisa laughed. "I've made a U-turn, to put it mildly. You won't believe what I'm doing right now."

"Helping the homeless?"

"Consorting with the rich. I'm going to the Hamptons for the weekend."

Riley laughed, too. "I always said you were too glamorous for Washington."

"Damn you, Riley," Annalisa said. "I miss you guys."

"You can always come back," Riley said.

"Too late," Annalisa said. She said goodbye and hung up the phone, twisting her auburn hair into her trademark ponytail. She went to the window and, pushing back the heavy gold drapes, looked out at the street. It was a long way down. She pushed at the window, longing for some fresh air in the overly air-conditioned suite, and remembered that the windows were bolted shut. She looked at her watch; it was three o'clock. She had two hours to pack and get to the heliport. It should have been plenty of time. But she didn't know what to pack. What did one wear to a weekend in the Hamptons?

"Paul, what should I bring?" she'd asked that morning.

"Oh, hell. I don't know," Paul had said. Paul was her husband.

He was engaged in getting out the door by seven A.M. on the dot, sitting on the edge of a hassock, pulling on thin silk socks and Italian loafers. Paul had never worn proper shoes before. He'd never had to, before New York. Back in Washington, he'd always worn leather Adidas tennis shoes.

"Are those new?" Annalisa asked, referring to the shoes.

"I can't say. What does new mean, exactly?" Paul asked. "Six months old? A day? These kinds of questions are only answerable if you know the context of the person asking."

Annalisa laughed. "Paul, you have to help me. They're your friends."

"Partners," Paul corrected. "Anyway, what difference does it make? You'll be the best-looking woman there."

"It's the Hamptons. They probably have a dress code."

"Why don't you call Sandy's wife, Connie?"

"I don't know her," Annalisa said.

"Sure you do. She's Sandy's wife."

"Oh, Paul," she said. It just doesn't work that way, she thought, but refrained from explaining. Paul wouldn't understand.

Paul leaned across the bed to kiss her goodbye. "Are you looking at apartments today?" he asked.

"I'm always looking at apartments. You'd think that with fifteen million dollars to spend, it would be easy."

"If it's not enough, spend more," Paul said.

"I love you," she called after him.

That morning, Annalisa had considered asking Emme, the real estate agent, what one wore in the Hamptons, but judging from Emme's appearance, Annalisa didn't think she'd like the answer. Emme was at least sixty years old but had a face that sported the latest in plastic surgery techniques. All morning, Emme's overarched eyebrows, plastic lips, and large white teeth kept distracting Annalisa, as did Emme's hair, which was coarse and dark at the roots and frayed blond on the ends. Emme was considered the best real estate agent on the Upper East Side. "I know you've got plenty of money," Emme said, "but money isn't the issue.

Everyone's got plenty of money these days. It's who you know that counts." Then she'd asked, "Who do you know?"

"How about the president of the United States?" Annalisa said, twisting her ponytail.

"Will he write you a letter?" Emme asked, not catching the sarcasm.

"Probably not," Annalisa said. "Considering I called his administration an embarrassment."

"Everybody says that," Emme said.

"Yes, but I said it on TV. I used to be a regular on *Washington Morning*."

"That's not a good answer," Emme said.

"How about Sandy Brewer?" Annalisa finally ventured.

"Who's he?" Emme asked.

"My husband works with him."

"But who *is* he?" Emme said.

"He runs a fund," Annalisa said cautiously, as Paul had told her repeatedly that she wasn't to talk about what he did or how he made his money. It was a secret community, he said, like Skull and Bones at Yale.

"So he's a hedge-fund manager," Emme guessed correctly. "Nobody knows who they are or wants to know them. Nobody wants them as a member of their club." She looked Annalisa up and down. "And it isn't just about your husband. It's about you, too. You have to be approved by the board."

"I'm a lawyer," Annalisa said. "I can't see anyone objecting to that."

"What kind of lawyer?" Emme asked.

"Class-action lawsuits. Among other things."

"I could see a lot of people objecting to you," Emme said. "Isn't that really a glorified kind of ambulance chasing?" She shook her head. "We'd better concentrate on brownstones. If you buy a brownstone, you won't have to worry about getting approved by a board."

The morning of the day Annalisa and Paul were going to the Hamptons, Emme had shown her three town houses. One was a mess, smelling of milk and dirty diapers, with toys strewn every-where. In the second town house, a woman of about thirty followed them around, holding a slippery two-year-old boy in her arms. "It's a fantastic house," the woman had said.

"Why are you moving?" Annalisa had asked.

"We're moving to the country. We've got a house there. We're putting on a big addition. It's better for kids in the country, don't you think?"

The third town house was larger and less expensive. The hitch was that it was broken up into apartments, most of which were occupied. "You'd have to get the tenants to leave. It usually isn't a problem. You pay them fifty thousand cash, and they're happy to have the money," Emme had explained.

"But where will they go?" Annalisa asked.

"They'll find a nice, clean studio apartment somewhere," Emme said. "Or they'll move to Florida."

"That doesn't seem right," Annalisa said. "Kicking people out of their apartments. It's against my moral code."

"You can't stop progress," Emme replied. "It's unhealthy."

And so another day passed during which she and Paul still didn't have a place to live and were stuck in the suite at the Waldorf.

Annalisa called Paul. "I can't find anything to buy. Maybe we should rent in the meantime."

"And move twice? It's ergonomically wasteful."

"Paul," she said, "I'm going to go out of my mind if we have to stay in this suite for one more day. Actually, I'll go out of my mind if I have to spend more time with Emme. Her face scares me."

"So let's change to a bigger suite. The staff can move our things."

"The cost," Annalisa said.

"Doesn't matter. Love you," he said.

She went downstairs into the bustle of the lobby. She had always stayed at the Waldorf when the law firm sent her to New York on business, and back then she'd thought the hotel lobby glamorous, with its grand staircases and brass and expensive wares displayed behind sparkling glass windows. The Waldorf was perfect for tourists and out-of-town businesspeople, but it was like a show-girl: One must enjoy the feathers and glitz without looking too closely. Otherwise, one saw the faded carpets and the dirty crystal in the chandeliers and the cheap polyester in the uniforms of the employees. One had time to observe these things, Annalisa noted, when one didn't have enough to do.

She was informed that a bigger suite was indeed available, and the manager was summoned. He had a soft face and jowls that pulled down the skin below his eyes; the available suite, he said, had two bedrooms and a living room and a bar and four bathrooms. It was twenty-five hundred a night, but if they were staying for a month, he'd give it to them for forty thousand. An odd feeling came over Annalisa, a rush of adrenaline, and she said she'd take it without seeing it first. It was the most exciting thing in weeks.

Back in the original suite, Annalisa opened the safe and put on the diamond-encrusted watch Paul had given her for her birthday. She couldn't imagine what it had cost, probably twenty thousand dollars, but it put some perspective on the cost of the suite, she supposed. The watch was a little flashy for her taste, but Paul would notice if she didn't wear it for the weekend. Under an attempt at a casual demeanor he had looked so eager and frightened and proud while she untied the ribbon on the blue handmade box with the beige suede lining. When she'd opened the box and removed the watch, Paul did the honors of closing the band around her wrist. "Do you like it?" he'd asked. "I love it," she'd said, lying. "I truly love it."

"Apparently, all the other wives have them. So you'll fit in," he said. And noting her expression, added, "If you want to."

"We don't fit in," she said. "That's why people love us."

Now she began to pack, placing a bathing suit and khaki shorts and three button-down shirts into a navy blue canvas roller bag. At the last minute, she tossed in a plain black sleeveless shift and a pair of black pumps with a sensible two-inch heel in case there was a fancy dinner. The dress wasn't summery but would have to do. She put on a white T-shirt, jeans, and yellow Converse sneakers; then she went downstairs again and waited in line for a taxi, arriving at the Twenty-third Street heliport at four-thirty, half an hour early. She was early to nearly everything these days and seemed to spend a lot of her time waiting. The heliport was located under the FDR Drive. The air was dense with the heat of July and the exhaust from the cars stalled on the highway and the stench of the East River. Annalisa walked to the edge of the dock and peered into the murky brown water, watching a plastic bottle lapping at the wood as a condom floated by.

She checked her watch again. Paul would be neither early nor late but exactly on time, arriving at 4:55, as he'd said he would. Indeed, at 4:55, a Town Car pulled in through the chain-link fencing, and Paul got out, leaning into the backseat of the car to take out his briefcase and a small hard-sided Louis Vuitton case covered in black goatskin. Until recently, Annalisa had no idea Paul cared for such things. He bought something pricey nearly every week now. Last week it had been a cigar box from Asprey, although Paul did not smoke.

He loped toward her, talking on his cell phone. Paul was tall and had the slight stoop of those accustomed to minding their heads. He managed to stay on his phone while waving to the pilot of the seaplane and overseeing the stowage of their luggage while a steward helped Annalisa from the dock into the plane. The interior held eight seats done up in plush pale yellow suede, and while Paul and Annalisa were the only passengers, Paul elected to sit in the row in front of her. He finally got off his call, and she said, hesitantly and a little bit hurt, "Paul?"

Paul wore glasses, and his soft, dark curling hair was always a bit unkempt. He was nearly handsome but for his hooded eyes and the slight gaps between his teeth. He was a mathematical genius, one of the youngest Ph.D.s at Georgetown ever, and there was always talk of him winning the Nobel Prize someday. But six months ago, he had taken a job with Sandy Brewer and, in two days, relocated to New York City at a small hotel on East Fifty-sixth Street. When they decided the move was permanent, Annalisa had joined him, but they'd lived long-distance for five months, and the residual effects were still there.

"Wouldn't you like to sit together?" Annalisa asked. She hated having to beg.

"These cabins are so small," he said. "Why be crowded? We're together the whole weekend anyway."

"You're right," she said. It was pointless pushing Paul on the small issues. Annalisa looked out the window. A middle-aged man was hurrying breathlessly toward the seaplane. Annalisa's first impression was of a man freckled and nearly hairless, like an exotic species of cat. The man was wearing spectator shoes and a white linen suit with a navy silk pocket square; in one hand was a woven hat. He gave his bag to the pilot and came up into the cabin, taking a seat in the row behind Annalisa. "Hello," he said, extending his hand over the top of the seats. "I'm Billy Litchfield."

"Annalisa Rice."

"I assume you're going to the Brewers' for the weekend. Are you a friend of Connie's?"

"My husband works for Sandy Brewer."

"Ah," Billy Litchfield said. "So you're an unknown element."

Annalisa smiled. "Yes."

"And that gentleman is your husband?"

Paul was reading something on his iPhone. "Paul," she said. He looked up briefly. "This is Billy Litchfield."

Paul gave Billy a curt smile and went back to his iPhone. He was never interested in strangers, and as usual, Annalisa tried to cover it up by being excessively friendly.

"Are you a friend of Connie's?" she asked.

"I'm a friend of both Brewers now. But yes, in answer to your question, Connie and I go way back."

There was a pause. Annalisa suddenly didn't know what to say, but Billy Litchfield smiled at her. "Have you been to the house before?" he asked.

She shook her head.

"You're in for a treat. It's magnificent, designed by Peter Cook. Peter can be over the top, but the Brewers' house is one of the best examples of his work."

"I see."

"You know who Peter Cook is, don't you?" he asked.

"Actually, I don't. I'm a lawyer, and—"

"Ah," Billy said, as if this explained everything. "Peter Cook is an architect. Some people say he ruined the East End with his McMansions, but eventually, they've all come round to him. Everyone uses him—he won't do a house for under ten million these days." The pilot started up the engines. "I love this moment of the week, don't you?" Billy said, leaning forward conspiratorially. "Taking off for greener pastures. Even if it is just for the weekend." He looked her over. "Do you live in New York?"

"We just moved."

"Upper East Side?" Billy asked.

"Nowhere, really."

"My dear," Billy said. "You and that magnificent husband of yours who is sporting a two-thousand-dollar Paul Smith shirt cannot be living in a cardboard box on the street."

"We're in the Waldorf. Until we find an apartment. Or a town house."

"Why the Waldorf?" Billy asked.

"I always used to stay there on business."

"Aha," Billy said.

Annalisa felt self-conscious, pinned under Billy's gaze. She was used to attention, having stood out all her life, with her auburn hair and her wide cheekbones and her light gray eyes. Men had a propensity to fall in love with her—foolishly—and she'd learned to ignore the undercurrents of male attraction. But with Billy, it was different. He seemed to be studying her as if she were a piece of fine china. Embarrassed, she turned away, leaving Billy to examine her profile. She's not a classic beauty, Billy thought, but a unique one. Having once seen her face, you wouldn't forget her. She wasn't wearing a stitch of makeup, and her hair was pulled back into a ponytail. Confident girl, he thought, to be so unadorned, save for the platinum-and-diamond Chopard watch on her wrist. That was a nice touch. He turned his attention to the husband, who was less interesting physically. Billy had already heard from Connie Brewer that Paul Rice was a mathematical genius. If he worked with Sandy Brewer, he was rich, and that was all that was required of a man in New York society—that he have money. It was the wives who mattered. As the seaplane taxied across the choppy waters of the East River, Billy sat back in his seat, satisfied. Annalisa and Paul Rice intrigued him. It would be an interesting weekend after all.

Picking up speed, the seaplane lifted off the water. They flew over Queens, over endless rows of tiny houses, and then straight up the middle of Long Island Sound, which sparkled as brightly as the diamonds on Annalisa's watch. They turned south over the rocky white lip of the North Fork, past the green pastures and corn-fields. Then they were over water again, and the plane was descending into an inlet.

Billy Litchfield tapped Annalisa on the shoulder. "This is a patch of paradise," he said. "I've been everywhere, and it's as beautiful here as it is in Saint-Tropez or Capri or any other place you can think of. It's why the Hamptons will never be over, no matter what anyone says."

The plane taxied to a pristine white dock. A lawn as perfectly manicured as a golf course sloped up a long hill, at the top of which sat an enormous shingled house with turrets that appeared to be made of pink stone. On the lawn next to the dock sat two golf carts.

Sandy Brewer met them on the dock. His most distinct feature was his name; without his name, he was disturbingly indistinct, with hair of no particular color and nondescript features. "Connie said to have you go straight up to the house," Sandy said to Billy. "She's having some problem with the dessert. I thought I'd take Paul and Annalisa on a tour of the property." Billy was driven away in one of the golf carts with the luggage.

Annalisa got into the back of the second golf cart. Paul sat in the front with Sandy. Sandy drove casually, turning back to talk to her. "Have you ever been to the Hamptons before?" he asked.

"I haven't, actually," Annalisa said.

"We've got fifty acres here," Sandy said. "It's an enormous amount of land. Connie and I just bought a ranch in Montana with a thousand acres, but Montana's different. If you don't have a thousand acres in Montana, you're a loser. In the Hamptons, you can have five acres and it's perfectly acceptable—you might even be a member of the Bath and Tennis in Southampton. But Connie and I don't like those kinds of places. We like to be private. When we're here, nobody knows it."

An hour later, after they were shown the two pools (one Olympic, one shaped like a pond with a waterfall), the guesthouse, the private zoo and aviary, the greenhouse where Sandy oversaw the cultivation of rare species of tulips, the miniature horse and goat barn, the three tennis courts complete with bleachers, the baseball diamond and basketball court, the children's Victorian summerhouse, the indoor squash court, the winery with state-of-the-art concrete casks, the five-acre vineyard, the orchard and vegetable garden and koi pond, Sandy ushered them into the house. Two grand staircases flanked the foyer. Paul went off with Sandy to talk business. A Guatemalan woman motioned for Annalisa to follow her up the stairs. They passed an upstairs sitting room and several closed doors. Annalisa was led into a room with an enormous four-poster bed and two bathrooms. French windows opened onto a balcony overlooking the lawn and the ocean. Her suitcase had been unpacked; her paltry supply of clothing for the weekend looked incongruous in the enormous cedar closet. Annalisa stepped inside, inhaling the odor of the wood. I've got to tell Paul about this, she thought, and went downstairs to find him.

Instead, she discovered Connie, Sandy's wife, and Billy Litchfield in a sunroom done up with pink silk chaises. "I'm sure you feel horrible," Connie was saying to Billy.

"Excuse me," Annalisa said, realizing she'd interrupted a tête-à-tête.

Connie sprang up. She was once a famous ballerina and wore her blond hair long and straight, hanging nearly to her tailbone. She had enormous blue eyes and a tiny nose and was as slim as a fairy. "I was about to check on you," she said. "Do you have everything you need?"

"Our room is wonderful, thank you. I was just looking for Paul."

"He's gone off with Sandy. They might be up to anything, but they're probably plotting how to take over the world. Come sit with us," Connie said. "We've heard you were a lawyer. Sandy said you had a very important job. Working for the attorney general."

"I clerked for him when I finished law school."

"You'll probably find us very boring then," Connie responded. "All the men ever talk about is business. And all we women talk about is children."

"Don't listen to her," Billy said to Annalisa. "Connie's an expert on contemporary art."

"Only because you taught me everything I know, Billy," Connie said. "My real love is jewelry. I love glittery things. I can't help myself. Do you have any passions you're ashamed of, Annalisa?"

Annalisa smiled. "My problem is that I'm probably too serious."

Connie rearranged herself on the chaise and said dramatically, "And mine is that I'm frivolous. I'm rich and silly. But I have a good time."

Billy stood up. "Shall we dress for dinner?" he asked. Annalisa walked with him to the stairs. "Connie is frivolous," Billy went on, "but they've only had their money for seven years. On the other hand, she doesn't have a mean bone in her body. If you become friends with her, you'll find her a useful ally."

"Am I going to need allies?"

"One always does," Billy said, and smiled.

He left Annalisa at the top of the landing. "I'll see you at cocktails. They start at eight on the veranda."

What a funny man, Annalisa thought, returning to her room. He was like someone out of the nineteenth century.

Paul came back while she was in a shower stall the size of a small room. She opened the glass door. "It's a steam shower," she called out to him. "Do you want to come in?" He got in, and she soaped his chest. "Did you see the cedar closet? And the towel warmers? And what about that bed?"

"Should we get a place like this?" Paul asked, tilting his head back to get the lather out of his hair.

"You mean our own ten-million-dollar Peter Cook house with pink stone and a little man like Billy Litchfield to teach us manners and art?" She jumped out of the shower and dried herself. Paul came out and stood dripping on the mat. She handed him a thick towel.

"Sure," he said. "Why not?"

"Paul," she said. "Is that what we're doing? Becoming Connie and Sandy Brewer? Are we going to be just like them but with newer money?"

"What are you talking about?" he asked.

"How old is our money, anyway? Six months? Maybe when it's a year old, we can have a birthday party to celebrate."

"You've lost me."

"Doesn't matter," she said. "It was just something odd that Billy Litchfield said. It's not important."

In a nearly identical room down the hall, Billy Litchfield lay on his back, arms folded carefully across his chest in order not to wrinkle his shirt. He closed his eyes, hoping to nap. Lately, he'd been tired all the time and yet found he couldn't sleep. For months, he'd felt psychically off; perhaps, he thought, he should try seeing an astrologer instead of a psychopharmacologist. After several more minutes of jangly exhaustion, he gave up and took a prescription bottle from his bag. Inside were several small orange pills. Billy broke one in half, swallowed it, and lay back down on the bed.

Within minutes, he relaxed and fell asleep. He napped longer than he'd planned, waking at ten minutes past eight.

Hurrying downstairs, he found Annalisa in the middle of a small clump of men. She was wearing a simple black shift that showed off her lanky, boyish figure, and her auburn hair swung free around her shoulders. Once again, she was without makeup, her only adornment the diamond-studded watch. As Billy passed by on his way to greet Connie, he overheard a snippet of the conversation. "Please don't tell me you're a Republican," Annalisa was saying to one of Sandy's associates. "If you have money and youth, it's your moral imperative to become a Democrat."

Billy paused and turned back to the group. Effortlessly inserting himself, he took Annalisa's arm. "Do you mind if I borrow you for a second?" he asked. "Have you met Connie's friends?"

Connie was sitting with three other women in a grouping of wide brown wicker couches. One of the women was surreptitiously smoking a cigarette; the others were talking about a shop in East Hampton. Connie looked up on their approach and patted the place next to her. "There's room here," she said to Annalisa, and indicated the woman who was smoking. "This is Beth. She went to Harvard as well. That's right, isn't it?"

"Harvard Law," Beth said, quickly stubbing out her cigarette. "What about you?" she asked Annalisa.

"Georgetown," Annalisa said.

"You still working?" Beth asked.

"No. I just quit."

"Beth quit her job years ago," Connie jumped in. "And you haven't looked back."

"I don't have time to work," Beth said. "When you're married to one of these guys"—she indicated the men—"it's a full-time job."

"Oh, but it's the kids, really," Connie said. "You don't want to miss a minute."

At nine o'clock, they were ushered in to dinner. They were served by a young man and woman dressed in black—college students earning extra money on their summer break. Annalisa was seated between Billy Litchfield and Sandy Brewer, occupying the place of honor next to the host. "Have you ever been to the Andes?" Sandy asked her. Beth, seated across from her, jumped in, prompting a lively discussion with Sandy about how the Andes were the "new" New Zealand. The conversation turned to the Bilbao art fair, a charity event to which Sandy had pledged a million dollars, and the best wine auction in the world. After dinner,

there was an endless game of pool in a paneled library. Sandy and
the other men smoked cigars. They were tipsy on fine wine and
champagne, and during a match between Billy and Paul, Billy's
voice carried across the room. "You'll make a ton of money," Billy
was saying, "bags and bags, more than you could ever imagine—and
it won't make a bit of difference. Because you'll be working as hard
as you were before, maybe harder, and you won't be able to stop,
and one day you'll look up and realize the only thing that's
changed in your life is your location. And you'll wonder why the
hell you spent your whole life doing it . . ."

All conversation went dead. Into the silence, like the bell in a
lighthouse, came the voice of Connie Brewer: "Well," she said
breathlessly, "you know what they say. It's all about location.
Location, location, location."

The guests breathed a sigh of relief. The time was noted and
exclaimed upon: It was two A.M. Everyone went upstairs to bed.

"What do you think got into that guy?" Paul said, taking off his
pants.

"Billy Litchfield?" Annalisa asked. "Probably too much alcohol."
The air conditioner was turned up high, and she snuggled under
the down comforter. "Anyway, I like him."

"That's good," Paul said, getting into bed.

"Do you think they liked us?" she asked.

"Why wouldn't they?"

"I don't know. The women are so different."

"They seemed nice enough."

"Oh, they're perfectly nice," Annalisa said.

"What's wrong?" Paul said, yawning loudly. "You sound insecure. That's not like you."

"I'm not insecure," she said. "Just curious." After a moment, she
said, "What if Billy Litchfield is right, Paul? About the money thing?"

But Paul was asleep.

The next morning at breakfast, Annalisa learned that they were
expected to play tennis in a small tournament with some of the
guests from the night before. Paul, who was not athletic, was

eliminated in the first match against Sandy. Annalisa sat in the bleachers, watching. She'd been a high school champion. Her competitive nature rose to the fore. I'm going to win this, she thought.

The tournament went on for five hours. The sun came out and the temperature rose. Annalisa won four matches in a row and was faced with Sandy in the final. As she stood on the baseline, bouncing the ball, she assessed her opponent. His playing style indicated that he'd had a lot of lessons, and his aggression made up for his lack of skill. But he didn't have a natural ability for tennis. She could win if she kept him off balance.

You might be rich, but I can still beat you, she thought, tossing the ball into the air. She brought her racket up behind her and, just before the moment of contact, flicked her wrist so the ball sliced across the net and bounced right on the sideline.

"Ace!" Billy Litchfield shouted.

Thirty minutes later, it was over. As they clustered around her, congratulating her, Annalisa thought, You can do this. You can really do this. You can succeed here as well.

"Good job," Paul said. He hugged her distractedly, with one eye on Sandy.

They all headed back to the house.

"Your wife moves well," Sandy said.

"She's good," Paul ventured.

"Yeah," Sandy said. "She'd be great in a war."

Billy Litchfield, who was strolling behind them, shuddered a little on hearing their conversation. At that moment, Annalisa stopped and turned, waiting for the group to catch up. She looked unabashedly triumphant. Billy took her arm. "Well done," he said. And then, apprising her of the age-old rule at house parties, said, "Of course, it's always a good idea to let the host win."

She stopped. "But that would be cheating. I could never do that."

"No, my dear," he said, steering her along the path. "I can see that you're the kind of girl who plays by her own rules. It's wonderful, and you must never change. But it's always wise to know what the rules are before you break them."

4

Billy Litchfield arrived back in the city at six o'clock on Sunday evening. Taking a taxi to his apartment, he was content, having had an unexpectedly fruitful weekend. Connie Brewer had agreed to buy a small Diebenkorn for three hundred thousand dollars, from which he would take a 2 percent commission. Mostly, though, he was thinking about Annalisa Rice. A girl like her rarely came along these days—she was a true original, from her auburn ponytail and light gray eyes to her keen mind. Feeling a little rush of excitement, Billy guessed that with his guidance, she might even become one of the greats.

Billy's apartment was located on Fifth Avenue between Eleventh and Twelfth Streets; his narrow brown building, a former residence for single ladies, was dwarfed into invisibility by the fine redbrick buildings on either side. His building had no doorman, although a porter could be summoned with a buzzer. Billy collected his mail and climbed the stairs to his apartment on the fourth floor.

In this building, every floor and every apartment were the same. There were four apartments per floor, and each apartment was a one-bedroom of approximately six hundred square feet. Billy liked to joke that it was an early-retirement home for spinsters such as himself. His apartment was comfortably cluttered, furnished with the castoffs of wealthy ladies. For the past ten years, he'd been telling himself that he would redecorate and find himself a lover, but he never seemed to be able to get around to either, and time passed and it mattered less and less. Billy had had no visitors for years.

He began opening his mail as a matter of course. There were several invitations and a couple of glossy magazines, a bill for his MasterCard, and a legal-size envelope that was hand-addressed, which Billy put aside. He picked out the most promising invitation, and instantly recognizing the heavy cream stationery, turned it over. The address on the back was One Fifth Avenue. The stationery came from Mrs. Strong's, and there was only one person he knew who still used it—Mrs. Louise Houghton. He opened the envelope and extracted a card on which was printed PRIVATE MEMORIAL SERVICE FOR MRS. LOUISE HOUGHTON, ST. AMBROSE CHURCH, with the date, Wednesday, July 12, written in calligraphy below. It was so Louise, Billy thought, to have planned out her memorial service in advance, down to the guest list.

He put the card in a place of honor on the narrow mantelpiece above the small fireplace. Then he sat down to the rest of his mail. Picking up the legal-size envelope, he saw that the return address was that of his building's management company. With growing dread, Billy opened it.

"We're happy to inform you . . . a deal has been closed . . . building will go co-op as of July 1, 2009 . . . you may purchase your apartment for market value . . . those not purchasing their apartments will be expected to vacate by the closing date . . ." A dull throb started up in his jaw. Where would he go? The market value of his apartment was at least eight hundred thousand dollars. He'd need two or three hundred thousand as a down payment, and then he'd have a mortgage payment and a maintenance fee. It would add up to several thousand a month. He paid only eleven hundred dollars a month in rent. The thought of finding another apartment and packing up and moving overwhelmed him. He was fifty-four. Not old, he reminded himself, but old enough to no longer have the energy for such things.

He went into the bathroom and, opening his medicine cabinet, took three antidepressants instead of his usual dose of two. Then he got into the tub, letting the water fill up around him. I can't move, he thought. I'm too tired. I'll have to figure out how to get the money to buy the apartment instead.

Later that evening, clean and in a better frame of mind, Billy called the Waldorf-Astoria, asking for the Rices' room. Annalisa answered on the third ring. "Hello?" she said curiously.

"Annalisa? It's Billy Litchfield. From this weekend."

"Oh, Billy. How are you?"

"I'm fine."

"Yes?"

"I was wondering," Billy said. "Have you ever heard the expression 'A lady should appear in the newspapers only three times in her life—her birth, her marriage, and her death'?"

"Is that true?"

"It was true a hundred years ago."

"Wow," Annalisa said.

"Well, I was wondering," Billy said. "Would you like to go to a funeral with me on Wednesday?"

$$\Psi$$

On Monday afternoon, back in her office after having spent the weekend with her family at Redmon and Catherine Richardly's house in the Hamptons, Mindy opened a new file on her computer. Like most jobs in the so-called creative glamour business, her work had become increasingly less creative and less glamorous and more organizational; a significant portion of her day was devoted to being kept in the loop or keeping others in the loop. Originality was met with smug politesse. Nevertheless, due perhaps to her perplexing weekend, Mindy had had an idea that she planned to pursue. It had popped into her head during the ride back to Manhattan in the rental car, with James driving and Mindy mostly looking at her BlackBerry or staring straight ahead. She would start a blog about her own life.

And why not? And why hadn't she thought of this before? Well, she had, but she'd resisted the idea of putting her mincey little thoughts out there on the Internet with her name attached for all to see. It felt so common; after all, anyone could do it and did. On the other hand, very good people were doing it these days. It was one of the new obligations, like having children, for smart people to make an effort to get some sensible opinions out there in the ether.

Now Mindy typed in the title of her new blog: "The Joys of Not Having It All." Not wholly original, perhaps, but original enough; she was quite sure no one else was nailing this particular female lament with such preciseness.

"Scenes from a weekend," she wrote. She crossed her legs and leaned forward, staring at the mostly blank computer screen. "Despite global warming, it was a spectacular weekend in the Hamptons," she typed. It had been nearly perfect—eighty degrees, the leaves a halo of dusky pinks and yellows, the grass still very green on the two-acre expanse of lawn on Redmon Richardly's property. The air was still and lazy with the peaty scent of decay, a scent, Mindy thought, that made time stand still.

Mindy and James and Sam had left the city late on Friday night to avoid the traffic, arriving at midnight to red wine and hot chocolate. Redmon and Catherine's baby, Sidney, was asleep, dressed in a blue onesie in a blue crib in a blue room with a wallpaper band of yellow ducks encircling the ceiling. Like the baby, the house was new but pleasantly reassuring, reminding Mindy of what she didn't have—namely, a baby and a pleasant house in the Hamptons to which one could escape every weekend, and to which one could someday make the ultimate escape: retirement. It was, Mindy realized, becoming harder and harder to justify why she and James didn't have these things that were no longer the appurtenances of the rich but only of the comfortable middle class. The ease of the Richardlys' life was made all the more enviable when Catherine revealed, in a private moment between her and Mindy in the eight-hundred-square-foot kitchen, where they were loading the dishwasher, that Sidney had been conceived without the aid of technology. Catherine was forty-two. Mindy went to bed with a pain in her heart, and after James fell asleep (immediately, as was his habit), Mindy was consumed with examining this riddle of what one got in life and why.

Just after her fortieth birthday, in the midst of a vague discontent, Mindy began seeing a shrink, a woman who specialized in a new psychoanalytropic approach called life adjustment. The shrink was a pretty, mature woman in her late thirties with the smooth skin of a beauty devotee; she wore a brown pencil skirt with a leopard-print shirt and open-toed Manolo Blahnik pumps. She had a five-year-old girl and was recently divorced. "What do you want, Mindy?" she'd asked in a flat, down-to-basics, corporate tone of voice. "If you could have anything, what would it be? Don't think, just answer."

"A baby," Mindy said. "I'd like another baby. A little girl." Before she'd said it, Mindy had had no idea what was ailing her. "Why?" the shrink asked. Mindy had to think about her answer. "I want to share myself. With someone." "But you have a husband and a child already. Isn't that so?" "Yes, but my son is ten." "You want life insurance," said the shrink. "I don't know what you mean." "You want insurance that someone is still going to need you in ten years. When your son has graduated from college and doesn't need you anymore." "Oh." Mindy had laughed. "He'll always need me." "Will he? What if he doesn't?" "Are you saying I can't win?" "You can win. Anyone can win if they know what they want and they focus on it. And if they're willing to make sacrifices. I always tell my clients there are no free shoes." "Don't you mean patients?" Mindy had asked. "They're clients," the shrink insisted. "After all, they're not *sick*."

Mindy was prescribed Xanax, one pill every night before bedtime to cut down on her anxiety and poor sleep habits (she awoke every night after four hours of sleep and would lie awake for at least two hours, worrying), and was sent to the best fertility specialist in Manhattan, who preferred high-profile patients but would take those recommended by other doctors of his ilk. At the beginning, he had recommended prenatal vitamins and a bit of luck. Mindy knew it wouldn't work because she wasn't lucky. Neither she nor James ever had been.

After two years of increasingly complicated procedures, Mindy gave up. She'd tallied their money and realized she couldn't afford to go on.

"I can count the days I've been truly content on one hand," Mindy wrote now. "Those are bad numbers in a country where pursuing happiness is a right so important, it's in our Constitution. But maybe that's the key. It's the pursuit of happiness, not the actual acquisition of it that matters."

Mindy thought back to her Sunday in the Hamptons. In the morning, they'd all gone for a walk on the beach, and she'd carried Sidney as they labored in the soft sand above the waterline. The houses, set behind the dunes, were enormous, triumphant testimonials to what some men could achieve and what others could not. In the afternoon, back at the house, Redmon organized a touch-football game.

Catherine and Mindy sat on the porch, watching the men. "It's a beautiful day, isn't it?" Catherine said for the tenth time.

"It's amazing," Mindy agreed.

Catherine squinted at the men on the lawn. "Sam is so cute," Catherine said.

"He's a good-looking boy," Mindy said proudly. "But James was cute when he was younger."

"He's still attractive," Catherine said kindly.

"You're very nice, but he isn't," Mindy said. Catherine looked startled. "I'm one of those people who won't lie to herself," Mindy explained. "I try to live with the truth."

"Is that healthy?" Catherine asked.

"Probably not."

They sat in silence for a moment. The men moved clumsily on the lawn with the heavy breath that marks the beginning of real age, and yet Mindy envied them their freedom and their willingness to pursue joy. "Are you happy with Redmon?" she said.

"Funny you should ask," Catherine said. "When we were pregnant, I was afraid. I had no idea what he'd be like as a father. It was one of the scariest times in our relationship."

"Really?"

"He still went out nearly every night. I thought, Is this what he's going to do when we have the baby? Have I made another terrible mistake with a man? You don't really know a man until you have a child with him. Then you see so much. Is he kind? Is he tolerant? Is he loving? Or is he immature and egotistical and selfish? When you have a child, it can go two ways with your husband: You love him even more, or you lose all respect for him. And if you lose respect, there's no way to get it back. I mean," Catherine said, "if Redmon ever hit Sidney or yelled at him or complained about him crying, I don't know what I'd do."

"But he'd never do those things. Redmon has so much pride in being civilized."

"Yes, he does, but one can't help thinking about those things when one has a baby. The protective gene, I suppose. How is James as a father?"

"He was great from the beginning," Mindy said. "He's not a perfect man . . ."

"What man is?"

"But he was so careful with Sam. When I was pregnant, he read all the parenting books. He's a bit of a nerd . . ."

"Like most journalists . . ."

"Well, he likes the details. And Sam has turned out great."

Mindy sat back in her chair, taking in the hazy warmth of the summer day. What she'd told Catherine about James was only half the truth. James had been neurotic about Sam, about what he ate and even the kind of diapers he wore, so much so that Mindy would find herself arguing with him about the best brand in the aisle of Duane Reade. Their resentment toward each other was always just under the surface. Catherine was right, Mindy thought: All the trouble in their marriage went back to those first few months after Sam was born. Likely, James was as scared as she was and didn't want to admit it, but she'd interpreted his behavior as a direct assault on her mothering abilities. She worried he secretly thought she was a bad mother and was trying to prove it by criticizing all her decisions. This, in turn, inflamed her own guilt. She'd taken her six weeks of maternity leave and not a day more, returning to work immediately, and the truth was, she secretly relished getting out of the house and getting away from the baby, who was so demanding that it scared her, and who elicited such love from her that it scared her, too. They'd adjusted, as most parents do, and having created little Sam together was ultimately big enough to astonish them out of their animosity. But still, the bickering over Sam had never quite gone away.

"I don't have it all, and I'm coming to the realization that I probably never will," Mindy wrote now. "I suppose I can live with that. Perhaps my real fear lies elsewhere—in giving up my pursuit of happiness. Who would I be if I just let myself be?"

Mindy posted her new blog entry on the website and, returning to One Fifth for the evening, caught sight of herself in the smoky mirror next to the elevators. Who is that middle-aged woman? she thought. "I have a package for you," said Roberto the doorman.

The package was big and heavy, and Mindy balanced it precariously on her forearm as she struggled with her keys. It was addressed to James, and going into the bedroom to change, she dropped it on the unmade bed. Seeing it was from Redmon Richardly's office, and thinking it might be important, she opened it. Inside were three bound galleys of James's new book.

She opened the book, read two paragraphs, and put it down, feeling guilty. What she'd read was better than expected. Two years ago, she'd read half of James's book in first draft and had become afraid. Too afraid to go on. She'd thought the book wasn't so good. But she hadn't wanted to hurt his feelings, so she'd said it wasn't her kind of material. This was easy to get away with, as the book was a historical novel about some character named David Bushnell, a real-life person who'd invented the first submarine. Mindy suspected that this David Bushnell was gay because he'd never married. The whole story took place in the seventeen hundreds, and if you weren't married back then, you were definitely homosexual. Mindy had asked James if he was going to explore David Bushnell's sexuality and what it might mean, and James had given her a dirty look and said no. David Bushnell was a scholar, he said. A farm boy who was a mathematical genius and had managed to go to Yale and then invented not just the submarine but underwater bombs. Which didn't quite work.

"So in other words," Mindy said, "he was a terrorist."

"I guess you could say that," James said. And that was the last conversation they'd had about the book.

But just because you didn't talk about something didn't mean it went away. That book, all eight hundred manuscript pages, had lain between them like a brick for months, until James finally delivered the copy to his publisher.

Now she found James on the cement pad in the back of the apartment, drinking a Scotch. She sat down next to him on a chair with metal arms and a woven plastic seat that she'd purchased from an online catalog years ago, when such transactions were new and marveled over ("I bought it online!" "No!" "Yes. And it was so easy!"), and wriggled her feet out of her shoes. "Your galleys have arrived," she said. She looked at the glass in his hand. "Isn't it a little early to start drinking?" she asked.

James held up the glass. "I'm celebrating. Apple wants to carry my book. They're going to put it in their stores in February. They want to experiment with books, and they've chosen mine as the first. Redmon says we're practically guaranteed sales of two hundred thousand copies. Because people trust the Apple name. Not the name of the author. The author doesn't matter. It's the opinion

of the computer that counts. I could make half a million dollars."
He paused. "What do you think?" he asked after a moment.

"I'm stunned," Mindy said.

That evening, Enid crossed Fifth Avenue to visit her stepmother,
Flossie Davis. Enid did not relish these visits, but since Flossie was
ninety-three, Enid felt it would be cruel to avoid her. Flossie could-
n't last much longer, but on the other hand, she'd been knocking at
death's door (her words) for the past fifteen years, and death had
yet to answer.

As usual, Enid found Flossie in bed. Flossie rarely left her two-
bedroom apartment but always managed to complete the grotesque
makeup routine she'd adopted as a teenaged showgirl. Her white
hair was tinted a sickly yellow and piled on top of her head. When
she was younger, she'd worn it bleached and teased, like a swirl of
cotton candy. Enid had a theory that this constant bleaching had
affected Flossie's brain, as she never got anything quite right and was
querulously insistent on her rightness even when all evidence
pointed to the contrary. The only thing Flossie had managed to get
partially right was men. At nineteen, she'd snatched up Enid's father,
Bugsy Merle, an oil prospector from Texas; when he passed away at
fifty-five from a heart attack, she'd married the elderly widower,
Stanley Davis, who had owned a chain of newspapers. With plenty
of money and little to do, Flossie had spent much of her life pursuing the goal of becoming New York's reigning socialite, but she'd
never developed the self-control or discipline needed to succeed.
She now suffered from heart trouble and gum infections, wheezed
when she spoke, and had only television and visits from Enid and
Philip to keep her company. Flossie was a reminder that it was terrible to get old and that there was very little to be done about it.

"And now Louise is dead," Flossie said triumphantly. "I can't say
I'm sorry. Nobody deserved death more than she. I knew she'd
come to a bad end."

Enid sighed. This was typical Flossie, completely illogical in her analyses. It came, Enid thought, from never having had to really apply herself.

"I would hardly call her death 'just deserts,'" Enid said carefully. "She was ninety-nine. Everyone dies eventually. It's not a punishment. From the moment we're born, life only goes in one direction."

"Why bring that up?" Flossie said.

"It's important to face the truth," Enid said.

"I never want to face the truth," Flossie said. "What's good about the truth? If everyone faced the truth, they would kill themselves."

"That might be true," Enid said.

"But not you, Enid," Flossie said, pushing herself up on her elbows in preparation for a verbal attack. "You never married, never had children. Most women would have killed themselves. But not you. You go on and on. I admire that. I could never be a spinster myself."

"'Single' is the word they use now."

"Well," Flossie said brightly, "I suppose you can't miss what you never had."

"Don't be ridiculous," Enid said. "If that were true, there would be no envy in the world. No *unhappiness*."

"I was not envious of Louise," Flossie said. "Everyone says I was, but I wasn't. Why would I be envious of her? She didn't even have a good figure. No bosom."

"Flossie," Enid said patiently. "If you weren't envious, then why did you accuse her of robbery?"

"Because I was right," Flossie said. Her wheezing increased, and she reached for an inhaler on the coffee table. "The woman," she said between gasps, "was a thief! And worse."

Enid got up and fetched Flossie a glass of water. When she returned, she said gently, "Drink your water. And forget about it."

"Then where is it?" Flossie said. "Where is the Cross of Bloody Mary?"

"There's no proof the cross ever existed," Enid said firmly.

"No proof?" Flossie's eyes bulged. "It's right there. In the painting by Holbein. It's hanging around her neck. And there are documents that talk about Pope Julius the Third's gift to Queen Mary for her efforts to keep England Catholic."

"There's one document," Enid said. "And that document has never been shown to be authentic."

"What about the photograph?"

"Taken in 1910. About as real as the famous photograph of the Loch Ness Monster."

"I don't know why you don't believe me," Flossie said, looking at Enid with hurt eyes. "I saw it myself. In the basement of the Met. I shouldn't have let it out of my sight, but I had the Pauline Trigère fashion show in the afternoon. And Louise did go to the Met that day."

"Flossie dear," Enid said firmly. "Don't you understand? You might just as easily have taken the cross yourself. If it exists at all."

"But I didn't take it," Flossie said stubbornly. "Louise did."

Enid sighed. Flossie had been beating this rumor drum for fifty years. It was her stubborn insistence that Louise had stolen this cross that had caused Flossie's eventual removal from the board of the Metropolitan Museum in a charge led by Louise Houghton, who had subtly suggested that Flossie suffered from a slight mental impairment. As this was generally believed to be true, Louise had prevailed, and Flossie had never forgiven Louise not only her supposed crime but also her betrayal, which had led to Flossie's permanent fall from grace in New York society.

Flossie could have worked her way back in, but she refused to let go of her crazy idea that Louise Houghton, a woman above reproach, had stolen the Cross of Bloody Mary and kept it hidden somewhere in her apartment. Even now Flossie pointed out the window and, with a wheeze, said, "I'm telling you, that cross is in her apartment right now. It's just sitting there, waiting to be discovered."

"Why would Louise Houghton take it?" Enid asked patiently.

"Because she was a Catholic. And Catholics are like that," Flossie said.

"You must give this up," Enid said. "It's time. Louise is dead. You must face the facts."

"Why?"

"Think about your legacy," Enid said. "Do you want to go to your grave with everyone thinking you were the crazy old woman who accused Louise Houghton?"

"I don't care what people think," Flossie said proudly. "I never have. And I'll never understand how my very own stepdaughter continued to be friends with Louise."

"Ah, Flossie." Enid shook her head. "If everyone in New York took sides over these petty, insignificant arguments, no one would have any friends at all."

"I read something funny today," the makeup artist said. "'The Joys of Not Having It All.'"

"Not having it all?" Schiffer asked. "I'm living it."

"A friend e-mailed it to me. I can e-mail it to you if you want."

"Sure," Schiffer said. "I'd love that."

The makeup artist stepped back to look at Schiffer in the long mirror. "What do you think?"

"It's perfect. We want it natural. I don't think a mother superior would wear much makeup."

"And after she has sex for the first time, we can make it more glamorous."

The red-haired PA, Alan, stuck his head into the makeup room. "They're ready for you," he said to Schiffer.

"I'm ready," she said, getting out of the chair.

"Schiffer Diamond is on her way," Alan said into a headset.

They walked down a short corridor, then went through the construction department. Two tall metal doors led to one of the six sets. Inside, behind a maze of gray plywood walls, was a white backdrop. Several director's chairs were set up a few feet away, clustered in front of a monitor. The director, Asa Williams, introduced himself.

He was a brooding, gaunt man with a shaved head and a tattoo on his left wrist. He'd directed lots of TV and, recently, two hit movies. Milling around was the usual crowd of crew and executives, all wondering, no doubt, what Schiffer was going to be like. Difficult or professional? Schiffer was friendly but removed.

"You know the drill, right?" Asa said. She was led onto the set. Told to walk toward the camera. Turn to the right. Turn to the left. The battery in the camera died. There was a four-minute break while someone replaced it. She walked away and stood behind the director's chairs. The executive producers were in a conversation with the network executives. "She still looks good."

"Yes, she looks great."

"But too pale, maybe."

She was sent back to the makeup room for an adjustment. Sitting in the chair, she recalled the afternoon when Philip had knocked on the door of her trailer. He was still put out that she'd called his movie lousy. "If you think my movie sucks, why are you in it?" he'd asked.

"I didn't say it sucked. I said it was lousy. There's a big difference. You're going to need much thicker skin if you're going to survive in Hollywood," she'd said.

"Who said I want to survive in Hollywood? And what makes you think I don't have thick skin?"

"And what do you know, anyway?" he asked later, when they were having drinks at the outdoor tiki bar in the hotel. "It's only your second movie."

"I'm a fast learner," she said. "How about you?"

He ordered two shots of tequila, then two more. There was a pool table in the back of the bar, and they used every excuse to accidentally touch each other. The first kiss happened outside the bathroom, located in a little hut. When she came out, he was waiting for her. "I was thinking about what you said, about how Hollywood corrupts."

She leaned back against the rough wood of the hut and laughed. "You don't have to take everything I say at face value. Sometimes I say things just to hear how they sound. Any crime in that?"

"No," he said, putting his hand on the wall above her shoulder. "But it means I'm never going to know when you're serious." Her head was tilted back to look at him, although he wasn't so much taller than she was—maybe six inches. But then his arm was around her back, and they were kissing, and his mouth was so soft. They were both startled and broke away, then went back to the bar and had another tequila shot, but the line had been crossed, and soon they were kissing at the bar and putting their hands on each other's faces and backs until the bartender said, "Get a room."

She laughed. "Oh, we have one."

Back in her room, they engaged in the long, delicious process of getting to know each other's bodies. When they took off their shirts and pressed together, the sensation of skin on skin was a revelation. They lay together for a while, like high school kids who have all the time in the world and don't need to go too far too fast; then they took off their pants and pantomimed sex—his penis touching her vagina through their undergarments. All through the night, they touched and kissed, dozing off and waking to the joy of finding the other in the bed, and then the kissing started again, and finally, in the early morning when it was right, he entered her. There was nothing like that first push, and it so overwhelmed them that he stopped, just let his penis be inside her, while they absorbed the miracle of two pieces that fit perfectly together.

She had a seven A.M. call, but at ten A.M., during a break in shooting, he was in her trailer and they were doing it on the small bed in the back with the polyester sheets. They did it three more times that day, and during dinner with the crew, she sat with her leg over his, and he kept putting his hand under her shirt to touch her waist. By then the whole crew knew, but set romances were a given in the intimacy and stress of getting a movie made. Though they usually ended when the movie wrapped, Philip came to L.A. and moved into her bungalow. They played house like any other young couple discovering the wonders of companionship, when the mundane was new and even a trip to the supermarket could be an adventure. Their anonymous bliss lasted only a short while, however, because then the movie came out, and it was huge.

Their relationship was suddenly public. They rented a bigger house with a gate in the Hollywood Hills, but they couldn't keep the outside world from creeping in, and that started the trouble.

Their first fight was over an article in a magazine that featured her on the cover. In the piece, she was quoted as saying, "I can't take making movies too seriously. In the end, it's not that different from what little girls do when they're playing dress-up." She came home from a meeting one afternoon and found the magazine on the coffee table and Philip in a foul mood over her quote. "Is that what you think about my work?" he said.

"It doesn't have anything to do with you."

"That's right," he said, "because everything is about you. Did you ever consider the fact that it's my movie you were talking about?"

"Don't take yourself so seriously. It's not attractive." But she had, it seemed, irrevocably bruised his ego. They continued on for a little longer, then he moved back to New York. A miserable month passed before he called her. "I've been thinking. It's not us. It's Hollywood. Why don't you come to New York?"

She'd been twenty-four then, willing to take on any adventure. But that was over twenty years ago, she thought now, staring at her reflection in the makeup mirror. In the harsh light of the bare bulbs, there was no denying that she no longer looked like that girl. Her face had matured; it was more angular and hollow, and no one would mistake her for an ingenue. But she knew a lot more about what she wanted from life and what no longer mattered.

But did Philip know? Leaning in to the mirror to check her makeup, she wondered what he'd thought when she'd run into him in the elevator. Did he see her as middle-aged? Did he still find her attractive?

The last time she'd seen him had been ten years ago. She'd been in New York doing publicity for a movie when she ran into Philip in the lobby of One Fifth. They hadn't talked in over a year, but they immediately fell into their old habits, and when she'd finished her last interview, they'd met for dinner at Da Silvano. At eleven o'clock there was a terrific thunderstorm, trapping everyone inside, and the waiters cleared away the tables and turned up the music, and everyone danced. "I love you," Philip said. "You're my best friend."

"You're my best friend, too."

"We understand each other. We'll always be friends."

They went back to her apartment. She had an antique four-poster bed she'd had shipped from England; that year she'd spent two months in London doing a play and become enamored with the idea of English country houses. Philip was propped up on his arms above her, his hair falling into her face. They made love hard and seriously, astounded by how good it still was, which once again brought up the issue of being together. He asked about her schedule. She was flying to Europe and was supposed to go directly back to L.A. but said she'd make a detour and spend at least a few days in New York. Then she went to Europe and got stuck there for an extra two weeks and had to go directly back to L.A. Then she started a movie that was shooting in Vancouver and India. Six months passed, and she heard from someone that Philip was getting married. She got on a plane and flew to New York to confront him.

"You can't get married," she said.

"Why not?"

"What about us?"

"There is no us."

"Only because you don't want there to be."

"Whether I want it or not is irrelevant. It doesn't exist."

"Who is she?" Schiffer demanded. "What does she do?"

Her name was Susan, and she taught at a private school in Manhattan. When Schiffer insisted, he showed her a photograph. She was twenty-six, pretty, and utterly bland. "After all the women you've been with, why her?" she asked.

"I'm in love with her. She's nice," Philip said.

Schiffer raged and then begged. "What does she have that I don't have?"

"She's stable."

"I can be stable."

"She's in the same place all the time."

"And that's what you want? Some little mouse who will do everything you say?"

"You don't know Susan. She's very independent."

"She's dependent. That's the real reason why you want to marry her. At least be truthful about your motives."

"We're getting married on September twenty-sixth."

"Where?"

"I won't tell you. I don't want you to crash the wedding."

"I'm not going to crash it. Why are you so worried? I bet you're getting married in her parents' backyard."

"Their country house, actually. In East Hampton."

She did crash the wedding by enlisting Billy Litchfield to help her. They hid in the hedges surrounding the property. She watched Philip in a white linen suit say "I do" to another woman. For months afterward, she justified her behavior by claiming Philip's marriage was like a death: One needed to see the dead body in order to believe the soul was really gone.

A little over a year had passed when she heard from an agent that Philip was getting divorced. His marriage had lasted fourteen months. But by then it was too late. Schiffer was engaged to the English marquis, an aging glamour boy who turned out to have a vicious drug habit. When he died in a boating accident in Saint-Tropez, she went back to L.A. to restart her career.

There was no work, her agent told her—she'd been away for too long, and she was over thirty-five. He said she ought to do what every other actress did and start having children. Being alone in L.A. without work to distract her from her husband's death slammed her into a deep depression, and one day she didn't bother to get out of bed. She stayed there for weeks.

Philip had come to L.A. in that time, but she'd made excuses not to see him. She couldn't see anyone. She could barely leave the house in Los Feliz. The thought of driving down the hill to the supermarket exhausted her, it took hours to work up the energy to gather her things, get in the car, and back it out of the garage. Steering the car along the hairpin turns, she looked for places where she might drive off the road and into a steep ravine, but she wasn't sure an accident would result in death, and it might leave her worse off than she already was.

Her agent forced her to lunch one afternoon at the Polo Club. She could barely speak and picked at her food. "What's wrong with you?" he asked. She shook her head, murmuring, "I don't know."

"I can't send you out like this. Hollywood is a cruel town. They'll say you'll never work again, if they're not saying it already. Why don't you go to the desert? Or Mexico. Even Malibu, for Christ's sake. Take a couple of weeks. Or a month. When you come back, I can probably get you a part playing someone's mother."

When the interminable lunch was over and she was back in her car driving down Sunset, she began to cry uncontrollably and couldn't stop for several hours. There was the unaccountable despair, but the shame was the worst of it. People like her weren't supposed to be depressed, but she felt broken and didn't know how to fix herself. Out of pity, her agent sent her a script for a TV series. She refused to meet the writer for lunch but allowed him to come to the house. His name was Tom, and he was younger than she and eager and sensitive and wasn't put off by her weakness. He said he wanted to help her, and she let him, and soon they were lovers, and shortly thereafter, he moved in. She didn't take the part in the series, but it was a hit, and Tom made money and stuck with her, and then they were married. She started working again, too, and made three independent movies, one of which was nominated for an Oscar, putting her back on the map. Things were good with Tom, too. He made another TV show, and it was a hit as well, but then he had to work all the time, and they became irritated with each other. She took nearly every part she was offered in order to get away from him and their marriage. They continued like that for another three years, and then she found out Tom was having an affair, and it was easy. They'd been married six years, and not once in those six years did she stop thinking about Philip or what her life would have been like if she were with him instead.

5

Lately, sex was weighing heavily on Mindy's mind. She and James didn't do it enough. In fact, they didn't do it at all. Looking at it optimistically, they did it once or twice a year. It was terrible and wrong and made Mindy feel like she was a bad wife, not doing her duty, but at the same time, it was such a relief not to do it.

The problem was, it hurt. She knew this could be an issue for women as they got older. But she thought it didn't happen until well after menopause. She'd never expected it to happen so soon. At the beginning, when she'd first met James, and even into their fourth or fifth year of marriage, she'd prided herself on being good at sex. For years after Sam was born, she and James would do it once a week and really make a night of it. They had things they liked to do. Mindy liked to be tied up, and sometimes she would tie James up (they had special ties they used for this practice—old Brooks Brothers ties James had worn in college), and when James was tied up, she would ride his penis like a banshee. Over time, the sex started to dwindle, which was normal for married couples, but they still did it once or twice a month, and then, two years ago, the pain came. She went to her female gynecologist and tried to talk about it, but the doctor said her vagina wasn't dried up and she wasn't going through menopause and she should use lotions. Mindy knew all about sex lotions, but they didn't work, either. So she bought a vibrator. Nothing fancy, just a plain slim tube of colored light blue plastic. She didn't know why she picked light blue. It was better than pink or purple, she supposed. On a Saturday afternoon when James was out with Sam, she tried to put the vibrator in her vagina but could get it no farther than an inch before the pain started. She began avoiding sex altogether. James never asked her about it, but the lack of sex in their marriage lay between them like a sack of potatoes. Mindy felt guilty and ashamed, although she told herself it didn't matter.

Now it looked like James was going to be successful, and it did matter. She wasn't stupid. She knew successful men had more choices. If she didn't give him sex, he might get it somewhere else. Arriving home from work on Tuesday evening, Mindy was determined to do it with James that night no matter how much it hurt. But real life intruded.

"Are you going to the funeral?" Roberto asked her as she came into the lobby of One Fifth.

"What funeral?" Mindy asked.

"Mrs. Houghton. It's tomorrow at St. Ambrose Church." Roberto, who was always smiling, laughed. "I hear it's private."

"Funerals aren't private," Mindy said.

"This one is. I hear you need an invitation."

"Where did you hear that?" Mindy said.

"I just heard, is all," Roberto said and laughed.

Mindy was furious. Instead of going to her apartment, she went up to Enid Merle's. "What's this about Mrs. Houghton's funeral?" she said.

"It's a memorial service, dear. Mrs. Houghton has already been laid to rest."

"Are you going?" Mindy asked.

"Of course."

"Why wasn't I invited? I'm the head of the board."

"Mrs. Houghton knew so many people. This is New York. Not everyone is invited to everything."

"Can you get me an invitation?" Mindy asked.

"I can't imagine why you would want to go," Enid said, and closed her door. She was still annoyed at Mindy for refusing to embrace her plan to split up Mrs. Houghton's apartment.

Downstairs, Mindy found James in his office. "I am so insulted," she said, plopping herself onto the old leather club chair. "It seems everyone in the building has been invited to Mrs. Houghton's memorial service. Everyone but me."

"Let it go," James said warningly.

This was not like James. Mindy asked what was wrong.

"Why didn't you tell me you were writing a blog?" he said.

"I did."

"You didn't."

"I did and you don't remember."

"Well, it's all over Snarker," James said.

"Is it good or bad?"

"What do you think?" James said.

Mindy got up and peered over his shoulder at the computer screen. The headline read: INTERNET MOGULETTE (NOT!) AND CORPORATE MEDIA SLUT MINDY GOOCH ASSAULTS WORLD WITH MUSINGS. Underneath was a hideous color photograph of her, taken as she was leaving her office building. She looked ragged and unkempt in an old black trench coat, with her sensible brown saddlebag slung over her shoulder. Her mouth was open; the angle of the photograph made her nose and chin appear especially pointy. Mindy's first thought was that the photograph was more devastating than the text. For much of her life, Mindy had made a considerable effort to avoid the sin of vanity, as she despised people who cared excessively about their looks; she considered it the height of shallowness. But the photograph instantly shattered her interior mirror. There was no way to pretend that you were pretty, that you still looked like a twenty-five-year-old, when the evidence to the contrary was available on any computer screen, accessible twenty-four hours a day, every day of the year, for years and years and years. Maybe even forever. Or at least until the oil ran out, the polar ice caps melted, and/or the world was destroyed by war, a meteorite, or a giant tsunami.

"Who wrote this?" she demanded. She peered at the name next to the text. "Thayer Core. Who the hell is he?"

"Let it go," James said.

"Why should I? How dare they?"

"Who cares?" James asked.

"I do," Mindy said. "It's my reputation, my image, at stake here. I'm not like you, James. When someone insults me, I don't just sit there. I do something."

"What?" James said, rolling his eyes.

"I'm going to have that kid fired."

James made a dismissive noise.

"What you don't understand is that all those websites are owned by corporations," Mindy said. "Or they will be soon. And I've got connections. In the corporate world. They don't call me 'corporate media slut' for nothing. I must put on Mozart." Lately, she'd found Mozart soothing, which could be yet another sign of middle age, she thought.

To put on the Mozart, she had to get up and go into her office next door. She chose *The Magic Flute* from a pile of CDs. The overture—the great booming drums and oboes, followed by the delicate string instruments—momentarily distracted her. But then she glanced over at her computer. Her screen saver was up, a photograph of Sam dressed as a dinosaur for Halloween. He'd been three and crazy about dinosaurs. She turned away, but the computer was calling her. Snarker was calling her. She pulled up the website and read the item again.

"Mindy," James said accusingly, coming into her office. "What are you doing?"

"Working."

"No, you're not. You're sitting here, reading about yourself." And then he went off on a tirade. "It's the neurosis of the new millennium. It's not self-absorption. It's self-addiction. And that's why"—he began sputtering—"that's why I wrote about David Bushnell."

"Huh?" Mindy said.

"David Bushnell wasn't about the self," James said. He sat down on her couch, leaning back as if preparing to engage in a long discussion about his book. "Unlike the bottom-feeders who now populate the world, the publicists, the stockbrokers, the lawyers, everyone trying to make a buck off someone else . . ."

Mindy stared at him, unable to fathom what the hell he was going on about. She changed the topic back to herself. "I can't get over it," she said. "How dare they? Why me? Why are they making fun of *me*?"

Once again, James thought, Mindy was refusing to talk about his book. Usually, he let it go. But this time, he wasn't in a mood to be solicitous to his wife. He stood up and started messing around with her CDs. "Why shouldn't they make fun of you?" he said, examining a CD of the Rolling Stones' greatest hits. "Mother's Little Helper" was on it, he noted; perhaps he should have a listen.

"Excuse me?" she said.

"Because you're special and better than everyone else?" James asked casually.

"I am genuinely hurt," Mindy countered. "I am *humiliated*." She gave James her most withering look.

"All I'm saying," James said, "is that in your twenty years as a journalist, you've never hurt anyone?"

"Are you saying this is some kind of retribution?" Mindy asked.

"It could be. Maybe it's karma."

Mindy snorted in derision. "Maybe it's just that young people these days are nasty and jealous. And disrespectful. What did I ever do to them?"

"You're somewhat successful. Or seen as successful, anyway," James said. "Don't you get it? We're the establishment now." He paused and, pointing a finger at her, said, "Us. You and me. We're the so-called adults now. The ones the young people want to knock down. And we were exactly like them when we were in our twenties."

"We were not."

"Remember the stories you used to write? About that billionaire. You made fun of his fingers! Woo-hooo. 'Short-fingered vulgarian,' you called him."

"That was different."

"It was exactly the same. You only think it was different because you wrote it. And every time you ripped someone, you said it was okay because they were successful, ergo, they were an asshole. And everyone thought you were so clever, and you got attention. It's the easiest way to get attention, Mindy. Always has been. Make fun of your betters. Disrespect the successful, and you put yourself on their radar. It's so fucking cheap."

Any normal person, James thought, would have been slain by this comment. But not Mindy. "And you're so much better?" she said.

"I never did *that*."

"No, James," Mindy said. "You didn't have to. You were a man. You wrote those long, endless pieces about . . . golf. That took a year to write. Ten thousand words about golf, and it takes a year? I was working, James. Making money. It was my *job*."

"Right," James said. "And now it's these kids' *job* as well."

"That's great, James," Mindy said. "I ask for your support. And you turn on me. Your own wife."

"I'm trying to put things into perspective," James said. "Don't you get it? These kids are just like us. They don't know it yet, but in twenty years, they'll wake up and they'll *be* us. It will be the last thing they were expecting. Oh, they'll protest now. Say it will never happen to them. They'll beat the odds. Won't change. Won't end up tired, mediocre, apathetic, and sometimes defeated. But life will take care of them. And then they'll realize they've turned into us. And that will be their punishment."

Mindy pulled at a strand of hair and examined it. "What are you really saying?" she asked. "Is there something wrong with *us*?"

The fight had gone out of James. "I don't know," he said. He slumped.

"What's going on?" a voice asked. Mindy and James looked up.

Their son, Sam, had come into the apartment and was standing in the door to Mindy's office.

"We were just talking," Mindy said.

"What about?" Sam asked.

"Your mother was on Snarker," James said.

"I know." Sam shrugged.

"Sit down," James said. "How do you feel about it?"

"I don't feel anything at all," Sam said.

"You're not feeling . . . traumatized?"

"No."

"Your mother's feelings are hurt."

"That's your generation. Kids my age don't get hurt feelings. It's just drama. Everyone's on their own reality show. The more drama you have, the more people pay attention to you. That's all."

James and Mindy Gooch looked at each other, thinking the same thing: Their son was a genius! What other thirteen-year-old boy had such insights into the human condition?

"Enid Merle wants me to help her with her computer," Sam said.

"No," Mindy said.

"Why?"

"I'm angry at her."

"Leave Sam out of it," James said.

"Can I go?" Sam asked.

"Yes," James said. When Sam left the room, he continued on his diatribe. "Reality TV, blogging, commentators, it's the culture of the parasite." Immediately, he wondered why he said these things. Why couldn't he embrace the new? This new human being who was self-centered and rabidly consumerist?

❦

Sam Gooch bore the harsh marks of budding adolescence and the scars of being a New York City kid. He wasn't innocent. He'd stopped being innocent between the ages of two and four, when he was applauded for making adult remarks. Mindy would often repeat his remarks to her coworkers, followed by the tagline (always delivered with appropriate awe): "How could he know such things! He's only [fill in the blank]."

Now, at thirteen, Sam also worried that he knew too much. Sometimes he felt world-weary and often wondered what would happen to him; certainly, things would happen to him, things happened to kids in New York City. But he also knew he didn't have the same advantages as the other children with whom he consorted. He lived in one of the best buildings in the Village but in the worst apartment in that building; he wasn't taken out of school to go to Kenya for three weeks; he'd never had a birthday party at the Chelsea Piers; he had never gone to see his father play lead guitar in a rock concert at Madison Square Garden. When Sam went out of town, it was always to stay at the country houses of kids with wealthier and more accomplished parents than his own. His dad urged him to go for the "experience," clinging to the quaint notion that part of being a writer was about having all kinds of experiences in life, although his dad didn't seem to have many experiences of his own. Now Sam had had some experiences he wished he hadn't had, mostly concerning girls. They wanted something he didn't know how to give. What they wanted, Sam suspected, was constant attention. When he went out of town to the country houses, the parents left the kids to their own devices. The boys posed and the girls acted crazy. At some point, there was crying. When he got home, he was exhausted, as if he'd lived two years in two days.

His mother would be waiting for him. After an hour or two would come the inevitable question: "Sam, did you write a thank-you note?" "No, Mom, it's embarrassing." "No one was ever embarrassed to get a thank-you note." "I'm embarrassed to write one." "Why?" "Because no one else has to write thank-you notes." "They're not as well brought up as you are, Sam. Someday you'll see. Someone will remember that you wrote them a thank-you note and give you a job." "I'm not going to work for anyone." And then his mother would hug him. "You're so smart, Sammy. You're going to run the world someday."

And so Sammy became a computer whiz, which impressed his

parents and all other adults born before 1985. "Sam was on the Internet before he could talk!" his mother boasted.

At six, having been admitted to one of New York City's most exclusive schools—a bonus secured by the often obnoxious, unwavering determination of his mother to set him on the right track (Mindy was one of those people of whom others eventually said, "It's easier to give in to her just to get her to go away")—Sam realized he would have to make his own pocket money in order to survive his artificially heightened status. At ten, he began his own computer business in the building.

Sam was tough but fair. He charged the residents, the Philip Oaklands, the quiet doctors and lawyers, the woman who managed the rock band, a hundred dollars an hour for his services, but he helped the doormen and porters for free. This was to make up for his mother. The doormen considered the most egregious residents the bad Christmas tippers, and Sam knew his mother was one such Scrooge. When she doled out the twenty- and fifty-dollar bills for Christmas tips, her mouth would turn down in an unhappy line. She would check and recheck her envelopes next to the list of the twenty-five doormen and porters, and if she found she'd made a mistake—and she usually had, in taking an extra fifty or twenty from the cash machine—she would snatch up the bill and carefully lay it in her wallet. But Sam's efforts paid off. Sam was loved in the building, and Mindy was tolerated, the word being that Mindy wasn't as bad as she seemed. "She has a nice son, after all, and that says a lot about a woman," the doormen said.

But now there was trouble between Mindy and Enid, which Sam would have to fix as well.

In the lobby, Sam ran into a strange girl standing before the elevators, looking down at her iPhone. He knew everyone in the building and wondered who she was, why she was there, and whom she was going to see. She was wearing a green halter top, dark jeans, and high-heeled sandals, and was a certain type of beautiful. There were girls in his school who were beautiful, and there were models and actresses and sometimes just pretty college girls on the street. But this girl, he thought, with her poochy lips turned up at the corners in a manner that was almost obscene, was a little different. Her clothes were expensive, but she was a little too perfect. She glanced down at Sam and looked away, back at her phone, as if she were embarrassed.

The girl was Lola Fabrikant, and she was on her way to her interview with Philip Oakland. Sam had caught Lola in a rare moment of vulnerability. The walk down Fifth Avenue to One Fifth had left her disconcerted. Having developed a keen sense of status, she was attuned to both blatant and subtle differences between all kinds of residences, products, and service providers, the result being that in strolling down Fifth Avenue, the glaring differences between this avenue and Eleventh Street, where she now resided, assaulted her sense of entitlement. Fifth Avenue was so much nicer than Eleventh Street—why didn't she live here? she wondered. And then coming upon the towering gray mightiness of One Fifth, with not one but two entrances and a wood-paneled lobby (like a men's club), and three doormen all over her in uniforms and white gloves (like footmen in a fairy tale), she thought again, Why don't I live in this building?

Waiting for the elevator, she decided that she would live here somehow. She deserved it.

She looked down and saw a teenaged boy staring at her. Did kids live in the building as well? Somehow she'd imagined New York City as a place for adults only.

The boy got into the elevator after her. He pressed the button for thirteen. "What floor?" he asked.

"Thirteen," she said.

Sam nodded. The girl was going to see Philip Oakland. It figured. His mother always said Philip Oakland had it easy, and life was unfair.

◈

Shortly before Lola arrived for her appointment, Philip got a call from his agent. "Oh, these people," the agent said.

"What's the problem?" Philip asked. Despite his trouble with the material, he'd managed to turn in a draft of *Bridesmaids Revisited* the day before.

"Nobody knows what the hell they're doing," the agent said. "I'm giving you a heads-up. The studio wants an emergency conference call this afternoon."

"Fuck them," Philip said. "Sounds like a power play."

"It's all a power play. If anyone knew how to make a good movie these days, we wouldn't be having this conversation."

His agent hung up, and an assistant from the studio called. Then he was on hold for ten minutes, waiting for the head of the studio to get on. She had graduate degrees in both business and law, degrees that should have been irrelevant when it came to understanding the creative process, but now seemed to be the equivalent of having won the Pulitzer Prize for fiction. "Philip," she said, not apologizing for keeping him waiting, "something happened between the last draft and the current one."

"It's called a rewrite," Philip said.

"We've lost something with the main character. She isn't likable anymore."

"Really?" Philip replied.

"She has no personality," said the studio head.

"That's because you've insisted I take out anything that would give her personality," Philip replied.

"We have to think about the audience. Women are very, very judgmental. As you know. They're harsh critics of other women."

"That's too bad," Philip said. "Maybe if they weren't, women would rule the world."

"I'll need another draft in two weeks. Just fix it, Philip," she said, and hung up.

Philip called his agent. "Can I quit this project?" he asked.

"Forget your ego and just give them what they want. Then it's their problem."

Philip put the phone down, wondering, as he often did these days, what had happened to his courage.

His intercom buzzed. "Miss Lola Fabrikant is downstairs," the doorman Fritz said. "Shall I send her up?"

Damn, Philip thought. In the confrontation with the studio, he'd forgotten about his appointment with the girl who'd e-mailed him requesting an interview. He'd seen ten candidates for the job, and every one had been a disappointment. This girl would likely prove another waste of time, but she was already downstairs. He'd give her ten minutes just to be polite. "Send her up," he said.

A few minutes later, Lola Fabrikant was perched on Philip's couch, attempting to be on her very best behavior. Philip Oakland was no longer as young as his author photo on the back cover of her tattered copy of *Summer Morning*, but he wasn't old, either, and he was certainly younger than her father, who would never wear a faded black T-shirt and Adidas tennis shoes and sport hair past his earlobes. Folded up in his chair, feet on his desk, Philip alternated between tapping a pen on a pile of papers and tucking his hair behind his ears. The girl who had given Lola his e-mail had been right—Philip Oakland was hot.

"Tell me about you," Philip said. "I want to know everything." He was no longer in a rush to get rid of Miss Lola Fabrikant, who was not what he'd been expecting and who, after his lousy day, was more than a welcome relief, almost like the answer to his prayers.

"Have you seen my Facebook page?" she asked.

"I haven't."

"I tried to look you up," she said. "But you don't have a page."

"Should I?"

She frowned at him as if concerned for his welfare. "Everyone has a Facebook page. How else can your friends keep up with you?"

How else indeed, he thought, finding her charming. "Do you want to show me your Facebook page?"

She tapped quickly on her iPhone and held it out to him.

"That's me in Miami." Philip stared at a photograph of a bikini-clad Lola standing on a small boat. Was he being seduced deliberately or inadvertently, he wondered. Did it matter?

"And then there's my bio," she said, coming up behind him to tap once again on the small machine. "See? My favorite color: yellow. My favorite quote: 'My way or the Henry Hudson Highway.' My dream honeymoon: sailing on a yacht around the Greek Islands." She swung her long hair, and a strand touched his face. She giggled. "Sorry."

"It's very interesting," he said, handing the iPhone back to her.

"I know," she said. "My friends are always saying big things are going to happen to me."

"What kinds of big things?" Philip asked, noting her smooth, unblemished skin. Her presence was turning him into an idiot, he thought.

"I don't know," she said, thinking how different Philip Oakland was from anyone she'd ever met. He was like a real person, but better, because he was a celebrity. She sat back down on the couch. "I know I should know, because I'm twenty-two, but I don't."

"You're a baby," Philip said. "You have your whole life ahead of you."

She dismissed this by blowing a small puff of air through her lips. "Everyone always says that, but it isn't true. These days you have to make it right away. Or you get left behind."

"Really?" Philip asked.

"Oh yes," she said, nodding her lovely head. "Things have changed. If you want something, a million other people want it as well." She paused, holding out her sandaled foot and cocking her head to admire her black toenail polish. "But it doesn't bother me. I'm very competitive. I like to win. And I usually do."

Aha, Philip thought, suddenly inspired. This was what his character was missing in *Bridesmaids Revisited*. This unbridled confidence of youth.

"So what is this job?" she asked. "What do I have to do? I won't have to pick up your dry cleaning or anything like that, will I?"

"Worse, I'm afraid," Philip said. "I'll expect you to do some research for me—but I'll also want you to be an assistant. When I'm on a conference call, you'll be on the other line and will take notes. If I make handwritten notes on a manuscript, you'll retype it. I'll expect you to read every draft before it goes out, checking for typos and continuity. And occasionally, I'll use you as a sounding board."

"Meaning?" Lola asked, tilting her head.

"For instance," Philip said, "I'm working on a screenplay now called *Bridesmaids Revisited*. I'm wondering how obsessed a twenty-two-year-old woman would be with her wedding."

"Haven't you ever seen *Bridezillas*?" Lola asked, flabbergasted.

"What's that?" Philip said.

"Ohmigod," Lola said, warming up to this discussion about reality shows, which was one of her favorite topics. "It's about these women who are totally obsessed with their weddings, to the point where they literally go crazy."

Philip tapped his pen. "But why?" he asked. "What's the big deal about getting married?"

"Every girl wants to get married now. And they want to do it while they're young."

"I thought they wanted to have careers and take over the world by thirty."

"That was older Gen Y," Lola said. "All the girls I know want to get married and have kids right away. They don't want to end up like their mothers."

"What's wrong with their mothers?"

"They're unhappy," Lola said. "Girls my age won't put up with unhappiness."

Philip felt an urgency to get back to work. He unfolded his legs from the desk and stood up.

"Is that it?" she said.

"That's it," he said.

She picked up her bag, a gray snakeskin pouch that was so large Philip guessed it must have been made from the entire skin of a boa constrictor. "Do I have the job?" she asked.

"Why don't we both think about it and talk tomorrow," Philip said.

She looked crushed. "Don't you like me?" she asked.

He opened the door. "I do like you," he said. "I like you very much. That's the problem."

When she was gone, he stepped out onto his terrace. His vista was south. A chunky, modern medieval landscape of gray-blues and terra cottas lay before him. Just below was Washington Square Park, a patch of green populated with tiny people going about their business.

You must not do this, he scolded himself. You must not hire that girl. If you do, you'll sleep with her, and it will be a disaster.

But he finally had a grip on his screenplay. And gathering up his things, he headed out to the small library on Sixth Avenue, which was open late and where he could work uninterrupted.

♦

Schiffer Diamond was finished on the stages at seven P.M., and during the ride back to the city, she found the attachment from Mindy's blog, sent by the makeup artist on her BlackBerry: "I don't have it all, and I'm coming to the realization that I probably never will. Perhaps my real fear lies elsewhere—in giving up my pursuit of happiness."

No, one must never do that, Schiffer thought, and arriving at One Fifth, she went right up to the thirteenth floor and rang Philip's bell. He wasn't home. Back in her apartment, her phone rang, and picking it up, she thought it might be Philip after all—he was one of the few people who had the number. Instead, it was Billy Litchfield. "A little bird told me you were in town," he scolded. "Why didn't you call me?"

"I've been meaning to. But I've been working nonstop."

"If you're not working right this minute, let's have a drink at Da Silvano. It's a gorgeous evening."

It was a gorgeous night, she realized. Why should she sit alone in her apartment? She would meet Billy and check back with Philip later. Maybe he'd be home.

She arrived first at Da Silvano, ordered a glass of wine, and thought about Billy. She loved Billy—everyone did. She felt proprietary in her friendship with him. Although years could go by during which she barely saw him, this was never a reflection of her feelings, especially as Billy was one of the first people she'd met in New York.

Indeed, if it weren't for Billy, she wouldn't be where she was today.

She'd been a student at Columbia, studying French literature with a minor in photography, when she'd wrangled an internship with a famous fashion photographer during the summer of her sophomore year. It was on one of these debauched photo shoots in a loft in SoHo that she'd met Billy, who was then an editor at large at *Vogue*. Champagne and cocaine were staples in those days, the model was three hours late, and, in the middle of the afternoon, engaged in sex with the photographer in his bedroom while an endless tape of Talk Talk played over and over.

"You know you're more beautiful than the model," Billy said to Schiffer while they waited for the photographer to finish his business.

"I know." Schiffer shrugged.

"Are you always this confident?"

"Why should I have to lie about my looks? I didn't choose them. They just are."

"You should be in front of the camera," Billy said.

"I'm too shy."

Nevertheless, when Billy insisted she meet his friend who was a casting director, she went along with it. And when the casting director set her up with an audition for a movie, she went along with it, and when she got the part, she didn't turn it down. She played a spoiled rich suburban girl, and on-screen, her beauty was riveting. Then she was on the cover of *Vogue*, and had a cosmetics campaign, and broke up with her boyfriend, a nice, good-looking boy from Chicago who was going to Columbia med school. She was signed by the biggest talent agent at ICM and told to move to Los Angeles, which she did, renting a small house off Sunset Boulevard. Right away she got the iconic part of the tragic ingenue in *Summer Morning*.

And met Philip, she reminded herself.

Now Billy, her dear old Billy, came hurrying down the sidewalk in a seersucker suit. She stood up to embrace him.

"I can't believe you're here. And I don't believe you'll stay in New York," Billy said, sitting down and motioning to the waiter. "Hollywood people always say they're going to stay, and they never do."

"But I never considered myself a Hollywood person," Schiffer said. "I always thought of myself as a New Yorker. It was the only way I managed to live in L.A. for so long."

"New York has changed," Billy said, a mournful tone creeping into his voice.

"I'm sorry about Mrs. Houghton," Schiffer said. "I know you were close."

"She was very old. And I think I may have found a couple for her apartment."

"That's nice," Schiffer said, but she didn't want to talk real estate. "Billy," she said, leaning forward. "Have you seen Philip Oakland?"

"That's exactly what I mean about New York changing," Billy said. "I almost never see him anymore. I see Enid, of course, at events. But not Philip. I've heard he's a bit of a mess."

"He was always a bit of a mess," Schiffer said.

"But at a certain point, the mess needs to go away. Even Redmon Richardly got married." Billy brushed a speck of dirt off his seersucker trousers. "That was one thing I've never understood. Why didn't you two end up together?"

"I have no idea."

"You didn't need him," Billy said. "A man like Philip wants to be needed. And you were a great actress . . ."

She shook her head. "I was never a great actress. I watch *Summer Morning* now, and I cringe."

"You were wonderful," Billy said.

"I sucked," Schiffer said with a self-deprecating laugh. "Do you know what Philip Oakland said to me once?" she asked. "He said I'd never be a great actress because I wasn't vulnerable."

"There's your answer," Billy said. "Philip was jealous."

"Can a man who's won a Pulitzer Prize and an Oscar be jealous?"

"Of course," Billy said. "Jealousy, envy, ego—those are the things success is made of. I see it all the time in these new people who come to New York. I suppose in that way, New York hasn't changed." Billy took a sip of his wine. "It's too bad about Philip Oakland, though, because he really was talented."

"That makes me sad," Schiffer said.

"My dear," Billy said, "don't waste your time worrying about Philip. In five years, he'll be fifty, and he'll be one of those old men who are always with young women, and the young women get worse and worse and more and more silly. While you, on the other hand, will probably have three Emmys. You won't be giving Philip Oakland a second thought."

"But I love Philip."

Billy shrugged. "We all love Philip. But what can you do? You can't change human nature."

Later, on her way home from Da Silvano, Schiffer thought about ringing Philip's bell again. But remembering what Billy had said about Philip, she decided it probably was pointless. Who was she kidding? Billy was right. Philip would never change. Coming into her apartment, she congratulated herself on for once doing the sensible thing.

6

"Why are you going to a funeral for a woman you don't even know?" Paul Rice asked.

That same evening, he and Annalisa were dining at La Grenouille. Paul adored the famous French restaurant, not for the food but simply because it was ridiculously expensive (sixty-six dollars for Dover sole) and close to the hotel, prompting him to refer to it as "the canteen."

"She's not just any woman," Annalisa said. "Mrs. Houghton was the city's most important socialite. Billy Litchfield asked me, and apparently, it's a very exclusive invitation."

Paul studied the wine menu. "Who's Billy Litchfield again?"

"Connie's friend," Annalisa said. She felt weary. "Remember? We spent the weekend with him."

"Right," Paul said. "The bald fruit."

Annalisa smiled. The comment was Paul's attempt at a joke. "I wish you wouldn't say things like that."

"What's wrong with it? He is gay, isn't he?"

"Someone might hear you. And get the wrong impression."

Paul looked around the restaurant. "Who?" he asked. "There's no one here."

"Billy says he can probably get us Mrs. Houghton's apartment. It's supposed to be spectacular—three floors with wraparound terraces—and the building is one of the best in the city."

The sommelier came to the table. "We'll have the Bordeaux," Paul said. He handed over the wine menu and continued to Annalisa, "I still don't get it. Why do you have to go to a funeral to get this apartment? Isn't cold hard cash enough?"

"It doesn't work that way," Annalisa said, tearing off a small piece of bread. "Apparently, it's all about who you know. That's why I'm going. To meet some of the other residents. Eventually, you'll have to meet them, too. And when you do, please don't call anyone a fruit."

"How much does he charge?" Paul asked.

"Who?"

"This Billy Litchfield character."

"I don't know."

"You hired him and didn't ask how much he cost?"

"He's not an object, Paul. He's a person. I didn't want to be rude."

"He's the help," Paul said.

"You're the one with the money. You talk to him," Annalisa said.

"The help is your area," Paul said.

"Do we have areas now?"

"We will. When we have children."

"Don't tease, Paul."

"I'm not," he said. The sommelier returned to the table and made a great show of opening the wine and pouring it into Paul's glass. Paul tasted it and approved. "By the way, I've been thinking about it. Now would be a good time to get started."

Annalisa took a sip of her wine. "Wow," she said. "I'm not sure I'm ready."

"I thought you wanted to have children."

"I do. I just wasn't thinking about having one so soon."

"Why not?" Paul said. "We've got plenty of money. And you're not working."

"I might go back to work."

"None of the other wives work," Paul said. "It's inconvenient."

"Says who?" Annalisa asked.

"Sandy Brewer."

"Sandy Brewer is an ass." Annalisa took another sip of wine. "It's not that I don't want to have a child. But we don't even have an apartment yet."

"That won't be a problem," Paul said. "You know you'll get this Mrs. Houghton's apartment if you put your mind to it." He picked up the menu and studied it, absentmindedly patting her hand.

※

"You're not going to work today?" James Gooch asked his wife the next morning.

"I told you. I'm going to Mrs. Houghton's memorial service."

"I thought you weren't invited," James said.

"I wasn't," Mindy said. "But when did that ever stop me?"

Upstairs, Philip Oakland knocked on his aunt's door. Enid greeted him dressed in black slacks and beaded black top. "I saw Sam Gooch yesterday," she said as they were riding down in the elevator. "He said you had a young lady in your apartment."

Philip laughed. "What if I did?"

"Who was she?" Enid asked.

"A young lady," Philip said teasingly. "I was interviewing her."

"Oh, Philip," Enid said. "I wish you wouldn't. You're getting to an age when you need to be sensible about women."

The elevator doors opened, and finding Mindy Gooch in the lobby, Enid put aside her concerns about Philip's love life. Mindy was also dressed in black, causing Enid to suspect that Mindy was going to try to crash Mrs. Houghton's memorial service. Enid decided to let this pass unnoticed as well. "Hello, Mindy dear," she said. "Sad day, isn't it?"

"If you want to look at it that way," Mindy said.

"Any outside interest in the apartment?" Enid asked casually.

"Not yet. But I'm sure there will be soon," Mindy replied.

"Don't forget about our interest," Enid said pleasantly.

"How can I?" Mindy said. She strode out of the building ahead of Enid and Philip, fuming.

The memorial service was at St. Ambrose Church on Broadway and Eleventh Street. There was a snarl of traffic in front of the entrance; a cacophony of honking horns was followed by the wail of a siren as a police car tried to disperse the traffic.

Mindy put her hands over her ears. "Shut up!" she screamed. After this outburst, she felt a little better. She joined the crowd in front of the church, slowly shuffling their way in. She passed a line of police barricades, behind which stood the usual pack of paparazzi. When she reached the steps, she was stopped by a massive security guard. "Invitation?" he asked.

"I left it at home," Mindy said.

"Step to the side, please," the guard said.

"Mrs. Houghton was a very good friend. We lived in the same building," Mindy said.

The security guard waved more people through, and Mindy took the opportunity to try to sneak in with the group ahead of her. The guard spotted her and stepped in front of her. "Move to the side, ma'am."

Chastised, Mindy moved a little to her right, where she had the pleasure of seeing Enid and Philip Oakland about to pass her by. At the last second, Enid spotted Mindy and, wiggling through the crowd, touched Mindy on the arm. "By the way, dear, I meant to tell you. Sam was such a help yesterday with my computer. Thank God for young people. We old people couldn't survive in this technological world without them."

Before Mindy could respond, Enid moved on, and Mindy's irritation nearly reached the boiling point. Not only had Enid insulted her by implying that she and Mindy were in the same age category ("old," Enid had said), but she had cruelly and deliberately left Mindy outside. Enid could have easily brought Mindy into the church, as no one said no to Enid Merle. Enid was what little girls called a fair-weather friend, Mindy thought, and planned to return the favor someday.

Strolling up Eleventh Street, Billy Litchfield spotted Mindy Gooch loitering on the edge of the crowd. Providence, he thought happily. This could be nothing less than a sign from Mrs. Houghton herself that Annalisa Rice was meant to get the apartment. Billy had been hoping to introduce Annalisa to Enid Merle and, through Enid, to make her introduction into One Fifth. But Mindy Gooch, the head of the board, was a much bigger—though less glamorous—fish. Approaching her, Billy couldn't help thinking, Poor Mindy. She'd been relatively pretty once, but over the years, her features had sharpened and her cheeks had sunk, as if literally eaten away by bitterness. Arranging his face into an appropriately mournful demeanor, he took her hands and kissed her on both cheeks. "Hello, Mindy dear," he said.

"Billy."

"Are you going in?" Billy asked.

Mindy looked away. "I thought I might pay my respects."

"Ah." Billy nodded, immediately guessing at the truth. There was, he knew, no possibility that Mrs. Houghton would have invited Mindy to her memorial service; although Mindy was the head of the board, Mrs. Houghton had never mentioned her and most likely had not known, or cared to know, of Mindy's existence. But Mindy, who was always full of misplaced and determined pride, would have found it necessary to attend in order to cement her status. "I'm waiting for a friend," he said. "Perhaps you'd like to go in with us."

"Sure," Mindy said. Say what you would about Billy Litchfield, she thought, at least he was always a gentleman.

Billy took Mindy's arm. "Were you very close to Mrs. Houghton?"

Mindy stared at him unflinchingly. "Not really," she said. "I mostly saw her in the lobby. But you were close, weren't you?"

"Very," Billy said. "I visited her at least twice a month."

"You must miss her," Mindy said.

"I do." Billy sighed. "She was an amazing woman, but we all know that." He paused, gauging Mindy's mood, and went in for the kill. "And that apartment," he said. "I wonder what will happen to it."

His gamble paid off. Mindy was much more interested in talking about Mrs. Houghton's apartment than about Mrs. Houghton herself. "Now, that's a good question," she said. Leaning forward intently, she whispered loudly, "There are some people in the building who want to split it up."

Billy took a step back in shock. "That would be a travesty," he said. "You can't split up an apartment like that. It's a landmark, really."

"That's what I think," Mindy said emphatically, pleased to discover that she and Billy were of one mind in the matter.

Billy lowered his voice. "I may be able to help you. I know someone who would be perfect for the apartment."

"Really?" Mindy said.

Billy nodded. "A lovely young woman from Washington, D.C. I would only say this to you, my dear, because you'll understand exactly what I mean. But she's definitely one of us."

Mindy was flattered but did her best not to show it. "Can she afford a twenty-million-dollar apartment?"

"Naturally, she comes with a husband. He's in finance. My dear," Billy said quickly, "we both know One Fifth has a great tradition of being home to creative types. But we also know what's happened to the real estate market. No one in the arts can afford an apartment like that anymore. Unless, as you said, you agree to split it up."

"I'll never let that happen," Mindy said, folding her arms.

"Good girl," Billy said approvingly. "In any case, you can meet my friend." Looking over Mindy's shoulder, he saw Annalisa getting out of a cab. "Here she comes now."

Mindy turned around. A tall young woman with auburn hair pulled back into a messy ponytail was approaching. She had a serious yet interesting face, the kind of face that other women appreciate as beautiful, possibly because it was the kind of beauty that appeared to be attached to a personality.

"This is Mindy Gooch," Billy said to Annalisa. "Mindy lives in One Fifth. She was also a friend of Mrs. Houghton's."

"Nice to meet you," Annalisa said. Her handshake was firm, and Mindy appreciated the fact that Annalisa didn't try to kiss her on the cheek in the faux European manner, and that Billy had referred to her as a friend of Mrs. Houghton's. Billy, Mindy thought, was a perfect example of how civilized Fifth Avenue residents ought to behave toward each other.

Inside the church, they took seats in a middle pew. Two rows ahead, Mindy recognized the back of Enid's coiffed and bleached blond hair (she had once been a brunette, but gray hair had eventually gotten the better of her) next to Philip's shiny brown bob. What kind of middle-aged man insisted on wearing his hair so long? They were a ridiculous pair, Mindy decided—the aging spinster and her silly nephew—with their attitudes and arrogance. It was too much. Enid Merle needed to be taught a lesson.

The church bell chimed mournfully ten times. Then the organ music began, and two priests in white robes, swinging balls of incense, came down the aisle, followed by the bishop in a blue gown and mitered hat. The congregation stood. Mindy bowed her head. Billy leaned toward her. "Who wants to break up the apartment?" he whispered.

"Enid Merle. And her nephew Philip."

Billy nodded. The bishop reached the altar, and the congregation sat down. The traditional Catholic ceremony, which was what Mrs. Houghton had wanted, continued in Latin and English. Billy let the words flow over him. On the surface, he found it hard to believe that Enid Merle would want to break up Mrs. Houghton's apartment. But there was a good reason Enid had survived as a gossip columnist for nearly fifty years. She wasn't as kindly as she appeared, and while it was generally understood that Enid and Louise Houghton had been bosom buddies, Billy suspected that wasn't the whole story. He recalled some trouble between them concerning Enid's stepmother, which might have been resolved when the stepmother moved out of One Fifth. It was possible Enid Merle didn't give a damn about preserving Louise Houghton's legacy.

Still, the situation presented a moral dilemma. Billy didn't want to thwart Enid, which might be dangerous, as Enid still controlled a segment of popular opinion through her syndicated column. And yet the apartment had been Mrs. Houghton's pride and joy. She had ruled over all of Manhattan society from her perch in the sky, and even in the seventies and eighties, when downtown lost its luster and the Upper East Side ruled, Mrs. Houghton wouldn't consider moving. When she relayed this information to Billy, she would tap on the floor with her marble-topped cane. "This is the center of New York Society," she would insist in her grand low voice. "Not up there in the provinces," she'd say, referring to the Upper East and West Sides of Manhattan. "Did you know it used to take an entire day to reach the Dakota? And then one was forced to spend the night in that Gothic monstrosity." She would tap her cane again. "Society began here, and it will end here. Never forget your origins, Billy."

A significant portion of society would end if Enid Merle had her way with the apartment, Billy thought. His mission was clear: As much as he admired Enid Merle, his loyalty must be to Mrs. Houghton's wishes.

There was more praying, and the congregation knelt. Mindy folded her hands in front of her face. "I was thinking," Billy whispered behind his closed palms. "What are you doing after this? Perhaps we could nip over to One Fifth and take a peek at the apartment."

Mindy looked at Billy in surprise. She'd suspected a motive behind his sudden kindness, but she hadn't expected him to go so far as to wheel and deal in the house of the Lord. But this was New York, where nothing was sacred. She peeked through her fingers at the back of her neighbors' heads, and her resentment flared. The bishop led the mourners in the sign of the cross. "In the name of the Father, the Son, and the Holy Spirit," Mindy said. She sat back in the pew and, staring straight ahead, whispered to Billy, "I think it can be arranged."

❖

Following the memorial service, Enid had organized a luncheon for twenty at the Village restaurant on Ninth Street, to which Philip Oakland accompanied his aunt. Although not technically open for lunch, the restaurant, where Enid had been a patron for years—along with almost everyone else who lived in the neighborhood—made an exception for Enid and the sad occasion. Philip was well acquainted with Enid's crowd, once New York's best and brightest. These people and their particular rituals—which included speaking to the woman on your right during the appetizer and the woman on your left during the main course; exchanging inside information on politics, business, the media, and the arts; and, lastly, standing and speechifying during coffee—was so much a part of Philip's life that he barely noticed how ancient these movers and shakers had become.

The conversation was, as usual, impassioned. Although the tragedy of Mrs. Houghton's unfortunate accident and her untimely death—"she had another five good years in her," most agreed—was part of the discussion, it eventually turned to the upcoming elections and the impending recession. Seated next to his aunt was an aged man who held himself stiffly upright in his chair. A former senator and speechwriter for Jack Kennedy, he held forth on the differences between the Democratic candidates' oracular styles. The second course came—veal in a lemon butter sauce—and without missing a beat in the conversation, Enid picked up her knife and fork and began to cut up the senator's meat. Her act of kindness terrified Philip. As he looked around the table, the scene was all at once garish to him, a picaresque grotesquery of old age.

He put down his fork. This was where his own life was headed; indeed, he was only a short hop away. His perceived reality panicked him, and everything that had recently gone wrong with his life came to the fore. There was trouble with his current screenplay; there would be trouble with the next one, if there was a next one, and if there was another book, he'd have trouble with that as well. Someday he'd be here, an impotent and insignificant windbag, needing someone to cut up his meat. And he didn't even have a woman to soothe him.

He stood up and made his excuses. He had a conference call from Los Angeles that couldn't be avoided—he'd only just gotten the message on his BlackBerry. "You can't stay for dessert?" Enid asked. Then she exclaimed, "Oh, damn. There go the numbers." His absence meant there would be an uneven number of men and women.

"Can't be avoided, Nini," he said, kissing her on her upturned cheek. "You'll manage."

He made it only halfway down the block before he called Lola. Her casual hello made his heart race, and he covered it up by becoming more serious than he'd intended. "This is Philip Oakland."

"What's up?" she said, although she sounded pleased to hear from him.

"I want to offer you the job. As my researcher. Can you start this afternoon?"

"No," she said. "I'm busy."

"How about tomorrow morning?"

"Can't," she said. "My mother's leaving, and I have to say goodbye."

"What time is she leaving?" he said, wondering how he'd gotten into this desperate-sounding exchange.

"I don't know. Maybe ten? Or eleven?"

"Why don't you come by in the afternoon?"

"I guess I could," Lola said, sounding uncertain. Sitting on the edge of the pool at Soho House, she dipped her toe into the warm, murky water. She wanted the job but didn't want to appear too eager. After all, even though Philip would technically be her employer, he was still a man. And in dealing with men, it was always important to keep the upper hand. "How's two o'clock?"

"Perfect," Philip said, relieved, and hung up the phone.

Back at Soho House, the waiter approached Lola and warned her that cell phones were not allowed in the club, even on the roof. Lola gave him an icy stare before texting her mother to tell her the good news. Then she slathered herself with more sunscreen and lay down on a chaise. She closed her eyes, fantasizing about Philip Oakland and One Fifth. Maybe Philip would fall in love with her and marry her, and then she'd live there, too.

"It's beautiful," Annalisa said, stepping into the foyer of Mrs. Houghton's apartment.

Billy clutched his heart. "It's a mess. You should have seen it when Mrs. Houghton lived here."

"I did see it," Mindy said. "It was very old-lady."

The apartment had been stripped of its antiques, paintings, rugs, and silk draperies; what was left were dust bunnies and faded wallpaper. At mid-afternoon, the apartment was flooded with light, revealing the chipped paint and scuffed parquet floors. The small foyer led to a bigger foyer with a sunburst inlaid in the marble floor; from there, a grand staircase ascended. Three sets of tall wooden doors opened to a living room, dining room, and library. Billy, lost in memories, stepped into the enormous living room. It ran the length of the front of the apartment, overlooking Fifth Avenue. Two pairs of French doors led to a ten-foot-wide terrace. "Oh, the parties she had here," he said, gesturing around the room. "She had it set up like a European salon, with couches and settees and conversational clusters. You could fit a hundred people in this room and not even know it." He led the way to the dining room. "She had everyone to dinner. I remember one dinner in particular. Princess Grace. She was so beautiful. No one had any idea that a month later, she'd be dead."

"People rarely do," Mindy said dryly.

Billy ignored this. "There was one long table for forty. I do think a long table is so much more elegant than those round tables for ten that everyone does these days. But I suppose there's no choice. No one has a large dining room anymore, although Mrs. Houghton always said one never wanted more than forty people at a sit-down dinner. It was all about making the guests feel they were part of a select group."

"Where's the kitchen?" Mindy asked. Although she'd been in the apartment once before, it had been only a cursory tour, and now she felt envious and intimidated. She had no idea Mrs. Houghton had lived so grandly, but the grand living appeared to have taken place before Mindy and James moved into the building. Leading the way through swinging doors, Billy pointed out the butler's pantry and, farther on, the kitchen itself, which was surprisingly crude, with a linoleum floor and Formica countertops. "She never came in here, of course," Billy explained. "No one did except the staff. It was considered a form of respect."

"What if she wanted a glass of water?" Annalisa asked.

"She would call on the phone. There were phones in every room, and each room had its own line. It was considered very modern in the early eighties."

Annalisa looked at Mindy, caught her eye, and smiled. Until then Mindy hadn't known what to make of Annalisa, who managed to appear self-contained and confident, without revealing a peep of information about herself. Perhaps Annalisa Rice had a sense of humor after all.

They went up to the second floor, examined Mrs. Houghton's master bedroom, large bathroom, and sitting room, where, Billy noted, he and Louise had spent many pleasant hours. They peeked into the three bedrooms down the hall and then went up to the third floor. "And here," Billy said, throwing open two paneled doors, "is the pièce de résistance. The ballroom."

Annalisa walked across the black-and-white-checkerboard marble floor and stood in the middle of the room, taking in the domed ceiling and the fireplace and the French windows. The room was overwhelmingly beautiful—she had never imagined that such a room, in such an apartment, could exist in a building in New York City. Manhattan was full of wonderful secrets and surprises. Gazing around, Annalisa thought that she had never desired anything in her life as much as this apartment.

Billy came up behind her. "I always say if one can't be happy in this apartment, one can't be happy anywhere." Even Mindy was unable to come up with a retort. The atmosphere was full of longing, Billy thought, what he called "the ache." It was part of the pain of living in Manhattan, this overwhelming ache for prime real estate. It could cause people to do all kinds of things—lie, stay in marriages that were over, prostitute themselves, even commit murder. "What do you think?" he asked Annalisa.

Annalisa's heart was racing. What she thought was that she and Paul must buy the apartment now, this afternoon, before anyone else saw it and wanted it as well. But her trained lawyerly mind prevailed, and she kept her cool. "It's wonderful. Certainly something for us to consider." She looked at Mindy. The key to getting the apartment lay in the hands of this jumpy neurotic woman whose eyes bulged slightly out of her head. "My husband, Paul, is so particular," Annalisa said. "He'll want to see the building's financials."

"It's a top-notch building," Mindy said. "We have the highest mortgage credentials." She opened the French doors and went onto the terrace. Looking over the side, she had a clear view of the corner of Enid Merle's terrace. "Have you seen this view?" she called to Annalisa.

Annalisa came outside. Standing on the terrace was like being on the prow of a ship sailing over a sea of Manhattan rooftops. "Gorgeous," she said.

"So you're from . . . ?" Mindy asked.

"Washington," Annalisa said. "We moved here for Paul's work. He's in finance." Billy Litchfield had whispered to her in the church to avoid "hedge-fund manager" and use "finance" instead, which was vague and classier. "When you talk to Mindy, emphasize how normal you are," Billy had advised.

"How long have you lived here?" Annalisa asked politely, turning the topic away from herself.

"Ten years," Mindy said. "We love the building. And the area. My son goes to school in the Village, so it makes things easier."

"Ah." Annalisa nodded wisely.

"Do you have children?" Mindy asked.

"Not yet."

"It's a very child-friendly building," Mindy said. "Everyone loves Sam."

Billy Litchfield joined them, and Annalisa decided now was the time to strike. "Is your husband James Gooch?" she asked Mindy casually.

"He is. How do you know him?" Mindy asked, looking at her in surprise.

"I read his last book, *The Lonesome Soldier*," Annalisa said.

"Only two thousand people read that book," Mindy countered.

"I loved it. American history is one of my obsessions. Your husband is a wonderful writer."

Mindy took a step back. She wasn't sure whether to believe Annalisa, but she liked the fact that Annalisa was making an effort. And considering James's coup with Apple, maybe Mindy had been wrong about his fiction abilities. It was true that James had once been a wonderful writer; it was one of the reasons she'd married him. Perhaps he was about to become a wonderful writer again. "My husband has a new book coming out," she said. "People in the business are saying it's going to be bigger than Dan Brown. If you can believe that."

Having said the words aloud, and having liked how they sounded, Mindy now began to believe James's success was a distinct possibility. That would really show Philip Oakland, she thought. And if the Rices took the apartment, it would be a blow to both Enid and Philip.

"I've got to get back to my office," Mindy said, holding out her hand to Annalisa. "But I hope we'll be seeing each other soon."

"I'm impressed," Billy said to Annalisa, when they were on the sidewalk in front of One Fifth. "Mindy Gooch liked you, and she doesn't like anyone."

Annalisa smiled and flagged down a taxi.

"Have you really read *The Lonesome Soldier?*" Billy asked. "It was eight hundred pages and dry as toast."

"I have," Annalisa said.

"So you knew James Gooch was her husband?"

"No. I Googled her on our way out of the church. There was an item that mentioned James Gooch was her husband."

"Clever," Billy said. A taxi pulled up, and he held open the door.

Annalisa slid onto the backseat. "I always do my homework," she said.

❖

As predicted, the job as Philip's researcher was easy. Three afternoons a week—on Mondays, Wednesdays, and Fridays—Lola met Philip at his apartment at noon. Sitting at a tiny desk in his large, sun-filled living room, Lola made a great pretense of working; for the first few days, anyway. Philip worked in his office with the door open. Every now and then, he would poke his head out and ask her to find something for him, like the exact address of some restaurant that had been on First Avenue in the eighties. Lola couldn't understand why he needed this information; after all, he was writing a screenplay, so why couldn't he just make it up the way he had the characters?

When she questioned him about it, he took a seat near her on the arm of the leather club chair in front of the fireplace and gave her a lecture about the importance of authenticity in fiction. At first Lola was mystified, then bored, and finally fascinated. Not by what Philip was saying but by the fact that he was speaking to her as if she, too, possessed the same interests and knowledge. This happened a few times, and when he went back to his office abruptly, as if he'd just thought of something, and she'd hear the tap of his fingers on his keyboard, Lola would tuck her hair behind her ears and, frowning in concentration, attempt to Google the information he'd requested. But she had a short attention span, and within minutes, she'd be off on the wrong tangent, reading Perez Hilton, or checking her Facebook page, or watching episodes of *The Hills*, or scrolling through videos on YouTube. If she'd had a regular job in an office, Lola knew, these activities would have been frowned upon—indeed, one of her college friends had recently been fired from her job as a paralegal for this particular infraction—but Philip didn't seem to mind. Indeed, it was the opposite: He appeared to consider it part of her job.

On her second afternoon, while looking at videos on YouTube, Lola came across a clip of a bride in a strapless wedding gown attacking a man with an umbrella on the side of a highway. In the background was a white limousine—apparently, the car had broken down, and the bride was taking it out on the driver. "Philip?" Lola said, peeking into his office.

Philip was hunched over his computer, his dark hair falling over his forehead. "Huh?" he said, looking up and brushing back the hair.

"I think I've found something that might help you."

"The address of Peartree's?"

"Something better." She showed him the video.

"Wow," Philip said. "Is that real?"

"Of course." They listened to the bride screaming epithets at the driver. "Now, that," Lola said, sitting back in her little chair, "is authenticity."

"Are there more of these?" Philip asked.

"There are probably hundreds," Lola replied.

"Good work," Philip said, impressed.

Philip, Lola decided, was book-smart, but despite his desire for authenticity, he didn't seem to know a lot about real life. On the other hand, her own real life in New York wasn't exactly shaping up to be what she'd hoped.

On Saturday night, she'd gone clubbing with the two girls she'd met in the human resources department. Although Lola considered them "average," they were the only girls she knew in New York. Clubbing in the Meatpacking District had been both an exciting and depressing adventure. At the beginning of the evening, they were turned away from two clubs but found a third where they could wait in line to get in. For forty-five minutes, they'd stood behind a police barricade while people in Town Cars and SUVs pulled up to the entrance and were admitted immediately— and how it stung not to be a member of that exclusive club—but during the wait, they saw six genuine celebrities enter. The line would begin buzzing like a rattlesnake's tail, and then all of a sudden, everyone was using their phones, trying to get a photo of the celebrity. Inside the club, there was more separation of the Somebodies and the Wannabes. The Somebodies had bottles of vodka and champagne at tables in roped-off tiers protected by enormous security guards, while the Nobodies were forced to cluster in front of the bar like part of a mosh pit. It took another half hour to get a drink, which you clutched protectively like a baby, not knowing when you'd be able to get another.

This was no way to live. Lola needed to find a way to break into New York's glamorous inner circle.

The second Wednesday of Lola's employment found her stretched out on the couch in Philip's living room, reading tabloid magazines. Philip had gone to the library to write, leaving her alone in his apartment, where she was supposed to be reading the draft of his script, looking for typos. "Don't you have spell-check?" she'd asked when he handed her the script. "I don't trust it," he'd said. Lola started reading the script but then remembered it was the day all the new tabloid magazines came out. Putting aside the script, she went out to the newsstand on University. She loved going in and out of One Fifth, and when she passed the doormen now, she would give them a little nod, as if she lived there.

But the tabloids were dull that week—no major celebrities had gone to rehab or gained (or lost) several pounds or stolen someone's husband—and Lola tossed the magazines aside, bored. Looking around Philip's apartment, she realized that with Philip gone, there was something much more interesting to do: snoop.

She headed for the wall of bookcases. Three entire shelves were taken up with Philip's first book, *Summer Morning,* in various editions and languages. Another shelf consisted of hardcover first editions of the classics; Philip had told her that he collected them and had paid as much as five thousand dollars for a first edition of *The Great Gatsby,* which Lola thought was crazy. On the bottom shelf was a collection of old newspapers and magazines. Lola picked up a copy of *The New York Review of Books* dated February 1992. She flipped through the pages until she came upon a review of Philip's book *Dark Star.* Boring, she thought, and put it back. On the bottom of the pile, she spied an old copy of *Vogue* magazine. She pulled it out and looked at the cover. September 1989. One of the headlines read: THE NEW POWER COUPLES. What was Philip doing with an old copy of *Vogue?* she wondered, and opened it up to find out.

Turning to the middle of the magazine, she found the answer. There was a ten-page spread of a much younger Philip and an even younger-looking Schiffer Diamond, standing in front of the Eiffel Tower, feeding each other croissants at a sidewalk café, strolling down a Paris street in a ballgown and a tux. The headline read: LOVE IN THE SPRINGTIME: OSCAR-WINNING ACTRESS SCHIFFER DIAMOND AND PULITZER PRIZE–WINNING AUTHOR PHILIP OAKLAND SHOW OFF THE NEW PARIS COLLECTIONS.

Lola took the magazine to the couch and studied the pictures more carefully. She'd had no idea Philip Oakland and Schiffer Diamond had once been together, and she was filled with jealousy. In the past week, she'd felt moments of attraction to Philip but had always hesitated because of his age. He *was* twenty years older. And while he looked younger and was in good shape—he went to the gym every morning—and there were tons of young women who married older celebrities—look at Billy Joel's wife—Lola still worried that if she "went there" with Philip, she might get a nasty surprise. What if he had age spots? Or couldn't get it up?

But as she flipped through the photo spread in *Vogue*, her estimation of him rose, and she began calculating how to seduce him.

At five P.M., Philip left the library and walked back to One Fifth. Lola should be gone, he figured, and another day would have passed during which he had managed not to attempt to sleep with the girl. He was attracted to her, which he couldn't help, being a man. And she seemed to be attracted to him, judging by the way she looked at him through a strand of hair she was always twisting in front of her face, as if she were shy. But she was a little young even for him and, despite her knowledge of everything celebrity and Internet, not very worldly. So far, nothing much had happened to her in life, and she was a bit immature.

Riding the elevator to his floor, he had an inspiration and hit the button for nine. There were six apartments on this floor, and Schiffer's was at the end. He walked down the hallway, reminded of the many times he'd been here at all hours of the day and night. He rang her bell and then rattled the door handle. Nothing. She wasn't home, of course. She was never home.

He went upstairs to his own apartment and, turning the key in the lock, was startled to hear Lola call out, "Philip?"

Inside the door was a small pink patent-leather overnight case. Lola was in the living room on the couch. She peeked over the back.

"You're still here," Philip said. He was surprised but not, he realized, unhappy to see her.

"Something really, really terrible has happened," she said. "I hope you won't be angry."

"What?" he asked in alarm, thinking it must have something to do with his screenplay. Had he gotten another call from the head of the studio?

"There's no hot water in my building."

"Oh," he said. Guessing at the meaning of the overnight case, he said, "Do you need to take a shower here?"

"It's not just that. Someone told me they're going to be working on the pipes all night. When I went home, there was all this banging."

"But surely they'll stop. After six, I would think."

She shook her head. "My building isn't like your building. It's a rental, so they can do whatever they want. *Whenever* they want," she added for emphasis.

"What do you want to do?" he asked. Was she angling to spend the night at his apartment? Which could be a very bad—or a very good—idea.

"I was thinking maybe I could sleep on your couch. It's only one night. They'll have to have the pipes fixed by tomorrow."

He hesitated, wondering if the pipes were an excuse. If so, he'd be a fool to resist. "Sure," he said.

"Oh, goody," she exclaimed, jumping up from the couch and grabbing her bag. "You won't even know I'm here, I promise. I'll sit on the couch and watch TV. And you can work, if you want to. Or whatever."

"You don't have to act like a little orphan girl," he said. "I'll take you to dinner."

While she was in the shower, he went into his office and scrolled through his e-mails. There were several he knew he ought to return, but hearing the shower running and imagining Lola's naked body, he couldn't concentrate and tried to read *Variety* instead. Then she appeared in the doorway, damp but clothed in a short tank-top dress, rubbing her hair in a towel. "Where do you want to go for dinner?" she asked.

He closed his computer. "I thought I'd take you to Knickerbocker. It's right around the corner, and it's one of my favorite restaurants. It's not fancy, but the food's good."

A little later, seated in a booth, Lola studied the extensive menu while Philip ordered a bottle of wine. "I always get the oysters and steak," he said. "Do you like oysters?"

"I love them," she said, putting down the menu and smiling at him eagerly. "Have you ever had an oyster shot? They take an oyster and put it in a shot glass with vodka and cocktail sauce. We had them all the time when I was in Miami."

Philip wasn't sure how to respond, having never had an oyster shot, which sounded disgusting but probably made sense to a twenty-two-year-old. "And then what happened?" he asked. It was a random question, but it prompted a response.

"Well," she said, putting her elbows on the table and resting her chin in her hands, "you get really wasted. And one girl—she wasn't one of my friends, but she was in our posse—got so drunk, she took off her shirt for *Girls Gone Wild*. And her father saw it. And he flipped out. Isn't that disgusting, knowing your father watches *Girls Gone Wild*?"

"Maybe he'd heard she'd done it. And he wanted to know for sure."

She frowned. "No one tells their father they did *Girls Gone Wild*. But some girls definitely do it to get guys interested. They think it makes them look hot."

"What do you think?" he asked.

"It's stupid. Yeah, a guy will sleep with you, but then what?"

Then what, indeed, Philip thought, wondering how many men she'd slept with. "Have you ever done it?" he asked.

"*Girls Gone Wild*? No way. I would maybe take my clothes off for *Playboy*. Or *Vanity Fair*, because those are classy. And you have photo approval."

Philip took a gulp of wine and smiled. She definitely wanted to sleep with him. Why else would she be talking about sex and taking her clothes off? She was going to drive him insane if she didn't stop.

A little angel on his shoulder, however, reminded him that he shouldn't have sex with her, while the devil on his other said, "Why not? She's obviously done it before, and probably quite often." As a compromise, he made the dinner last as long as possible, ordering another bottle of wine, dessert, and after-dinner drinks. When the inevitable moment arrived and it was time to go home, Lola stood up and fumbled for her snakeskin bag, obviously tipsy. Leaving the restaurant, he put his arm around her to steady her, and when they got outside, she slipped her arm around his waist and leaned in to his body, giggling. In response, his cock swelled against his thigh.

"That was so much fun," she said. And then becoming serious, added, "I had no idea the movie business was so hard."

"But it's worth it," he said. After the sex talk, and feeling loose from the wine, he'd told her all about his troubles with the studio, while she'd listened, rapt. He moved his hand up from her shoulder to the back of her neck. "It's time to get you to bed," he said. "I don't want you to be hungover tomorrow."

"I already will be." She giggled.

Back in his apartment, she made a great show of going into the bathroom to get changed, while he put a pillow and blanket on the couch. They both knew she wasn't going to sleep there, but it was probably a good idea to pretend, Philip thought. She came out of the bathroom barefoot in a short baby-doll nightgown with silk ribbon stitched around the neckline, unbuttoned just enough to expose her cleavage. Philip sighed. And, summoning all his resistance, he stopped in front of her, kissed her on the forehead, and went into his room. "Good night," he said. And somehow forced himself to close the door.

He took off his clothes save for his boxer shorts and got into bed, leaving the light on and picking up a copy of Buddenbrooks. Once again, he couldn't concentrate, not with Lola on the other side of the door in that tiny baby-doll nightgown. Frowning at the page, he reminded himself that she was only twenty-two. He could sleep with her—and then what? She couldn't work for him if they were having sex. Or could she? He could always fire her and find another researcher. After all, it was probably easier to find another researcher than it was to find a gorgeous twenty-two-year-old who wanted to have sex.

But what now? Should he get up and go to her? For a moment, he had a disquieting thought: What if he was wrong? What if she didn't want to sleep with him at all, and the excuse about the broken pipes in her apartment building was real? What if he went out there and she rejected him? It would be doubly awkward to have her around, and then he really would have to fire her. Another minute or two passed. And there it was—his answer—a knock on the door.

"Philip?" she said.

"Come in," he called.

She opened the door as he took off his reading glasses. Acting as if she didn't want to disturb him, she leaned against the door frame with her hands crossed in front of her like a child. "Can I have a glass of water?"

"Sure," he said.

"Can you get it for me? I don't know where the glasses are."

"Follow me." He got out of bed, realizing he was wearing only his boxer shorts, and realizing he didn't care.

She stared at his chest, at the patch of dark curling hairs that made a neat pattern above his pectoral muscles. "I didn't mean to disturb you."

"You're not disturbing me," he said, going to the kitchen. She followed him, and he took out a glass and filled it with tap water. When he turned, she was standing right next to him. He was about to hand her the glass but suddenly put it down and put his arm around her shoulder. "Oh, Lola," he said. "Let's stop pretending."

"What do you mean?" she asked coyly, putting her hand in the hair on his chest.

"Do you want to sleep with me?" he whispered. "Because I want to sleep with you."

"Of course." She pressed her body against his as they kissed. He could feel her firm, full breasts through the thin fabric of her nightgown; he could even, he thought, feel the poke of her erect nipples. He put his hands under the nightgown, sliding them along the sides of her panties and up her stomach to her breasts, where his fingers played with her nipples. She groaned and leaned back, and he pulled the nightgown over her head. God, she was beautiful, he thought. He lifted her onto the counter and, parting her legs, stood between them, kissing her. He moved his hand down to her crotch and pulled aside her panties, which were also silk and lacy, and then, surprised by what he felt, stopped and took a step back.

"No hair?" he said.

"Of course not," she said proudly. Like all the girls she knew, she had a Brazilian wax once a month.

"But why?" he said, touching the exposed skin.

"Because men like it," she said. "It's supposed to be hot." She took a breath. "Don't tell me you've never seen one before?" She laughed.

"I like it," he said, examining her hairless vagina. It was like one of those soft, hairless cats, he thought. He lifted her again and carried her to the couch. "You're spectacular," he said.

Placing her on the edge of the couch, he pushed her legs open and began licking the purplish skin. "Stop," she said suddenly.

"Why?" he asked.

"I don't like it."

"That's only because no one's ever done it properly," he said. The kissing "down there" seemed to go on for hours, and finally, she gave in, with her legs shaking and her vagina pulsating. Then she was overcome and burst into tears.

He kissed her on the mouth, and she could taste herself on his lips and tongue. Reason told her she ought to be repulsed, but it wasn't so bad; more, she thought, like clean, slightly damp clothes just out of the dryer. She put her hands in his hair, which was softer and finer than her own. She stared into his eyes. Would he tell her he loved her?

"Did you like it?" he whispered.

"Yes," she said.

Then he went into the kitchen.

"Is that it?" she asked, wiping her cheeks and laughing. "Aren't you going to . . . ?"

He came back with two shots of vodka. "Sustenance," he said, handing her the tiny glass. "It doesn't have an oyster in it, but it'll do." He took her hand and led her into the bedroom and removed his boxer shorts. His penis was fat, with a thick vein on the underside, and his balls swung slightly in the sack of prickly pink skin. She lay on her back, and he crunched her knees up to her chest, kneeling between her legs. When he pushed his penis in, she braced herself for some pain, but surprisingly, there was none, only a pulse of pleasure. "Lola, Lola, Lola," he said, repeating her name. Then his body stiffened, his back arched, and he collapsed on top of her. Lola put her arms around him, kissing his neck.

In the middle of the night, he woke her up, and they made love again. She fell asleep, and the next morning, she awakened to find him staring at her. "Ah, Lola," he said. "What's going to happen with you?"

"With me?"

"With me and you."

Lola wasn't sure she liked the sound of that. "Philip?" she said shyly, teasing his penis with the tip of her nail. In the next second, he was on top of her again. Lola opened her legs, and after he'd come and was lying on top of her, exhausted, she whispered, "I think I love you."

His head jerked up and he looked at her with surprise. Smiling and kissing the tip of her nose, he said, "'Love' is a big word, Lola." He stretched and got out of bed. "I'm going to get us some breakfast. How about bagels? What kind of bagel do you like?"

"What's the best kind?" Lola asked.

He laughed, shaking his head at her remark. "There is no best. It's whatever kind you like."

"What do you like?" she asked.

"Sesame."

"I'll have sesame, too."

He pulled on his jeans and, looking at Lola lying naked on his bed, smiled. This was what was so great about New York, he thought. You never knew what was going to happen. One's life could literally improve overnight.

While he was gone, Enid Merle, having heard suspicious noises coming from Philip's apartment the night before, decided to check in on him. She went through the small gate that separated their terraces and knocked on the French door. Her worst fears were confirmed when a young lady, wearing only what appeared to be one of Philip's T-shirts—with probably nothing underneath—came to the door. She looked at Enid curiously. "Yes?" she said.

Enid pushed past her. "Is Philip here?"

"I don't know," the girl said. "Who are you?"

"Who are you?" Enid said, not unpleasantly.

"I'm Philip's girlfriend," the girl said proudly.

"Really?" Enid said, thinking that was quick. "I'm Philip's aunt."

"Oh," the girl said. "I didn't know Philip had an aunt."

"And I didn't know he had a girlfriend," Enid said. "Is he here?"

The girl folded her arms as if realizing she was practically naked. "He went to get bagels."

"Tell him his aunt stopped by, will you?"

"Sure," Lola said. She followed Enid to the French door and watched her go through the gate to her own terrace.

Lola went inside and sat down on the couch. So Philip had a relative who lived right next door. She hadn't expected that—somehow she'd assumed that people like Philip Oakland didn't have relatives. Idly opening a magazine, she recalled the cold look on Enid's face but told herself it didn't matter. The aunt was ancient. How much trouble could an old lady be?

7

"James, what is wrong with you?" Mindy asked the next morning.

"I don't think I'm suited for fame," James said. "I can't even figure out what to wear."

Mindy rolled over in the bed and looked at the clock. It was just after six A.M. I am depressed, she thought. "Could you be a little quieter?" she said. "I'm tired."

"It's not my fault."

"Do you have to rattle the hangers so loudly? Can't you try on clothes silently?"

"Why don't you get up and help me?"

"You're a grown man, James. You ought to be able to figure out what to wear."

"Fine. I'll wear what I always wear. Jeans and a T-shirt."

"You could try a suit," Mindy said.

"Haven't seen that suit in three months. The dry cleaners probably lost it," James said in a slightly accusatory tone, as if this might be her fault.

"Please, James. Stop. It's only a stupid picture."

"It's my publicity photograph."

"Why are they doing it so early?"

"I told you. Some famous fashion photographer is taking the picture. He's only available from nine to eleven."

"Jesus. I could have taken your picture. With my cell phone. Oh, please," Mindy said. "Can't you be quiet? If I don't sleep, I'm going to go insane."

If you haven't already, James thought, gathering up a pile of clothes and leaving the room in a huff. It was *his* big day. Why did Mindy have to make everything about her?

He took the pile into his office and dropped the clothes on a chair. Viewed from this angle, his clothing looked like something you'd find in the cart of a homeless person. The publicist in Redmon's office, who possessed the improbable moniker of Cherry, had instructed him to bring three choices. Three shirts, three pairs of pants, a jacket or two, and a couple pairs of shoes. "But I mostly wear sneakers. Converse," James had said. "Do your best," Cherry had replied. "The photograph should be a reflection of you."

Great, James thought. It'll be a photograph of a balding, middle-aged man. He went into the bathroom and studied his appearance. Perhaps he should have shaved his head. But then he'd look like every other middle-aged guy who was balding and trying to cover it up. Besides, he didn't believe he had the face for the no-hair look. His features were irregular; his nose appeared as if it might have been broken once and healed badly, but it was only the Gooch nose, passed down through generations of ordinary hardship. He wished he looked like someone specific, though; he would have been happy with the brooding, hooded look of an artist. He narrowed his eyes and turned down his mouth, but this only made him appear to be making a face. Resigned to his visage, James shoved as many clothes as he could into one of Mindy's carefully folded shopping bags from Barneys and went out into the lobby.

It was raining. Hard. From the little windows in the back of his apartment, it was difficult to gauge the weather, so that one might arrive outside and find it was much better, although usually much worse, than one expected. It was not yet seven A.M., and already James felt defeated by the day. He went back into his apartment to get an umbrella, but all he could find in the jumbled hall closet was a flimsy fold-up affair, which, when opened, revealed four sharp spokes. Back in the lobby, James peered out anxiously at the pouring rain. A black SUV was idling at the curb. Behind him, the doorman Fritz was rolling out a plastic runner. Fritz stopped for a moment and joined James. "It's really pouring out there," he said, looking concerned. "You need a cab?"

"I'm okay," James said. He did need a taxi, but he never allowed the doormen to get him one. He knew how the doormen felt about Mindy's tipping, and he felt guilty asking them to perform the normal duties they did for other, better-tipping residents. If he made money from his book, he thought, he'd be sure to give them extra this year.

The elevator door opened, and Schiffer Diamond came out. James suddenly felt excited and diminished. She had her hair in a ponytail and was wearing a shiny green trench coat and jeans and low-heeled black boots. She didn't necessarily look like a movie star, James thought, but she somehow looked better than a regular person, so that no matter where she went, people would think, This woman is someone, and they would look at her curiously. James didn't know how a person could stand that, always being looked at. But they must get used to it. Wasn't that the reason, after all, that people became actors in the first place—to be gaped at?

"Bad weather, eh, Fritz?" Schiffer said.

"It's only going to get worse."

James stepped outside and stood under the awning. He looked up the street. Nothing. No taxis at all.

Schiffer Diamond came out behind him. "Where are you going?" she asked.

James jumped. "Chelsea?" he asked.

"Me, too. Come on, I'll give you a ride."

"No, I—"

"Don't be silly. The car's free. And it's pouring." Fritz came out and opened the door. Schiffer Diamond slid across the backseat.

James looked at Fritz. What the hell, he thought, and got in.

"Two stops," she said to the driver. "Where are you going?" She turned to James.

"I, uh, don't know exactly." He fumbled in his jeans pocket for the slip of paper on which he'd written the address. "Industria Super Studios?"

"I'm going to the same place," she said. "One stop, then," she informed the driver. She reached into her bag and pulled out an iPhone. James sat stiffly beside her; luckily, there was a console between them so it wasn't as uncomfortable as it might have been. Outside, the rain was coming down in buckets, and there was a rumble of thunder. This is nice, James thought. Imagine never having to worry about getting a taxi. Or taking the subway.

"Horrible weather, isn't it?" she said. "It's so wet for August. I don't remember it being this rainy in the summer. I remember ninety-degree heat. And snow at Christmas."

"Really?" James said. "It doesn't usually snow until January now."

"I guess I have a romantic memory of New York."

"We haven't had snow in years," James said. "Global warming." I sound like a putz, he thought.

She smiled at him, and James wondered if she was one of those actresses who seduced every man. He remembered a story about a journalist friend, a real regular guy, who had been seduced by a famous movie star during an interview.

"You're Mindy Gooch's husband, right?" she asked.

"James," he said. She clearly wasn't going to introduce herself, knowing, obviously, there was no need.

She nodded. "Your wife is . . ."

"The head of the board. For the building."

"She writes that blog," Schiffer said.

"Do you read it?"

"It's very touching," Schiffer said.

"Really?" James rubbed his chin in annoyance. Even here, in an

SUV with a movie star going to a photo shoot, it was still about his wife. "I try not to read it," he said primly.

"Ah." Schiffer nodded. James had no idea what the nod meant, and for a few blocks, they rode in stiff silence. Then Schiffer brought the topic back to his wife. "She wasn't the head of the board when I moved in. It was Enid Merle then. The building was different. It wasn't so . . . quiet."

James winced at Enid's name. "Enid," he said.

"She's a wonderful character, isn't she? I adore her."

"I don't really know her," James said carefully, caught in the middle of betraying his wife and alienating a movie star.

"But you must know her nephew Philip Oakland," Schiffer insisted. There she went again, she thought, bringing up Philip's name, digging for information. "Aren't you a novelist as well?" she asked.

"We're different. He's much more . . . commercial. He writes screenplays. And I'm more . . . literary," James said.

"Meaning you sell five thousand copies," Schiffer said. James was crushed but tried not to show it. "Please," she said, touching his arm. "I was kidding. It's my bad sense of humor. I'm sure you're a wonderful writer."

James didn't know whether to agree or disagree.

"Don't take anything I say seriously. I never do," she said.

The car stopped at a red light. It was his turn to come up with a conversational gambit, but James couldn't think of one.

"What's happening with Mrs. Houghton's apartment?" she asked.

"Oh," he said, relieved. "It's been sold."

"Really? That was quick, wasn't it?"

"The board meeting is this week. My wife says they're as good as approved. She likes them. They're supposedly a regular couple. With millions of dollars, of course," he added.

"How boring," Schiffer said.

The car arrived at the destination. There was another awkward moment as they stood waiting for the elevator. "Are you working on a movie?" James asked.

"TV show," she said. "I never thought I'd do TV. But you look around at your peers and think, Is that how I want to end up? With the plastic surgery and the adoptions and the crazy tell-all books that no one really wants to read? Or else with the dull husband who cheats."

"I'm sure it's difficult," James said.

"I like to work. I stopped for a while, and I missed it."

They got into the elevator. "Do you shoot the TV show here?" he inquired politely.

"I'm here for a photo shoot. For the cover of one of those over-forty magazines."

"Don't you get nervous?" James said.

"I just pretend I'm someone else. That's the secret to all this." The elevator door opened, and she got out.

An hour later, James, having submitted his face to the basting and flouring of makeup, sat on a stool in front of a blue roll of paper, his face stiffened in a death mask of a smile.

"You are famous author, no?" asked the photographer, who was French and, although a good ten years older than James, in possession of a full head of hair, as well as a wife thirty years his junior, according to the makeup artist.

"No," James said between gritted teeth.

"You will be soon, eh?" said the photographer. "Otherwise your publisher wouldn't pay for me." He put down his camera and called to the makeup artist, who was hovering on the side. "He is so stiff. Like a corpse. I cannot take a picture of a corpse," he said to James, who smiled uncomfortably. "We must do something. Anita will make you relax." The makeup artist came up behind James and put her hands on his shoulders. "I'm fine," James said as the young woman dug her fingers into his back. "I'm married. Really. My wife wouldn't like it."

"I don't see your wife here, do you?" Anita asked.

"No, but she—"

"Shhhhh."

"I can see you are not used to the attention of beautiful ladies," said the photographer. "You will learn. When you are famous, you will have the women all over you."

"I don't think so," James said.

The photographer and the makeup artist began laughing. Then it seemed that everyone in the studio was laughing. James reddened. He suddenly felt eight years old. He was playing on the Little League team at the neighborhood baseball diamond and had let the ball roll through his legs for the third time in a row. "C'mon, buddy," the coach said to James as he was laughed off the field. "It's all about picturization. You got to picture yourself a winner. Then you can *be* one." James sat on the bench for the rest of the game with his rheumy eyes and his runny nose (he had hay fever) and tried to "picturize" himself hitting a home run. But all he saw was that ball rolling between his legs again and again, and his father asking, "How'd it go, son?" and James replying, "Not so good." "Again?" "That's right, Dad, not so good." Even when he was eight, it was obvious to him that he was never going to be more than Jimmy Gooch, the kid who didn't quite fit in.

James looked up. The photographer was hidden behind his camera. He clicked off a shot. "That's very good, James," he said. "You look sad. Soulful."

Do I? James thought. Maybe he wasn't so bad at this famous-author business after all.

⬥

That evening, Schiffer knocked on Philip's door again, hoping to catch him at home. When he didn't answer, she tried Enid. "Philip?" Enid called out.

"It's Schiffer."

"I was wondering when you'd come to see me," Enid said, opening the door.

"I have no excuse."

"Perhaps you thought I was dead," Enid said.

Schiffer smiled. "I'm sure Philip would have told me."

"Have you seen him?"

"Only in the elevator."

"That's a shame. You haven't been to dinner?"

"No," Schiffer said.

"It's that damn girl," Enid said. "I knew this was going to happen. He hired some little twit to be his researcher, and now he's sleeping with her."

"Ah." Schiffer nodded. For a moment, she was taken aback. So Billy had been right after all. She shrugged, trying not to show her disappointment. "Philip will never change."

"You never know," Enid said. "Something might hit him over the head."

"I doubt it," Schiffer said. "I'm sure she finds him fascinating. That's the difference between girls and women: Girls find men fascinating. Women know better."

"You thought Philip was fascinating once," Enid said.

"I still do," Schiffer said, not wanting to hurt Enid's feelings. "Just not in the same way." She quickly changed the subject. "I heard a new couple is moving into Mrs. Houghton's apartment."

Enid sighed. "That's right. And I'm not very happy about it. It's all Billy Litchfield's fault."

"But Billy is so sweet."

"He's caused a great deal of trouble in the building. He was the one who found this couple and introduced them to Mindy Gooch. I wanted the bottom floor for Philip. But Mindy wouldn't hear of it. She called a special meeting of the board to push them through. She'd rather have strangers in the building. I saw her in the lobby, and I said, 'Mindy, I know what you're up to, changing the meeting,' and she said, 'Enid, you were late three times last year with your maintenance payments.'

"She has something against Philip," Enid continued. "Because Philip is successful, and her own husband is not."

"So nothing has changed."

"Not a bit," Enid said. "Isn't it wonderful? But you've changed. You've come back."

A few days later, Mindy was in her home office, looking through the Rices' paperwork. One of the pluses of being the head of the board of a building was access to the financial information of every resident who had moved into the building in the last ten years. The building required applicants to pay 50 percent of the asking price in cash; it also required they have an equivalent amount left over in bank accounts, stocks, retirement funds, and other assets; basically, an applicant had to be worth the full price of the apartment. The rules had been different when Mindy and James had moved in. Applicants had needed only 25 percent of the asking price and merely had to prove that they had liquid assets to cover the cost of the maintenance fee for five years. But Mindy had pushed through a referendum for change. There were, she argued, too many layabout characters in the building, the unseemly residue from the eighties when the building had been filled with rock-and-rollers and actors and models and fashion types and people who had known Andy Warhol, and it was the premier party building in the city. During Mindy's first year as head of the board, two of these residents went bankrupt, another died of a heroin overdose, and yet another committed suicide while her five-year-old son was asleep. She'd been a sometime model and girlfriend to a famous drummer who had married someone else and moved to Connecticut, abandoning the girlfriend and child in a two-bedroom apartment where she couldn't afford the maintenance. She'd taken sleeping pills and put a dry-cleaning bag over her head, Roberto reported.

"A building is only as good as its residents," Mindy had said in what she considered her famous address to the board. "If our building has a bad reputation, we all suffer. The value of our apartments suffers. No one wants to live in a building with police and ambulances rushing in and out."

"Our residents are creative types with interesting lives," Enid had countered.

"There are children living in this building. Overdoses and suicides are not 'interesting,'" Mindy said, glaring at her.

"Perhaps you'd be happier in a building on the Upper East Side. It's all doctors, lawyers, and bankers up there. I hear they never die," Enid said.

In the end, Enid was defeated by a vote of five to one.

"We clearly have very different values," Mindy said.

"Clearly." Enid nodded.

Enid was nearly forty years older than Mindy. So how was it that Enid always made Mindy feel like she was the old lady?

Shortly thereafter, Enid had retired from the board. In her place, Mindy installed Mark Vaily, a sweet gay man from the Midwest who was a set designer and had a life partner of fifteen years and a beautiful little Hispanic girl adopted from Texas. Everyone in the building agreed that Mark was lovely, and most important, he always agreed with Mindy.

The meeting with the Rices would include Mindy, Mark, and a woman named Grace Waggins, who had been on the board for twenty years, worked at the New York Public Library, and lived a quiet life in a one-bedroom apartment with two toy poodles. Grace was one of those types who never changed but only aged and had no apparent expectations or ambitions other than the wish that her life should remain the same.

At seven o'clock, Mark and Grace came to Mindy's apartment for a premeeting. "The bottom line is, they're going to pay cash," Mindy said. "They're financially sound. They're worth about forty million dollars . . ."

"And they're how old?" Grace asked.

"Young. Early thirties."

"I always hoped Julia Roberts would buy the apartment. Wouldn't it be lovely to have Julia Roberts here?"

"Even Julia Roberts probably doesn't have twenty million dollars cash to buy an apartment," Mark said.

"It's a shame, isn't it?"

"Actresses are not good tenants," Mindy said. "Look at Schiffer Diamond. She left her apartment empty for years. It caused a huge mouse problem. No," she went on, shaking her head. "We need a nice, stable couple who will live in the building for twenty years. We don't want any more actors or socialites or someone who will attract attention. It was bad enough when Mrs. Houghton died. The last thing we need are paparazzi camped outside the building."

The Rices arrived at seven-thirty. Mindy brought them into the living room, where Mark and Grace were sitting stiffly on the couch. Mindy had brought out two wooden chairs and motioned for the Rices to sit. Paul was more attractive than Mindy had imagined he'd be. He was sexy, with the kind of dark curly hair that reminded Mindy of a young Cat Stevens. Mindy distributed small bottles of water and perched between Mark and Grace. "Shall we begin?" she said formally.

Annalisa took Paul's hand. She and Paul had made several visits to the apartment with the real estate agent, Brenda Lish, and Paul was as enamored of the apartment as she was. Their future lay in the hands of these three odd people staring at them with blank, slightly hostile faces, but Annalisa was not afraid. She'd survived rigorous job interviews, had appeared in debates on TV, and had even met the president.

"What's your typical day like?" Mindy asked.

Annalisa glanced at Paul and smiled. "Paul gets up early and goes to work. We're trying to start a family. So I'm hoping to be busy with a baby soon."

"What if the baby cries all night?" Grace asked. She was childless herself, and while she adored children, the reality of them made her nervous.

"I hope he—or she—won't," Annalisa said, trying to make a joke. "But we'd have a nanny. And a baby nurse at first."

"There's certainly enough room in that apartment for a baby nurse," Grace said, nodding agreeably.

"Yes," Annalisa said. "And Paul needs his sleep as well."

"What do you do in the evenings?" Mindy said.

"We're very quiet. Paul gets home at about nine, and we either go out to dinner or we eat something at home and go to bed. Paul has to be up at six in the morning."

"Do you have a lot of friends?" Mark asked.

"No," Paul said. He was about to say "We don't like a lot of people," but Annalisa squeezed his hand. "We don't do a lot of socializing. Except on the weekends. Sometimes we go away."

"One has to get out of the city," Mark agreed.

"Do you have any hobbies we should know about?" Grace asked. "Play any musical instruments? You should know that there's a rule in the building—no playing of musical instruments after eleven P.M."

Annalisa smiled. "That rule must be left over from the jazz era. And One Fifth was built a little before that fun was over—Was it in 1927? The architect was . . ." She paused as if thinking, although she knew the answer by rote. "Harvey Wiley Corbett," she continued. "His firm also designed much of Rockefeller Center. He was considered a visionary, although his plans for elevated sidewalks in midtown didn't work out."

"I'm impressed," Grace said. "I thought I was the only one who knew the building's history."

"Paul and I love this building," Annalisa said. "We want to do everything we can to maintain the historical integrity of the apartment."

"Well," Mindy said, looking from Grace to Mark, "I think we're all in agreement." Mark and Grace nodded. Mindy stood up and held out her hand. "Welcome to One Fifth," she said.

▽

"That was easy. It was so easy, wasn't it?" Annalisa said to Paul in the Town Car, riding back to the hotel.

"How could they reject us?" Paul said. "Did you see them? They're freaks."

"They seemed perfectly nice to me."

"What about that Mindy Gooch?" Paul asked. "She's one of those bitter career women."

"How do you know?"

"I see them all the time. In my office."

Annalisa laughed. "There aren't any women in your office. There are hardly any women in your industry."

"There are," Paul said. "And they're all like Mindy Gooch. Dried-up husks who spend their whole lives trying to be like men. And not succeeding," he added.

"Don't be so hard on people, Paul. And what difference does it make? We'll probably never see her."

Back at the hotel, Annalisa sat on the bed, reading through the bylaws of the building, which Mindy had put together into a neat, printed pamphlet for new occupants. "Listen to this," Annalisa said as Paul brushed and flossed his teeth. "We have a storage room in the basement. And there's parking. In the Mews."

"Really?" Paul said, removing his clothes.

"Maybe not," Annalisa said, reading on. "It's a lottery. Every year, they pick one name out of a hat. And that person gets a parking spot for a year."

"We'll have to get one," Paul said.

"We don't have a car," Annalisa said.

"We'll get one. With a driver."

Annalisa put the pamphlet aside and playfully wrapped her legs around his waist. "Isn't it exciting?" she said. "We're starting a new life."

Knowing she wanted to have sex, Paul kissed her briefly, then moved down to her vagina. Their lovemaking was slightly clinical and always consisted of the same routine. Several minutes of cunnilingus, during which Annalisa climaxed, followed by about three minutes of intercourse. Then Paul would arch his back and come. She would hold him, stroking his back. After another minute, he would roll off her, go to the bathroom, put on his boxer shorts, and get into bed. It wasn't exactly exciting, but it was satisfying as far as orgasms went. This evening, however, Paul was distracted and lost his hard-on.

"What's the matter?" she asked, raising herself up on her elbow.

"Nothing," he said, pulling on his shorts. He began pacing the room.

"Do you want me to give you a blow job?" she asked.

He shook his head. "Just thinking about the apartment," he said.

"Me, too."

"And that parking spot. Why does it have to be a lottery? And why do you only get it for a year?"

"I don't know. Those are the rules, I guess."

"We have the biggest apartment in the building. And we pay the most maintenance. We should get precedence," he said.

❦

Three weeks later, when Annalisa and Paul Rice had closed on the apartment, Mrs. Houghton's lawyer called Billy Litchfield and asked to see him in his office.

Mrs. Houghton might have chosen an attorney from an old New York family to manage her legal affairs, but instead had retained Johnnie Toochin, a tall, pugnacious fellow who had grown up in the Bronx. Louise had "discovered" Johnnie at a dinner party where he was holding court as the city's brightest up-and-coming young lawyer in a case of the city versus the government over school funding. Johnnie had won, and his future was doubly assured when Mrs. Houghton hired him on retainer. "There are as many criminals in the 'establishment' as there are in the ghettos," Mrs. Houghton was fond of saying. "Never forget that it's easy for a man to hide his bad intentions beneath good clothes."

Happily for Mrs. Houghton, Johnnie Toochin had never been well dressed, but after exposure to money and superior company, he had definitely become establishment. His office was nearly a museum of modern furniture and art, containing two Eames chairs, a sharkskin coffee table, and on the walls, a Klee, a DeKooning, and a David Salle.

"We should see each other more often," Johnnie said to Billy from behind a massive desk. "Not like this, though. The way we used to at parties. My wife keeps telling me we ought to go out more. But somehow there's no time. You're still out and about, though."

"Not as much as I used to be," Billy said, quietly resenting the conversation. It was the same conversation he seemed to have often now, every time he ran into someone he hadn't seen in ages and likely wouldn't in the future.

"Ah, we're all getting old," Johnnie said. "I'll be sixty this year."

"Best not to talk about it," Billy said.

"You still live in the same place?" Johnnie asked.

"Lower Fifth," Billy said, wishing Johnnie would get on with whatever it was that had caused him to call this meeting.

Johnnie nodded. "You lived close to Mrs. Houghton. Well, she adored you, you know. She left you something." He stood up. "She insisted I give it to you in person. Hence the visit to my office."

"It's no trouble," Billy said pleasantly. "It's nice to see you."

"Well," Johnnie said. He stuck his head out the door and called to his assistant. "Could you get the box Mrs. Houghton left for Billy Litchfield?" He turned back to Billy. "I'm afraid it's not much. Considering all the money she had."

Best not to talk about that, either, Billy thought. It wasn't polite. "I wasn't expecting anything from her," he said firmly. "Her friendship was enough."

The assistant came in carrying a crude wooden box that Billy recognized immediately. The piece had sat incongruously among priceless bibelots on the top of Mrs. Houghton's bureau. "Is it worth anything, do you think?" Johnnie asked.

"No," Billy said. "It's a sentimental piece. She kept her old costume jewelry in it."

"Perhaps the jewelry's worth something."

"I doubt it," Billy said. "Besides, I wouldn't sell it."

He took the box and left, balancing it carefully on his knees in the taxi going home. Louise Houghton had always been proud of the fact that she came from nothing. "Dirt-poor farmers we were in Oklahoma," she said. The box had been a gift from her first beau, who had made it for her back in school. Louise had taken the box with her when she'd left at seventeen, carting it all the way to China, where she worked as a missionary for three years. She had come to New York in 1928, looking for money to support the cause, and had met her first husband, Richard Stuyvesant, whom she had married, much to the consternation of his family and New York society. "They considered me a little farm girl who didn't know my place," she'd tell Billy on the long afternoons they used to spend together. "And they were right. I didn't know my place. As long as one refuses to know one's place, there's no telling what one can do in the world."

Back in his apartment, Billy set the box down on his coffee table. He opened the lid and extracted a long string of plastic pearls. Even as a penniless young girl, Louise had had style, sewing her own clothes from scraps of material and adorning herself with glass beads, cheap metals, and feathers. She was one of those rare women who could take the tackiest item and, by wearing it with confidence, make it look expensive. Of course, after she took New York by storm, she didn't need to wear costume jewelry and acquired a legendary collection of jewelry that she kept in a safe in her apartment. But she never forgot her roots, and the box of costume jewelry was always on display. On afternoons when they sat in her bedroom, where Louise felt it was safe to gossip, she and Billy would sometimes engage in a silly game of dress-up, decorating themselves in various pieces of costume jewelry and pretending they were other people. Now Billy stood up, and staring into the mirror over the mantelpiece, he wrapped the pearls around his neck and made a face. "No, no," Louise would have said, laughing. "You look like that awful Flossie Davis. Pearls aren't for you, darling. How about a feather?"

Billy went back to the couch and began carefully laying out each piece on the coffee table. Some of the pieces were ninety years old and falling apart; Billy decided he would wrap each piece in tissue paper and bubble wrap to keep them from suffering further injury. Then he picked up the box, meaning to put it on his own bureau, where it would be the last thing he saw before he went to sleep and the first thing he saw in the morning; in that way, he might keep Louise and her memory close to him. As he lifted the box, the top slammed shut on his finger. Billy opened the lid and glanced inside. He had never examined the box empty, and now he saw a small latch tucked into the back. No wonder Louise had always kept the box, he thought. She would have found it romantic—a box with a hidden compartment. It would have been a magical piece for a bright fourteen-year-old girl who had only fairy tales to nourish her dreams.

It was a small, simple latch made of bronze, a tongue held in place by a tiny knob. Billy unhooked the latch and, using a nail file for leverage, lifted out the wooden shelf. There was indeed something in the hidden compartment, something wrapped in a soft, gray pouch fastened with a black cord. Billy warned himself not to get too excited: Knowing Louise, it was probably a rabbit's foot.

He untied the cord and peeked inside.

What he saw made him immediately want to tie the cord again and pretend he'd never seen it. But a perverse curiosity prevailed, and slowly, he inched off the pouch. There was old gold, rough-cut emeralds and rubies, and in the center, an enormous crudely faceted diamond. The piece was as big as his hand. Billy began to shake with excitement, to which was quickly added fear and confusion. He picked up the piece and carried it over to the window, where he could examine it more closely in the light. But he was quite sure of what he held in his hand. It was the Cross of Bloody Mary.

Act
Two

Act
Two

8

Enid Merle liked to say she could never stay angry at anyone for long. There were exceptions, of course, such as Mindy Gooch. Now, when Enid saw Mindy in the lobby, she cut her, deliberately turning her head away, as though she literally didn't see her. Nevertheless, she kept up with Mindy's comings and goings through Roberto, the doorman, who knew everything about everyone in the building. She found out that Mindy had purchased a dog—a miniature cocker spaniel—and that the Rices were hoping to install through-the-wall air-conditioning units in their apartment, a request that Mindy planned to turn down. Why was it, Enid wondered, that the first thing everyone wanted these days was air-conditioning?

Although she had yet to forgive Mindy, Enid's ire at the Rices themselves had fizzled with the hot August weather. Mostly because Enid found Annalisa Rice, with her auburn hair and curious wide mouth, intriguing. Several times a day, Enid caught glimpses of Annalisa Rice on her terrace, dressed in a smudged T-shirt and shorts, taking a break from unpacking boxes. Annalisa would lean over the railing to try to catch a breeze, shaking her long hair out of its ponytail for a second before twisting it back up on top of her head. On Thursday, the hottest afternoon of the year so far, Enid left Roberto a note to pass on to "Mrs. Rice."

Ever helpful, Roberto delivered the envelope to Mrs. Rice's door himself. As he handed her the missive, he attempted, not very subtly, to peek around her, hoping to get a glimpse of the apartment. Without the furniture or rugs, it appeared vast and echoey, although Roberto was able to see only into the second foyer and the dining room beyond. Annalisa thanked Roberto, firmly closed the door, and opened the envelope. Inside was a light blue card, across the top of which was embossed ENID MERLE, in no-nonsense gold lettering. Underneath was written: "PLEASE COME BY FOR TEA. AT HOME TODAY FROM THREE TO FIVE."

Annalisa immediately set to work at making herself presentable. She clipped and filed her fingernails and scrubbed her body with a loofah. She put on a pair of khakis and a white shirt, tying the tails around her waist. The effect was casual but neat.

Enid's apartment wasn't what Annalisa was expecting. She'd assumed the apartment would be filled with chintz and heavy drapes, like Louise Houghton's, but instead, it was a museum of seventies chic, with white shag carpeting in the living room and a Warhol above the fireplace. "Your apartment is beautiful," Annalisa said after she'd shaken hands with Enid and been invited inside.

"Thank you, dear. Is Earl Grey tea okay?"

"Anything's fine."

Enid went into the kitchen, and Annalisa sat down on the white leather couch. In a few minutes, Enid returned, carrying a papier mâché tray, which she set on the coffee table. "I'm so happy to meet you properly," she said. "Usually, I meet all our newcomers first, but unfortunately, that wasn't possible in your case."

Annalisa stirred a spoonful of sugar into her tea. "It all happened so quickly," she said.

Enid waved this fact away. "It's not your fault. Mindy Gooch rushed your application through. I'm sure it will work out for the best. No one wants a lot of potential buyers trooping through the building—it's extra work for the doormen and irritating to the other residents. But we like to take our time approving applicants. We kept one gentleman waiting a year."

Annalisa smiled tensely, not sure of what to make of Enid Merle. She knew who Enid was, but given Enid's comments about their entry into the building, Annalisa had yet to discern whether she was friend or foe.

"He was a so-called fertility specialist," Enid continued, "and we were right to wait. It turned out he was impregnating his patients with his own sperm. I kept telling Mindy Gooch there was something unsavory about the man, although I couldn't quite put my finger on it. Mindy couldn't see it at all, but it wasn't her fault, poor dear. She was trying to get pregnant herself then, and she wasn't thinking clearly. And when the scandal broke, she had to admit I'd been right all along."

"Mindy Gooch seems very nice," Annalisa said cautiously. She'd been looking for an opening to talk more about Mindy. Paul mentioned the parking spot in the Mews nearly every other day, and Annalisa wanted to find a way to secure it for him, guessing that Mindy Gooch was the key.

"She *can* be nice," Enid said, taking a sip of her tea. "But she can also be difficult. Bullheaded. She's very determined. Unfortunately, it's the kind of determination that doesn't always lead to success." She leaned forward and whispered, "Mindy lacks people skills."

"I think I see what you mean," Annalisa replied.

"But she'll be nice to you—at first," Enid said. "She's always nice, as long as she's getting what she wants."

"And what does she want?" Annalisa asked.

Enid laughed. Her laugh was unexpected, a great joyous whoop. "That's a good question," she said. "She wants power, I suppose, but other than power, I don't think she has a clue. And that's the problem with Mindy. She doesn't know what she wants. You never know what you're going to get with her." Enid poured more tea. "On the other hand, the husband, James Gooch, is as mild as toast. And their boy, Sam, is brilliant. He's some kind of computer whiz, but all children are these days—it's quite frightening, don't you think?"

"My husband's what one might call a computer whiz as well."

"Naturally." Enid nodded. "He's in finance, isn't he? And they do all that wheeling and dealing on computers these days."

"Actually, he's a mathematician."

"Ah, numbers," Enid said. "They make my eyes glaze over. But I'm just a silly old woman who was barely taught anything in school. They didn't used to teach girls mathematics, other than addition and subtraction, so one could make change, if necessary. But your husband appears to have done well. I heard he works for a hedge fund."

"Yes, he's a new partner," Annalisa said. "But please don't ask me what he does. All I know is that it involves algorithms. And the stock market."

Enid stood up. "Let's stop kidding ourselves," she said.

"Excuse me?" Annalisa said.

"It's four o'clock in the afternoon. I've been working all day, and you've been unpacking boxes. And it's ninety-six degrees. What we both need is a nice gin and tonic."

Several minutes later, Enid was telling Annalisa about the former owners of the penthouse apartment. "Louise Houghton didn't like her husband at all," she said. "Randolf Houghton was a bastard. But he was her third husband, and that's why they moved downtown in the first place. Louise assumed correctly that a twice-divorced woman wouldn't be completely accepted in Upper East Side society. She convinced Randolf to move here, which was considered very bohemian and original and made everyone forget that Randolf was her third husband."

"Why was he a bastard?" Annalisa asked politely.

"The usual reasons." Enid smiled and finished her cocktail. "He drank. He cheated. Two qualities a woman could live with in those days but for the fact that Randolf was impossible to live with. He was rude and arrogant and quite possibly violent. They had terrible fights. I think he may have hit her. There were servants in the house at the time, but no one ever said a word."

"And she didn't divorce him?"

"She didn't have to. Louise was lucky. Randolf died."

"I see."

"The world was a much more dangerous place back then," Enid continued. "He died from sepsis. He was in South Africa, trying to get into the diamond business, when he cut his finger. While he was traveling back to the States, the cut got infected. He made it back to One Fifth, but a few days later, he was dead."

"I can't believe her husband died from a cut," Annalisa said.

Enid smiled. "Staph. It's a very dangerous bacteria. We had an outbreak in the building once. Years ago. Spread by a pet turtle. Aquatic creatures don't belong in apartment buildings. But no matter. Louise had her grand apartment and all of Randolf's money and the rest of her life to live unencumbered. Marriage was considered a bit of a trial for women back then. If a woman could manage to live independently, free of the matrimonial noose, it was considered a blessing."

That evening, Annalisa bought a bottle of wine and a pizza and set this feast out for Paul on paper plates.

"I had the most interesting day," she said eagerly, sitting cross-legged in the dining room on the recently stained parquet floors. The setting sun made the wood glow like the last embers of a fire. "I met Enid Merle. She invited me to tea."

"Does she know anything about the parking space?"

"Let me get to that. I want to tell you everything." Annalisa tore at a piece of pizza. "First we had tea and then gin and tonics. It turns out that all is not well between Mindy Gooch and Enid Merle. Enid says the only reason the Gooches got into the building at all is because of the real estate crash in the early nineties. The board decided to sell off six little rooms on the ground floor that used to be the coat-check room and tiny bedrooms for the staff and the place where they stored the luggage when the building was a hotel. 'If it weren't for baggage, the Gooches wouldn't be here at all,'" Annalisa said, imitating Enid's voice. "You should have seen her. She's a real character."

"Who?" Paul asked.

"Enid Merle. Paul," Annalisa said, "can you please pay attention?"

Paul looked up from his pizza and, trying to satisfy his wife, said, "As long as she doesn't give us any trouble."

"Why would she give *us* trouble?"

"Why would anyone give us trouble?" Paul said. "As a matter of fact, I just saw Mindy Gooch. In the lobby. She told me we weren't allowed to put through-the-wall air conditioners in the apartment."

"That's just crap," Annalisa said. "Was she at least nice about it?"

"What do you mean by 'nice'?"

Annalisa picked up the paper plates. "Don't fight with her, is all. Enid said Mindy can be tricky. Apparently, the way to get to her is through her son, Sam. He's a computer whiz—works on everyone's computers in the building. I could e-mail him."

"No," Paul said. "I can't have some kid messing with my computer. Do you know what's on my hard drive? Billions of dollars' worth of financial information. I could destroy a small country if I felt like it."

Annalisa turned and bent over to kiss Paul on the forehead. "I know how you boys love to play spy," she said. "But I wasn't thinking about your computer. I was thinking about mine."

As she turned to go into the kitchen, Paul called after her, "Can't we do this the old-fashioned way? Isn't there someone in the building we can bribe?"

"No, Paul," Annalisa said. "We're not going to do that. Just because we have money doesn't mean we're going to get special treatment. Let me try it Enid's way. We're in a new place, and we have to respect the culture."

Down below, in the kitchen of the Gooches' stifling apartment, Mindy Gooch was cutting up vegetables. "Paul Rice basically told me to shove it," she said to James.

"Did he use those exact words, 'Shove it'?" James asked.

"No. But you should have seen the expression on his face when I said no to the through-the-wall air conditioners. His expression said, 'Shove it.'"

"You're being paranoid," James said.

"I'm not," Mindy said. Her new puppy, Skippy, jumped up on her leg. Mindy fed him a bit of carrot.

"You shouldn't feed the dog people food," James said.

"It's health food. No one ever got sick from eating a carrot." She picked up the dog and cuddled it in her arms.

"You were the one who insisted on letting them into the building," James said. "They're your responsibility."

"Don't be ridiculous," Mindy said. She carried the little dog to the door and put him out onto the cement slab that was their patio. Skippy sniffed around the edges of the slab, then squatted down and urinated.

"What a good dog!" Mindy exclaimed. "Did you see that, James? He peed outside. We've only had him for three days, and already he's house-trained. What a smart doggie!" she said to Skippy.

"And that's another thing. Skippy. He's your responsibility, too," James said. "You can't expect me to walk him. Not with my book coming out." James wasn't sure how he felt about Skippy. He'd never had a dog growing up, or any pet, for that matter, as his parents didn't believe in having animals in the house. "Peasants have animals in the house," his mother always said.

"Can't I have one thing, James?" Mindy asked. "One thing of my own? Without you criticizing it?"

"Sure," James said.

The puppy ran through the kitchen and into the living room. James chased after him. "Skippy!" he commanded. "Come!" Skippy ignored him and skittled into Sam's room, where he jumped on Sam's bed.

"Skippy wants to visit you," James said.

"Skipster. Dude," Sam said. He was seated at his little desk in front of his computer. "Check this out," he said to his father.

"What?" James said.

"I just got an e-mail from Annalisa Rice. Paul Rice's wife. Isn't that the guy Mom was arguing with?"

"It wasn't an argument," James said. "It was a discussion." He went into his own little office and closed the door. There was a small high window, and in the window was an old air conditioner that snuffled like a child's runny nose. James pulled his chair around and sat beneath the warmish air, trying to get cool.

※

Tink, tink, tink went the noise. It was eight in the morning, and Enid Merle looked over the side of her terrace and frowned. Outside the building, the scaffolding was going up, thanks to the Rices, who were about to start renovating their apartment. The scaffolding would be up by the end of the day, but it was only the beginning. Once the actual construction began, there would be weeks of a cacophony of drilling, sanding, and hammering. Nothing could be done about the noise: The Rices had the right to improve their apartment. So far, they had done everything to the letter, including sending out notices to the other residents of the building, informing them of the construction and the length of time estimated to do the work. The apartment would be rewired and replumbed for a washer and dryer and restaurant-quality appliances and, according to Roberto, "high-powered computer equipment." Mindy had won the first round on the air conditioners, but the Rices were still pushing. Sam told Enid that Annalisa had employed him to construct a website for the King David Foundation, which provided music and art classes for underprivileged teens. Enid was familiar with the charity, which had been started by Sandy and Connie Brewer. At last year's gala, they were rumored to have raised twenty million dollars at a live auction in which hedge-funders were falling all over themselves to outbid each other on prizes like a live concert by Eric Clapton. So Annalisa was making her way in the new society, Enid thought. It was going to be a very busy and noisy fall.

In the apartment next door, Philip and Lola were awakened by the noise.

"What is that?" Lola complained, putting her hands over her ears. "If it doesn't stop, I'm going to jump out of my skin."

Philip rolled over and stared at her face. There was, he thought, nothing like those first mornings of waking up with someone new and finding yourself both surprised and happy to see them.

"I'll make you forget about it," he said, putting his hand on her breast. Her breasts were especially firm, due to the implants. She'd received them as a present from her parents for her eighteenth birthday—a ritual that was apparently now considered a standard milestone for girls approaching adulthood. The surgery had been celebrated with a pool party where Lola had revealed her new breasts to her high school pals.

Lola pushed his hand away. "I can't concentrate," she said. "It sounds like they're hammering into my head."

"Ha," Philip said. Although he and Lola had been lovers for only a month, he'd noticed that she had an acute sensitivity to all physical maladies, both real and imagined. She often had headaches, or felt tired, or had a strange pain in her finger—probably, Philip had pointed out, the result of too much texting. Her pains required rest or TV watching, often in his apartment, which Philip did not object to at all, because the rest periods usually led to sex.

"I think you've got a hangover, kiddo," Philip said, kissing her on the forehead. He got out of bed and went into the bathroom. "Do you want aspirin?"

"Don't you have anything stronger? Like a Vicodin?"

"No, I don't," he said, once again struck by the peculiarities of Lola's generation. She was a child of pharmacology, having grown up with a bevy of prescription pills for all that might ail her. "Don't you have something in your purse?" he asked. He'd discovered that Lola never went anywhere without a stash of pills that included Xanax, Ambien, and Ritalin. "It's like *Valley of the Dolls*," he'd said, alarmed. "Don't be stupid," she'd replied. "They give kids this stuff. And besides, the women in *Valley of the Dolls* were drug addicts." And she'd given a little shudder.

Now she said, "Maybe," and crawled across the bed, leaning over the side in a seductive manner and feeling around on the floor for her snakeskin bag. She hauled it up and began digging around inside. The sight of her naked body—spray-tanned bronze and perfectly formed (in an unguarded moment, she'd let slip that she'd also had a tiny bit of lipo on her thighs and tummy)—filled Philip with joy. Ever since Lola had turned up at his apartment that July afternoon, his fortunes had changed. The studio loved his rewrite of *Bridesmaids Revisited*, and they were going to start shooting in January; off this good news, his agent got him a gig writing a historical movie about an obscure English queen known as Bloody Mary, for which he'd be paid a million dollars. "You're on a roll, baby," his agent said after delivering the news. "I smell Oscar."

Philip had gotten the phone call the day before, and he'd taken Lola to the Waverly Inn to celebrate. It was one of those evenings when everyone was there and the booths were filled with celebrities, some of whom were old friends. Before long, their table expanded to include a glamorous, boisterous group that drew envious glances from the other patrons. Lola kept introducing herself as his researcher, and full of everything that was good in life, he corrected her and claimed she was his muse, squeezing her hand across the table. They drank bottle after bottle of red wine, finally stumbling home at two in the morning through a foggy hot night that made the Village look like a Renaissance painting.

"Come on, sleepyhead," he said now, bringing her two aspirins.

She slipped under the covers and curled into a fetal position, holding out her hand for the tablets. "Can't I stay in bed all day?" she asked, staring up at him like a beautiful dog who always got its way. "I've got a headache."

"We've got work to do. I have to write, and you have to go to the library."

"Can't you take the day off? They can't expect you to start writing right away, can they? You just got the job. Doesn't that mean you get two weeks off? I know," she said, sitting up. "Let's go shopping. We could go to Barneys. Or Madison Avenue."

"Nope," he said. He would have revisions on *Bridesmaids Revisited* until they started shooting, and he needed to finish the first draft of the Bloody Mary script by December. Historical movies about royals were all the rage, his agent said, and the studio wanted to go into production as soon as possible. "I need that research," Philip said, playfully pulling her toe.

"I'll order some books from Amazon. Then I can stay here with you all day."

"If you stay here with me, I won't get any work done. Hence, it's off to the stacks." He pulled on jeans and a T-shirt. "I'm going out for a bagel. You want anything?"

"Could you bring me back a green-tea-and-apple VitaWater?" she said. "And make sure it's green-tea-and-apple. I hate the green-tea-and-mango. Mango is gross. Oh, and could you get me a frozen Snickers bar? I'm hungry."

Philip went out, shaking his head over the indulgence of eating a candy bar for breakfast.

On the sidewalk, he ran into Schiffer Diamond, who was being helped out of a white van by a Teamster. "Hey!" he exclaimed.

"You're in a good mood," she said, kissing him on the cheek.

"Sold a screenplay yesterday. About Bloody Mary. You should be in it."

"You want me to play a cocktail?"

"Not the cocktail. The queen. First daughter of Henry the Eighth. Come on," Philip said. "You get to cut off everyone's head."

"And have my own head cut off at the end? No, thank you," she said, walking toward the entrance to One Fifth. "I just spent the whole night shooting in a goddamn church on Madison with no air-conditioning. I've had enough of Catholics for the moment."

"I'm serious," he said, realizing she'd be perfect for the part. "Will you at least consider it? I'll personally deliver the screenplay when it's finished, along with a bottle of Cristal and a tub of caviar."

"Cristal's out, schoolboy. Make it a magnum of Grande Dame and I'll think about it," she called over her shoulder. She was always walking away from him, he thought. Wanting more of their banter, he asked where she was going.

She folded her hands and lay them next to her chin. "Sleep," she said. "I've got a six P.M. call."

"Catch you later, then," Philip said. As he walked away, he was reminded of why it had never worked out with Schiffer. She wasn't available for him. Never had been and never would be. That was what was so great about Lola. She was always available.

Back in Philip's apartment, Lola dragged herself out of bed and went into the kitchen. She idly thought about surprising Philip by making coffee, but after finding the bag of whole coffee beans next to a small grinder, decided it was too much trouble. She went into the bathroom and carefully brushed her teeth, then pulled her lips back into a grimace to check their whiteness. She thought about the trek up to the library at Forty-second Street on what was going to be another hot day, and she felt irritated. Why had she taken this job as Philip's researcher? For that matter, why did she need to have a job at all? She was only going to quit as soon as she got married. But without an engagement, her mother wouldn't let her stay in New York without a job—"it would look whorish," she'd said. Continuing on her path of random thoughts, Lola reminded herself that if she hadn't taken the job, she wouldn't have met Philip and become, as he'd put it, his muse. It was incredibly romantic, being the muse of a great artist, and what always happened was the great artist fell in love with his muse, insisted upon marrying her, and had beautiful children with her.

Until then, being wise in the matter of cliques and social order, Lola could already see that in Philip's world, this muse business might not be enough. It was one thing to be around famous people, quite another to have them accept you as one of their own. In particular, she recalled an interaction last night with the world-famous movie star who'd sat at their table. He was a not particularly attractive middle-aged man who was distinctly before her time; she couldn't recall exactly who he was or which movies he'd starred in. But since everyone else was making a huge fuss of him, hanging on his every word like he was Jesus, she realized she ought to make some effort. As it happened, he was squeezed into a chair next to her, and when he finished a long soliloquy about the beauty of seventies movies, she asked him, "Have you lived in New York long?"

He slowly turned his head and stared at her, and the fact that it took him about a minute to complete this movement made her wonder if she was supposed to be afraid of him. She wasn't—and if he thought he could intimidate Lola Fabrikant with a look, he had another thing coming.

"And what do you do?" he asked, mocking the tone of her question. "Don't tell me you're an actress."

"I'm Philip's researcher," she replied with the edge to her voice that usually silenced strangers. But not this man. He looked from her to Philip and back again. He grinned. "A researcher, eh?" He laughed. "And did I tell you I'm Santa Claus?"

The whole table erupted in laughter, including Philip. Sensing this was not a good time to go into high dudgeon, Lola laughed along gamely, but really, she told herself, it was too much. She wasn't used to being treated this way. She would let it go this once but not again. Of course, she planned to bring it up with Philip, but would be careful about how she did so. In general, it wasn't a good idea to complain about a man's friends to his face—it could hurt his feelings, and then he would associate you with negativity.

In the meantime, she thought, she should find a way to be taken a bit more seriously. No man wanted a woman whom other people thought silly—in which case, a visit to the library might not be a bad idea after all.

When Philip returned to the apartment, however, he found Lola had gone back to bed and appeared to be in a deep sleep. He went into his office and quickly knocked off five pages. From the other room, he heard the sound of Lola's gentle snoring. She was so natural, he thought. Reading through his pages, which were excellent, he decided she was his good-luck charm.

❦

The Rices' apartment was slowly taking shape. The once empty dining room now held an ornate table with six Queen Anne chairs that Billy had mysteriously conjured from a friend's storage bin

somewhere on the Upper East Side. The table was on loan until a
proper (meaning larger) table could be found; in the meantime, it
was strewn with decorating books and color swatches, both fabric
and paint, and Internet printouts of various pieces of furniture.
Annalisa looked at the table and smiled, recalling something Billy
Litchfield had said to her weeks ago.

"My dear," he'd admonished her when she brought up the fact
that she might, in the future, go back to work as a lawyer, "how do
you expect to do two jobs?"

"Excuse me?"

"You already have a job," he explained. "From now on, your life
with your husband is your job." He corrected himself. "It's more
than a job. It's a career. Your husband makes the money, and you
create the life. And it's going to take effort. You'll rise each morning and exercise, not simply to look attractive but to build
endurance. Most ladies prefer yoga. Then you will dress. You'll
arrange your schedule and send e-mails. You'll attend a meeting for
a charity in the morning, or perhaps visit an art dealer or make a
studio visit. You'll have lunch, and then there are meetings with
decorators, caterers, and stylists; you'll have your hair colored twice
a month and blow-dried three times a week. You'll do private
tours of museums and read, I hope, three newspapers a day: *The
New York Times*, *The New York Post*, and *The Wall Street Journal*. At
the end of the day, you'll prepare for an evening out, which may
include two or three cocktail parties and a dinner. Some will be
black-tie charity events where you'll be expected to wear a gown
and never the same dress twice. You'll need to have your hair and
makeup done. You'll also plan vacations and weekend outings. You
may purchase a country house, which you will also have to organize, staff, and decorate. You will meet the right people and court
them in a manner both subtle and shameless. And then, my dear,
there will be children. So," Billy concluded, "let's get busy."

And busy they had been. There were so many tiny details to put
together: bathroom tiles handmade in South Carolina to comple-
ment the marble floors (the apartment held five bathrooms, and

each needed its own theme), rugs, window treatments, even door handles. Most of Annalisa's days were spent in the furniture district in the East and West Twenties, but there were all the antique shops on Madison that had to be explored, as well as the auction houses. And then there were the renovations themselves. One by one, each room was being torn apart, rewired, replastered, and put back together. For the first month, Annalisa and Paul had moved an air mattress from one room to another to get out of the way of the construction, but now, at least the master bedroom was finished, and she was, as Billy said, "beginning to put together a bit of a closet."

The intercom buzzed exactly at noon. "A man is here to see you," Fritz said from below.

"Which man?" Annalisa asked, but Fritz had hung up. The intercom was in the kitchen, on the first floor of the apartment. Annalisa ran through the nearly empty living room and up the stairs to the bedroom, where she quickly tried to finish dressing.

"Maria?" she said, sticking her head out of the bedroom door and calling down the hall to the housekeeper, whom she'd heard rustling around in one of the back bedrooms.

"Yes, Mrs. Rice?" Maria asked, coming out into the hall. Maria was from an agency and cooked and cleaned and ran errands and would even, supposedly, walk your dog if you had one, but so far Annalisa hadn't felt comfortable asking her to do much of anything, not being used to having a live-in housekeeper.

"Someone's coming up," Annalisa said. "I think it's Billy Litchfield. Do you mind answering the door?"

She went back to the bedroom and into the large walk-in closet. The beginnings of the closet were not the closet itself but its contents. According to Billy, she was to have an array of shoes, bags, belts, jeans, white shirts, suits for luncheons, cocktail dresses, evening gowns, resort clothes for both mountain and island, and any sport in which one might be called upon to participate: golf, tennis, horseback riding, parasailing, rappelling, white-water rafting, and even hockey. To help her get her wardrobe together, Billy had hired a famous stylist named Norine Norton, who would pick out clothing and bring it to her apartment. Norine was famously busy and wasn't able to schedule their first appointment for two weeks, but Billy was thrilled. "Norine is like the best plastic surgeons. It can take six months to get an appointment with her—and that's only for a consultation."

In the meantime, one of Norine's six assistants had begun the task of dressing Annalisa, and on a low shelf were arranged several shoe boxes with a photograph of the shoe pasted on the front of the box. Annalisa selected a pair of black pumps with a four-inch heel. She hated wearing high heels during the day, but Billy had said it was necessary. "People expect to see Annalisa Rice, so you must give them Annalisa Rice."

"But who is Annalisa Rice?" she'd asked jokingly.

"That, my dear, is what we're going to find out. Isn't this fun?"

Right now the visitor was not Billy Litchfield but the man coming to see about Paul's aquarium. Annalisa led him upstairs to the ballroom and glanced regretfully at the ceiling, painted in the whimsical Italian view of heaven, with puffy clouds in a halo of pink on which sat fat cherubs. Sometimes, when she had a moment, Annalisa would come up here for a brief rest, lying on the floor in a patch of sunlight, utterly contented, but Paul had declared the ballroom his private space and planned to turn it into "command central," from where, Annalisa teased him, he could take over the world. The French windows were to be reglazed with a new electrical compound to render them completely opaque with the touch of a button—thus thwarting any attempts to photograph the room or the actions of its occupant by the employment of a long-lens camera from a helicopter—while a three-dimensional screen would be installed above the fireplace. On the roof, a special antenna would scramble cell and satellite transmissions. There would be a state-of-the-art aquarium, twenty feet long and seven feet wide, which would allow Paul to pursue his new hobby of collecting rare and expensive fish. It was a shame to destroy the room, but Paul wouldn't consider any arguments to the contrary. "You can do what you like with the rest of the apartment," he'd said. "But this room's mine."

The aquarium man began taking measurements, asking Annalisa about voltage and the possible construction of a subfloor to support the weight of the aquarium. Annalisa did her best to answer his questions but then gave up and fled downstairs.

Billy Litchfield had arrived, and five minutes later, they were sitting in the back of a crisp new Town Car heading downtown.

"I have a welcome surprise for you, my dear," he said. "After all that furniture, I thought you might like a break. Today we're looking at art. Last night I had a brilliant idea." He took a breath. "I'm thinking, for you, feminist art."

"I see."

"Are you a feminist?"

"Of course," Annalisa said.

"Either way, it doesn't matter. For instance, I doubt you're a cubist, either. But think how much cubist art is worth now. It's unaffordable."

"Not for Paul," Annalisa said.

"Even for Paul," Billy said. "It's only for the multibillionaire, and you and Paul are still working your way into the multimillionaire category. Cubist art isn't chic, anyway. Not for a young couple. But feminist art—that's the future. It's just about to break, and most of the really great work is still available. Today we're going to look at a photograph. A self-portrait of the artist nursing her child. Wonderful shock value. And striking colors. And there's no waiting list."

"I thought a waiting list was good," Annalisa said cautiously.

"The waiting list is excellent," Billy said. "Especially if it's a particularly difficult list to get on. And you do have to pay cash up front for a painting you've never seen. But we'll get to that in time. In the meantime, we need one or two spectacular pieces that will increase in value."

"Billy?" Annalisa asked. "What do you get out of this?"

"Pleasure," Billy said. He looked at her and patted her hand. "You mustn't worry about me, my dear. I'm an aesthete. If I could spend the rest of my life looking at art, I'd be happy. Every piece of art is unique, made by one person, one mind, one point of view. In this manufactured world, I suppose I take solace in it."

"That's not what I meant," Annalisa said. "How do you get paid?"

Billy smiled. "You know I don't talk about my finances."

Annalisa nodded. She'd tried to bring up the topic several times, but every time, he changed the subject. "I need to know, Billy. Otherwise, it's not right, your spending so much time with me. People ought to be paid for their work."

"On art, I take a two percent commission. From the dealer," Billy said, pressing his lips together.

Annalisa was relieved. Billy occasionally mentioned a million-dollar sale in which he'd been involved, and after doing the math, she came up with twenty thousand dollars as his fee. "You must be rich, Billy," she'd said, half joking.

"My dear," Billy said, "I can barely afford to live in Manhattan."

Now, in the gallery, Billy took a step back and, folding his arms, nodded at the photograph as if he approved. "It's very modern, but the composition is classic mother and child," he said. The photograph was a hundred thousand dollars. Annalisa, feeling the sharp pang of guilt that was always under the surface due to her own good fortune, bought it. She paid with a MasterCard, which Billy said everyone used for large purchases in order to get extra airline miles. Not that any of these people needed airline miles, as most of them flew in private planes. Nevertheless, leaving the gallery with the bubble-wrapped photograph in the trunk of the car, Annalisa reminded herself that it was two thousand dollars in Billy's pocket. It was the least she could do.

Lola sat at the long counter in the window of Starbucks, reading through a printout of an article she'd found on the Internet. She hadn't been able to work herself up for a trip to the library after all. As she'd suspected, it would have been a waste of time anyway. There was plenty of information online. Lola adjusted her glasses and prepared to read. On the way to Starbucks, she'd purchased a pair of black frames in order to appear more serious. Apparently, the glasses were working. As she was reading about Queen Mary's obsession with Catholicism, a nerdy young man sat down next to her, opened a laptop, and kept jerking his head above it to stare at her. Lola did her best to ignore him, keeping her head down and pretending to be absorbed in the text. From what she could gather, Queen Mary, who was described as "sickley and fraile," which Lola interpreted as anorexic, was some kind of sixteenth-century fashionista who never appeared in public without wearing millions of dollars' worth of jewelry in order to remind the masses of the power and wealth of the Catholic Church. Lola looked up from her reading and saw that the nerd was staring at her. She looked down at the pages, and when she looked up, he was still staring. He had reddish-blond hair and freckles but was better-looking than her first assessment. Finally, he spoke.

"Did you know those are men's?" he asked.

"What?" she said, giving him a glare that should have sent him away.

The nerdle wasn't put off. "Your glasses," he said. "Those are men's glasses. Are they even real?"

"Of course they're real," she said.

He rolled his eyes. "Do they have a real prescription in them? Or are they just for show?"

"It's none of your business," she said, adding, for good measure, a threatening, "if you know what I mean."

"All you girls wear glasses now," the young man continued on, unabated. "And you know they're fake. How many twenty-two-year-olds need glasses? Glasses are for old people. It's another one of those fake things that girls do."

She sat back on her stool. "So?"

"So I was wondering if you were one of those fake girls. You look like a fake girl. But you might be real."

"Why should you care?"

"I think you're kind of cute?" he asked sarcastically. "Maybe you can give me your name, and I can leave you a message on Facebook?"

Lola gave him a cold, superior smile. "I already have a boyfriend, thanks."

"Who said I wanted to be your boyfriend? Christ, girls in New York are so arrogant."

"You're pathetic," she said.

"Uh-huh," he said. "And look at you. You're wearing designer clothes at a Starbucks, your hair is blown dry, and you have a spray tan. Probably from City Sun. They're the only ones who do that particular shade of bronze."

Lola wondered how this kid knew about the subtleties of spray tans. "And look at you," she said in her most patronizing tone of voice. "You're wearing plaid pants."

"Vintage," the kid said. "There's a difference."

Lola gathered her papers and stood up.

"Leaving?" the kid asked. "So soon?" He stood up and fished around in the back pocket of his hideous plaid pants. They were not even Burberry plaid, Lola thought, which she could have excused. He handed her a card. THAYER CORE, it read. In the bottom right-hand corner was a 212 phone number. "Now that you know my name, will you tell me yours?" he said.

"Why would I do that?" Lola asked.

"New York's a tricky place," he said. "And I'm the joker."

9

A few weeks later, James Gooch sat in the office of his publisher. "Books are like movies now," Redmon Richardly said, waving his hand as if to dismiss the whole lot. "You get as much publicity as you can, have a big first week, and then drop off from there. There's no traction anymore. Not like the old days. The audience wants something new every week. And then there are the big corporations. All they care about is the bottom line. They push the publishers to get new product out there. Makes them feel like their people are doing something. It's heinous, corporations controlling creativity. It's worse than government propaganda."

"Uh-huh," James said. He looked around Redmon's new office and felt sad. The old office used to be in a town house in the West Village, filled with manuscripts and books and frayed Oriental carpets that Redmon had taken from his grandmother's house in the South. There was an old down-filled yellow couch that you sat on while you waited to see Redmon, and you leafed through a pile of magazines and watched the pretty girls go in and out. Redmon was considered one of the greats back then. He published new talent and edgy fiction, and his writers were going to be the future giants. Redmon made people believe in publishing for a while—up until about 1998, James reckoned, when the Internet began to take over.

James looked past Redmon and out the plate-glass window. There was a view of the Hudson River in the distance, but it was small consolation for the cold, generic space.

"What we're publishing now is an entertainment product," Redmon continued. Redmon hadn't lost his ability to pontificate about nothing, James thought, and found comfort in this fact. "Oakland's a perfect example. He's not so great anymore, but it doesn't matter. He still sells copies—even for him, not as many. But it's the same story with everyone." Redmon threw his hands into the air. "There's no art anymore. Fiction used to be an art form. No more. Good, bad, it doesn't matter. The public is only interested in the topic. 'What's it about?' they ask. 'Does it matter?' I say. 'It's about life. All great books are about only one thing—life.' But they don't get that anymore. They want to know the topic. If it's about shoes or abducted babies, they want to read it. And we don't do that, James. We couldn't even if we wanted to."

"We certainly couldn't," James agreed.

"'Course not," Redmon said. "But what I'm saying is . . . Well, you've written a great book, James, an actual novel, but I don't want you to be disappointed. We'll definitely get on the list, right away, I hope. But as to how long we'll stay on the list . . ."

"It doesn't matter to me," James said. "I didn't write the book to sell copies. I wrote it because it's a story I needed to tell." And I won't be corrupted by Redmon's cynicism, he thought. "I still believe in the public. The public knows the difference. And they'll buy what's good," he added stubbornly.

"I don't want you to have your heart broken," Redmon said.

"I'm forty-eight years old," James said. "My heart's been broken for about forty years."

"There is good news," Redmon said. "Very good news. Your agent and I agreed that I should be the one to tell you. I can offer you a million-dollar advance on your next book. Corporations are bad, but they're also good. They have money, and I intend to spend it."

James was so shocked, he couldn't move. Had he heard correctly?

"You'll get a third on signing," Redmon continued, as if he gave away million-dollar advances all the time. "With that and the money we'll get from the iStores' placement, I think you can expect to have a very good year."

"Great," James said. He still wasn't sure how to react. Should he jump out of his chair and do the watusi?

But Redmon was being calm about it. "What will you do with the money?" he asked.

"Save it. For Sam's college education," James said.

"That will about use it up," Redmon agreed. "Six, seven hundred thousand dollars—what does it get you these days? After taxes . . . Christ. And with those guys on Wall Street buying Picassos for fifty million." He put up his hands as if to push away this reality. "It's our new world order, I suppose."

"I suppose," James agreed. "But one could always pursue the teenage fantasy. Buy a little sailboat in the Caribbean and disappear for a few years."

"Not me," Redmon said. "I'd be bored in two days. I can hardly stand to take a vacation. I like cities."

"Right," James said. He looked at Redmon. How lucky to know one's own mind. Redmon was always pleased with himself, James thought. While James did not, he realized, know his own mind at all.

"I'll walk you out," Redmon said. Standing, he made a face and put his hand to his jaw. "Damn tooth," he said. "Probably needs another root canal. How are your teeth? It's extraordinary, getting old. It is as hard as people say." Exiting the office, they came out into a maze of cubicles. "But there are advantages," Redmon continued, his overweening confidence firmly back in place. "For instance, we know everything now. We've seen it all before. We know there's nothing new. Have you noticed that? The only thing that changes is the technology."

"Except we can't understand the technology," James said.

"Bullshit," Redmon said. "It's still a bunch of buttons. It's only a matter of knowing which ones to press."

"Like the panic button that blows up the world."

"Wasn't that disabled?" Redmon said. "Why can't we have another cold war? It was so much more sensible than a real war." He pushed the button for the elevator.

"Mankind is going backward," James said. The elevator came, and he got on.

"Say hi to your family for me," Redmon called out with genuine urgency as the doors were closing.

Redmon's admonishment struck James as extraordinary. Family concerns were something Redmon never would have considered ten years ago, when he was out bedding a different woman in publishing every night and drinking and doing cocaine until dawn. For years, people had postulated that something terrible would happen to Redmon—he appeared to deserve it, although what the terrible thing was, no one could say—rehab, maybe? Or some kind of death? But nothing terrible ever did happen to him. Instead, he slid into his new life as a married father and corporate man with the agility of a skier. James had never understood it, but he thought perhaps Redmon, instead of being a source of consternation, ought to be considered an inspiration. If Redmon could change, why not he?

I have money now, James thought, the reality hitting him at the same time as the crisp September air. At least New York appeared to be having a real fall this year. Ordinary occurrences were now a pleasure and a relief to him, a reminder that in some ways, life could go on as before.

But would it now that he had money? Passing the chain stores that lined lower Fifth Avenue with their wares displayed in great glass cases like a middle-class shopper's dream, he reminded himself that it wasn't so much money. Not enough even to buy a tiny studio apartment in this great and expensive metropolis. But he had a bit of money. He was no longer—for this moment, anyway—a loser.

At Sixteenth Street, he passed Paul Smith and, out of habit, stopped for a second and gazed into the windows. Paul Smith's clothing was a status symbol, the choice for the sophisticated, urbane downtown male. Mindy had bought him a Paul Smith shirt years ago, for Christmas, when she was feeling proud of him and, apparently, had decided he was worth a splurge. Staring into the window at a pair of velvet pants, it occurred to James that for the first time in his life, he could afford anything in this store. This new feeling empowered him, and he went in.

Almost immediately, his phone rang. It was Mindy.

"What are you doing?" she said.

"Shopping."

"You? Shopping?" Mindy said with faux astonishment that was edged ever so slightly with disdain. "What are you buying?"

"I'm in Paul Smith."

"You're not going to actually buy anything, are you?" Mindy said.

"I might," he said.

"You'd better not. That store is too expensive," she said. James had thought he'd call Mindy first thing about his advance, but he surprised himself by wanting to keep it to himself.

"When are you coming home?" she asked.

"Soon."

"How did it go? With Redmon?"

"Great," he said, and hung up. He shook his head. Both he and Mindy had a quaint, puritan approach to money. Like it was always about to run out. Like it shouldn't be squandered. One's feelings about money were a gene one inherited. If your parents were afraid about money, then you'd be afraid. Mindy came from New England stock, where it was considered tacky to spend a lot of money. He came from immigrant stock, where money was needed for food and education. They'd survived in New York because they saved and didn't get their self-esteem from their outward appearances. But maybe that wasn't the solution. Because, James thought, neither he nor Mindy seemed to have much self-esteem at all.

James looked around the store and, walking to a rack of jackets, fingered a fine cashmere overcoat. He did not know what it was like to have money. Not having money had kept him tied to Mindy's apron strings. He knew it, had known it for years, had denied it, had rationalized it, had been ashamed of it, but what was most shameful was that he'd never been willing to do anything about it. Because, he'd told himself, he believed in the purity of his pursuit of literature. He'd been willing to sacrifice his manhood for this higher ideal. He'd taken succor in the fact that he was an honorable struggler.

But he had money now! He looked around the store, inhaling the manly scent of leather and cologne. The shop was like a stage set, with its wood-paneled walls—a cornucopia of anything a man with taste, sophistication, and style might want. And, he thought, looking at the three-thousand-dollar price tag on a cashmere jacket, a sense of irony at how much money it cost to keep warm.

In an act of defiance, he took the jacket off the hanger and carried it into the dressing room. He took off his own jacket, which was a sensible navy wool bought during a sale at Barneys five years ago, and looked at his body. He had the advantage of height, but he was a gangle of limbs with a soft belly. His legs were still firm, but his butt was flat, and his chest was flabby ("man boobs" was the current term, he believed), but all this could be hidden with the right clothing. He slipped his arms into the sleeves and buttoned the jacket across his chest. He was transformed into a man who had something big going on in his life.

He stepped out of the dressing room and ran into Philip Oakland. James's confidence dispersed like a mist. He did not belong in this store, he thought in panic. Even a store was about a tribe, and he was not part of this tribe; Philip Oakland was sure to sense this. James often saw Philip in the lobby or on the streets around One Fifth. Philip never acknowledged him, but perhaps he'd have to in this store, wearing this jacket, the kind of jacket Philip himself might own. Indeed, Philip Oakland looked up from a pile of sweaters and, as if they were casual friends, said, "Hey."

"Hey," James said.

That might have been the end of it if it weren't for the girl, the beautiful girl who was with Philip and whom James had seen around the building, coming in and out at odd hours during the day. He'd always wondered who she was and what she was doing in One Fifth, but now it made sense: She was Philip's girl-friend.

She spoke, startling James. "That looks good," she said to him.

"Really?" James said, staring at the girl. She had the unassailable confidence that comes from having been pretty her whole life.

"I know everything about clothes," she said boldly. "My friends are always saying I should have been a stylist."

"Lola, please," Philip said.

"It's true," Lola said, turning to Philip. "You look so much better since I started helping you with your clothes."

Philip shrugged and rolled his eyes at James, as if to say, "Women."

James took the opportunity to introduce himself. "I've seen you before," Lola said. "Yes," James said. "I live in One Fifth, too. I'm a writer."

"Everyone's a writer in One Fifth," she said with a dismissive arrogance that made James laugh.

"We should be going," Philip said.

"But we didn't buy anything," she protested.

" 'We,' " Philip said to James. "Notice that? Why is shopping with women always a group sport?"

"I don't know," James said. He glanced over at Lola, wondering how one managed to get a girl like that. She was saucy. He liked the way she stood up to the great Philip Oakland and wondered how Philip felt about it.

"Men never know what to buy on their own," she replied. "My mother let my father go shopping once, and he came back with an acrylic striped sweater. She said, 'Never again.' What do you write?" she asked James, not missing a beat.

"Novels," James said. "I have a book coming out in February." He was pleased to be able to deliver this information in front of Philip. Take that, he thought.

"We have the same publisher," Philip said, perhaps, James thought, finally figuring out who he was. "What's your print run?"

"Don't know," James said. "But we've got two hundred thousand copies going out to iStores in the first week."

Philip looked suitably bothered. "Interesting," he said.

"It is," James said. "I'm told it's the future of publishing."

Lola was suddenly bored. "If we're not buying anything here, can we please go to Prada?"

"Sure," Philip said. "See you around," he said to James.

"Right," James said.

As they walked away, Lola turned back to James. "You should buy that jacket. It looks great."

"I will," James said.

James paid for the jacket. As the salesman was putting it into a garment bag, James had an inspiration. "Don't bother," he said. "I'm going to wear it home."

▼

That afternoon, Norine Norton, the stylist, came to Annalisa's apartment for their third appointment. Norine, with her hair extensions and her subtle facial work and seemingly encyclopedic knowledge of the latest bag, shoe, designer, fortune-teller, trainer, and cosmetic procedure, made Annalisa uncomfortable. Her nickname, she informed Annalisa during their first meeting, was "the Energizer Bunny"—an energy that, Annalisa suspected, might be drug-induced. Norine never stopped talking; no matter how often Annalisa tried to remind herself that Norine was a woman, an actual human being, Norine always managed to convince her otherwise.

"I have something you'll die for," Norine said. She snapped her fingers and pointed to her assistant, Julee. "The gold lamé, please."

"The golf outfit?" Julee asked. She was a frail girl with spindly blond hair and the fearful eyes of a rabbit.

"Yes," Norine said with faux patience. With her assistant, Norine appeared to be on the edge of snapping at any moment. But when she turned back to Annalisa, it was with all the solicitude of a merchant presenting his wares to a grand lady.

Julee held up a clear plastic hanger from which hung a tiny gold top and matching miniskirt.

Annalisa regarded the garment with dismay. "I don't think Paul will like that."

"Listen, sweetie," Norine said. She sat down on the edge of the four-poster bed with the pleated silk canopy that had recently arrived from France, and patted the place next to her. "We need to talk."

"Do we?" Annalisa asked. She didn't want to sit next to Norine; nor did she want one of Norine's lectures. So far, she had forced herself to tolerate them, but she wasn't in the mood today.

Annalisa looked from Norine to Julee, who was still standing there, holding up the hanger like one of those girls on a game show. Her arm had to be tired. Annalisa felt bad for her. "Fine," she said, and went into the bathroom to try it on.

"You're so shy," Norine called after her.

"Huh?" Annalisa said, poking her head out the door.

"You're so shy. Changing in the bathroom. You should change in here so I can help you," Norine said. "You don't have anything I haven't seen before."

"Right," Annalisa said and shut the door. She turned to look at herself in the mirror and grimaced. How the hell had she gotten herself into this situation? It had sounded like such a good idea at first, hiring a stylist. Billy said everybody did it these days, meaning everyone with money or status who had to go out and be photographed. It was the only way, Billy said, to get the best clothes. But this was out of control. Norine was always calling or sending e-mail attachments of the clothes, accessories, and jewelry she photographed while shopping or visiting designer showrooms. Annalisa had had no idea there were so many lines. Not just spring and fall but resort, cruise, summer, and Christmas. Each season required its own look, and getting the look required as much planning as a military coup. Clothing had to be chosen and ordered months in advance, otherwise it would be gone.

Annalisa held the gold lamé up to her chin. No, she thought. This has gone too far.

But perhaps everything had gone too far. Despite the progress she'd made on the apartment, Paul was unhappy. The lottery had been held for the parking space in the Mews, and Paul hadn't won. Coupled with this disappointing news was a letter from Mindy Gooch, officially informing them that their request for through-the-wall air-conditioning units had been denied.

"We'll make it work without them," Annalisa had said, trying to soothe him.

"I can't."

"We have to."

Paul glared at her. "It's a conspiracy," he insisted. "It's because we have money and they don't."

"Mrs. Houghton had money," Annalisa said, trying to reason with him. "And she lived here without any trouble for years."

"She was one of them," Paul countered. "And we're not."

"Paul," she said patiently. "What are you talking about?"

"I'm making real money now," he said. "And I expect to be treated with a certain amount of respect."

"I thought you were making real money six months ago," she said, attempting to lighten the situation.

"Forty million isn't real money. A hundred million is getting there."

Annalisa felt queasy. She knew Paul was making a lot of money and planned to make more. But somehow it had never hit her that it was going to become a reality. "That's insane, Paul," she protested. But it also excited her, the way looking at dirty pictures excited you even though you didn't want to feel turned on and felt guilty about the excitement. Perhaps too much money was like too much sex. It crossed the line and became pornographic.

"Come on, Annalisa. Open the door. Let me *see* you," Norine said.

There was something pornographic in this, too. In this being seen, this unrelenting demand to be constantly seen everywhere. Annalisa felt worse than naked, as if her private parts were on display, open to all for examination.

"I don't know," Annalisa said, coming out. The gold lamé golf suit consisted of a skirt cropped mid-thigh and a shirt cut like a polo shirt (they'd been Lacoste shirts when she was a kid; she'd called them "alligator shirts," a testament to how blissfully unfashionable she'd been growing up), pulled together by a wide belt slung low on the hips. "What am I supposed to wear under this?" she asked.

"Nothing," Norine said.

"No underpants?"

"Call them panties, please," Norine said. "If you want, you wear gold lamé panties. Or maybe silver lamé. For contrast."

"Paul would never allow it," Annalisa said firmly, hoping to put an end to the discussion.

Norine took Annalisa's face in her hands, holding it between her manicured fingers, and squeezed Annalisa's face like a child's. She shook her head, pursing her lips. "You mustn't, mustn't say that again," she said in a baby voice. "We don't care what Daddy Paulie likes or dislikes. Repeat after me: 'I will choose my own clothes.'"

"I will choose my own clothes," Annalisa said reluctantly. Now she was stuck. Norine never seemed to understand that when Annalisa said Paul wouldn't like something, it meant she didn't like it but didn't want to offend Norine.

"Very good," Norine said. "I've been doing this a long time—too long—but the one thing I know is that men never mind what their wives are wearing as long as the wives are happy. And look great. Better than the other men's wives."

"But what if they don't?" Annalisa said, thinking she'd had enough of this exercise.

"That's why they have me," Norine said with unbridled confidence. She snapped her fingers at her assistant. "Photo, please," she said.

Julee held up her phone and snapped Annalisa's picture.

"How is it?" Norine asked.

"Good," Julee said, clearly terrified. She passed the phone to Norine, who peered at the tiny image.

"Very good," Norine said, showing Annalisa the photograph.

"Ridiculous," Annalisa said.

"I think it's fabulous," Norine said. She handed Julee the phone and crossed her arms, preparing for another lecture. "Look, Annalisa," she said. "You're rich. You can do anything you want. There's no bogeyman around the corner who's going to punish you."

"I thought God punished us," Annalisa said under her breath.

"God?" Norine said. "I've never heard of such a thing. Spirituality is only for show. Astrology, yes. Tarot cards, yes. Ouija boards, Kundala, Scientology, and even born-agains, yes. But a real God? No. That would be inconvenient."

⧫

In her office, Mindy wrote: "Why do we torture our husbands? Is it necessary or the inevitable result of our inherent frustration with the opposite sex?" She sat back in her chair and regarded the sentence with satisfaction. Her blog was a success—over the past two months, she'd received 872 e-mails congratulating her on her courage in addressing topics that were off-limits, such as whether a woman really needed her husband after he had given her children. "It's all about the existential question," Mindy wrote. "As women, we're not allowed to ask existential questions. We're supposed to be grateful for what we have, and if we're not, we're losers. Can't we take a break from imposed happiness and admit that despite what we have, it's okay to feel empty? It's okay to feel that something is missing and life may be meaningless? Instead of feeling bad about it, why can't we admit it's normal?"

This same unsentimental eye was applied to men and relationships. Mindy's conclusion was that marriage was like democracy—imperfect but still the best system women had. It was certainly better than prostitution.

Mindy reread her opening sentence for the week's blog entry and considered what she wanted to say next. Writing a blog was a bit like going to a shrink, she thought—it forced you to examine your real feelings. But it was also better than a shrink, because you got to do your navel-gazing in front of an audience of several thousand as opposed to one. And in her experience, that one—the shrink—was usually half asleep and expected money. "This week, I realized I spend at least thirty minutes a day nagging my husband," she wrote. "And to what end? There are no consequences." She looked up and saw that her assistant was standing in front of her desk.

"Do you have an appointment with a Paul Rice?" the assistant asked, as if Paul Rice were a thing as opposed to a person. Catching the surprise on Mindy's face, she said, "I didn't think so. I'll have security send him away."

"No," Mindy said a little too eagerly. "He's from my building. Send him up."

She put her feet back in her shoes and stood, smoothing her skirt and rearranging her blouse, over which she was wearing a woolly vest. The vest was not sexy, and she debated taking it off but wondered if it would be obvious that she had made an effort. Then she realized she was being ridiculous: Paul Rice wouldn't know she'd been wearing the vest all day. She took it off. She sat down behind her desk and fluffed her hair. She rummaged in the top drawer of her desk, found an old lip gloss, and rubbed a dab on her mouth.

Paul Rice appeared in her doorway. He was dressed in a beautifully tailored suit with a crisp white shirt. He looked, Mindy noted, expensive. More like a sophisticated European as opposed to an ink-stained mathematician. But mathematicians wouldn't be ink-stained anymore. They did their work on computers, like everyone else.

Mindy stood up and leaned over the desk to shake his hand.

"Hello, Paul," she said. "This is a surprise. Have a seat." She gestured to the small armchair in front of her desk.

"I don't have long," Paul said. He pointedly held out his wrist and looked at his watch, a large vintage gold Rolex. "Exactly seven minutes, to be precise. Which should be the amount of time it takes my driver to circle the block."

"Not at four-thirty in the afternoon," Mindy disagreed. "It will take him at least fifteen minutes in rush-hour traffic."

Paul Rice stared at her, saying nothing.

Mindy began to feel slightly excited. "What can I do for you?" she asked. Since she'd met Paul at the board meeting, it had crept up on her that she was secretly affected by him. She found him sexy. Mindy had always been a sucker for a man of genius, and Paul Rice was rumored to be one. Plus, there was all his money. Money didn't matter, but men who made a lot of it were always interesting.

"I need those air conditioners," he said.

"Now, Paul," Mindy said, sounding slightly schoolmarmish to her own ears. She leaned back in her chair and crossed her legs and began picturing herself as a Mrs. Robinson type. She smiled. "I thought I explained this in my letter. One Fifth is a landmark building. We're not allowed to alter the face or the structure of the building in any way."

"What does that have to do with me?" Paul said, narrowing his eyes.

"It means you can't have in-the-wall air-conditioning units. No one can," Mindy said.

"An exception will have to be made."

"I can't do that," Mindy said. "It's illegal."

"I have a lot of expensive computer equipment. I need to keep my apartment at a precise temperature."

"And what would that be?" Mindy said.

"Sixty-four point two degrees."

"I'd like to help you, Paul, but I can't."

"How much money will it take?" Paul asked.

"Are you suggesting a bribe?"

"Call it whatever you like," Paul said. "I need my air conditioners. And the parking spot in the Mews. Let's make this as easy as possible for both of us. Name your price."

"Paul," Mindy said slowly. "This is not about money."

"Everything is about money. It's all about numbers."

"In your world, maybe. But not in One Fifth," Mindy said in her most patronizing tone. "It's about preserving a historical landmark. That's something money can't buy."

Paul remained impassive. "I paid twenty million dollars for that apartment," he said. "So you will approve my air conditioners." He looked at his watch again and stood up.

"No," Mindy said. "I will not." She stood up as well.

"In that case," Paul said, taking a step closer, "it's war."

Mindy gasped involuntarily. She knew she should have sent the Rices the official letter denying the air conditioners weeks ago, when they'd first presented their plans for the renovation, but she'd liked having an excuse to talk about something with Paul when she ran into him in the lobby. But this was not how the game was supposed to play out. "Excuse me?" she asked. "Are you threatening me?"

"I never threaten anyone, Mrs. Gooch," Paul said, emotionless. "I merely state the facts. If you don't approve my air conditioners, it's war. And I will win."

10

"Look," Enid Merle said the next afternoon. "Schiffer Diamond's new TV series premiered with a two point oh share. And four million viewers."

"Is that good?" Philip asked.

"It's the highest cable opening in history."

"Oh, Nini," Philip said. "Why do you pay attention to these things?"

"Why don't you?" Enid asked. "Anyway, it's a hit."

"I've read the reviews," Philip said. SCHIFFER DIAMOND SHINES, declared one. DIAMOND IS FOREVER, gushed another.

"Schiffer is a star," Enid said. "She always was, and she always will be." She put down *Variety*. "I do wish . . ."

"No, Nini," Philip said firmly, knowing what she was getting at. "It's not going to happen."

"But Schiffer is so . . ."

"Wonderful?" Philip said with an edge of sarcasm. Enid looked hurt. "I know you adore her," Philip said. "But it's impossible to be with an actress. You know that."

"But you've both grown up," Enid countered. "And I'd hate to see you—"

"End up with Lola?" Philip said. It could happen. Lola was crazy about him. "I wish you'd try to get to know her a little better. It would mean a lot to me."

"We'll see," Enid said.

Philip went back to his apartment. Lola was curled up on the couch, watching TV. "Where were you?" she asked.

"Visiting my aunt."

"But you just saw her yesterday."

Philip felt snappish. "You call your mother every day."

"But she's my mother."

Philip went into his office and closed the door. After a couple of minutes, he got up from his desk, opened the door, and stuck his head out. "Lola," he said. "Can you please turn down that damn TV?"

"Why?"

"I'm trying to work," he said.

"So?" She yawned.

"I've got a rewrite due in four days. If I don't get it finished, we don't start shooting on time."

"What's the problem?" she asked. "They'll wait. You're Philip Oakland. They have to wait."

"No, they do not," Philip said. "It's called a contract, Lola. It's called being an adult and honoring your commitments. It's called people are counting on you to produce."

"Then write," she said. "What's stopping you?"

"You are," he said.

"All I'm doing is sitting here. Watching TV."

"That's the point. I can't concentrate with the TV on."

"Why should I have to stop doing what I want to do so you can do what you want to do?"

"What I *have* to do."

"If you don't want to do it, if it doesn't make you happy, then don't do it," Lola said.

"I need you to turn off the TV. Or at least turn it down."

"Why are you criticizing me?"

Philip gave up. He closed the door. Opened it again. "You need to do some work, too," he said. "Why don't you go to the library?"

"Because I just got a manicure. And a pedicure." She held up a foot and wiggled her toes for his inspection. "Isn't it pretty?" she asked in her baby-girl voice.

Philip went back to his desk. The noise from the TV continued unabated. He put his hands in his hair. How the fuck had this happened? She'd taken over his apartment, his life, his concentration. His bathroom was littered with makeup. She never put the cap back on the toothpaste. Or bought toilet paper. When the toilet paper ran out, she used paper towels. And stared at him accusingly, as if he had fallen down on the job of making her life easy. Every one of her days was a never-ending orgy of pampering. There were hair-styling appointments and massages and exercise classes in obscure Asian martial arts. It was, she explained, all in preparation for some great, future, unnamed, and undefined event that would inevitably happen to her and would change her life, for which she needed to be ready. Camera-ready. And he couldn't get her to go home.

"You could go back to your apartment," he'd suggest.

"But your apartment is so much nicer than mine."

"Your apartment is so much nicer than most twentysome-things'," he'd point out. "Some of them live in the outer reaches of Brooklyn. Or New Jersey. They have to cross the river by ferry."

"What are you saying, Philip? That it's *my* fault? Am I supposed to feel guilty about other people's lives? I don't have anything to do with their lives. It doesn't make sense."

He tried to explain that one ought to feel guilty about other people's hardships and struggles because that was how decent people felt about the world, it was called a conscience, but when pressed by her, he had to admit that feeling guilty was a legacy of his generation, not hers. She was, she explained, a child of choice—her parents chose to have her. Unlike previous generations in which parents, like his mother, didn't have a choice about having kids, and therefore made their children feel guilty about coming into the world. As if it were the kid's fault!

Sometimes it was like trying to argue with someone from another planet.

He got up and opened the door again. "Lola!" he said.

"What is wrong with you?" she said. "I haven't done anything. You're in a bad mood because your writing isn't going well. Don't you dare blame that on me. I won't tolerate it." She got up.

"Where are you going?" he said.

"Out."

"Fine," he said. He shut the door. But now he did feel guilty. She was right, she hadn't done anything wrong. And he was in a bad mood. About what, he didn't know.

He opened the door. She was carefully sliding her feet into ballet flats. "You don't have to go."

"I'm going," she said.

"When are you coming back?"

"I have no idea." And she left.

In the elevator, Lola checked her Facebook page. Sure enough, there was a message from Thayer Core. He left her messages regularly, although she rarely responded. From her Facebook page, he'd found out she was from Atlanta and, from the photos she'd posted, seemed to think she was a party girl. "Hey Southern Girl," he'd written. "Let's hook up." "Why?" she'd texted back. "Because you're crazy about me," he wrote. "All girls are."

"IDTS," she responded. Which meant "I don't think so."

Now, however, might be a good time to take Thayer Core up on his offer. The best way to get back at a man was to make him jealous, although she wasn't sure Thayer Core would make Philip squirm. Still, Thayer was young, he was hot, and he was better than nothing. "What are you doing?" she texted Thayer.

A reply came back immediately. "Torturing the rich."

"Let's hang," she wrote. He texted back his address.

His apartment was on Avenue C and Thirteenth Street, in a low brick building with a dirty Chinese restaurant below. Lola rode a narrow elevator to the third floor. The hallway was tiled with large squares of brown linoleum. A door opened at one end of the short hallway, and a bristled man in a stained wifebeater stared at her briefly and went back inside.

Another door opened, and a pimply-faced kid stuck his head out. "You here to see Thayer?" he asked.

"Yes," Lola said. "What was that about?" She indicated the occupant of the other apartment.

"Pay no attention. The guy's a drug addict. Probably jonesing for his dealer to bring him a fix," the kid said casually, as if thrilled to be in possession of such knowledge. "I'm Josh," he said. "Thayer's roommate." The apartment was all that Lola had been expecting and worse. A board atop two plastic crates made a coffee table; in one corner was a futon with eggplant-colored sheets, barely visible under a pile of clothes. Pizza boxes, Chinese food containers, bags of Doritos, a bong, dirty glasses, and a bottle of vodka littered the counter that separated the tiny living room from the kitchen area. The place smelled of dirty socks, nighttime emissions, and marijuana.

"Are you Thayer's new girlfriend?" Josh asked.

"Hardly."

"Thayer's juggling three or four girls right now. I can't keep track of them, and neither can he." Josh knocked at a flimsy wooden door in the middle of a makeshift plywood wall. "Thay?"

"What the fuck?" came a voice from inside.

"Thayer's a serious writer," Josh said. "He's probably working."

"I'm going to go," Lola said.

Suddenly, the door opened and Thayer Core came out. He was taller than Lola remembered, at least six-two, and was wearing madras pants, flip-flops, and a ripped pink Lacoste shirt. Ironic preppy, Lola thought.

"Hey," Thayer said.

"Hey," Lola replied.

"I was telling Lola that you're a writer. He's a real writer," Josh said, turning to Lola.

"Meaning?"

"I get paid to write shit," Thayer said, and grinned.

"He's published," Josh said.

"You wrote a book?" Lola asked.

"Josh is an idiot."

"He's a writer for Snarker," Josh said proudly.

"Give me your stuff, Josh," Thayer said.

Josh looked annoyed. "There's hardly anything left."

"So? Give it to me. I'll get more later."

"That's what you said last night."

"Give me a break. I had that obscene cocktail party at Cartier, where they wouldn't let us in. Then some art party at the Whitney, where they wouldn't let us in, either. Then the Box. Which was groovy. Full of hipsters. But no pot. Only coke. Dammit, Josh, come on. I need your stash."

Josh reluctantly reached into his pocket and handed over a small bag of marijuana.

"You carry it with you? You're such a skive," Thayer said.

"I never know when I might need it."

"Like now," Thayer said.

"I'm going," Lola said.

"Why?" Thayer asked. "I thought you wanted to hang out. You have someplace better to go? This is the best spot in Manhattan. Center of the universe here. Going to destroy Manhattan from this tiny rat-infested three-thousand-dollar-a-month shithole."

"That's nice," Lola said.

Thayer handed her the bong, and she took a hit. She hadn't meant to smoke marijuana, but it was there and she was there and she thought, Why not? Plus, Thayer irritated her in an intriguing sort of way. He didn't seem to understand she was superior to him.

"Where's your boyfriend?" Thayer said.

"I'm pissed at him."

"You see, Josh?" Thayer said. "All roads lead to me."

Lola's phone rang. She looked at the number. It was Philip. She hit ignore.

"Who was that?" Thayer asked.

"None of your business."

Thayer took a hit from the bong. "Bet it was the boyfriend," he said to Josh. "Bet he's some boring premed student from the South."

"He isn't," Lola said proudly. "He's famous."

"Oooooh, Joshie boy. Did you hear that? He's famous. Nothing but the best for our Southern princess. Would I know him?" Thayer asked Lola.

"Of course," she said. "Philip Oakland? The novelist?"

"That guy?" Thayer said. "Baby, he's old."

"Got to be over forty, at least," Josh agreed.

"He's a man," Lola said.

"You hear that, Josh? He's a man. And we're not."

"You're certainly not," Lola said to Thayer.

"What am I?"

"An asshole?" Lola said.

Thayer laughed. "Didn't used to be," he said. "Until I came here. Until I got into this stinking, corrupt business called media."

"You still have your book," Josh said. "Thayer's going to be a great writer."

"I doubt it," Lola said.

"I like that you're sleeping your way to the top," Thayer said. "I'd do it if I could. But I don't relish the thought of a dick up my ass."

"It's the metaphorical dick that counts," Josh said.

"What do you talk to Oakland about?" Thayer asked. "He's an old man."

"What does any girl talk to you about?" Josh said. "I thought talking wasn't the point."

"As if you'd know," Thayer said, looking at Josh in disgust.

It went on like this for a while, and then some other people showed up. One was a girl with very pale skin and dyed black hair and a face that resembled a pug's. "I hate beauty queens," she screamed when she saw Lola.

"Shut up, Emily. Lola's okay," Thayer said.

More time passed. Thayer played seventies music, and they drank the vodka and danced in weird ways, and Josh filmed it on his cell phone. Then two guys and a girl came in. They were tall and pretty, like models, but Thayer said they weren't models, they were the rich-kid offspring of some famous New Yorkers, and if their kids didn't look like models, they would disown them. The girl was named Francesca, and she had long, narrow hands that she moved around when she talked. "I've seen you before," she said to Lola. "At that Nicole Kidman screening."

"Yes," Lola said loudly, over the music. "I was with my boyfriend, Philip Oakland."

"I love Nicole." The girl sighed.

"Do you know her?" Lola asked.

"I've known her my whole life. She came to my third birthday party." Francesca took Lola into the bathroom, and they put on lipstick. The bathroom smelled of damp towels and vomit. "Philip Oakland is cool," Francesca said. "How'd you meet him?"

"I'm his researcher," Lola said.

"I dated my teacher when I was sixteen. I love older men."

"Me, too," Lola said, glancing out at Thayer and Josh, who were pretending to box each other. She rolled her eyes and decided she'd tortured Philip long enough. "I have to go," she said.

When she got back to One Fifth, she found Philip in the kitchen, pouring himself a glass of wine. "Kitty," he exclaimed. He put down the glass and immediately gave her a hug, then he tried to make out with her and put his hand on her breast. She stiffened and pulled away. "What's wrong?" he said. "I tried to call you."

"I was busy."

"Really?" he asked, as if surprised that she might have something else to do. "Where were you?"

She shrugged. "With friends." She took out a glass and poured herself some wine, taking the glass with her into the bedroom.

He waited a beat and then followed her. "Kitty?" he said, sitting next to her on the bed. "What are you doing?"

"Reading *Star* magazine."

"You don't have to be pissed off," he said, trying to pull the magazine away.

"Stop it," she said, swatting at his hand and pretending to concentrate on an ad for Halloween costumes. "I have to figure out what I should be for Halloween." She paused. "I could be Lindsay Lohan or Paris Hilton, but then I don't know what you would be. Or I could be a dominatrix. Then you could be a businessman, like that guy who lives in the penthouse. The one you hate."

"Paul Rice?" Philip said. "A scumbag hedge-fund guy? Lola." He stroked her leg. "I will do nearly anything for you. But I will not dress up for a child's holiday."

She sat up and glared at him. "It's Halloween," she said pointedly, as if the subject wasn't open for discussion. "I want to go to parties. That's what people do on Halloween. It's the biggest holiday of the year."

"Tell you what," Philip said. "You can dress up however you want for me. We'll stay home and have our own Halloween."

"No," Lola said. "What's the point of dressing up if no one sees you?"

"I'll see you," Philip said. "Am I no one?"

Lola looked away. "I want to go out. There's a Halloween party at the Bowery Hotel. This guy Thayer Core told me about it."

"Who's Thayer Core?"

"He's this kid who works for Snarker."

"What's Snarker?" Philip asked.

Lola sighed dramatically and jumped off the bed, throwing down the magazine. She went into the bathroom. "How come we never do what I want to do? Why do we always have to go out with *your* friends?"

"My friends happen to be very interesting," Philip said. "But it's okay. If you want to go to this Halloween party, we'll go."

"Will you dress up?"

"No," he said.

"Then I'll go by myself."

"Fine," he said, and went out of the room. What was he doing, playing this game? He was too old for this, he decided. He picked up the phone and called the director of *Bridesmaids Revisited*, who happened to be home, and got into a discussion with him about the film.

A few minutes later, Lola came into his office and stood in front of him with her arms crossed. Philip looked at her, looked away, and went back to his conversation. Lola went into the living room, steaming. Trying to think of a way to push his buttons, she remembered the spread of him and Schiffer Diamond in *Vogue* magazine. Removing the magazine from the shelf, she banged it down noisily on the coffee table and opened it up.

Sure enough, Philip came in a few minutes later, looked at her, saw what she was reading, and stiffened. "What are you doing?" he demanded.

"What does it look like I'm doing?"

"Where did you get that?" he said, standing over her.

"It was on your bookshelf," she said innocently.

"Put it back," he said.

"Why?"

"Because I'd like you to," he said.

"Who are you? My father?" she asked teasingly, pleased to have gotten such a big reaction out of him.

He grabbed the magazine out of her hands. "This is off-limits," he said.

"Are you embarrassed about it?"

"No."

"Oh, I get it," Lola said, narrowing her eyes. "You're still in love with her." She jumped up and ran into the bedroom and started pounding on a pillow.

"Lola, stop," Philip said.

"How can you be in love with me when you're still in love with *her*?" Lola shrieked.

"It was a long time ago. And I never said I was in love with you, Lola," he said firmly, then immediately realized his mistake.

"So you're not in love with me?" she asked, her voice rising in outrage.

"I didn't say I wasn't in love with you. I'm saying we've only known each other for two months."

"More than that. Ten weeks. At least."

"Okay." Philip sighed. "Ten weeks. What's the difference?"

"Were you in love with her?" Lola said.

"Come on, Kitty," Philip said. "You're being silly." He went up to her, but she tried—not very hard, Philip noted—to push him away. "Listen," he said. "I'm very, very fond of you. But it's too soon to say 'I love you.'"

She crossed her arms. "I'm going to leave."

"Lola," he said. "What do you want from me?"

"I want you to be in love with me. And I want to go to that Halloween party."

He sighed. Relieved to be off the topic of his feelings for her, he said, "If you want to go to the party, we'll go."

This seemed to mollify her, and she put her hands in the waistband of his jeans. She unzipped his pants, and unable to object, he put his hands in her hair as she knelt in front of him. At one point, she pulled her mouth away from his penis and, looking up at him, said, "Will you dress up?"

"Huh?" he said.

"For Halloween?"

He closed his eyes. "Sure," he said, thinking, If it means more blow jobs, why not?

❦

In the week before Halloween, the city was hit by a cold snap. The temperature dropped to thirty degrees, causing people to remark that maybe global warming wasn't such an issue. For Thayer Core, the weather simply put him in a bad mood. He didn't own an overcoat, and the cold air reminded him that he was about to experience his third winter in New York, in which his lack of proper attire would make him hate the cold, hate the businessmen in their long cashmere coats and cashmere scarves and thick, leather-soled loafers. He hated everything about winter: the giant puddles of slush on the street corners and the disgusting puddles of dirty water in the subway and the puffy coat filled with acrylic batting that he was forced to wear when the temperature dropped below forty. His only protection against the icy weather was this silly ski jacket his mother had given him for his birthday the year he'd moved to New York. She'd been so excited about the gift, her flat brown eyes exuding a rarely seen sparkle of anticipation that had hurt him because his mother was pathetic, and irritated him because he was her son. Still, she loved him no matter what he did. She loved him although she had no idea who he was or what he really thought. Her assumption that he would love the gift of a ski coat for its practicality annoyed him and made him want to drink and drug away his infuriation, but when winter came to New York, he wore the coat. He had nothing else.

In the middle of the day in the middle of the week, when he imagined most people in America were wasting the company's time at their dull and unrewarding office jobs, Thayer Core took the subway to Fifty-first Street and walked up Fifty-second to the Four Seasons, where he would eat caviar and drink champagne under the pretense of reporting on how the privileged filled up their many hours of free time.

It was his third attendance at such a lunch, which appeared to be a regular once-a-week event, the purpose of which was the promotion of a movie (independent, often worthy, and usually boring). The guests were supposed to discuss the movie, like one of those middle-aged-lady book clubs that his mother belonged to, but no one ever did. Instead, they cooed over each other about how fabulous they were, which was especially galling to Thayer, who saw them as old and frightening and misguided. Nevertheless, he had managed to keep himself invited each week by not yet writing about the event in Snarker. He would have to soon. But in the meantime, he planned to enjoy his free lunch.

Thayer was always one of the first people to arrive, in order to do so anonymously. He took off his coat and was about to hand it to the coat-check man when he saw that Billy Litchfield had come up behind him. The sight of Billy filled Thayer with bile. Billy, Thayer had decided, was what could happen to a person who stayed too long in New York. What was his point? He appeared to do nothing but go to parties. He was a hanger-on to the rich and privileged. Didn't he get bored? Thayer had been going to parties for only two years, and already he was bored out of his mind. If he wasn't careful, time would pass, and he would end up like Billy Litchfield.

And now Billy had seen his coat.

"Hello, young man," Billy said pleasantly.

"Hello," Thayer muttered. No doubt Billy Litchfield couldn't remember his name. He held out his hand aggressively, forcing Billy to take it. "I'm Thayer Core," he said. "From Snarker?"

"I know exactly who you are," Billy replied.

"Good," Thayer said. Giving Billy a backward glance, he bounded up the steps ahead of him, if only to remind himself— and Billy—of his youth and energy. Then he took up his usual position at the bar, where he could observe and overhear and largely be ignored until lunch.

Billy handed his overcoat to the coat-check man, wishing he could have avoided shaking the hand of Thayer Core. Why was he here? Billy wondered. Thayer Core was a blogger on one of those vicious new websites that had popped up in the last few years, displaying a hatred and vitriol that was unprecedented in civilized New York. The things the bloggers wrote made no sense to him. The readers' comments made no sense to him. None of it appeared to be written by humans, at least not humans as he knew them. This was the problem with the Internet: The more the world opened up, the more unpleasant people seemed to be.

It was one of the reasons he'd begun taking the pills. Good old-fashioned Prozac. "Been around for twenty-five years. Babies take it," the shrink said. "You've got anhedonia. Lack of pleasure in anything."

"It's not a lack of pleasure," Billy protested. "It's more a horror of the world."

The doctor's office was located on Eleventh Street in a two-bedroom town house apartment. "We've met before," the doctor said the first time Billy walked in.

"Have we?" Billy said. He was so hoping this wouldn't be true, that he and his psychiatrist would have no acquaintances in common.

"You know my mother."

"Do I?" Billy said, trying to put him off. But there was a degree of comfort in the information.

"Cee Cee Lightfoot," the doctor said.

"Ah. Cee Cee," Billy said. He knew Cee Cee well. The muse to a famous fashion designer who had died of AIDS back in the days when fashion designers had muses. How he missed those times, he thought. "What happened to your mother?" he asked.

"Oh, she's still around," the doctor said with a mixture of what sounded like despair and amusement. "She still has a one-bedroom apartment here. And a house in the Berkshires. She spends most of her time there."

"What does she do?" Billy asked.

"She's still very, very active. She's involved with charity. She rescues horses."

"How wonderful," Billy said.

"How are *you* feeling?" the doctor asked.

"Not so good," Billy said.

"You've come to the right place," the doctor said. "We'll have you feeling good in no time."

And the pills—they actually worked! No, they didn't solve your problems, didn't make them go away. But one no longer cared quite so much.

Now Billy took a seat at the bar and ordered a glass of water. He stared at Thayer Core and briefly felt sorry for him. What a terrible way to earn a living. The young man must be filled with self-loathing. He was only a few feet away, but an enormous ocean of thirty years of knowledge separated them like two continents in which neither population understood the other's customs and mores. Billy decided he didn't care about that, either, and, glass of water in hand, went off to work the room.

Thirty minutes later, the luncheon was in full swing. "I love your TV show," shrieked a woman dressed in a beaded suit to Schiffer Diamond, leaning across Billy to address her.

Schiffer looked at Billy and gave him a wink. "I thought no one was going to talk about the TV show. I was promised."

Ever since *Lady Superior* had aired three weeks ago on Showtime, Schiffer had been invited everywhere and decided to enjoy herself in the little playground of New York society. Everyone wanted to fix her up. So far she'd dated a famous billionaire who'd been more intelligent and pleasant than she'd expected, but who, after a three-hour dinner, had said he didn't believe they were suited to each other and should move on; and a famous movie director who was desperately looking for a third wife. Today she was seated next to Derek Brumminger, who was sixty-three years old and rugged and pockmarked (by both acne and life, Schiffer decided), who had been fired two years before from his position as CEO of a major media corporation and been given eighty million dollars in compensation. He had just returned from a yearlong worldwide journey on which he had tried to find himself and failed. "I realized I wasn't ready to retire. I don't want to get off the stage. And that's why I came back," he said. "What about you?"

"I'm not ready to get off the stage, either," she said.

At the next table, Annalisa Rice was sitting next to Thayer Core. "That must be a very interesting job, blogging," she said.

"Have you ever done it?" Thayer asked.

"I've sent e-mails," she said.

"It's the kind of thing anyone can do. And does," Thayer replied with a mix of disdain and loathing.

"I'm sure that's not true."

"It is," Thayer said. "It's a bullshit way to make a living."

"Being a lawyer might be worse," she joked.

"It might be," he agreed. "I thought I was going to be a novelist. What did you think you'd be?"

"I always wanted to be a lawyer. Once you're a lawyer, you're always a lawyer, I suppose. But today I went to see a piece of art—everyone was talking about it—and it turned out to be a pair of running shoes and a plastic dinosaur glued to a baby's blanket. For half a million dollars."

"Doesn't that piss you off? It pisses me off. We live in a world full of douchebags."

"I guess one person's baby blanket is another person's art," Annalisa said, smiling at him.

"That's not a very original thought," he said, finishing off his third glass of champagne.

"Oh, I'm not trying to be original," she said without malice. "This room is full of original people. I'm still trying to figure out New York."

Thayer thought Annalisa was one of the most decent people he'd met at one of these things in a while. "If you were an emoticon, what would it be? A smiley face?" he asked.

Annalisa laughed. "I'd be perplexed. A K with a colon underneath."

"Because of the baby's blanket. For half a million dollars. You didn't buy it, I hope."

"No," she said. "But my husband is building a giant aquarium in our apartment."

"Where do you live?" Thayer asked casually.

"One Fifth," she said.

Thayer put it together: Annalisa Rice was one half of the couple who'd bought Mrs. Houghton's apartment. Her husband was Paul Rice, some scummy hedge-fund guy who was only thirty-two years old and already worth millions. The purchase had been noted in the real estate section of *The New York Observer*.

After the lunch, Thayer Core returned to his apartment. It was especially depressing, coming from the clean glamour of the Four Seasons. The windows were closed, and steam hissed from the old radiator. His roommate, Josh, was asleep on the pile of clothing he called his bed, his mouth open, wheezing in the deadly dry air.

Who was Thayer kidding? Josh was a loser—he would never make it in this town. It was the assholes who cleaned up, like Paul Rice, sitting in his giant apartment on Fifth Avenue looking at fish, while his beautiful, gracious wife, who was clearly too good for him, was forced to spend her time looking at fraudulent art with that creep Billy Litchfield. In this state of moral indignation, Thayer went into his room and sat down in front of his computer, ready to write a blistering attack on the Rices and Billy Litchfield and the lunch at the Four Seasons. Usually, his ire carried him through five hundred words of nasty hyperbole, but all at once, his anger deserted him and was replaced by a rare circumspection. He remembered Annalisa's face, smiling at him with what appeared to be delight in his charm, and completely innocent of his true intentions. Yes, he "hated" those people, but hadn't he come to New York to be one of them?

He was the next F. Scott Fitzgerald, he reminded himself, and someday he would write the Great American Novel and they'd bow down before his genius. In the meantime, Annalisa Rice would be his Daisy Buchanan.

"Every now and then, one meets a creature of the female persuasion who is so natural, so lovely, it's enough to make one consider not quitting this hellhole that is New York," he wrote.

Two hours later, his blog entry appeared on Snarker, earning him twenty dollars. In the meantime, Mindy Gooch, sitting in her generic office in midtown Manhattan, was also working on her blog. "When my son was born," she wrote, "I discovered I wasn't Superwoman. Especially when it came to my emotions. Suddenly, I no longer possessed the emotional energy for everyone, including my husband. All my emotions went to my son. My emotions, I learned, were limited, not limitless. And my son used them up. There was nothing left for my husband. I knew I should have felt guilty. And I did feel guilty. But not for the right reasons. I felt guilty because I was perfectly happy."

She sent the file to her assistant. Then she began surfing through her regular rotation of blogs: The Huffington Post, Slate, The Green

Thumb (an obscure site about gardening that Mindy found soothing), and finally, steeling herself against shock, horror, and
degradation, Snarker.

Each week, Snarker made fun of her blog in a feature called
"Middle-aged Mommy Crisis." It wasn't healthy to read hateful
comments about oneself (some of the comments said simply, "I
hate her. I wish she would die"), but Mindy was hooked. The
comments fed her demons of self-hatred and insecurity. It was,
she thought, the emotional version of cutting yourself. You did
it so you could feel. And feeling awful was better than feeling
nothing.

Today, however, there were no items about her. Mindy was
relieved—and slightly disappointed. It would make her evening
with James more dull, with nothing to rail about. As she was about
to close the website, a new item popped up. Mindy read the first
sentence and frowned. It was all about Annalisa Rice. And Paul
Rice. And his aquarium.

This, Mindy thought, was exactly what she didn't want to
happen. When it came to One Fifth, no publicity was good publicity.

Early the next morning, Mindy Gooch stationed herself at the
peephole, intending to confront Paul Rice when he passed through
the lobby on his way to work. Skippy, the cocker spaniel, was by
her side. Perhaps it was the atmosphere in his home and not his
inherent personality, but Skippy had developed a vicious streak. He
was perfectly pleasant for hours, and then, without warning, he
would attack.

At seven A.M. on the dot, Paul Rice came out of the elevator.
Mindy opened her door. "Excuse me," she said. Paul turned.
"What?" he demanded. At that moment, Skippy slipped out the
door. Baring his teeth, he closed in on Paul's pant leg. Paul turned
white. "Get your dog off me," he shouted, hopping on one leg
while he tried to shake Skippy free. Mindy waited for a moment,
then came out, pulling Skippy away from Paul's leg. "I could sue
you for that," Paul said. "Dogs are perfectly legal in this building,"

Mindy said, baring her own teeth. "But I'm not sure about fish. Oh yes," she said, noting the look of surprise on Paul's face. "I know all about your aquarium. There are no secrets in this building." She went back inside and kissed Skippy on the top of his head. "Good dog," she cooed. And from then on, a routine was established.

The Halloween party Lola insisted she and Philip attend wasn't at the Bowery Hotel after all, but in an abandoned building on the next block. Lola was dressed as a showgirl, in a sequined bra and panties, fishnet stockings, and high heels. She looked sensational, like a girl on the cover of a men's magazine. "Are you sure you want to go out like that?" Philip asked.

"What's wrong with it?"

"You're practically naked."

"No more naked than I am at the beach." She wrapped a feather boa around her neck. "Is that better?"

Trying to get into the spirit of things, Philip was dressed as a pimp, in a striped suit, white sunglasses, and a fur hat. On Eighth Street, Lola had bought him an imitation diamond necklace, at the bottom of which dangled a diamond-encrusted skull.

"Isn't this fun?" Lola exclaimed, walking to the party. The streets were filled with revelers dressed in every kind of costume. Yes, Philip thought, taking her hand. This was fun. He hadn't allowed himself to have this kind of silly fun for years. What had happened to him? When had he become so serious?

"You're going to love Thayer Core," she said, tugging on his hand to hurry him along.

"Who's he?" And seeing Lola's irritated expression, said, "I know, I know—the young impresario who wants to be a writer."

"Not wants, *is*," Lola said. "He writes every day for Snarker."

Philip smiled. Lola seemed incapable of making distinctions between the artist and the hack, the real and the wannabe. In her mind, a blogger was the same as a novelist, a star on a reality show was equal to an actress. It was her generation, he reminded himself. They had grown up in a culture of insistent democracy in which everyone was the same and everyone was a winner.

A large crowd was gathered in front of a decrepit building. Gripping Lola's hand, Philip pushed through. At the entrance were two guys with pierced faces, a transvestite in a pink wig, and Thayer Core himself, smoking a cigarette. He shook Philip's hand. "It's a destructor party, man," Thayer said. "Building's going to be torn down tomorrow. We do our best to destroy the place until the police get here."

Philip and Lola went in the door and up a wooden staircase. The air was hot and thick with smoke, lit by a single bulb. There was the sound of retching, and upstairs, music thumped out of two speakers set in the windows. The room was packed. "What is the point of this?" Philip said into Lola's ear.

"There is no point. Isn't it great?" Lola said.

They pushed their way up to a makeshift bar, where they were handed a slosh of vodka and cranberry juice in a red plastic cup, no ice. "When can we get out of here?" Philip shouted over the music.

"You want to leave already?" Lola said.

Philip looked around. I don't know one person here, he thought. And they were all so young, with their smooth faces and their attitudes, preening and shouting at each other. And the music. Loud, thumping, with no discernible melody. Yet they were all dancing, moving their hips while keeping their upper bodies still. I can't do this, Philip thought.

"Lola," he shouted into her ear. "I'm going home."

"No," she shrieked.

"You stay. Have a good time. I'll meet you back at the apartment in an hour."

Walking back to One Fifth, Philip was relieved and then perplexed. He couldn't imagine anything worse than being stuck at that crowded, hot, filthy party. How was that possibly fun? But he had gone to parties like that when he was twenty-two, and they *were* fun. There were scavenger hunts in limousines, endless evenings in tiny, smoke-filled clubs or in enormous spaces with a different theme every night; there was a club in an old church where you danced on the altar, and another one containing an abandoned subway tunnel where people went to take drugs. Manhattan was a giant playground where there was always music, always a party. One hot August night, he and Schiffer had crashed a party of transvestites on a decaying pier on the Hudson River, where several people fell in and had to be rescued by the fire department. He and Schiffer had laughed and laughed, laughed until they were crying. "Hey, schoolboy," she'd gasped, bent over in hilarity, "let's do this forever. Let's never work again and become twenty-four-hour party people. Wouldn't that be glamorous? And when we've had enough, we'll live in an old farmhouse in Vermont."

What happened to those days? he wondered. Coming into One Fifth and catching a glimpse of himself in the mirror next to the elevators, he realized he looked a fool, a middle-aged man trying to pretend he was young. When had he gotten so old?

"Philip?" He heard a voice. "Philip Oakland, is that you?" Followed by the familiar peals of laughter.

He turned. Schiffer Diamond had come in and was standing with a pile of scripts folded across her chest. It was obvious she'd just come from the set, in full hair and makeup, wearing jeans, fuzzy boots, and a bright orange parka. A white cashmere scarf was tied around her neck. She looked good—her mocking, amused expression was reminiscent of how she'd looked when he'd first met her. How was it that she seemed not to have aged at all, while he'd become such an obvious victim of time? "Schoolboy," she said. "It *is* you. What the hell are you wearing?"

"It's Halloween," he said.

"I know that. But what are you supposed to be?"

Philip felt embarrassed and irritated. "Nothing," he said, pressing the button for the elevator.

The doors opened and they got in. "Like the hat," she said, looking him up and down. "But you were never good at disguises,

Oakland." The elevator stopped on her floor. She looked again at his getup, shook her head, and got out. And once again, he thought, she was gone.

Hanging out with Thayer at the party, Lola lost track of time. Thayer seemed to know everyone and kept introducing her to people. She sat on his lap. "Can you feel my hard-on?" he said.

Francesca showed up. She and Lola went into the stairwell and smoked marijuana. Then they found someone with a bottle of vodka. One of the speakers fell out the window. The night went on and on.

At three A.M. the room lit up with the red and white lights of several police cars. The cops came in with flashlights, and Lola ran as fast as she could down the stairs and up Third Avenue. At Fifth Street, she stopped, finding herself alone outside in the dead of night. It was cold and her feet hurt and her mouth was dry and she couldn't think of what to do.

She began walking, wrapping her arms around her chest to keep warm. The streets were still filled with people and taxis, and it struck her as funny that she was walking around outside in little more than a bra and panties. "I love your ass," Thayer Core had kept telling her. If she weren't with Philip Oakland, she just might go after Thayer. But that would make her desperate. She'd go crazy hanging out in Thayer's terrible apartment, with that awful Josh there all the time. That's how it was for most girls. They were lucky if they found a guy who was interested, and then he lived in a terrible place. She could never live in New York like that. As her mother would say, "That isn't living, it's surviving."

She finally made it to Fifth Avenue. The street was deserted, yellow and spooky under the streetlights. She'd never come into the building so late and found the door was locked. She banged on it in a panic, rousing the doorman, who'd been sleeping in a chair. He didn't know her and gave her a hard time, insisting on ringing

Philip on the house phone. When she finally got upstairs, Philip was standing in the hallway in his boxer shorts and a Rolling Stones T-shirt.

"Jesus Christ, Lola. It's three in the morning," he said.

"I was having fun." She giggled.

"I can see that."

"I tried to call you," she protested innocently. "But you didn't answer your phone."

"Uh-huh," Philip said.

"It's not my fault," she insisted. "This is what happens when you don't answer your phone."

"Good night," Philip said coldly. He turned and went into the bedroom.

"Fine," she said. She went into the kitchen. She was angry. This wasn't the reception she'd been expecting. She marched into the bedroom to confront Philip about his attitude. "I had fun, okay?" she said. "Is that such a big deal?"

"Go to sleep. Or go to your own apartment."

She decided to try a different tactic. She slipped her hand under the covers and put her fingers over his penis. "Don't you want to have fun?"

He pointedly removed her hand. "Go to bed. Please. If you can't sleep, go to the couch."

Lola glared at him, slowly took off her clothes, and got into bed. Philip was lying there with his eyes shut tight. She lay down next to him. Then she rolled onto her side. Then she accidentally kicked him with her foot.

He sat up. "I mean it," he said. "If you can't sleep, you should go to the couch."

"What is your problem?" she said.

"Look," he said. "I need to get some sleep. I have a big day tomorrow."

"Take it easy," she said. "I'll take a sleeping pill."

"That's always the solution, isn't it?" Philip muttered. "A pill."

"You're the pill," Lola said.

She didn't fall asleep right away. She lay in the dark, hating Philip. He was no fun, and she probably should break up with him and go out with Thayer. But then she thought about Thayer's apartment again, and how he had no money and was basically an asshole. If she broke up with Philip, she'd be back where she was when she started in New York. Living in that tiny apartment on Eleventh Street and going to destructor parties every night. There would be no movie openings, no dinners at the Waverly Inn, no rubbing shoulders with glamour. She needed to stay with Philip for at least a little while. Either until he married her, or something happened and she became famous in her own right.

The next morning, Philip greeted her with a chilly "Good morning." Lola's head felt like a bowling ball, but for once, she didn't complain, knowing she needed to mollify him. She dragged herself out of bed and went into the bathroom, where he was shaving. She sat down on the toilet seat, put her arms between her legs, and looked up at him through her mess of dark hair. "Don't be mad at me," she said. "I didn't know you'd be so upset."

Philip put down his razor and looked at her. Last night, after the embarrassment of running into Schiffer and then lying alone in his bed waiting for Lola to come home, he'd begun to wonder what he'd gotten himself into. Maybe Nini was right: He was too old to be dating a twenty-two-year-old. But what was he supposed to do? Schiffer Diamond was obsessed with her career and didn't need him. He supposed he could find a nice, accomplished woman who was his age, like Sondra, but that might mean accepting the fact that the exciting part of his sex life was over. He couldn't do it. It was the equivalent of giving up.

And here was gorgeous Lola Fabrikant, in his bathroom, contrite and pliable. He sighed. "Okay, Lola," he said. "Just don't do it again."

"I won't," she said, jumping up. "I promise. Oh, Philip, I love you so much." And she went back to bed.

Philip smiled. Where did she pick up her crazy ideas about love? he wondered. "Hey, Lola," he called. "Why don't you make us some breakfast?"

She laughed. "You know I don't cook."

"Maybe you should learn."

"Why?" she asked. Philip finished shaving, examining his skin in the mirror. He'd had young girlfriends before, but none had been quite like Lola, he thought. Usually, the young women were much more accommodating. He took a step back and patted his face, shaking his head. Who was he kidding? Schiffer Diamond had been much wilder than Lola. But he'd been in love with Schiffer, so her antics had driven him crazy—once she'd even suggested they have sex with another man. She might have been joking, but he never knew for sure. On the other hand, he wasn't in love with Lola, so, he told himself, he was safe—her actions couldn't really affect him.

He went into the bedroom. Lola was lying on her stomach, naked under the covers, as if she were waiting for him. "Oh, hello," she said, turning her head to greet him. Pulling back the covers, he forgot all about Schiffer Diamond as he surveyed Lola's body. She opened her legs invitingly. He dropped his towel and, kneeling behind her, lifted her hips and slipped his cock in from behind.

He came quickly and felt the sleepy calm that followed the satiation of pleasure. He closed his eyes. Lola rolled over and began playing with his hair. "Philip?" she asked sweetly. "What are you doing for Thanksgiving? Do you want to come to Atlanta with me?"

"Maybe," he said before he fell asleep.

II

The drilling had begun again in the Rices' apartment. Enid Merle got up from her desk in annoyance and went outside. On the terrace above was a pile of copper pipes. So the Rices still hadn't finished the renovations on their bathrooms. Or maybe the pipes were for the aquarium Paul Rice was rumored to be installing in Mrs. Houghton's ballroom. Enid hoped the renovation wouldn't drive her into becoming one of those particular types of old people who, with little in their lives on which to focus, become obsessed with their neighbors. She turned on the History Channel to distract herself. The programs were a reminder of the true nature of human beings—while there were always a few who strived for greatness, most of humankind was engaged in the crude art of staying alive, reproduction, and indulgence in the baser instincts, including murder, paranoia, and war.

Her bell rang. Expecting Philip, she opened the door and found Mindy Gooch standing in the hallway. Mindy's arms were crossed, and she wore her usual grim expression. "I need to talk to you about something," she said.

"Come in." Enid held open the door so Mindy could pass. Mindy's visit was curious, Enid thought, as they hadn't spoken since Mrs. Houghton's funeral.

"I think we have a problem," Mindy said.

Enid smiled. "I've lived in this building my entire life, dear," she said, thinking that Mindy was referring to their lack of communication. "I was here before you moved in. And I expect to be here after you move out. If we don't speak for the next five years, it won't be an issue for me."

"I'm not talking about you," Mindy said. "I mean the Rices. Something has to be done about them."

"Is that so," Enid said coldly.

"Paul Rice came by my office last week."

"Trying to be friendly, I suppose."

"Trying to bribe me to approve his in-the-wall air conditioners."

"And what did you say?"

"I told him no."

"Well, then," Enid said. "What's the problem?"

"This," Mindy said. She opened her hand and held up a tiny green plastic toy soldier thrusting a bayonet.

"I don't understand," Enid said.

"This morning, when I opened my door to get the newspaper, I found a whole troop of them arranged on the mat."

"And you think Paul Rice did it," Enid said skeptically.

"I don't think he did it. I know he did it," Mindy said. "He told me if I didn't approve his air conditioners, it was war. If this isn't a sign," she continued, shaking the little green army man in Enid's face, "I don't know what is."

"You must confront him," Enid said.

"I can't do it alone," Mindy said. "I need your help."

"I don't see how I can help you," Enid said calmly. "Dealing with unpleasant residents is your job. After all, you are the president of the board."

"You were the president of the board for fifteen years," Mindy said. "There must be something we can do. Some way to get them out."

Enid smiled. "They've only just moved in."

"Look, Enid," Mindy said, beginning to lose patience. "We were friendly once."

"Yes, we were." Enid nodded. "We were friendly for a long time. We were even friendly after you conspired to have me removed as president."

"I thought you didn't want the job anymore," Mindy protested.

"I didn't, and that's why I forgave you. I thought, If she wants the job that much, why not let her have it?"

Mindy looked away. "What if the approval was a mistake?" she asked tentatively.

Enid sighed. "There's nothing we can do. The only way we can force them out is if they don't pay their maintenance. And given the circumstances, I'd say that's highly unlikely."

"I'm not sure I can live in the same building with this man," Mindy said.

"Then perhaps you'll have to move," Enid said. She held open her door. "So sorry I can't help you, dear. Have a good day."

Lola put down the novel *Atonement* and, opening the door to the terrace, stepped out onto the icy surface in her high-heeled Chloé boots. She peered over the edge and, still seeing no sign of Philip, went back inside. She closed the book and glared at the cover. It was a gift from Philip, although "gift" probably wasn't the right word. "Suggestion" was more like it. He had given her the book after they'd had a disastrous dinner with one of his old friends. "This is a great book," he'd said. "I thought you might enjoy it."

"Thank you," she'd said gratefully, although she knew exactly what he was up to. He was trying to educate her, and while she thought it was sweet of him, she couldn't understand why he found it necessary. As far as she was concerned, it was Philip who needed educating. Every time she mentioned a hot new actor or some YouTube video everyone was talking about, or even when she played music for him off her iPod, he claimed never to have heard of any of it. This was frustrating, but she always refrained from criticizing him. She at least had the decency not to hurt his feelings and make him feel old.

In adopting this attitude, she'd found she could pretty much get Philip to do whatever she wanted. Today, for instance, they were going to visit the set of Schiffer Diamond's new TV show. Everyone was talking about the show, and knowing Philip was, as he put it, "old friends" with Schiffer, Lola had wondered why he hadn't gone to see her. Philip seemed to wonder, too, and, with her urging, went down to her apartment and left her a note. One evening, Schiffer called, and Philip went into his office and talked to her on the phone for an hour with his door closed while Lola waited impatiently outside. When he came out, he said he was going to see Schiffer on the set, but Lola shouldn't bother coming with him, as it would be dull and she would be bored. This after it was her idea to go in the first place! Then she'd given him a foot massage and, while she was rubbing his feet, pointed out that a set visit would be good for her education. As his researcher and girl-friend, naturally, she wanted to understand everything about his work. "You know what I do," he'd protested, but only mildly. "I sit at a computer all day."

"That's not true," she said. "You're going to Los Angeles for two weeks in January. And I'll probably come out for a week. I'll have to go to the set with you then—you can't expect me to sit in a hotel room all day."

"I thought we discussed L.A.," he said, tensing his foot. "It's going to be a nightmare. The first two weeks of production always are. I'll be working sixteen-hour days. It won't be fun for you at all."

"You mean I won't see you for two weeks?" she'd exclaimed. He must have felt guilty, because almost immediately, he agreed to take her with him to the set of *Lady Superior* after all. She was so pleased, she didn't even mind about him not going to her parents' house for Thanksgiving; she told herself it was too soon in their relationship to be spending holidays with each other's families. She wouldn't have wanted to spend Thanksgiving with Enid, which was what Philip had done, taking his aunt to a boring lunch at the Century Club. Philip had dragged Lola there once, and she'd vowed never to return. Everyone was over eighty. So Lola happily went back to Windsor Pines and met up with her girlfriends and stayed up until two A.M. on Friday night and showed off pictures of her and Philip and Philip's apartment. One of her friends was engaged and planning a wedding; the others were trying to get their boyfriends to marry them. They looked at the photographs of Philip and his apartment and sighed in envy.

That was three weeks ago, and now it was nearly Christmas, and Philip had finally come up with a day for the set visit. Lola spent two days getting ready. She'd had a massage and a spray tan, her dark hair was highlighted with strands of gold, and she'd bought a dress at Marc Jacobs. After the purchase, her mother called, wondering if she had indeed just spent twenty-three hundred dollars. Lola accused her mother of using her credit card to spy on her. They had had a rare fight, and Lola hung up, felt terrible, then called her mother back. Beetelle was nearly in tears. "Mommy, what's wrong?" Lola demanded. When her mother didn't respond, Lola asked in a panic, "Are you and Daddy getting a divorce?" "Your father and I are fine." "So what's the problem?" "Oh, Lola," her mother said, sighing. "We'll talk about it when you come home for Christmas. In the meantime, try to be careful with money."

This was very strange, and Lola hung up, perplexed. But then she decided it wasn't important. Her mother got upset about money every now and again, but she always got over it and, feeling guilty, usually bought Lola a trinket like Chanel sunglasses.

❦

Philip, meanwhile, was around the corner, getting his hair cut. He'd frequented this particular salon, located on Ninth Street off Fifth, for thirty years. His mother started coming to the salon in the seventies, when the clients and stylists would play music on a boom box and snort cocaine. Naturally, the proprietor was a dear friend

of his mother's. Everyone was a dear friend of his mother's. She'd
had that charming neediness that made people want to take care of
her. She'd been a trust fund girl and considered a great beauty, but
there was an air of tragedy about her that only increased her fascination. No one was surprised when she killed herself in 1983.

The proprietor, Peter, had been giving Philip the same haircut
for years and was nearly finished, but Philip was trying to kill time.
Peter had recently recovered from cancer and had begun to work
out at a gym every day, so they talked about his routine. Then
they talked about Peter's house upstate in the Catskills. Then they
talked about how the neighborhood was changing. Philip was
dreading the set visit and the impending meeting of his former love
and his current lover. There was a bald difference between "love"
and "lover," the first being legitimate and honorable, the second
being temporary and even, he thought, when it came to Lola,
slightly embarrassing.

This unpleasant reality had come to light during the dinner
with the Yugoslavian director. The director, who happened to have
won two Academy Awards, was an elderly man who drooled, and
whose Russian wife, dressed in gold Dolce & Gabbana (and twenty
years younger, about the same difference in age, Philip guessed, as
he and Lola), had had to feed him his soup. The director was a cur-
mudgeon, and his wife was ridiculous, but still, the man was a
legend, and despite his age (which couldn't be helped) and his silly
wife, Philip had the utmost respect for him and had been looking
forward to the dinner for months.

Lola, intentionally or not, was on her worst behavior. During a
long discourse during which the director explained his next project (a movie about an obscure civil war in Yugoslavia in the
thirties), Lola had attended to her iPhone, sending texts and even
taking a call from one of her girlfriends in Atlanta. "Put it away,"
Philip had hissed at her. She gave him a hurt look, signaled to the
waiter, and asked for a Jell-O shot, explaining to the table that she
didn't drink wine, as it was for old people. "Stop it, Lola," he said.
"You do drink wine. You'll have what everyone else is having." "I

don't drink red wine," she pointed out. "Besides, I need something strong to get through this dinner." She'd asked the director if he'd ever worked on any popular movies. "Popular?" he'd asked, startled. "Vat is zat?"

"You know," Lola said. "Movies for regular people."

"Vat is regular people?" the director asked, insulted. "I think my tastes are too sophisticated for a young lady such as yourself."

The old man hadn't meant to be insulting, but it had come out that way. And Lola took the bait.

"What's that mean?" she'd said. "I thought art was for the people. If the people can't understand it, what's the point?"

"This is zee problem with America," the director said. He'd lifted his glass of wine to his mouth, his hand shaking so violently he spilled half the glass. "Too much democracy," he exclaimed. "It's zee death of art."

For the rest of the evening, everyone ignored Lola.

In the taxi on the way back to One Fifth, Lola was fuming, staring out the window and playing with her hair.

"What's wrong now?" Philip had asked.

"No one paid any attention to me."

"What are you talking about?" he said.

"I was ignored, Philip. Why should I be there if I'm going to be ignored?"

"You wouldn't have been ignored if you hadn't made that stupid remark about his films."

"He's an insignificant old man. Who cares about him and his movies? Oh, excuse me," she added with vehemence, "his *films*."

"He's a genius, Lola. He's allowed his idiosyncracies. And he's earned his respect. You need to learn to honor that."

"Are you criticizing me?" she said warningly.

"I'm pointing out that you could stand to learn a thing or two about life."

"Listen, Philip," she'd said. "In case you haven't figured it out, I don't put anybody above me. I don't care what they've accomplished. I'm as good as anyone. Even if they have won two

Academy Awards. Do you really think that makes a person better than other people?"

"Yes, Lola, I do," he said.

They went into the building in stony silence. It was yet another spat that ended in sex. She seemed to have a sixth sense about when he might be angry with her, and she always managed to divert his attention with some new sexual trick. That evening, she came out of the bathroom in crotchless panties, showing off the Brazilian wax she'd had that afternoon, as a "special treat" for him. He was helpless in the face of such sexual temptation, and the next morning, they went on as before.

Now, as he shook his head about Lola while the stylist brushed the clipped hair from his shoulders, who should walk by the plate-glass window but James Gooch. Was Philip always going to run into James Gooch now, too? he wondered. How had this happened? They'd lived in the same building for years and had managed to coexist peacefully, without the acknowledgment of each other's presence, and all of a sudden, ever since that afternoon at Paul Smith, he ran into James nearly every other day. He did not wish to increase his acquaintance with James, but it was probably inevitable, as James struck him as one of those men who, knowing he is not wanted, only becomes more insistent on pushing his way in. Sure enough, James spotted him through the selection of wigs in the shop window and, with a look of surprise, came into the salon.

"How are you?" he asked eagerly.

Philip nodded, trying not to speak. If he spoke, it was all over.

"I didn't know they cut men's hair here," James said, taking in the purple velvet chairs and the fringed wall hangings.

"Been doing it forever," Philip murmured.

"It's so close to the building. Maybe I should start coming here. I still go to a guy on the Upper West Side."

Philip politely inclined his head.

"We used to live up there," James said. "I tell everyone my wife rescued me from my studio apartment and loft bed. If it weren't for her, I'd probably still be there."

"I hope not." Philip stood up.

"What about you?" James asked. "Have you always lived downtown?"

"I've always lived in One Fifth," Philip said. "I grew up there."

"Nice," James said, nodding. "What do you think about the Rices, by the way? Guy seems like an asshole to me. He hassles my wife, and then he's putting in a two-thousand-gallon aquarium."

"I've learned not to get involved in the altercations of the other residents," Philip said dryly. "That's my aunt's area."

"I thought you knew Schiffer Diamond, though," James said. "Didn't you two used to date?"

"A long time ago," Philip said. He handed the cashier forty dollars and tried to get away from James by quickly slipping out the door. But James followed him. Now Philip was stuck with James for the two-block walk back to One Fifth. It seemed an eternity. "We should have dinner sometime," James said. "My wife and I, you and your girlfriend. What's her name again?"

"Lola," Philip said.

"She's young, isn't she?" James asked nonchalantly.

"Twenty-two," Philip said.

"That is young," James said. "She could be your daughter."

"Luckily, she isn't," Philip said.

They reached the building, and James repeated his offer of dinner. "We can go someplace in the neighborhood. Maybe Knickerbocker?"

Philip couldn't see a way out. What could he say? "I never want to have dinner with you and your wife"? "Maybe after Christmas," he said.

"Perfect," James said. "We'll do it the first or second week after New Year's. My book comes out in February, so I'll be away after that."

❧

"What are you doing for Christmas?" Brumminger asked Schiffer Diamond over the phone.

"No plans," Schiffer said, leaning forward in the makeup chair.

She'd had four dates with Brumminger; after the fourth dinner, they'd decided to sleep together to "get it out of the way" and ascertain whether or not they were compatible. The sex was fine—adult and technically correct and slightly passionless but not unsatisfying—and Brumminger was easy and intelligent, although somewhat humorless. His lack of humor came from a residual bitterness over being fired from his position as CEO two years ago, then struggling with his perceived loss of status. If he wasn't CEO, if he didn't have a title after his name, who was he? Brumminger's yearlong hejira had taught him one thing: "Soul searching is good, but achievement is better." He, too, had returned to New York to start over, trying to put together some deals with other former CEOs who'd been put out to pasture at sixty. "The First CEOs Club," he joked.

Now he said: "Want to go to Saint Barths? I've got a villa from the twenty-third until January tenth. If you can leave on the twenty-third, I can give you a lift. I'm flying private."

Alan, the PA, stuck his head into the room. "You have visitors," he mouthed. Schiffer nodded. Philip and his young girlfriend, Lola, came into the room. Philip had mentioned he'd be bringing her, and Schiffer had agreed, curious about this girl who had managed to hold on to Philip longer than Schiffer had expected.

Stating the obvious, Philip said, "I brought Lola."

Schiffer held out her hand. "I've heard about you from Enid."

"Really?" Lola said, looking pleased.

Schiffer held up one finger and went back to her phone call. "What do you think?" Brumminger asked.

"It's a great idea. I can't wait," Schiffer said, and hung up.

"Can't wait for what?" Philip asked with the curious familiarity of having once had an intimate relationship.

"Saint Barths. At Christmas."

"I've always wanted to go to Saint Barths," Lola said, impressed.

"You should get Philip to take you," Schiffer said, looking at Philip. "It's one of his favorite islands."

"It's one of everyone's favorite islands," Philip grumbled. "Who're you going with?"

"Brumminger," Schiffer said, looking down so the makeup artist could apply mascara.

"Derek Brumminger?" he asked.

"That's right."

"Are you seeing him now?"

"Sort of."

"Oh," Philip said. He sat down on the empty chair beside her. "So when did that happen?"

"It's new," Schiffer said.

"Who's Brumminger?" Lola asked, inserting herself into the conversation.

Schiffer smiled. "He's a man who was once rich and powerful and now isn't quite as powerful. But definitely richer."

"Is he old?" Lola asked.

"Positively ancient," Schiffer said. "He may even be older than Oakland."

"They're ready," Alan said, poking his head in.

"Thanks, darling," Schiffer said.

Schiffer took Lola and Philip to the set. Walking through the maze of hallways, Lola kept up a pleasant patter about how excited she was to be there, oohing and ahing over a backdrop of the Manhattan skyline, the number of people milling around, the plethora of cables and lights and equipment. Schiffer wasn't surprised Enid hated the girl—Lola seemed to have Philip wrapped around her black polished fingernail—but she wasn't so bad. She was perfectly friendly and seemed to have some spunk. She was just so young. Being with her made Philip look slightly desperate. But it wasn't, Schiffer reminded herself, her problem. Both she and Philip had moved on years ago. There was no going back.

With a glance at Lola, who was sitting blithely in the director's chair, completely unaware of her faux pas, Schiffer stepped onto the set and tried to put Philip and his girlfriend out of her mind. The scene she was shooting took place in her office at the magazine and involved confronting a young female employee who was having an office affair with the boss. Schiffer sat down behind her desk and put on a pair of black-framed reading glasses from the props department.

"Settle," the director called out. "And action."

Schiffer stood up and took off her reading glasses as the young actress approached the desk.

"Ohmigod. It's Ramblin Payne," Lola squealed from behind the monitors.

"Cut!" the director shouted. He looked around, spotted the interloper in his chair, and strode over to confront Lola.

Schiffer scooted out from behind the desk and tried to intervene. "It's okay. She's a friend."

The director stopped, looked at her, and shook his head, then saw Philip standing next to Lola. "Oakland?" he said. He went over and shook hands with Philip and patted him on the back. "Why didn't you tell me Oakland was here?" the director said to Schiffer.

"I wanted to surprise you."

"How're you doin', man? I hear you're getting *Bridesmaids Revisited* made."

"That's right," Philip said. "We start shooting in January."

The director looked at Lola in confusion. "Is this your daughter?" he asked.

Schiffer tried to catch Philip's eye, but he refused to look at her. Poor Philip, she thought.

Later, in the car going back to the city, a black cloud of melancholy descended over Philip of which Lola was seemingly unaware. She chattered away, ignorant of his silence, nattering on and on about how she'd had an epiphany standing on the set. It was, she realized, where she belonged. She could see herself in front of the cameras, doing what Ramblin Payne did, which wasn't so hard, really. It didn't look hard. But maybe she'd be better off on a reality show. They could do a reality show about her life—about a young woman taking on the big city. After all, she pointed out, she did have a glamorous life, and she was pretty—as pretty as all the other girls on reality shows. And she was more interesting. She was interesting, she asked Philip, wasn't she?

"Sure," Philip said, his response automatic. They were crossing the Williamsburg Bridge into lower Manhattan, which presented a very different view than the famous midtown skyline. Here, the buildings were brown and gray, low-slung, in disrepair; one thought of desperation and resignation as opposed to renewal and the fulfillment of one's dreams. The sight of these buildings caused Philip to have his own epiphany. Schiffer Diamond had returned to New York and taken up her new life with ease; she was celebrated and had even found a relationship. But what, Philip thought, of his own life? He hadn't moved on at all; he'd taken no new steps in years. The subject matter of his work changed, his girlfriends changed, but that was it. Thinking ahead to Christmas, he became more aware of his discontent. His Christmas would be spent with his aunt—usually, they went to the Plaza for dinner, but the Plaza was no longer the Plaza, under renovation as an exorbitantly priced condominium—and now he didn't know where they'd go. Schiffer was going to Saint Barths. Even Lola was going home to her parents'. He felt old and left behind and had to forcibly remind himself that this wasn't like him. And then he saw a way out of his depression.

"Lola," he said, taking her hand. "How would you like to go to the Caribbean for New Year's?"

"Saint Barths?" she asked eagerly.

"No," he said, not wishing to spend the holiday running into Schiffer Diamond and her new lover. "Not Saint Barths. But someplace just as good."

"Oh, Philip," she said, throwing her arms around him. "I'm so happy. I was so worried we weren't going to do anything for New Year's—I thought maybe you forgot. But I guess you were saving it as a surprise."

Unable to contain her excitement, she immediately called her mother to give her the good news. Her mother had been funny lately, and Lola thought this would cheer her up.

Three days later, Lola, in a haze of excitement, flew down to Atlanta. Her thoughts were concentrated on her trip with Philip; she would leave on the twenty-seventh and fly directly to Barbados, where she would meet up with him and fly to Mustique. Everyone knew that when a man took you on vacation, he was testing you to see how you got along when you were together all day for several days; if the trip went well, it could lead to an engagement. And so, in the week before she left for the trip, she had almost as much to do as a bride: She needed to buy bathing suits and resort wear, wax herself from head to toe, have her calluses scraped and her elbows scrubbed and her eyebrows threaded. Sitting on the plane, she imagined her wedding day. She and Philip would marry in Manhattan; that way they could invite Schiffer Diamond and that funny novelist James Gooch, and the wedding would get into *The New York Times* and the *Post* and maybe even the tabloid magazines, and the world would begin to know about Lola Fabrikant. With these happy thoughts firmly in mind, Lola collected her bags from the carousel and met her mother at the curb. Each of her parents drove a new Mercedes, leased every two years, and Lola felt a swelling of pride at the easy superiority of their lives.

"I missed you, Mother," Lola said, getting into the car. "Can we go to the Buckhead Mall?" This was a Christmas tradition for mother and daughter. Ever since Lola had gone away to Old Vic University, she and Beetelle would go straight to the mall when Lola came home for the holidays. There, mother and daughter would bond over shoes and accessories and the various outfits Lola tried on while Beetelle waited outside the dressing room to exclaim over the "cuteness" of a pair of jeans or a Nicole Miller dress. But this year, Beetelle was not dressed for shopping. It was her personal edict never to appear in public without her hair straightened and blown dry and her makeup applied, and wearing midpriced designer clothes (usually slacks and a blouse and often an Hermès scarf and several heavy gold necklaces), but today Beetelle wore jeans and a sweatshirt, her naturally curly hair pulled back in a scrunchy. This was her "work" outfit, donned only at home when she jumped in and helped the housekeeper with special chores, such as polishing the silver and washing the Tiffany crystal and moving the heavy oak furniture for a thorough vacuuming of the rugs. "A scrunchy, Mother?" Lola said with affection and annoyance—living in New York had made her mother's flaws all too apparent—"You can't go to the mall like that."

Beetelle concentrated on maneuvering the car through the line of holiday pickups. She'd been preparing for this scene with her daughter for days, rehearsing it in her head like the psychologists suggested in anticipation of a difficult conversation. "Things are a little different this year," she said.

"Really?" Lola said. She was deeply disappointed, having imagined getting started on her shopping spree right away. But then she was distracted by the satellite radio, tuned to seventies hits. "Oh, Mother," she said. "Why do you listen to this sentimental crap?"

Beetelle had adjusted to Lola's dismissive remarks long ago, brushing them away with reminders that this was her daughter who loved her and could never mean to be deliberately hurtful; Lola was, after all, like all young people, occasionally unaware of the feelings of others. But this time the characteristic remark hit Beetelle like a blow to her solar plexus.

"Mother, can we please change the station?" Lola said again.

"No," Beetelle said.

"Why not?"

"Because I like it."

"But it's so awful, Mother," Lola whined. "It's so . . . out of touch."

Beetelle took her eyes off the road for a second to regard her daughter, sitting impatiently in the front seat, her eyes narrowed in annoyance. An irrational anger overwhelmed her; all at once, she hated her daughter. "Lola," she said. "Will you please shut up?"

Lola's mouth opened like that of a little fish. She turned to her mother, unable to fathom what she'd just heard. Beetelle's face was hard, set in an expression Lola saw rarely and only in brief flashes, as when the head of the school board had dismissed Beetelle's suggestions to serve only organic lettuce. But her ire was never turned on Lola herself, and Lola was shocked.

"I mean it," Beetelle said.

"All I said was . . ." Lola protested.

Beetelle shook her head. "Not now, Lola," she said.

They were on the highway. Beetelle thought about the forty-minute drive in traffic and decided she couldn't go on. Lola had to be told. Beetelle took the next exit. "Mother!" Lola screamed. "What is wrong with you? This isn't our turn."

Beetelle pulled in to a gas station and parked the car. She reminded herself that she was a courageous person, a person of honor, who could face the most devastating of circumstances and come out a winner.

"What's going on?" Lola demanded. "It's Daddy, isn't it? He's having an affair."

"No," Beetelle said. She looked at her daughter, wondering what Lola's reaction would be to the news. She would likely scream and cry. Beetelle had screamed and cried when she'd first heard as well. But she'd gotten used to it—the way, she'd been told by the hospice patients she occasionally visited, one got used to constant physical pain.

"Lola," Beetelle said gently. "We're broke. We've lost all our money. There. I've said it, and now you know."

Lola sat silently for a moment, then erupted into hysterical laughter. "Oh, Mother," she said. "Don't be so dramatic. How can we be broke? I don't even know what that means."

"It means we don't have any money," Beetelle said.

"How can that be? Of course we have money. Did Daddy lose his job?" Lola asked, beginning to panic.

"He quit," Beetelle said.

"When?" Lola asked in alarm.

"Three months ago."

"Why didn't you tell me?" Lola said accusingly.

"We didn't want to upset you," Beetelle said. "We didn't want to distract you from your work."

Lola said nothing, allowing the irony of the situation to sink in. "Daddy can get another job," she muttered.

"He might," Beetelle said. "But it won't solve our problems. Not for a long time."

Lola was too frightened to ask her mother what that meant. Beetelle started up the car, and they rode the rest of the way in silence.

Windsor Pines was an idea more than an actual town—a continuation of the strip malls and fast-food restaurants that spoked out from Atlanta like the legs of a spider. But in Windsor Pines, the shops were upscale, and the downtown strip sported Mercedes, Porsche, and Rolls-Royce dealerships. There was a Four Seasons hotel and a new town hall built of white brick and set back from the road and fronted by a wide green lawn with a bandshell. The "town" of Windsor Pines, incorporated in 1983, had fifty thousand residents and twelve golf courses, the most golf courses per capita in Georgia.

The Fabrikant manse sat on the edge of one of these golf courses in a gated community. The house was an amalgamation of styles— mostly Tudor, because Beetelle loved all things "English countryside," with a nod to the great plantation architecture in the form of tall white columns flanking the entrance. There was a three-car garage and, above it, an entertainment center that had a pool table, a giant flat-screen TV, a bar, and sectional leather couches. The large kitchen had marble countertops and opened into the great room; in addition, the house had formal living and dining rooms (hardly ever used), four bedrooms, and six bathrooms. A white gravel driveway, replenished and resurfaced each spring, made a sweeping turn to the columned entrance. As they came up the road to the house, Lola gasped. A FOR SALE sign was poked into the lawn on either side of the driveway.

"You're selling the house?" she asked, aghast.

"The bank's selling it."

"What does that mean?" Lola asked. It began to dawn on her that her mother was serious after all. Dread rose to her throat; she could barely speak.

"They take all the money," Beetelle said.

"But why?" Lola wailed.

"We'll talk about it later," Beetelle said. She popped open the trunk and wearily lifted out Lola's suitcases. She began carrying them into the house, pausing on the landing, where she appeared dwarfed by the columns, by the house, and by the enormity of her situation.

"Lola," she asked. "Are you coming?"

Sam Gooch never looked forward to Christmas. Everyone he knew went away, while he was stuck in the city with his parents. Mindy said it was the best time in New York, with everyone gone and just the tourists, who rarely ventured into their neighborhood. Sam would return to school after New Year's to find a classroom full of kids chattering about their exotic vacations. "Where'd you go, Sam?" one of them would joke. Someone else would answer, "Sam took a tour of the Empire State Building."

One year, the Gooches had gone away to Jamaica. But Sam was only three then, and he barely remembered it, although Mindy sometimes brought it up with James, making a negative reference to an afternoon he spent with a Rastafarian.

Walking back to One Fifth from Washington Square Park, where Sam had taken Skippy to the dog run (Skippy had attacked a Rottweiler, which gave Sam a perverse sort of pride), he wondered why they couldn't go away this year. After all, his father was supposedly getting money from his book—but it hadn't changed their Christmas plans. As usual, they would drive to Pennsylvania early on Christmas morning to visit his mother's parents; after a traditional Christmas dinner of roast beef and Yorkshire pudding, they would drive to Long Island to see James's father. James's family was Jewish and didn't celebrate Christmas, so they would have dinner at a Chinese restaurant.

Skippy was attached to a retractable leash; when walked, he liked to be as far away from his owner as possible. He ran into One Fifth several feet ahead of Sam; by the time Sam got into the building, Skippy had tangled his leash around Roberto's legs. "You've got to train that dog, man," Roberto said.

"He's my mother's dog," Sam reminded him.

"She thinks that dog is a child," Roberto said. "By the way, Mrs. Rice was looking for you. Something's wrong with her computer."

Annalisa Rice was on the phone when Sam knocked on her door. "I'm so sorry, Mom," she was saying. "But Paul wants to go away with these people . . ." She motioned for Sam to come in.

Every time Sam stepped into the Rices' apartment, he'd try to summon up a nonchalance at his surroundings, but he was always awed. The floor in the foyer was a sparkly white marble; the plaster walls were yellow cream and looked like frosting. The foyer was deliberately spare, though an astounding photograph hung on one wall: an image of a large dark hairy woman nursing an angelic blond baby boy. The woman's expression was both maternal and challenging, as if she were daring the viewer to deny that this was her child. Sam was mesmerized by the woman's enormous breasts, with areolas the size of tennis balls. Women were strange creatures, and out of respect for his mother and Annalisa, he pulled his eyes away. Beyond this foyer was another entry with a grand staircase, the likes of which one saw only in black-and-white movies. There were a few duplexes in the building, but they had narrow, sharply turning staircases, so anyone over the age of seventy-five always moved out. This staircase, Sam guessed, was at least six feet wide. You could have an entire party on the staircase.

"Sam?" Annalisa asked. She had a sharp, intelligent face, like that of a fox, and she was a fox, too. When she'd first moved into the building, she'd worn jeans and T-shirts, like a regular person, but now she was always dressed. Today, she was wearing a white blouse and a gray pencil skirt and velvet kitten-heeled shoes and a soft, thick cashmere cardigan that Sam, from his experience with private-school girls, surmised cost thousands of dollars. Usually, when he came up to help her with the website, she spent time talking to him, telling him about when she was a lawyer and had advocated for runaway girls, who were usually running away from abuse, and how they often ended up in jail. She'd traveled to every state to help these girls, she'd said, and sometimes it made her question human nature. There were people out there who were capable of terrible things, of abandoning their children or beating them to death. To Sam, the people she talked about must have lived in a different era, but Annalisa said it was happening every minute—somewhere in America, a girl was abused every nineteen seconds. And then sometimes she'd tell the story of meeting the president. She'd met him twice—once when she was invited to a reception at the White House, and another time when she'd spoken before a Senate committee. It sounded much more interesting to Sam than Annalisa's life now. Just last week, she told him, she'd gone to a lunch for a new handbag. She found the concept funny and said she was surprised the handbag hadn't been given its own chair and a glass of champagne.

Annalisa always made jokes about it, but Sam suspected she wasn't thrilled with this new life. "Oh, I am," she said, when he asked her about it. "I'm happy to organize a luncheon to raise money to send computers to disadvantaged children in Africa. But all the women attend in their fur coats, and after the luncheon, they all leave in their chauffeured SUVs."

"New York's always been that way," Sam volunteered helpfully. "There's no use fighting it. And there's always some other lady who'd be happy to take your place."

Today, however, Annalisa was in a rush. "Thank God you're here, Sam," she said, starting up the stairs. "I didn't know what I was going to do. We're leaving tonight," she said over her shoulder.

"Where're you going?" Sam asked politely.

"So many places it's insane. London. China. Then Aspen. The Aspen part is supposed to be the vacation, I think. Paul has a lot of business in China, and the Chinese don't celebrate Christmas, obviously. We'll be gone for three weeks."

Annalisa led him down the hall to the cheerful little room, done up in light blues and greens, that she called her office. She flipped open the top of her computer. "I can't get on the Internet," she said. "I'm supposed to have some kind of advanced wireless system that allows you to go online anywhere in the world. But it's not much use if I can't even get online in my own apartment."

Sam sat down in front of the computer. His hands flew over the keys. "That's funny," he said. "The signal is scrambled."

"What does that mean?"

"In layperson's terms, it means there's a giant computer, maybe even a satellite, that's scrambling the signal. The question is, where is the satellite system coming from?"

"But aren't there satellites everywhere?" Annalisa asked. "For GPS? And those satellite images of people's neighborhoods?"

"This one's stronger," Sam said, frowning.

"Could it be coming from upstairs? From my husband's office?"

"Why would he have a satellite system?"

Annalisa shrugged. "You know how men are. For him, it's another toy."

"A satellite is not really a toy," Sam said with adult authority. "Governments have them."

"In a large or small country?" Annalisa asked, attempting to make a joke.

"Is your husband home? We could ask him," Sam said.

"He's almost never home," Annalisa said. "He's at his office. He's planning to go from his office to the airport."

"I should be able to fix it without him," Sam said. "I'll change your settings and reboot, and you should be fine."

"Thank God," Annalisa said. She knew Paul would have been irritated if Sam had had to go into his office, but on the other hand, if he had, she simply wouldn't have told Paul. Exactly what did he have in that office, anyway, besides his fish? What if something went wrong while they were away? They had enough trouble in the building as it was—the in-the-wall air-conditioning units hadn't been approved, so Paul had had the French doors cut in half and air-conditioning units installed in the bottom portion, which was what he should have done in the first place—but Mindy Gooch still refused to talk to her. When Annalisa approached her in the lobby, Mindy would say coldly, "Enjoying the apartment, I hope," and walk away. Even the doormen, who had been friendly at first, had become somewhat aloof. Paul suspected the doormen didn't deliver their packages on time, and although she said he was being paranoid, he wasn't all wrong. There had been a contretemps over a beaded Chanel jacket worth thousands of dollars that the messenger service had sworn was delivered; it was finally discovered two days later, having been left in Schiffer Diamond's apartment by mistake. True, the bag hadn't been labeled properly, but even so, it did make Annalisa wonder if the other residents disliked them. Now she was worried about Paul's computers. What if something happened while they were halfway around the world in China?

"Sam?" she said. "Can I trust you? If I gave you my keys—to keep, just while we're away, in case something happens—could you keep it a secret? Not tell your mother or anyone? Unless there was a real emergency. My husband's a little paranoid . . ."

"I get it," Sam said. "I'll guard the keys with my life."

And moments later, he was headed downstairs with the keys to the magnificent apartment hanging heavy in the pocket of his jeans.

▼

Later, at the house in Windsor Pines, Beetelle sat at the vanity in her powder room and rubbed the last of the La Mer cream into her face. Cem, she knew, would be hiding in the entertainment center, where he now spent all his time. Ever since the foreclosure notice had come from the bank two weeks ago, Cem had taken to spending the night on the couch, falling asleep in front of the giant flat-screen TV. Lola, Beetelle imagined, was in her room, trying to digest the reality of the situation.

But how could Lola understand when Beetelle could barely comprehend it herself?

Beetelle dug out the last of the precious cream with her manicured fingernail. When had the trouble started? Six months ago? She'd known Cem wasn't happy at his company. He'd never said so specifically—Cem kept his thoughts to himself—and although she'd sensed something was wrong, she'd ignored her feelings, convincing herself instead that, thanks to the cell-phone alert system Cem had invented, they were about to become very rich. But three months ago, Cem had come home unexpectedly early from work. "Are you sick?" she'd asked. "I quit," he'd said. He had his pride, he said. A man could take only so much. "So much of what?" she cried. "Disrespect." Eventually, she got it out of him: He'd quit because his boss was claiming Cem's invention as his own. The boss claimed the company owned the patent, and Cem wouldn't get a penny. Beetelle and Cem had hired a patent lawyer from Atlanta who came highly recommended, but he was no use at all. The lawyer, Beetelle discovered, was oily—and not only because his skin glistened against his navy blue pin-striped suit and red tie. Their one-hour meeting had cost them seven hundred dollars. Then the lawyer supposedly looked over the case. "There's no evidence that Cem developed this on his own," he said over the phone. "But he did. I saw him working on it," Beetelle protested. "How?" the lawyer asked. "On his computer." "I'm afraid that doesn't give us much of a case, Mrs. Fabrikant. You can proceed, if you'd like, but it'll cost you hundreds of thousands of dollars to take this to court. And you'll probably lose." Hanging up the phone, Beetelle suspected Cem had been lying to her all along. The cell-phone alert wasn't solely his invention; it was merely something he'd worked on with other people. But why would he lie? To please her, she guessed, to make himself more important in her eyes. She was such a dynamo, perhaps he'd felt emasculated and lied to make himself look better. He made a good salary, three hundred and fifty thousand a year, but after the first week of Cem's unemployment, she realized his salary was only more smoke and mirrors: They were living paycheck to paycheck and had three mortgages on the house, the last one taken out six months ago to enable Lola to move to New York. They owed over a million dollars. They might have survived by selling the house, but the market had dropped. The house that was worth one point two million a year ago was now worth only seven hundred thousand. "So you see," the banker had said while she and Cem sat trembling before him, "you actually owe three hundred thirty-three thousand dollars. And forty-two cents," he added.

Three hundred thirty-three thousand dollars. And forty-two cents, she repeated in her head. She'd said it over and over so many times it no longer had any effect. It was just a number, unattached to real life.

New York, Beetelle thought with a pang. If only circumstances had been different. What a life she'd have now, free from the horror of penury. Lucky Lola had moved to New York with every advantage, not the way Beetelle had when she'd gotten her first job as a medical technician at Columbia Hospital, making twelve thousand dollars a year. She'd lived in a run-down two-bedroom apartment with three other girls, and she'd loved every minute. But it didn't last long. After three happy months, she'd met Cem at the old convention hall on Columbus Circle, where there was now a fancy office tower with a mall. It hadn't been fancy then. Aisle after aisle of booths constructed of plasterboard sold everything from ball bearings for heart valves to magnets that would cure anything. Back then technology was only a little more advanced than witchcraft and sorcery. And so, in between the valves made of titanium and the magnets to reverse cancer, she'd found Cem.

He'd asked her for directions to the exit, and the next thing she knew, they were going out for coffee. The afternoon stretched into the early evening, and they meandered into the bar at the Empire Hotel, where he was staying. They were full of youth and career aspirations and New York City, drinking tequila sunrises while they looked at the view of Lincoln Center. It was spring, and the fountain was going, gushing great glittery streams of water.

Afterward they had sex—the kind of sex people had in 1984 when they didn't know better. Her breasts were heavy and full, the type of breasts that sagged almost immediately but had one season of ripeness with which to attract, and what she attracted was Cem.

He was sexy then. Or he was to her untested mind. She had had no experience, and the fact that Cem was interested in her thrilled her. For the first time, she was living life—a secret, unexplored, forbidden life. The next morning, feeling free and modern, she woke up expecting never to see Cem again. He was going back to Atlanta in the afternoon. But for days afterward, he pursued her, sending flowers, calling, even writing a postcard. She tucked them away, but by then she'd met another man and fallen in love, and she stopped responding to Cem's entreaties.

The man was a doctor. For the next few weeks, she did everything to keep him interested. Made a fool of herself playing tennis. Cleaned his kitchen. Showed up at his office with a sandwich. She managed to only let him kiss her (and then go to second and third base) for six weeks. And then she gave in. The next morning, he told her he was engaged to someone else.

She was confused and, when he wouldn't take her calls, devastated.

A week later, during a routine visit to the gynecologist, she discovered she was pregnant. She should have known, but she'd confused her nausea with the giddiness that comes from being in love. At first she thought the baby was the doctor's, and she constructed scenes in her head of when and how she would inform him, after which he would realize she was the one for him after all and would marry her. They'd have to do it quickly, before anyone suspected. But when the pregnancy test came in, the gynecologist informed her that she was almost three months pregnant. Beetelle counted backward, feeling her entire life switch into reverse. It wasn't the doctor's child. It was Cem's. The doctor said she ought to have it, as she was nearly too far gone for an abortion.

Beetelle cried and then called Cem. Over the phone, she told him she was pregnant. He was ecstatic and flew to New York for the weekend; he took a hotel room at the Carlyle (setting a pattern for spending money he didn't have) and took her to romantic restaurants. He bought her a half-carat diamond ring at Tiffany's, claiming he only ever wanted her to have the best. Two months later, they were married by a justice of the peace at her parents' house in Grand Rapids. After the ceremony, they went to dinner at the country club. And then Lola was born, and Beetelle understood it had all happened for a reason.

How she loved Lola. And naturally, while Beetelle no longer harbored feelings for the doctor, there were times when, seeing Lola so beautiful and bright, a curious sensation overcame her. A tiny part of her still believed, still hoped, that somewhere a mistake had been made, and Lola actually was the child of Leonard Pierce, a famous oncologist.

Beetelle got up from the vanity and went into the bedroom, standing before the bay window that looked out over the golf course. What would become of her and Lola now? There were times in the past when she'd considered what she would do if something happened to Cem. When he was late or driving home from Florida on his yearly pilgrimage to visit his mother, the thought crossed her mind that he could be killed in an accident with a tractor trailer. She pictured herself in mourning in Windsor Pines, dressed in black with a black pillbox hat and veil, although no one wore hats or veils anymore, holding a memorial service for Cem at the big nondenominational church to which everyone in their set belonged. She would never marry again. But along with the loss was a little fantasy. She would sell the house and be free to do with her life as she pleased. She might move to Italy, like that girl who wrote *Under the Tuscan Sun*.

But that was possible only if the house was worth something. Bankruptcy was not part of the bargain, and there were moments now, terrible moments, when she wondered if she wouldn't be better off without Cem. It had crossed her mind that if she did leave, she could move to New York and live with Lola in that sweet little apartment on Eleventh Street.

But there wasn't even enough money for that. They could no longer afford the apartment, and somehow, Lola had to be told this as well.

Beetelle was startled by the sudden presence of Lola in the room. "I've been thinking things over, Mother," she said, seating herself carefully on the edge of the bed. A quick survey of the house had revealed that things were worse than she'd thought— in the refrigerator was supermarket cheese instead of gourmet; the wireless Internet service had been canceled and their cable plan reduced to basic. "I don't have to work for Philip. I could get a real job, I suppose. Maybe do something in fashion. Or I could take acting classes. Philip knows everyone—he'll know the best teacher. And I'm sure I could do it. I watched Schiffer Diamond, and it didn't look hard at all. Or I could try out for a reality show. Philip says they're shooting more and more reality in New York. And doing a reality show doesn't take any talent at all."

"Lola, darling," Beetelle said, overcome by her daughter's desire to help out, "that would all be wonderful. If only we could afford to keep you in New York."

Lola's eyes narrowed. "What do you mean?" she asked.

Beetelle shook her head. "We can't afford the apartment any-more. I've been dreading telling you this, but we've already told the management company. They're going to let us out of the lease at the end of January."

Lola gasped. "You got rid of my apartment behind my back?"

"I didn't want to upset you," Beetelle said.

"How could you do such a thing?" Lola demanded.

"Darling, please. I didn't have a choice. As it is, both Mercedes are going to be repossessed in January . . ."

"How could you let this happen, Mother?"

"I don't know," Beetelle wailed. "I trusted your father. And this is what he does to us. And now we'll all have to live in a condo someplace—where no one knows us—and I guess we'll try to start over . . ."

Lola gave a harsh laugh. "You expect me to live in a condo? With you and Daddy? No, Mother," she said firmly. "I can't do that. I won't leave New York. Not when I've made so much progress. Our only hope is for me to stay in New York."

"But where will you live?" Beetelle cried. "You can't survive on the streets."

"I'll live with Philip," Lola said. "I practically live with him anyway."

"Oh, Lola," Beetelle said. "Living with a man? Before you're married? What will people think?"

"We don't have any choice, Mother. And when Philip and I get married, no one will remember that we lived together. And Philip has loads of money now. He just got paid a million dollars to write a screenplay. And once we're married"—Lola looked over at her mother—"we'll figure something out. He probably would have asked me to marry him by now if it weren't for his aunt. She's always around, checking up on him. Thank God she's old. Maybe she'll get cancer or something and have to give up her apartment. Then you and Daddy could move in."

"Oh, darling," Beetelle said, and tried to hug her. Lola moved away. If her mother touched her, Lola knew she would fall apart herself and start crying. Now was not the time to be weak. And seeming to channel some of her mother's former legendary strength in the face of adversity, she stood up.

"Come on, Mother," she said. "Let's go to the mall. We may not have money, but that doesn't mean I can let myself go. You must have some credit left on your MasterCard."

12

Billy Litchfield was on the train to Springfield, Massachusetts, when he got the call from his sister informing him that their mother had fallen down and broken her hip and was in the hospital. She'd been carrying groceries when she slipped on a patch of ice. She would live, but her pelvis was shattered. The surgeons would put the pelvis back together with metal plates, but it would take a long time to heal, and she could be in a wheelchair for the rest of her life. She was only eighty-three; she might easily live for another ten or fifteen years. "I don't have time to take care of her," Billy's sister, Laura, wailed on the phone. Laura was a corporate lawyer and single mom, twice divorced with two children, eighteen and twelve. "And I can't afford to put her in a nursing home. Jacob's going to college next year. It's too much."

"It'll be fine," Billy said. He was taking the news more calmly than he would have expected.

"How can it be fine?" his sister said. "Once something like this happens, it's downhill all the way."

"She must have some money," Billy said.

"Why would she have money?" his sister said. "Not everyone is like your rich friends in New York."

"I'm aware of how other people live," Billy said.

"You're going to have to move back to Streatham and take care of her," his sister said warningly. "She was grocery shopping for you. She normally only shops on Thursday mornings," she added accusingly, as if the accident had been his fault. "She made a special trip for you."

"Thanks, dear," Billy said.

He hung up and looked out the window. The train was pulling in to New Haven, where the landscape was depressing and familiarly bleak. Going home made him sad and uncomfortable; he'd had neither a happy childhood nor a happy home. His father, an orthodontist who believed homosexuality was a disease and that women were second-class citizens, was despised by both Billy and his sister. When his father passed away fifteen years ago, they said it was a blessing. Nevertheless, Laura had always resented Billy, his mother's favorite. Billy knew Laura thought him frivolous and couldn't forgive their mother for allowing Billy to study useless pursuits in college, like art and music and philosophy. Billy, on the other hand, thought his sister a dreary bore. She was absolutely ordinary; he couldn't comprehend how nature could have supplied him with such a dull sibling. She was a drone—the very epitome of everything Billy feared a human life could become. She had no passions, either in her life or for her life, and therefore tended to exaggerate every tiny event out of proportion. Billy guessed his sister was making a bigger deal out of his mother's fall than was necessary.

But when he got to the hospital on the outskirts of Springfield, he found his mother was worse than he'd hoped. She was always robust, but the accident had turned her into a colorless old lady under white hospital bedding, although she'd colored and permed her hair in preparation for his Christmas visit. "Ah, Billy." She sighed. "You came."

"Of course I came, Mother. What made you think I wouldn't?"

"She's on morphine," the nurse said. "She's going to be confused for a few days, aren't you, dear?"

His mother began to cry. "I don't want to be a burden to you and your sister. Maybe they should put me to sleep."

"Don't be ridiculous, Mother," Billy said. "You're going to be fine."

When visiting hours were over, the doctor pulled him aside. The operation had gone fine, but they wouldn't know when or if his mother would be able to walk. In the meantime, she'd have to be in the wheelchair. Billy nodded and picked up his Gaultier bag, thinking how incongruous the expensive French luggage looked in this sad local hospital, then waited outside in the cold for thirty minutes for a taxi that took him the twenty miles to his mother's house. The taxi cost a hundred and thirty dollars, and Billy winced at the price. With his mother injured, he would need to start saving money. In the snow next to the driveway, he saw the imprint of his mother's body where she had fallen.

The back door was unlocked, and entering the kitchen, Billy found two bags of groceries on the counter, obviously placed there by a kind paramedic. Although he'd always considered himself a cynic, recently Billy had noticed that random acts of human kindness now caused him to become sentimental. Feeling heavy of heart, he began unpacking the groceries. In one bag was a warm container of light cream. This was what would have caused his mother's unfortunate trip to the store. Billy still insisted on using light cream in his coffee.

He arrived at the hospital the next morning at nine. His sister came shortly thereafter, accompanied by her younger child, Dominique, a scrawny girl with thin blond hair and a nose like a beak; she looked just like her father, a local carpenter who had grown marijuana in the summers and eventually gotten arrested.

Billy tried to talk to the girl, but she was either not interested or not educated. She admitted that she hated reading books and hadn't read *Harry Potter*. What did she do, then? Billy asked. She talked to her friends on the Internet. Billy raised his eyebrows at his sister, but she shrugged. "I can't keep her off it. No one can keep their kids off it, and frankly, no one has time to monitor their kids every minute. Especially me."

Billy had some feeling for the girl—after all, she was a blood relative—but was saddened by her as well. The little girl was on the border of becoming white trash, he decided, and he was struck by the irony of how hard his own parents had worked to be upper-middle-class, to make sure their children were educated, to expose them to culture (his father had played Beethoven in his office), only to produce a granddaughter who would not even read. The Dark Ages, Billy thought, were just around the corner.

He spent a long day with his mother. She was in a cast from her knee to her waist. He held her hand. "Billy," she said. "What's going to happen to me?" "You're going to be fine, Ma, you'll see." "What if I can't drive?" "We'll figure it out." "What if I have to go into a nursing home? I don't want to go to a nursing home. I'll die there." "I won't let it happen, Ma." His stomach churned with fear. If it came to that, how could he prevent it? He had no means to do otherwise.

His sister asked him to dinner at her house—nothing fancy, macaroni and cheese. Laura lived a short distance away from their mother in a large ranch house that their father had bought her after her first divorce. It was a mystery to the family why Laura, who was a lawyer, could never manage to make ends meet, but since she was a writer of legal briefs, Billy suspected she didn't make as much money as her law degree would imply. And she was a spender. Her house had wall-to-wall carpeting, a dinette set, display cases of porcelain figurines, a collection of teddy bears, four TVs, and in the living room, a modular sofa in which each piece had cupholders and retractable footrests. The thought of spending the evening in such an environment filled Billy with dread—he knew it would leave him unbearably depressed—and so he invited Laura and her daughter to their mother's house instead.

He made an herb-roasted chicken, roasted potatoes with rosemary, haricots verts, and an arugula salad. He had learned to cook from the private chefs of his wealthy friends, for he always made it a point to mix with the staff in the kitchen. His niece, Dominique, was fascinated—apparently, she'd never seen anyone cook before.

Studying the girl, Billy decided she might have potential. Her eyes were wide-set, and she had a pretty smile, although her incisors were as pointy as a dog's. "What will Dominique do when she grows up?" he asked his sister when they were in the kitchen, cleaning up after the meal.

"How should I know? She's twelve," Laura said.

"Does she have any interests? Special talents?"

"Besides pissing me off? She says she wants to be a vet when she grows up. I said the same thing when I was twelve. It's something all little girls say."

"Do you wish you were a vet now?" Billy asked.

"I wish I was married to Donald Trump and lived in Palm Beach," Laura said. She smacked herself on the forehead. "I knew I forgot something. I should have married a rich guy."

"You might think about sending Dominique to Miss Porter's in Connecticut."

"Right," Laura said. "So *she* can marry a rich guy. Of course. There's only one problem. It takes money to get money, remember? Unless one of your rich-lady friends wants to give her a scholarship."

"I have connections," Billy said. "I might be able to make it happen."

His sister turned on him. "Connections?" she said. "What planet do you live on, Billy? Mom is in the hospital, and all you can think about is sending my daughter to a private school to learn how to sip tea?"

"You might find life more tolerable if you learned to speak to people in a civilized manner," Billy responded.

"Are you saying I'm not civilized?" Laura threw a dish towel on the counter. "I'm sick of it. All you do is come back here with your snotty New York attitude and act like everyone is below you. Like you're something special. And what have you done with your life? You don't even have a job. Unless you call escorting old ladies a job." She was standing in the middle of the kitchen, straddling the slate-tiled floor like a prizefighter. "And don't you even think about going back to New York," she hissed. "You're not going to leave me here to clean up the mess. I've been taking care of Ma for the last fifteen years. I'm done. It's your turn."

They stared at each other with hatred.

"Excuse me, Laura," Billy said, pushing past her. "I'm going to retire for the evening." And he went up to his room.

It was his old room, unchanged, although their mother had turned Laura's room into a guest bedroom. He lay on the bed, a four-poster with Ralph Lauren bedding from the early eighties, when Ralph had just ventured into home furnishings. The bedding was vintage, as, Billy realized, was he. He took a Xanax to soothe his anxiety and, at random, picked out a book from the shelves encasing one window. He turned it over and looked at the title: *Death in Venice* by Thomas Mann.

This was all too apt, and he put the book aside, wishing he'd bought the tabloid magazines at the supermarket. He took an Ambien, turned off the light, and prepared for the obscurity of sleep, but it wouldn't come. Instead, the reality of his troubles grew, and he imagined them like boulders being placed, one after another, on top of his body, slowly crushing him until eventually, his chest caved into his spinal cord and he was painfully suffocated to death.

But then an idea caused him to sit up and turn on the light. He got out of bed and began pacing in front of the fireplace. He could fix his problems, his mother's problems, even his sister's problems with one simple transaction. He could sell the Cross of Bloody Mary. It might easily fetch three million dollars or more. He could pay for private nurses to care for his mother, send Dominique to private school, even buy his apartment. If he owned his apartment outright, he could live out his days on lower Fifth Avenue in a pleasant cocoon of civilized behavior. But in the next moment, reality intruded. He could never sell the cross. It was a purloined antiquity, as dangerous as a loaded gun. There were people who dealt with such items, smuggling them around the world to the highest bidders, who would salivate at the possibility of getting their hands on it. But selling antiquities was an international crime, and people did get caught. Just last month, a smuggler had been arrested in Rome and sentenced to jail for fifty years.

The next morning, his mother was worse; an infection had set in. She might be in the hospital another week or more. Her insurance would run out, and she'd have to go on Medicaid, which meant she'd be moved to a less expensive hospital in the center of Springfield. "I'm sorry, Billy," she said, squeezing his hand. She was exhausted, and her eyes were full of fear. "Who would have thought our lives would come to this?" she whispered.

When she fell asleep, Billy went out for some fresh air. He bought a pack of cigarettes at a newsstand, although he'd given up smoking years ago, when hostesses stopped allowing it in their apartments. He sat down on a bench. It was another cold, gray New England day, threatening snow that would not come. He inhaled deeply. The sharp smoke hit his lungs, and immediately he felt dizzy and a little nauseated. He took a breath and kept smoking.

Over the next few days, while his mother remained in the hospital, Billy began smoking again to ease his stress. When he smoked, he had the same conversation with himself: No matter what he did, he was ruined. If he didn't sell the cross—out of misguided morality—his mother would suffer needlessly and probably die. If he did sell the cross, he would suffer his conscience. Even if he didn't get caught, he would feel like a criminal among the rarefied set in which he moved. He reminded himself that his kind of morality was old-fashioned, though. Nobody cared anymore.

On the third day, a nurse walked by. "Merry Christmas," she said.

"Merry Christmas," he replied, remembering that it was Christmas morning. He ground out his cigarette with the tip of his Prada loafer. He would sell the cross. He didn't have a choice. And if he could find the right private buyer, he just might get away with it.

Mindy loved the holidays in New York City. Every year, she put up a tree purchased from the deli around the corner—everything was so convenient in Manhattan!—bought four new ornaments at the local gift shop, wrapped the base of the tree in an old white sheet, and set up a crèche nestled into the folds. There sat Mary and

Joseph, five sheep, the baby Jesus in the manger, the three wise men, and right above the scene, on the lowest branch of the tree, the carefully hung Star of David. And every year, James looked at the crèche and shook his head.

Then there were the traditional family outings. They had to go skating at the Wollman rink ("I'm going to hug you, Sammy," Mindy said, chasing after him on her skates and embarrassing the hell out of him while James clung to the boards on the side) and to *The Nutcracker* at the New York City Ballet. Sam had been trying to get out of the performance for the past three years, claiming he was too old, but Mindy wouldn't hear of it. When the tree grew onstage and the scenery changed to a fantasy woodland glade complete with snow, she even cried. Sam slunk down in his seat, but there was nothing he could do about it. After the performance, they went to Shun Lee West, where Mindy insisted on behaving like a tourist by admiring the sixty-foot-long gold papier-mâché dragon that had been transported to Manhattan in pieces in the late seventies. She ordered a dish called "Ants Climb on Tree," which was only beef with broccoli. But—she reminded James and Sam—she couldn't resist the name.

This year was like every other year, with one small difference: Sam had a secret.

Through a chance remark by Roberto, the doorman, Mindy discovered that Sam had gone up to the Rices' apartment just before Christmas to help Annalisa with her computer. Normally, Sam discussed such incidents with her, but Christmas came and went without a peep from Sam. This was odd, and Mindy discussed it with James. "Why would he lie?" she asked.

"He hasn't lied. He's omitted to tell you. There's a difference," James said.

During the meal at Shun Lee West, Mindy decided the omission had gone on long enough. "Sam?" she said. "Is there something you want to tell me?"

Sam looked briefly alarmed. He immediately guessed what Mindy was getting at, and cursed himself for not having told

Roberto to keep it to himself. Everyone in One Fifth was so damn nosy. Why couldn't they all mind their own business? "Nope," Sam said, stuffing his mouth with a shrimp dumpling.

"Roberto said you went up to the Rices' apartment before Christmas."

"Oh, that," Sam said. "Yeah. That lady, what's-her-name, couldn't turn on her computer."

"Please don't call women 'that lady,'" Mindy said. "Always call women 'women.'"

"Okay," Sam said. "That *woman* was having *trouble* with her Internet *connection*."

Mindy ignored the sarcasm. "Is that all?"

"Yes," Sam said. "I swear."

"I want to hear all about it," Mindy said. "If there's anything new or different in that apartment, I need to know."

"There's nothing different." Sam shrugged. "It's just an apartment."

Sam hadn't told Mindy about his visit for one simple reason: He still hadn't learned how to lie effectively to his mother. Eventually, she would get it out of him that Annalisa Rice had given him the keys, and then Mindy would insist he turn the keys over to her, and she would sneak into the apartment.

That was exactly what happened. "Sam?" Mindy said slyly when they were back home. "What are you hiding?"

"Nothing," Sam said.

"Why are you acting so strangely?" Mindy said. "You saw something. And Annalisa Rice told you not to tell me. What is it?"

"Nothing. She just gave me her keys, is all," he blurted out.

"Give them to me," Mindy demanded.

"No," Sam said. "She gave the keys to me, not you. If she'd wanted you to have the keys, she would have given them to *you*."

Mindy put the issue aside until the next morning, when she started in on him again. "As the head of the board, it's my duty to make sure there isn't anything untoward going on in that apartment."

"Untoward?" James said, looking up from his cereal. "The only untoward element in this building is you."

"Besides, they have a housekeeper. She's probably in the apartment," Sam said.

"She's away. Went back to Ireland for the holidays," Mindy said. "Roberto told me."

"It's a good thing Roberto doesn't work for national security," James remarked.

"Are you going to help me, James?" Mindy said.

"No, I'm not. I refuse to engage in illegal activities. Sam," James said, "give your mother the keys. There won't be any peace in this house until you do."

Sam reluctantly turned over the keys. At which point Mindy immediately boarded the elevator for the penthouse apartment.

Riding up, she recalled with a pang of envy how she'd never been one of the anointed few who'd been invited to Mrs. Houghton's apartment for tea, or even to her annual Christmas party. Despite Mindy's position in the building, Mrs. Houghton had largely ignored her—although, to be fair, when the Gooches moved in, Mrs. Houghton was nearly ninety and mostly housebound. But every now and then, she would descend from above like an angel (or perhaps like one of the Greek goddesses) to walk amongst regular humans. She would ride down in the elevator in her sable wrap, diamonds and pearls slung around her neck—it being rumored that she always wore real jewelry, so confident was she in her fame and reputation as to never worry about being mugged—standing erect on her rickety old legs like a determined general. The nurse or housekeeper would call down ahead to alert the doormen that Her Majesty was "coming down," and when the elevator doors opened in the lobby, Mrs. Houghton would be greeted by at least two doormen, a handyman, and the super. "Can I help you, Mrs. Houghton?" the super would ask, offering his arm to walk her out to her ancient Cadillac limousine. On the occasions of Mrs. Houghton's coming down, Mindy would do her best to be in the vicinity, and even though she refused on principle to bow or scrape to anyone, she found herself doing just that with Mrs. Houghton.

"Mrs. Houghton?" she'd say meekly, shrinking her shoulders into a sort of bow. "I'm Mindy Gooch. I live here? I'm on the board?" And even though Mindy could tell Mrs. Houghton had no idea who she was, she never let on. "Yes, dear!" she'd exclaim, as if Mindy were a long-lost relative. She'd touch Mindy on the wrist. "How are you?" But the brief exchange never evolved into a conversation. And before Mindy could think of what to say next, Mrs. Houghton had moved on to one of the doormen.

And now, instead of the gracious Mrs. Houghton in the building, they had the despicable Paul Rice. Mindy had admitted him to the building; therefore, she reasoned, she had every right to sneak into his apartment. Paul Rice was probably engaging in illegal and nefarious activities. It was her duty to protect the other residents.

She had a hard time with the keys, which were electronic, in itself a possible violation of a building rule. When the door finally opened, she nearly fell into the foyer. Mindy wasn't into art ("You can't be into everything in this city, otherwise you have no time for accomplishments" was something she'd written recently in her blog), and so she barely noticed the lesbian photograph. In the living room, sparsely furnished, either on purpose or because they were still decorating, a freestanding mobile with papier-mâché renderings of cars blocked the view of the fireplace. Kids' stuff, Mindy thought with disdain, and went into the kitchen. Here again she was disappointed. It was just another high-end kitchen with marble countertops and restaurant-quality appliances. She peeked into the maid's room. Another bland pro-forma room with a single bed and a flat-screen TV. The bed had a profusion of pillows and a down comforter, and lifting up the corner, Mindy saw the sheets were from Pratesi. This was slightly irritating. These people really know how to waste money, she thought. She and James had had the same sheets for ten years, purchased on discount at Bloomingdale's. Mindy went upstairs. She passed two bedrooms—empty—and a bathroom. She continued down the hall and went into Annalisa's office. On top of a bookcase were several framed photographs, possibly the only personal items in the apartment. There was a large, schmaltzy photograph of Annalisa and Paul on their wedding day. Paul was wearing a tux and was leaner than he was now. Annalisa wore a small beaded tiara from which extended a lace veil. They looked happy, but who didn't on their wedding day? There were also some snapshots of Paul and Annalisa at a birthday party wearing paper cones on their heads; a photograph of Paul and Annalisa with what appeared to be her parents in front of a town house in Georgetown; Paul in a kayak; Annalisa on the Spanish Steps in Rome. All so disappointingly normal, Mindy thought.

She went into the bedroom. This room had a fireplace and built-in bookshelves. She admired the grand canopied bed, but the sheets made her shudder—gold! Mindy thought, How gauche, as she moved on to the bureau, on top of which were several bottles of perfume on a silver tray. Mindy picked up a small bottle of Joy. It was the actual perfume and not the eau de cologne, which James and Sam had given to her for Mother's Day several years ago and which she never wore because she never remembered about girly things like perfume. But in here, in another woman's bedroom, Mindy carefully pried open the stopper and put a dab behind each ear. She sat on the edge of the bed, looking around the room. What would it be like to be Annalisa Rice, to never have to worry about money? But those fantasies always came with a price, in this case the price being Paul Rice. How could a woman live with a man like that? At least Mindy could boss James around. James wasn't perfect, but she could always be herself around James, and that had to be worth more in life than Pratesi sheets.

Mindy got up and, seeing the closet door was slightly ajar, pushed it open. Inside was a huge walk-in closet, at least three times the size of Sam's bedroom. Along one wall were shelves stacked with shoe boxes; another shelf held handbags, scarves, and belts; and along the other wall was a rack of clothes, some still sporting their price tags. She fingered a leather jacket that cost eighty-eight hundred dollars and felt angry. This was but a tiny example of how the rich really lived. There was no longer any chance of keeping up with the Joneses, not when the Joneses could spend eight thousand dollars on a leather jacket they would never wear.

She was about to leave the closet when she spied a small cluster of worn, misshapen pantsuits on wire hangers. Aha, Mindy thought, these were Annalisa's clothes from her former life. But why had she kept them? To remind herself from whence she'd come? Or was it the opposite: She had kept them thinking someday she might have to go back?

Mindy threw up her hands, reassuring herself that these rich people were nothing but dull. She and James were a hundred times more interesting, even with a hundred times less money. She left the bedroom and went upstairs to the ballroom. At the top of the steps was another marble foyer and two tall paneled-wood doors. The doors were locked, but Mindy guessed she had the key. She pushed open the doors and paused. Inside, the light was dim, as if the room were heavily curtained, yet Mindy saw no curtains. She stepped carefully into the room and looked around.

So this was what had happened to Mrs. Houghton's legendary ballroom. She would be turning over in her grave. Probably all that remained of the original room were the fireplace and the ceiling. The famous paneled walls, painted with scenes from the Greek myths, were gone, covered over by plain white plasterboard. In the center of the room was the enormous aquarium, but it was empty. Above the fireplace was a black metal frame. Mindy moved in closer and stood on her toes to examine it. Inside the rim were pinhead-sized colored lights. It was a 3-D projection screen, Mindy decided, like something out of a futuristic spy movie. She wondered if it actually worked or was just for show. There was a closet on either side of the fireplace, but these were locked, and Mindy did not have the key. She put her ear up to the wood and heard a tiny, high-pitched humming sound. Dammit, she thought. There was nothing here at all. Sam was right, it was just an apartment.

In annoyance, she sat down at Paul's desk. The swivel chair was upholstered in chocolate suede, very modern and sleek, like the desk, which was a long slab of polished wood. There was practically nothing on the desk, save for a small pad of paper from a hotel, a sterling-silver container holding six number-two pencils with the erasers neatly pointing into the air, and a silver framed photograph of an Irish wolfhound. Probably Paul's childhood pet. No doubt Paul's Rosebud, Mindy thought with disgust.

She replaced the frame and picked up the pad of paper. It was from the Four Seasons hotel in Bangkok. The top page was blank, but the next two were filled with mathematical equations written in pencil of which she could not make heads or tails. On the fourth page, she came across something written in English, in minuscule box letters. Holding it up to her face, she read: WE ARE THE NEW RICH.

And you're an asshole, Mindy thought. She pocketed the pad of paper, thinking that when Paul Rice came home from vacation and found his pad missing, he'd know someone had been in his apartment, and that would be her little message to him.

Her own apartment felt cluttered and messy in comparison to the clean restraint of the Rice abode. The Rices' apartment was like a hotel room, she decided as she sat down at her desk to blog. "Today I discovered another one of the joys of not having it all: not *wanting* it all," she wrote with relish.

❖

Don't think, do, Philip reminded himself. This was the only possible philosophy when it came to women. If one thought about them too much, if one really considered a relationship and what it meant, one usually got into trouble. Someone (usually the woman) was disappointed, although (usually) through no fault of the man. A man couldn't help it if he loved women and loved sex. And so this morning, he had finally capitulated and asked Lola to move in with him.

He immediately realized he might have made a mistake. But the words were out, and there was no taking them back. Lola jumped up and put her arms around him. "There, there," he said, patting her back. "We're not getting married. We're only living together. It's an experiment."

"We're going to be so happy," she said. And then she went to her suitcase to dig out her bikini. Wrapped in a tiny sarong tied fetchingly around her hips, she'd practically skipped with him down to the beach.

And now she was frolicking in the waves like a puppy, looking back at him over her shoulder and gesturing for him to join her. "It's too early," he called from his lounge chair.

"It's eleven o'clock, silly," she said, splashing water at him.

"I don't like to get wet until after lunch," he replied.

"You shower in the morning, don't you?" she said playfully.

"That's not the point." He smiled indulgently and went back to reading *The Economist*.

Lola was so *literal*, he thought. But did it really matter? Don't think, he reminded himself. She was moving in with him, and if it worked, great, and if not, they'd move on. It wasn't such a big deal. He flipped the pages of the magazine—Time Warner was breaking up, he saw—and then put it down in the sand. He closed his eyes. He needed a vacation. With Lola sorted out now, perhaps he could finally rest.

The prospect had appeared unlikely when he'd met Lola at the airport in Barbados two days ago. Amid the bustle of holiday travelers in gaudy resort wear, she was sitting forlornly on her suitcase—a Louis Vuitton rollerboard—her hair fallen across a pair of large white-framed sunglasses. As he came up beside her, she stood and removed her sunglasses. Her eyes were puffy. "I shouldn't have come," she said. "I didn't know what to do. I wanted to call you, but I didn't want to ruin your Christmas. And I didn't want to disappoint you. There was nothing I could do, anyway. It's all so depressing."

"Did someone die?" he asked.

"I wish," she said. "My parents are bankrupt. And now I have to leave New York."

Philip didn't understand how her parents could have lost all their money. Didn't people have savings? His impression of Fabrikant mère and père was that, while superficially silly, they were simple, practical people who would never allow themselves to be involved in any kind of scandal. Especially Beetelle. The woman was too voluble, too impressed with her narrow circle of life, but also far too judgmental to get into a position in which she might be unfavorably judged herself. But Lola insisted it was true. She would have to leave New York; she didn't know where she would go, but not with her parents. Worst of all, she wouldn't be able to continue to work for him.

He understood immediately what she was angling for. With a word, he could solve all her problems. Taking care of Lola wouldn't be a burden financially, as he had plenty of money and no children. But was it the right thing to do? His instincts told him no. She wasn't his responsibility; if she moved in with him, she would be.

When they arrived at the Cotton House hotel in Mustique, they immediately made love, but just as he was about to come, she started crying silently, turning her head away as if she didn't want him to see. "What's wrong?" he said. Her legs were over his shoulders.

"Nothing," she whimpered.

"Something's wrong," he said. "Am I hurting you?"

"No."

"I'm about to come," he said.

"This might be one of the last times we make love. It makes me sad," she said.

His hard-on dissipated, and he lay down next to her.

"I'm sorry," she said, stroking his face.

"We've got a whole week to make love," he said.

"I know." She sighed and got off the bed and went to the mirror and distractedly began brushing her long hair over her naked breasts, wistfully looking at herself, and him, in the background. "But after this week, we might never see each other again."

"Oh, Lola," he said. "That kind of thing only happens in movies. Or Nicholas Sparks's books."

"Why do you always make a joke when I'm being serious?" she asked. "Obviously, you don't care if I stay in New York or not."

"That isn't true," he said.

Thinking it would make her happy, he took her to Basil's Bar, famous for being one of Mick Jagger's favorite haunts. Mick Jagger was even there, but Lola acted as if she didn't notice or care, drinking her rum punch through a straw and staring determinedly out at the harbor, where several yachts were anchored. She answered his questions in monosyllables, and finally, he got up and talked to Mick and got him to come over and meet Lola, but she only looked up at him with big, sad eyes and limply held out her hand as if Philip were secretly abusing her.

"You met Mick Jagger," Philip said after Mick walked away. "Aren't you excited?"

"I guess." She shrugged. "But what difference does it make? It's not like he can help me."

They went back to the Cotton House. She took a walk on the beach alone, saying she needed to think. He tried to take a nap. The bed was surrounded by a canopy of mosquito netting, but he couldn't manage to get it closed properly, and after being bitten three times, he gave up, went into the bar, and had a few more drinks. At dinner, Lola ordered a three-pound lobster and picked at it. When the waiter saw the uneaten lobster and came over to ask if anything was wrong, Lola began to cry silently.

The next day wasn't much better. They went to the beach, where Lola alternately moped on her towel and tried to make him jealous by flirting with two young Englishmen. Philip realized he would either have to give in or let her go. Why did women always have to force the issue?

In the afternoon, while he was having a massage, she said she was going to take a nap. When he got back to their bungalow, she wasn't there. He panicked. What if he'd underestimated her and she had done something after all? He tried calling her on her cell phone but found she'd left it in the room, along with her purse. This was more troubling, and he went to the main house and found a porter who drove him around the property in a golf cart, looking for her. They searched for an hour; Lola, it seemed, had mysteriously disappeared. The porter reassured him that she couldn't have gone far—they were on an island, after all. But this only made Philip more nervous, bringing to mind the American girl who'd disappeared on a small Caribbean island two years before. Perhaps she'd gone shopping, the porter suggested. Philip took a taxi to the port, searching the bar and the row of tiny shops. He returned to the Cotton House, defeated. What was he supposed to do now? Call her parents and say, "I heard you lost all your money, and I'm sorry about it, but you just lost your daughter as well"? He called her cell phone again, for the hell of it, hoping she'd come back to the room while he was gone, but it only rang and rang in her purse. He hung up, unable to tolerate the abandoned electronic bleat.

Finally, at six P.M., she came into the bungalow. Her eyes were sad, but her skin was glowing, as if she'd been swimming. "Ah, Philip," she said dully. "You're back."

"Of course I'm back," he said. "Where were you? I've been searching the island for the past three hours."

She momentarily brightened at this information but then went back to being depressed. "I figured you probably wanted some time away from me."

"What are you talking about?" he said. "I went to get a massage."

"I know. But I've been such a downer. I don't want to ruin your vacation as well."

"Where were you?" Philip said.

"In a cave."

"A cave?" he exclaimed.

"I found a little cave. In the rocks down by the water."

"You've been in a cave for the past three hours?" he repeated.

She nodded. "I needed a place to think. And I realized, no matter what happens, I love you. I always will. I can't help myself."

Philip felt protective. She was so young. And innocent. He could shape her. What was wrong with him? He pulled her to him. She made love vigorously, sucking his cock while teasing his asshole with her finger. He exploded, gasping with pleasure. How could he give this up?

For some reason, he couldn't bring himself to ask her to move in with him that night. But during dinner, Lola was nearly back to her old self, texting through dinner and flirting with the waiter and rubbing Philip's foot with her toe. She didn't bring up their relationship, her disappearance that afternoon, or her parents' financial woes, and neither did he.

But the next morning, when he woke up, he found her packing. "What are you doing?" he said.

"Oh, Philip." She sighed. "One of the things I realized in the cave is that I love you too much to go on like this. If we're not going to be together, there's no point in falling more in love with you and being hurt worse in the end. So I'm going to go. My mother needs me, and I'm not sure you do."

She was right, he realized. He couldn't go on like this, either. She bent over to rifle through her suitcase and he remembered the sex they'd had the night before. "Lola," he said. "You don't have to go."

"Oh, but I do, Philip," she said, not looking up.

"I mean"—he hesitated—"you can move in with me. If you want to," he added, as if it weren't his decision.

Now, on the beach, Philip leaned back in his lounge chair, folding his arms under his head. Of course she'd said yes. She loved him.

His reverie was broken by the chirrup of his cell phone. It was a 212 number, probably Enid calling him to wish him a happy New Year. He felt a momentary dismay. He would have to tell Enid that Lola was moving in. Enid wouldn't like it.

"Hello?"

The caller was a welcome surprise. "Schoolboy," Schiffer exclaimed. "How are you? What are you doing?"

"What are you doing?" he asked, sitting up. "I thought you were in Saint Barths."

"Couldn't do it," she said. "I thought about it and changed my mind. Why pursue a relationship with a man I'm not in love with? I don't need the guy, do I?"

"I don't know," Philip said. "I thought . . ."

She laughed. "You didn't think I was serious about Brumminger?"

"Why not?" Philip said. "Everyone says he's a great guy."

"Get real, Oakland," she said. Changing the subject, she asked, "Where are you, anyway? If you're around, I thought maybe we could get together with Enid. I've been neglecting her."

Philip swallowed. "I can't," he whispered.

"Why?" she said. "Where are you? I can hardly hear you. Speak up, schoolboy, if you want to be heard."

"I'm in Mustique," he said.

"What?"

"Mustique," he shouted.

"What the hell are you doing there?"

He felt his shoulders sag. "I'm with Lola."

"Ahhhhh," she said, getting it.

"I thought . . . you and Brumminger . . . Anyway, I've asked her to move in with me."

"That's great, Oakland," she said, not missing a beat. "It's about time you settled down."

"I'm not settling down. I just—"

"I get it, schoolboy," she said. "It's not a big deal. I was only calling you to see if you wanted to have a drink. We'll get together when you get back."

She hung up. Philip looked at his phone and shook his head. He would never understand women. He put the phone away and looked for Lola. She was still splashing around in the water, but in the European tradition, she had taken her top off. Everyone on the beach was staring while Lola bounced around, pretending to be oblivious to the attention. From the other side of the short beach, two white-haired old men were making a beeline for her. "Come on, girly," one of the men shouted in an English accent. "Let's have some fun."

"Lola!" Philip shouted sharply. He was about to tell her to put her top on, then realized how old it would make him sound—like her father. Instead, he smiled and stood up, making as if to join her in the water. He folded his sunglasses and placed them carefully on the table under the umbrella. He was, he thought, looking across the sand at Lola, either the luckiest man in the world or the world's biggest fool.

Act
Three

13

"Listen to this," Mindy said, coming into the bedroom. "'Is sex *really* necessary?'"

"Huh?" James said, looking up from his sock drawer.

"'Is sex really necessary?'" Mindy repeated, reading from the printout of her blog. "'We take the importance of sex as a given. Popular culture tells us it's as essential to survival as eating or breathing. But if you really think about it, after a certain age, sex isn't necessary at all . . .'"

James found two socks that matched and held them up. The only thing that wasn't necessary, he thought, was Mindy's blog.

"'Once you're past the age of reproduction, why bother?'" she continued reading. "'Every day, on my way to my office, I pass at least five billboards advertising sex in the form of lacy lingerie . . .'"

Pulling on the socks, James imagined how Lola Fabrikant would look in lacy lingerie. "'As if,'" Mindy continued, "'lacy lingerie is the answer to our dissatisfactions with life.'" It might not be, James thought, but it couldn't hurt. "'I say,'" Mindy went on, "'rip down the billboards. Burn the Victoria's Secret shops. Think about how much we could accomplish as women if we didn't have to worry about sex.'" She paused triumphantly and looked at James. "What do you think?" she asked.

"Please don't write about me again," James said.

"I'm not writing about you," Mindy said. "Did you hear your name mentioned?"

"Not yet, but I'm sure it will be."

"As a matter of fact, you're not in this particular blog."

"Any chance we can keep it that way in the future?"

"No," Mindy said. "I'm married to you, and you're my husband. The blog is about my life. Am I supposed to pretend you don't exist?"

"Yes," James said. It was a rhetorical answer, however. For reasons unfathomable to him, Mindy's blog had become more and more popular—so popular, in fact, that she'd even had a meeting with a producer from *The View*, who was considering featuring Mindy on a regular basis.

Since then there had been no stopping her. Never mind that he had a book coming out, that he'd just landed a million-dollar advance, that he was finally about to become a success. It was still all about Mindy.

"Couldn't you at least change my name?" he asked.

"How can I do that?" she said. "It's too late. Everyone knows you're my husband. Besides, we're both writers. We understand how it works. Nothing in our lives is off-limits."

Except, James thought, for their sex life. And that was only because they didn't have one. "Shouldn't you be getting ready for dinner?" he said.

"I am ready," Mindy said, indicating her woolly gray slacks and turtleneck sweater. "It's only dinner in the neighborhood. At Knickerbocker. It's ten degrees out. And I'm not going to dress up for some twenty-two-year-old chippy."

"You don't know that Lola Fabrikant is a chippy."

"That is such a typical male remark," Mindy said. "Neither you nor Philip Oakland can see the truth. Because you're both thinking with your little heads."

"I'm not," James said innocently.

"Is that so?" Mindy said. "In that case, why are you wearing a tie?"

"I always wear ties."

"You never wear ties."

"Maybe it's a new me," James said. He shrugged, trying to make light of it.

Luckily, Mindy didn't seem too concerned. "If you wear a tie with that V-neck sweater, you look like a dork," she said.

James took off the sweater. Then he gave up and removed the tie.

"Why are we having this dinner again?" she asked for the fourth or fifth time that day.

"Oakland invited us. Remember? We've been living in the same building for ten years, and we've never gotten together. I thought it would be nice."

"You like Oakland now," Mindy said skeptically.

"He's okay."

"I thought you hated him. Because he never remembered who you were."

Marriage, James thought. It really was a ball and chain, keeping you forever tethered to the past. "I never said that," he said.

"You did," Mindy said. "You said it all the time."

James went into the bathroom to try to get away from Mindy and her questions. Mindy was right—he had lied to her about the circumstances of the dinner. Philip hadn't asked them to dinner at all; indeed, for the first two weeks of January, he seemed to be trying to avoid the possibility by rushing past James when they passed in the lobby. But James had been insistent, and finally, Philip had to give in. James couldn't stand Philip, but he could stand Lola. Ever since he'd met her in Paul Smith with Philip, James had nursed an irrational belief that she might be interested in him.

Reminding himself that in a few minutes, he'd be seeing the lovely Lola Fabrikant in the flesh, James took off his glasses and leaned in to the mirror. His eyes had a naked quality, as if they belonged to one of Plato's cave dwellers who had yet to see the light. In between his eyes were two deep furrows, where the seeds of his life's discontent had been planted so often they'd become permanent. He tugged on the skin, erasing the evidence of his unhappiness. He went to the bathroom door. "What's that stuff?" he asked Mindy.

"What stuff?" Mindy said. She had taken off the slacks and was pulling on a pair of heavy black tights.

"That stuff that socialites use. To get rid of wrinkles."

"Botox?" Mindy said. "What about it?"

"I was thinking I might get some." On Mindy's look of astonishment, he added: "Might be good for the book tour. Couldn't hurt to look younger. Isn't that what everyone says?"

❦

Lola hated the Knickerbocker restaurant, which was filled with old people and Village locals—a motley crew, she thought, and not at all glamorous, with their pilled sweaters and reading glasses. If this turned out to be her life with Philip, she would kill herself. She consoled herself with the fact that they were having dinner with James Gooch, who had a book coming out that everyone was supposedly talking about, although Philip claimed he couldn't understand why. James Gooch was a second-rate writer, he said. Even if he was, Lola still didn't understand why Philip didn't like James. James was sweet, she decided, and easily manipulated. He kept glancing over at her, catching her eye, and then looking away.

His wife, Mindy Gooch, was another story. Every time Mindy spoke, Lola felt her hackles rising. Mindy couldn't be bothered to disguise the fact that she was deliberately behaving as if Lola were not sitting in the same booth right next to her. Mindy wouldn't even turn her head to look at her, instead focusing all her attention on Philip. Not that Lola wanted to talk to Mindy anyway. Mindy was a little scary, with her eighties bob and her pointy nose and pale skin, and most mysterious of all, she acted as though she were pretty. It crossed Lola's mind that perhaps a million years ago, when Mindy was eighteen, she was attractive. If so, her looks had faded quickly. Lola believed that any girl could be pretty at eighteen, but the real test of beauty came with age. Were you still pretty at twenty-two? Thirty? Even forty? This reminded her of Schiffer Diamond and how Philip claimed she was still a great beauty at forty-five. Lola had disagreed on principle. Philip claimed she was jealous. She denied this, insisting it was the reverse—other women were jealous of her. Philip didn't buy it, and eventually, she'd had to concede that Schiffer Diamond was beautiful "for her age."

With Mindy Gooch, there was no possibility of jealousy. Lola only wanted to stab her with a fork. "I'd like my steak well done," Mindy was saying to the waiter. "With steamed vegetables. Steamed, not sautéed. If I see butter, I'll send it back."

"Of course, ma'am," the waiter said.

If I ever turn out like Mindy Gooch, I will kill myself, Lola thought.

Apparently, Mindy was like this all the time, because Philip and James were ignoring this exchange, caught up in their own one-upmanship. "What is the function of the artist in today's society?" James was asking. "Sometimes I wonder if he really has a point anymore."

"He?" Mindy interjected. "What about she?"

"He used to reflect man," James continued. "The artist held up a mirror to society. He could show us the truth or inspire."

"If it's about reflecting society, we don't need artists anymore," Philip countered. "We have reality TV for that. And reality TV does it better."

"Has anyone ever seen *My Super Sweet 16*?" Lola asked. "It's really, really good."

"I have," James said.

"And what about *The Hills*?" Lola asked. "How great is that?"

"What the hell is *The Hills*?" Mindy grumbled. James caught Lola's eye and smiled.

After the dinner, James found himself on the sidewalk outside the restaurant, alone with Lola. Mindy was in the bathroom, and Philip had run into some people he knew. Lola was buttoning her coat. James looked up and down the street, trying not to stare at her. "You must be cold," he said.

"I don't get cold," she said.

"Really? My wife is always cold."

"That's too bad," Lola said, not interested in discussing Mindy. "When does your book come out?"

"In six weeks. Exactly," James said.

"You must be so excited. I can't wait to read it."

"Really?" James said in surprise, thinking about how interesting Lola was. Mindy was completely wrong. Lola wasn't a little chippy at all. She was smart. "I could get you an advance copy," he said.

"Sure," she said with what James perceived as genuine enthusiasm.

"I can bring it upstairs. Tomorrow. Will you be home?"

"Come by at ten," Lola said. "That's when Philip goes to the gym. I'm always so bored in the mornings."

"Ten o'clock," James said. "Sure."

She took a step closer. James saw that she was shivering. "Are you sure you're not cold?" he asked.

She shrugged. "Maybe a little."

"Take my scarf." He unwound the striped woolen scarf he'd purchased from a street vendor. Glancing into the restaurant and seeing neither Mindy nor Philip, he tenderly placed the scarf around Lola's neck. "That's better," he said. "You can give it back to me tomorrow."

"I may not give it back at all," she said, looking up at him. "It's not every day a girl gets a scarf from a famous author."

"There you are," Mindy said, coming out the door with Philip behind her.

"Anyone want a nightcap?" James asked.

"I'm beat," Mindy said. "It's only Tuesday, and I've got a long week ahead of me."

"Might be fun," James said to Philip.

"I'm done, too," Philip said. He took Lola's arm. "Some other time, maybe."

"Sure," James said. He felt crushed.

Lola and Philip strolled home a few feet ahead of him and Mindy. Lola walked with youthful energy, tugging on Philip's arm. Every now and then, she'd look up at Philip and laugh. James wished he knew what was entertaining her. He longed to stroll down the sidewalk with a girl, having fun. Instead, he had Mindy next to him. She was, he knew, freezing, refusing to wear a hat because it messed up her hair, walking silently with her shoulders hunched and her arms crossed against the cold. When they reached the lobby of One Fifth, Philip and Lola went right up in the elevator with vague murmurings of doing dinner sometime again in the future. Mindy went into the bedroom and changed into flannel pajamas. James thought more about Lola and how he was going to see her the next day.

"Damn," Mindy said. "I forgot about Skippy."

"Don't worry," James said. "I'll walk him."

He took the dog into the cobblestone street of the Washington Mews next to the building. While Skippy did his business, James stared up at the top of the building, as if he might catch a glimpse of Lola hundreds of feet above his head. All he saw, however, was the imposing facade of gray stone, and when he returned to the apartment, Mindy was in bed, reading *The New Yorker*. She lowered the magazine when he came in. "What was that business, anyway?" she asked.

"What business?" he said, taking off his shoes and socks.

"About watching *My Super Sweet 16*." Mindy turned off her light. "Sometimes I really do not get you. At all."

James didn't feel tired, so he left the room and went into his office. He sat at his desk, his feet bare, looking out the small window that framed the tiny courtyard. How many hours had he spent at this desk, looking out this window, and laboring on his book one word at a time? And for what? A lifetime of seconds wasted in front of his computer, endeavoring to re-create life when life was all around him.

Something's got to change, he thought, remembering Lola.

He got into bed and lay stiffly next to his wife. "Mindy?" he said.

"Mmmm?" she asked sleepily.

"I do need sex," he said. "By the way."

"Fine, James," she said into her pillow. "But you're not getting it from me. Not tonight."

Mindy fell asleep. James lay awake. Several pernicious sleepless seconds ticked by, then minutes and probably hours. James got up and went into Mindy's bathroom. He rarely ventured there; if Mindy caught him in her bathroom, she would demand to know what he was "doing in there." He'd better not be relieving himself, she would warn.

This time he did relieve himself, urinating carefully into the bowl without lifting the toilet seat. Searching for aspirin, he opened Mindy's medicine cabinet. Like everything else in their lives, it hadn't been cleaned out in years. There were three nearly empty tubes of toothpaste, a greasy bottle of baby oil, makeup in smudged containers, and a dozen bottles of prescription pills, including three bottles of the antibiotic Cipro dated October 2001—which Mindy had obviously hoarded for the family in case of an attack after 9/11—along with a bottle of malaria pills and antihistamines (for bites and rashes, the label read), and a container of sleeping pills, on which DANGER OF OVERDOSE was typed. Here was Mindy, he thought, prepared for any emergency, including the necessity of death. But not sex. He shook his head, then took one of the pills.

Back in his bed, James immediately fell into a brilliant Technicolor dream-filled sleep. He flew over the earth. He visited strange lands where everyone lived on boats. He swam across a warm salty sea. Then he had sex with a movie star. Just as he was about to come, he woke up.

"James?" Mindy said. She was already up, folding laundry before she went to the office. "Are you all right?"

"Sure," James said.

"You were talking in your sleep. Moaning."

"Ah," James said. For a moment, he wished he could go back to his dream. Back to flying and swimming and having sex. But he was seeing Lola, he reminded himself, and got out of bed.

"What are you doing today?" Mindy demanded.

"Don't know. Stuff," he said.

"We need paper towels and Windex and garbage bags. And aluminum foil. And dog food for Skippy. The Eukanuba mini-chunks. Mini. It's very important. He won't eat the big chunks."

"Can you make a list?" James asked.

"No, I cannot make a list," Mindy said. "I'm done with doing everything and being everyone's mama all the time. If you need a list, make it yourself."

"But I'm the one doing the shopping," James protested.

"Yes, and I appreciate it. But you need to do the whole job, not half of it."

"Huh?" James said, thinking that this was yet another great beginning to a typical day in the life of James Gooch.

"I've given it a lot of thought," Mindy said. "As you know, writing my blog has made me examine things I haven't wanted to confront."

Perhaps it had, James thought, but it didn't appear to have made Mindy any more sensitive. She just went on and on, running people over.

"And I've come to the conclusion," she continued, "that it's crucial to be married to another adult." Before he could respond, Mindy rushed out of the room. "Aha!" he heard her exclaim, indicating that she'd had a burst of inspiration about her blog.

"One of the joys of not having it all is not *doing* it all," Mindy wrote. "This morning I had a *Network* epiphany. 'I'm not going to take it anymore!' The constant doing: the laundry, the shopping, the folding, the lists. The endless lists. We all know what that's like. You make a list for your husband, and then you have to spend as much time making sure he follows the list as it would have taken you to do the job yourself. Well, those days are over. Not in my household! No more."

Satisfied, she went back into the bedroom for another round of hounding James. "One more thing," she said. "I know your book comes out in six weeks, but you need to start writing another one. Right away. If the book is a success, they're going to want a new one. And if it's a failure, you need to be working on another project."

James looked up from his underwear drawer. "I thought you didn't want to play mama anymore."

Mindy smiled. "Touché. In that case, I'll leave your future up to you. But in the meantime, don't forget about the mini-chunks."

After she left, James dressed carefully, changing his jeans and shirt several times, finally settling on an old black turtleneck cashmere sweater that had just the right amount of dash and writerly seriousness. Looking in the mirror, he was pleased with the result. Mindy might not be interested in him, but it didn't mean other women weren't.

On his way to the gym that morning, Philip ran into Schiffer Diamond in the deli. She'd been on his mind ever since her phone call on New Year's Eve. He told himself that he hadn't done anything wrong, and yet still felt a need to apologize—to explain. "I've been meaning to call," he began.

"You're always meaning to call, aren't you?" she replied. Now that Lola was moving in to his apartment, it should have been the absolute end of Schiffer's feelings for Philip. Unfortunately, her feelings hadn't gone away, causing an irrational irritation toward him. "Too bad you never do."

"You could call me," Philip said.

"Oakland." She sighed. "Have you noticed we're grown-ups now?"

"Yeah. Well," he said, shifting through a display of PowerBars.

This reminded him of the dozens of times he'd been in this deli with her in the past—buying ice cream and bread after sex, coffee and bacon and *The New York Times* on Sundays. There was a comfort and peace in those moments that he couldn't recall having had again. He'd assumed then that they'd be together forever doing their Sunday-morning routine when they were eighty. But there were the other times, like after a fight, or when she'd left again for L.A. or a movie location after making no plans for their future, when he'd stood here bitterly, buying cigarettes, and promising himself he'd never see her again.

"Listen," he said.

"Mmmmm?" she asked. She picked up a magazine with her face on the cover.

He smiled. "Do you still collect those things?" he asked.

"Not the way I used to," she said. She bought the magazine and headed out of the store.

He followed. "The thing about Lola," he began.

"Philip," she said. "I told you. It's none of my business." But she only ever called him by his name when she was angry with him.

"I want to explain."

"Don't."

"It wasn't my choice. Her parents lost all their money. She didn't have anyplace to live. What was I supposed to do—put her out on the street?"

"Her parents lost all their money? Come on, Philip," she said. "Even you're not that gullible."

"They did," he insisted, realizing how ridiculous it sounded. He unwrapped his PowerBar and said defensively, "You were with Brumminger. You can't be mad at me about Lola."

"Who said I was mad?"

"You're the one who's never around," Philip said, wondering why women were always so difficult.

"I'm here now, Philip," she said, stopping on the corner of Eighth Street and Fifth Avenue. "And I've been here for months."

She's still interested, Philip thought. "So let's have dinner."

"With Lola?" Schiffer said.

"No. Not with Lola. How about next Thursday? Enid's taking Lola to the ballet."

"That's an honorable plan," she said sarcastically.

"It's two old friends having dinner together. Why can't we be friends? Why do you always have to make such a big deal out of everything?"

"Fine, schoolboy," she said. "We'll have dinner. I'll even cook."

Meanwhile, upstairs in One Fifth, James Gooch was preparing to make love to Lola Fabrikant. Not actual love—not sex, which he knew was most likely beyond the realm of possibility—but verbal love. He wanted her interest and appreciation. At ten-ten, not wanting to appear too eager, he rode the elevator to the thirteenth floor. He was thinking only of Lola, but when she opened the door, some of his attention was diverted by Philip's apartment and the inevitable comparisons to his own. Oakland's place was a real apartment. No string of boxlike rooms for him. There was a foyer and a large living room, a fireplace, hallways, and when James followed Lola into the living room, he caught a glimpse of a proper-sized kitchen with granite countertops and a table large enough for four. The place smacked of old money, personal taste, travel, and a decorator, encapsulating that mix of antique and contemporary. James took in the Oriental rug, African sculpture, and leather club chairs in front of the fireplace. How often did Oakland sit there with Lola, drinking Scotch and making love to her atop the zebra rug? "I brought you my book," he said awkwardly. "As promised."

Lola was wearing a fancy T-shirt, even though it was winter—but didn't all young girls bare their almighty flesh in all kinds of weather these days?—and plaid pants that hugged her bottom, and on her feet, pretty little blue velvet slippers embroidered with a skull and crossbones. As she held out her hand for the book, she must have caught him looking at her feet, for she touched the heel of one slipper with the toe of the other and said, "They're last year's. I wanted to get the ones with the angels or butterflies—but I couldn't. They're six hundred dollars, and I couldn't afford them." She sighed and sat down on the couch. "I'm poor," she explained.

James did not know how to respond to this flood of random information. Her cell phone rang, and she answered it, followed by several "ohmigods" and "fucks," as if he weren't in the room. James was slightly hurt. In the run-up to this encounter, he'd imagined she truly was interested and the delivery of the book partly ruse, but now he wasn't sure. After ten minutes, he gave up and headed toward the door. "Wait," she said. She pointed to the phone, making a talking motion with her hand as if it were out of her control. She held the phone away from her ear. "Are you leaving?" she asked James.

"I guess so," he said.

"Why?"

"I don't know."

"You don't have to go. I'll be off in a minute." James doubted this but sat down anyway, as hopeful as an eighteen-year-old boy who still thinks he has a chance to get laid. He watched her pacing the room, fascinated and frightened by her energy, her youth, her anger, and mostly by what she might think about him.

She got off the phone and threw it onto the couch. "So," she said, turning to him, "two socialite girls got into a fight at a club, and a bunch of people videotaped it and put it on Snarker."

"Oh," James said. "Do girls still do those things?"

She looked at him like he was crazy. "Are you kidding? Girls are vicious."

"I see," James said. A painful pause ensued. "I brought you my book," he said again, to fill up the silence.

"I know," she said. She put her hands over her eyes. "I'm just so confused."

"You don't have to read it if you don't want to," James said. The book was sitting on the coffee table between them. On the cover was a color rendering of New York harbor circa 1775. The title of the book, *Diary of an American Terrorist*, was written across the top in raised red type.

She took away her hands and stared at him intently, then, remembering the book, picked it up. "I want to read it. I really do. But I'm upset about Philip."

"Oh," James said. For a moment, he'd forgotten all about Philip.

"He's just so mean."

"He is?"

She nodded. "Ever since he asked me to move in with him. He keeps criticizing everything I do." She readjusted herself on the couch. "Like the other day. I was doing a salt scrub in the bathroom, and some of the salt got on the floor. And then I had to do something right away—like go to the drugstore—and Philip came home and slipped on the salt. So when I came back, he started yelling at me about being messy."

James moved closer to her on the couch. "I'm sure it's nothing," he said. "Men are like that. It's an adjustment period."

"Really?" she asked, looking at him curiously.

"Sure," he said, bobbing his head. "It always takes men awhile to get used to things."

"And that's especially true of Philip," she said. "My mother warned me. When men get older, they get set in their ways, and you just have to work around them."

"There you go," James said, wondering how old she thought he was.

"But it's hard for me," she continued. "Because I'm the one taking all the risks. I had to give up my apartment. And if things don't work out, I don't know what I'll do."

"I'm sure Philip loves you," James said, wishing that Oakland did not and that he could take his place. But that wasn't possible unless Mindy decided to get rid of him as well.

"Do you really think so?" she asked eagerly. "Did he tell you that?"

"No . . ." James said. "But why wouldn't he?" he added quickly. "You're so"—he hesitated—"beautiful."

"Do you really think so?" she asked, as if she were insecure about her looks.

She's sweet, James thought. She really doesn't know how gorgeous she is.

"I wish Philip would tell me that," she said.

"He doesn't?"

She shook her head sadly. "He never tells me I'm beautiful. And he never says 'I love you.' Unless I force him."

"All men are like that," James said wisely. "I never tell my wife I love her, either."

"But you're married," Lola protested. "She knows you love her."

"It's complicated," James said, sitting back on the couch and crossing one leg over the other. "It's always complicated between men and women."

"But the other night," Lola began. "You and your wife—you seem so happy together."

"We have our moments," James said, although at that moment, he couldn't remember any. He recrossed his legs, hoping she couldn't see his hard-on.

"Well," she said, jumping up, "I've got to meet Philip."

James stood reluctantly. Was the visit over so soon? And just when he thought he was making progress.

"Thank you for bringing me your book," she said. "I'll start reading it this afternoon. And I'll let you know what I think."

"Great," James said, thrilled that she wanted to see him again.

At the door, he attempted to kiss her on the cheek. It was an awkward moment, and she turned her head away, so his kiss landed somewhere in her hair. Overcome by the sensation of her hair on his face, he took a step backward, tripping on the corner of the rug.

"Are you okay?" she asked, grabbing his arm.

He adjusted his glasses. "I'm fine." He smiled.

"See you soon." She waved and closed the door, then turned back into the apartment. It was cute the way James Gooch was so obviously interested in her. Naturally, she didn't return his feelings, but James was the kind of man who might do anything she wanted. And he was a best-selling author. He might come in very handy in the future.

Meanwhile, James stood waiting for the elevator, feeling his descending hard-on poke against his pants. Philip Oakland was a fool, he thought fiercely, thinking of Lola's breasts. Poor kid, she probably had no idea what she was getting into.

❦

On the floor above, Annalisa Rice placed a large red stamp on the corner of an envelope and passed it to her neighbor. Six women, including Connie Brewer, sat around her dining room table, stuffing envelopes for the King David charity ball. The King David Foundation was the Brewers' personal charity, and had grown from a dinner party at a Wall Street restaurant into a multimedia extravaganza held in the Armory. All the new Wall Streeters wanted to know Sandy Brewer, wanted to rub shoulders with him and do business, and were willing to pay the price by supporting his cause. Connie had asked Annalisa to be a cochair. The requirements were simple: She had to buy two tables at fifty thousand dollars each— for which Paul had happily written a check—and be involved in the planning.

Annalisa had thrown herself into the work with the same passion she'd brought to being a lawyer. She'd studied the financials—last year, the event had raised thirty million dollars, an extraordinary amount, and this year they hoped to raise five million dollars more. She went to tastings and examined floral arrangements, went over lists of invitees, and sat through hours of committee meetings. The work wasn't exciting, but it gave her a purpose beyond the apartment and kept her mind off Paul. Ever since the trip to China, where Paul and Sandy had done business during the day while Connie and Annalisa were driven around in a chauffeured Mercedes with a guide who took them on tours of temples and museums, Paul had become increasingly secretive and withdrawn. When he was home, he spent most of his time in his office on lengthy phone calls or making graphs on his computer. He refused to discuss his business, saying only that he and Sandy were on the verge of doing a groundbreaking deal with the Chinese that would change the international stock market and make them billions of dollars.

"What do you know about this China deal?" Annalisa asked Connie one afternoon when they were first back in New York.

"I stopped asking those questions a long time ago," Connie said, flipping open her tiny laptop. "Sandy tried to explain it a few times, and I gave up."

"Doesn't it bother you, not knowing what your husband really does?" Annalisa asked.

"No," Connie replied, studying a list of names for the benefit.

"What if it's illegal?" Annalisa said. She didn't know why this thought crossed her mind.

"Sandy would never do anything illegal. And neither would Paul. He's your husband, Annalisa. You love him, and he's wonderful."

Spending so much time with Connie had given Annalisa a new perspective on her character. Connie was naively romantic, a simple optimist who admired her husband and believed she could get everything she wanted with sugar as opposed to vinegar. She took Sandy's money for granted, as if she'd never considered what life would be like if she had less. Her attitude was due, Annalisa discovered, not to arrogance but to a lack of complexity. From the age of six, Connie's life had been dedicated to one thing—dance—and having become a professional dancer at eighteen, she'd never finished high school. Connie wasn't dumb, but she knew everything by rote. When it came to analysis, she was lost, like a child who has memorized the names of the states but can't picture where they are in relation to one another.

Having the stronger personality, Annalisa had quickly come to dominate Connie, who seemed to accept Annalisa's alpha status as a given. She made sure Annalisa was invited to lunches and the nightly cocktail parties in boutiques; she gave her the names of the people who would come to her house to cut and style her hair and perform waxing, manicures, and pedicures—"so you don't have to be seen in public with that tissue between your toes," Connie said—and even highlighting. Connie was obsessed with her own image and assumed Annalisa was as well, printing out photographs of Annalisa from the society websites she checked every morning. "There was a great picture of you in *Women's Wear Daily* today," Connie would crow with childish excitement. Or "I saw the best pictures of us from the perfume launch last night." Then she would dutifully ask if Annalisa wanted her to messenger the prints to her apartment. "It's okay, Connie, I can look them up myself," Annalisa would say. Nevertheless, two hours later, the doorman would buzz and an envelope would be delivered upstairs. Annalisa would look at the photos and put them in a drawer. "Do you really care about these things?" she'd asked Connie one day.

"Of course," Connie had said. "Don't you?"

"Not really," Annalisa said. Connie looked hurt, and Annalisa felt bad, having inadvertently dismissed one of Connie's great pleasures in life. And Connie took such pride in the fact that Annalisa was *her* friend, boasting to the other women about how Annalisa had written a scholarly book in college and appeared on *Charlie Rose*, how Annalisa had met the president, and how she had *worked* in *Washington*. In turn, Annalisa had become protective of Connie's feelings. Connie was such a tiny thing, reminding Annalisa of a fairy with her small bones and graceful hands. She loved everything sparkly and pretty and pink and was always nipping into Harry Winston or Lalaounis. Displaying her recent jewelry acquisitions, she would insist that Annalisa try on a yellow diamond ring or a necklace of colored sapphires, pressing Annalisa to borrow the piece.

"No," Annalisa always said firmly, handing the jewelry back. "I'm not going to walk around wearing a ring worth half a million dollars. What if something happened?"

"But it's *insured*," Connie would say, as if insurance mitigated one from all responsibility.

Now, sitting in her dining room in her grand penthouse apartment, stuffing envelopes with Connie and the other women on the committee, Annalisa glanced around and realized they were like children working on a craft project. She placed another stamp on another envelope as the women chitchatted about the things women always talked about—their children and their husbands, their homes, clothes, hair, a piece of gossip from the night before— the only difference being the scale of their lives. One woman was debating sending her daughter to boarding school in Switzerland; another was building a house on a private island in the Caribbean and was urging the other women to do the same "so they could all be together." Then one of the women brought up the story in the latest *W* that had dominated the conversation of this clique for the past three weeks. The story had been a roundup of possible socialites who might take the place of the legendary Mrs. Houghton, and Annalisa had been named third in the running. The story was complimentary, describing Annalisa as the "flame-haired beauty from Washington who had taken New York by storm," but Annalisa found it embarrassing. Every time she went out, someone mentioned it, and the story had increased her visibility so that when she appeared at an event, the photographers shouted her name, insisting that she stop and pose and turn. It was harmless, but it freaked Paul out.

"Why are they taking your picture?" he'd demanded, angrily taking her hand at the end of a short red carpet behind which sat posters with the logos of a fashion magazine and an electronics company.

"I don't know, Paul," she'd said. Was it possible Paul was this naive about the world of which he'd insisted they become a part? Billy Litchfield often said these parties were for the women—the dressing up, the showing off of jewelry—so perhaps Paul, being a man, simply didn't understand. He had always been terrible at anything social, having nearly no ability to read people or make small talk. He became stiff and angry when he was in a situation he didn't understand, and would thrust his tongue into his cheek, as if to forcibly prevent himself from speaking. That evening, seeing his cheek bulge, Annalisa had wondered how to explain the rules of this particular society. "It's like a birthday party, Paul. Where people take photographs. So they can remember the moment."

"I don't like it," Paul said. "I don't want pictures of me floating around on the Internet. I don't want people to know what I look like or where I am."

Annalisa laughed. "That's so paranoid, Paul. Everyone has their picture taken. Even Sandy's photograph is everywhere."

"I'm not Sandy."

"Then you shouldn't go out," she said.

"I'm not sure you should, either."

His remark had infuriated her. "Maybe we should move back to Washington, then," she'd said sharply.

"What's that supposed to mean?"

She shook her head, frustrated but knowing it was useless to fight with him, which she'd discovered early on in their marriage. When they disagreed, Paul picked apart the exact words she'd used, managing to divert attention away from the topic so it could never be resolved and they could never agree. Paul wouldn't give in on principle. "Nothing," she said.

She did stay home three nights in a row, but Paul wouldn't make any adjustments to his schedule, so she was alone in the big apartment, wandering from room to room until Paul came home at ten o'clock, ate a peanut-butter sandwich that the housekeeper, Maria, prepared, and went upstairs to work. Billy Litchfield was still at his mother's house, and Annalisa felt the sharp emptiness of being alone in a big city where everyone else seemed to have something important to do. On the fourth night, she gave up and went out with Connie, and the photographers took more pictures, and Annalisa put the prints in her drawer and didn't tell Paul.

Now one of the women, obsessed with the story in *W,* turned to Annalisa and casually said, "How did you get on that list? And only having been in New York for six months."

"I don't know," Annalisa said.

"Because she *is* going to be the next Mrs. Houghton," Connie said proudly. "Billy Litchfield says so. Annalisa would make a much better Mrs. Houghton than I would."

"I certainly would not," Annalisa said.

"Did Billy put you up for it?" asked one of the women.

"I love Billy, but he can be pushy," said another.

"I don't know why anyone cares," Annalisa said, pressing another stamp onto another envelope. She still had a pile of at least a hundred in front of her. "Mrs. Houghton is dead. Let her rest in peace."

The other women twittered at the outrageousness of this remark. "No, really," Annalisa said, getting up to ask Maria to bring in lunch. "I don't understand why it's a goal."

"It's only because you don't want it," one of the women replied. "It's always the people who don't want things who get them."

"That's right," Connie agreed. "I wouldn't give Sandy the time of day when I met him, and we ended up getting married."

"Maria," Annalisa said, pushing through the swing door into the kitchen. "Could you serve the Waldorf chicken salad and the cheese biscuits, please?" She returned to the table and began to attack the pile of envelopes again.

"Did you get the parking space yet?" Connie asked idly.

"No," Annalisa said.

"You have to be adamant with the people in your co-op," said one of the women. "You can't let them walk all over you. Did you make it clear you'd pay extra money?"

"It's not that kind of building." Annalisa felt the beginnings of a headache. The parking space, like the air conditioners, had been yet another disaster. Paul had gone to the resident who had won the lottery for the parking space, a quiet man who was a heart surgeon at Columbia, and asked if he could buy it from him. The doctor had complained to Mindy, and Mindy had sent Paul a note asking him not to bribe the other residents. When Paul saw the note, he turned white. "Where did she get this?" he demanded, indicating the paper on which the note was written. It was a sheet from a notepad from the Four Seasons hotel in Bangkok. "She was in our apartment," Paul said, his voice rising. "That's where she got the paper. From my desk."

"Paul, don't be crazy."

"Then where did she get this?" Paul demanded.

"I don't know," Annalisa said, remembering how she'd given Sam the keys over Christmas. So Sam, who had returned the keys, had given them to his mother after all. But she couldn't tell Paul that, so she insisted the paper had to be a coincidence. It was another thing she'd had to lie to Paul about, and it made her feel horribly guilty, as if she'd committed a crime. Paul had the locks changed, but it only increased his hatred of Mindy Gooch and made him vow to get "that woman" out of the building one way or another.

Maria brought in the lunch and set it out on the table with silver cutlery from Asprey and the Tiffany china, which Billy said was still the best. "Cheese biscuits," one of the women exclaimed, looking doubtfully at the golden biscuits piled up on the crystal platter. "Annalisa, you shouldn't have," she scolded. "I swear to God, you're trying to make us all fat."

14

As if he weren't neurotic enough to begin with, in the weeks leading up to the publication of his book, James became more so. He hated himself for it, having always disdained writers who checked their Amazon and Barnes & Noble ratings every half hour and scoured the Internet for reviews and mentions. His obsession left him harrowed, as if he were an insane person who believed he was being pursued by imaginary wraiths. And then there was Lola. In his occasional moments of sanity, James concluded that she was some kind of master lure, a shiny bright irresistible thing lined with hooks on both sides. On the surface of things, their relationship was still well within the concept of perfectly innocent, for nothing had happened other than the exchange of text messages and a few impromptu visits to his apartment. About twice a week, she would show up at his place unexpectedly, languishing on the folding chair in his office like a sleek black panther. She would have easily caught him under any circumstances, but in this case, the snare was made doubly secure by the fact that she had immediately read his book and wanted to discuss it while at the same time seeking his advice about Philip.

Should she marry Philip? Of course she loved him, but she

didn't want him to marry her under the wrong circumstances—those being that he felt obligated. On this question, James was as torn as Solomon. He wanted Lola for himself, but he wanted her in the building more, no matter what the circumstances. As he couldn't kick out his own wife and install Lola, having her upstairs was better than nothing. And so he lied, finding himself in the unexpected position of giving relationship advice to a twenty-two-year-old girl.

"I believe it's generally understood that one is supposed to give these things a try," James said, floundering like a fish. "They say you can always get divorced."

"I could never do that," she said. "It's against my religion."

Which religion was that? James wondered. "But since you say you love Philip . . ."

"I say I *think* I do," she corrected him. "But I'm only twenty-two. How am I supposed to know? For sure?"

"You can never know for sure," James said, thinking of Mindy. "A marriage is something that goes on and on unless one person really puts an end to it."

"You're so lucky." She sighed. "You've made your decision. And you're a genius. When your book comes out, you'll make millions of dollars."

The secret visits continued for several weeks, and then the Wednesday came when James's publisher was to receive his early review from *The New York Times Book Review*. Lola came by the apartment bearing a gift—a stuffed teddy bear "for good luck," she said—but James was too nervous to acknowledge the gift and absentmindedly shoved it in the back of the overcrowded coat closet.

Everything was riding on his review in the *Times*. As an author whose previous book had sold seventy-five hundred copies, he would need exorbitant praise to smash through the glass ceiling of previous book sales. He pictured this smashing as akin to smashing through the roof of Willie Wonka's chocolate factory in the great glass elevator, and he wondered what was happening to his brain.

"You must be so excited," Lola said, following him to his office. "You're going to get a great review. I just know it."

James didn't just know it, but poor Lola was too young to understand that usually, things did not work out as one hoped. His mouth was dry with nerves. All morning, his mood had veered between elation and despair. He was now on the downward cycle of this emotional roller coaster. "Everyone always wants to think he's a winner," he said thickly. "Everyone thinks if they only behave the way people do in the movies, or on *Oprah*, or in those so-called inspiring memoirs, and never give up, that they'll triumph in the end. But it isn't true."

"Why shouldn't it be true?" Lola said with irritating confidence.

"The only guarantee of success is hard work," James said. "Statistically speaking, that is. But even then, it's not a sure bet. The truth is, there are no sure bets."

"That's why there's true love," Lola said.

James's mood turned and his emotions began to chug upward like the little train that could. What a darling, he thought, looking at Lola. She didn't know a thing about life, but still, she believed in herself so purely, it *was* almost inspirational. "It's all about the numbers," he said, nodding at this realization. "Numbers upon numbers upon numbers. Maybe it always was," he went on musingly.

"Was what?" Lola asked. She was bored. The conversation had taken an unexpected turn not only away from her but into an area she equated with taxes. Meaning something she hoped never to think about.

"Ratings. Bottom lines," James said, thinking he wouldn't mind seeing Lola's bottom line. But he couldn't exactly say that, could he?

Or could he?

"I have to go," she said. "Hug your teddy. Kiss him for luck. And text me later. I can't wait to read the review."

After she left, James got back on the Internet. He checked and rechecked his e-mails, his Amazon ranking, his Google ranking, and looked up his name on any possible media-related website, including The Huffington Post, Snarker, and Defamer. The next five hours passed in this most unpleasant manner.

Finally, at three-fifteen, his phone rang. "We did it," Redmon said, his voice filled with triumph. "You got the cover of *The New York Times Book Review*. And they called you a modern-day Melville."

At first James was too shocked to speak. But after a moment, he found his voice and, as if he had books on the cover of *The New York Times Book Review* all the time, said, "I'll take that."

"Damn right we'll take it," Redmon said. "It couldn't be better if we'd written it ourselves. I'll have my assistant e-mail you the review."

James hung up. For the first time in his life, he was a success. "I am a man of triumph," he said aloud. Then he began to feel dizzy—with joy, he told himself—and then oddly nauseated. He hadn't thrown up in years, not since he was a boy, but the nausea increased, and he was finally forced to go into the bathroom to perform that most unmasculine of all rituals—spitting up into the toilet bowl.

Still unsteady on his feet, he went back to his office, opened the attachment on his computer, and printed it out, eagerly reading each page as it shot from the machine. His talent was at last recognized, and no matter how many books he sold, it was this acknowledgment of his place in the literary pantheon that mattered. He had won! But what was he supposed to do now? Ah—sharing the news. That's what one did next.

He began to dial Mindy's number but hesitated. Plenty of time to tell her, he thought, and there was one person who would appreciate the news more: Lola. She was the one who ought to hear first, who had sweated out this most fateful of days with him. Grabbing the three pages of the review, he went into the lobby, impatiently waiting for the elevator, planning exactly what he might say to her ("I did it"? "You're going to be proud of me"? "You were right"?) and what might happen afterward. (She would hug him, naturally, and that hug might turn into a kiss, and the kiss might turn into . . . ? God only knew.) At last the elevator arrived from the top of the building, and he got on and sent it right back up, looking back and forth from the slow ticking off of the floors to the words printed in the review and now imprinted on his brain: "Modern-day Melville."

Full of brio, he pounded on the door of Apartment 13B. He heard scuffling inside and, expecting Lola, was shocked when Philip Oakland opened the door. Seeing James, Philip's face became cold and annoyed. "Gooch," he said. "What are you doing here?"

It was, James thought, a scene straight out of the schoolyard. He tried to peer unobtrusively around Philip, hoping to catch sight of Lola. "Can I help you with something?" Philip asked.

James did his best to recover. "I just got a great review in *The New York Times Book Review*." The pages flapped uselessly in his hand.

"Congratulations," Philip said, making as if to close the door.

"Is Lola home?" James asked in desperation. Philip looked at him and gave a half-sardonic, half-pitying laugh as if he at last understood James's true mission. "Lola?" he said, calling out behind him.

Lola came to the door, wrapped in a silk robe, her hair wet, as if she'd just come out of the shower. "What?" she said. She casually slipped her hand into the back of Philip's jeans.

James awkwardly held out the pages. "Here's the review in the *Times*," he said. "I thought you might want to see it."

"Oh, I do," she said, as nonchalantly as if she hadn't been in his apartment hours before, had never been in his apartment ever, and hardly knew him at all.

"It's a good one," James said, knowing he was beaten but not wanting to acknowledge defeat. "It's great, as a matter of fact."

"That's so cute of you, James," she said. "Isn't that cute?" she asked, addressing Philip.

"Very nice," Philip said, and this time, he did close the door.

James wondered if he'd ever felt quite so foolish.

Back in his apartment, it took him several minutes to recover from this disquieting scene, and it was only because his phone rang. Mindy was on the line. "I just heard," she said accusingly.

"About what?" he said, falling into their old married habits like a grown-up visiting his parents.

"The cover of *The New York Times Book Review?*" she said. "Why didn't you tell me? I have to read about it on a blog?"

James sighed. "I only just found out myself."

"Aren't you excited?" Mindy demanded.

"Sure," he said. He hung up the phone and sat down in his chair. He hadn't expected the pleasure of his triumph to last forever, but he'd never imagined it would be so short-lived.

❦

Billy Litchfield returned to Manhattan a few days later. His mother was better, but they both understood she'd begun to make the inevitable descent into death. Nevertheless, his month in the remote suburbs on the edge of the Berkshire Mountains had taught him a great deal—namely, how lucky he'd been in life. The reality was that he wasn't to the manor born, but to the suburb, and the fact that he'd managed to escape the suburbs for over thirty years was extraordinary. His relief at being back in Manhattan, however, was brief. When he walked into his apartment building, he found an eviction notice on his door.

Restitution involved a trip to housing court on State Street, where he mingled among the hoi polloi of Manhattan. This was the real Manhattan, where everyone had a ragged sense of his own importance and his rights as a person. Billy sat among a hundred such people in a molded plastic chair in a windowless room until his case was called.

"What's your excuse?" the judge asked.

"My mother was sick. I had to leave town to take care of her."

"That's negligence."

"Not from my mother's point of view."

The judge frowned but appeared to take pity on him. "Pay the rent due and the fine. And don't let me see you in here again."

"Yes, Your Honor," Billy said. He waited in another long line to pay cash, then took the subway uptown. The warm, putrid air in the subway car clamped down on his mood like a vise. Scanning the faces around him, he was struck by the pointlessness of so many lives. But perhaps it was his own expectations that were too high. Maybe God hadn't intended for life to have a point beyond reproduction.

In this mood, he met Annalisa in front of One Fifth and got into her newly purchased green Bentley, complete with a chauffeur, which Billy had helped to arrange through a service. Not having seen her in a while, he was struck by her appearance, thinking how much she'd changed from the tomboyish woman he'd met nine months ago. But she still had that knack for appearing natural, as if she were wearing no makeup and hadn't had her hair styled and wasn't wearing five-thousand-dollar trousers, all the while, he knew, putting a great deal of time and effort into her appearance. It was no wonder everyone wanted her at their events and the magazines always featured her photographs. But he found himself feeling surprisingly hesitant about her budding success. This caution was new for him, and he wondered if it was due to recent events or to the realization that his own years of striving had added up to nearly nothing. "A photograph is only an image. Here today, gone tomorrow," he wanted to say. "It won't satisfy your soul in the long run." But he didn't. Why shouldn't she have her fun now, while she could? There would be plenty of time for regrets later.

The car took them to the Hammer Galleries on Fifth Avenue, where Billy sat on a bench and took in the recent paintings. In the clean white rarefied air of the gallery, he began to feel better. This was why he did what he did, he thought. Although he couldn't afford art himself, he could surround himself with it through those who could. Annalisa sat next to him, staring at Andrew Wyeth's famous painting of a woman in a blue room at the beach. "I'll never understand how a painting can cost forty million dollars," she said.

"Oh my dear," he said. "A painting like this is priceless. It's absolutely unique. The work and vision of one man, and yet in it, one sees the universal creative hand of God."

"But the money could be spent to really help people," Annalisa said.

Her argument made Billy feel weary. He'd heard it so many times before. "That's true, on the surface of things," he said. "But without art, man is an animal, and a not very attractive animal at that. Greedy, striving, selfish, and murderous. Here is joy and awe and regard." He indicated the painting. "It's nourishment for the soul."

"How are you, Billy?" Annalisa asked. "Really?"

"Just peachy," Billy replied.

"If there's anything I can do to help your mother—" She hesitated, knowing how Billy hated talking about his financial situation. But charity got the better of her. "If you need money . . . and Paul is making so much . . . He says he's on the verge of making billions"—she smiled as if it were an uncomfortable joke— "and I would never spend ten million dollars on a painting. But if a person needs help . . ."

Billy kept his eyes on the Wyeth. "You don't have to worry about me, my dear. I've survived in New York this long, and I reckon I'll survive a little longer."

When he got back to his apartment, the phone was ringing. It was his mother. "I asked the girl to bring me cod from the supermarket, and it had turned. You'd think a person would know if fish were bad or not."

"Oh, Ma," he said, feeling defeated and frustrated.

"What am I supposed to do?" she asked.

"Can't you call Laura?" he said, referring to his sister.

"We're not speaking again. We were only speaking because you were here."

"I wish you would sell the house and move to a condo in Palm Beach. Your life would be so much easier."

"I can't afford it, Billy," she said. "And I won't live with strangers."

"But you'd have your own apartment."

"I can't live in an apartment. I'd go crazy."

Billy hung up the phone and sighed. His mother had become impossible, as, he supposed, all elderly people were when they refused to accept that their lives had to change. He had hired a private nurse to visit his mother twice a week, as well as a girl who would clean her house and run errands. But it was only a temporary solution. And his mother was right—she couldn't afford to sell her house and buy a condo in Florida. During his month in the Berkshires, he'd consulted a real estate agent who'd informed him that the housing market had plummeted and his mother's house was worth maybe three hundred thousand dollars. If she'd wanted to sell two years ago, it would have been a different story—the house might have sold for four-fifty.

But he hadn't been concerned about his mother's situation two years ago. She was okay for the moment, but eventually, she'd have to go into some kind of assisted living facility, the cost of which, he'd been informed by his sister, was upward of five thousand dollars a month. If she sold the house, the money from the sale would last about four years. And then what?

He looked around his little apartment. Was he about to lose his own home as well? Would he, too, become a charity case? The fact that Annalisa Rice had asked him if he needed money was a bad sign. Was it apparent to all how desperate he was? Once people sensed his weakness, he'd be cut off. "Did you hear what happened to Billy Litchfield?" they'd ask. "He lost his apartment and had to leave New York." They'd talk about it for a little while, but then they'd forget about him. No one cared to think about the people who didn't make it.

He went into his bedroom and opened the wooden box Mrs. Houghton had left him. The Cross of Bloody Mary was still in its suede pouch in the hidden compartment. He'd considered renting a safe deposit box in which to store the cross, but he worried that this action alone might arouse suspicion. So he had kept it, as Mrs. Houghton had, on top of his bureau. Unwrapping the cross, he recalled something Mrs. Houghton had once said: "The problem with art is that it doesn't solve people's problems, Billy. Money, on the other hand, does."

Billy put on his reading glasses and examined the cross. The diamonds were crudely cut by today's standards and were far from perfect in color or clarity, with cloudy occlusions. But the stones were old and enormous. The diamond in the middle was at least twenty carats. On the open market, the cross might be worth ten to twenty million dollars.

This particular circumstance dictated that he mustn't be greedy, however—the more money he demanded, the more likely the sale would attract attention. He would ask for only three million dollars—just enough, he reasoned, to take care of his mother and ensure his relatively modest lifestyle in New York.

Then the reality of what he was about to do caused his body to react in fear. He felt a damp sweat beginning to form in his armpits, and leaving the cross on the bed, he went into the bathroom, took two Xanaxes, and stepped into the shower.

Afterward, patting himself dry with a heavy white towel, he sternly told himself that he must be resolute in his decision. He would have preferred to sell the cross to Annalisa Rice, whom he trusted completely, but Annalisa was a lawyer and would know the transaction was illegal. That left one other choice—Connie Brewer. Connie's blithe lack of intelligence might prove to be his downfall someday, but on the other hand, she was good at following instructions. As long as he constantly reminded her to keep quiet, he would probably be safe. Wrapping himself in his paisley silk robe, he reminded himself if the thing be done, it best be done quickly. Picking up the phone next to his bed, he called Connie.

She was collecting her children from school but would meet him at four o'clock. At four-thirty, his bell rang, and Connie came fluttering into his cramped apartment. "You're being so mysterious, Billy," she said.

He held up the cross.

"What is it?" she squealed, thrusting her head forward to get a better look. "Is it real? Can I hold it?" She put out her hand, and he placed it in her palm. She gasped. "Are those diamonds?"

"I hope so," he said. "It belonged to a queen."

"Oh, Billy, I want it. I want it," she repeated. "I have to have it. It's mine." She held the cross to her chest and stood to look at herself in the mirror above the mantelpiece. "It's speaking to me. Jewelry speaks to me, you know—and it's saying it belongs to me."

"I'm so glad you like it," Billy said casually. Having begun the transaction, he felt calm. "It's special. It needs the right home."

Connie became businesslike, as if fearful that the cross might get away from her if she didn't buy it right away. "How much do you want for it?" she asked, sitting on the couch and taking her iPhone out of her handbag. "I can call Sandy right now and have him write you a check."

"That would be lovely, my dear. But I'm afraid it's a bit more complicated than that."

"I want it now," she insisted. Billy let her take it with her, and was almost relieved to have it out of his apartment. Now all he needed was the money.

He had a cocktail party that evening but stayed home to wait for Sandy.

At eight o'clock, Sandy rapped impatiently on the door. He'd never been in Billy's apartment, and he looked around, surprised and possibly shocked, Billy thought, by how small it was. "When you get the money, I guess you'll be buying a bigger place," Sandy said, opening his briefcase.

"No," Billy said. "I like it here."

"Suit yourself," Sandy said, pulling out a yellow legal pad. He began outlining the particulars, and within twenty minutes, he and Billy had come to an agreement.

Afterward, Billy got into bed, exhausted. Sandy, no doubt, found the need for secrecy strange, but he'd assumed the cross was merely a bibelot, and Billy eccentric. But the arrangements were easy enough, and the money couldn't be traced to the sale of the cross. Sandy would open an investment account for him at a bank in Geneva, Switzerland, and would transfer the three million dollars into the account in increments of just under ten thousand dollars a day over the next ten months, which would avoid alerting the authorities, who tracked only transactions of over ten thousand dollars. Wrapping up their business, Sandy jokingly suggested Billy make a will.

"Why?" Billy said, taken aback.

"If something happens to you, the government will try to claim the money," Sandy said, snapping his briefcase shut.

Billy closed his eyes. It was done now, and there was no going back. He promptly fell asleep and didn't wake until morning. It was the first night in weeks he'd been able to fall asleep without taking a pill.

Two nights later, however, he had a terrible fright. It was the opening night of Balanchine's *Jewels* at the New York City Ballet, and Billy decided to go alone, wanting an evening off from the obligation of having to maintain his persona in front of other people. He should have known better—as soon as one left one's apartment, there was no privacy in New York—and strolling through the promenade in the State Theater during the first intermission, Billy ran into Enid Merle, accompanied, incongruously, by a cookie-cutter young beauty with enormous teeth. Enid didn't introduce the girl and was, in fact, distinctly unfriendly. "Ah, Billy" was all she said before she turned away.

Billy didn't put too much emphasis on it, reminding himself that Enid could be that way. Besides, he thought, rationalizing her behavior, like everyone else he'd known in New York for years, Enid Merle was finally old.

In the next second, he was distracted by a pat on the shoulder. Billy turned and found himself face-to-face with David Porshie, the director of the Metropolitan Museum. David Porshie was a bald man with olive skin and deep bags under his eyes; at fifty-five, he was relatively young to hold such a position, the hope of the board being that he might remain the head of the Met for another thirty years. "Billy Litchfield," David said, folding his arms and looking at Billy scoldingly, as if he'd done something wrong.

Billy was terrified. As the director of the Met, David would know all about the mystery of the Cross of Bloody Mary, and it crossed Billy's mind—irrationally—that somehow David had found out that Mrs. Houghton had had the cross and given it to him. But he was only being paranoid, because David said, "I haven't seen you in ages. Where have you been keeping yourself?"

"I've been around," Billy said cautiously.

"I never see you at our events anymore. Ever since Mrs. Houghton passed—God rest her generous soul—I suppose you don't think we're important enough."

Was he somehow digging for information? Billy wondered. Struggling to maintain his composure, he said, "Not at all. I've got my calendar marked for the gala next month. I'm arranging to bring Annalisa Rice. She and her husband bought Mrs. Houghton's apartment."

He didn't need to say more. David Porshie immediately understood the ramifications of bringing a potential donor into the fold. "Well done," he said, pleased. "We can always count on you to have the inside track."

Billy smiled, but as soon as David walked away, he rapidly made his way to the men's room. Was it going to be like this from now on? Was he always going to be looking over his shoulder, wondering if people like David Porshie suspected him? Everyone in the art world knew him. He would never be able to avoid them, not as long as he lived in Manhattan.

He felt around in his pocket for an orange pill and slipped one in his mouth, swallowing it dry. It would only take a few minutes for the pill to take effect, but he decided it was too late. The evening was spoiled. There was nothing to do but go home. And passing through the promenade on his way out, he again spotted Enid Merle. She looked up at him briefly. He waved, but she didn't wave back.

⬙

"Who was that?" Lola asked.

"Who, dear?" Enid said, ordering two glasses of champagne.

"That man who waved to you."

"I don't know who you're talking about, dear," Enid replied. She knew exactly to whom Lola was referring, but she still felt a residual annoyance at Billy Litchfield over Mrs. Houghton's apartment. She'd always considered Billy a good friend—so he should have come to her first and at least have had the courtesy to inform her of what he was planning to do with the Rices.

But she didn't want to think about Billy Litchfield or the Rices and their apartment. She was at the ballet now. Attending the ballet was one of the great pleasures in Enid's life, and she had her rituals. She always sat in the first row in the first ring in seat 113, which she considered the best seat in the house, and she always treated herself to a glass of the most expensive champagne during the intermissions. The elegant first act, "Emeralds," was over, and after paying for the champagne, she turned to Lola. "What did you think of it, dear?" she asked.

Lola stared at the piece of strawberry in her glass. The ballet, she knew, was supposed to be the height of culture. But the first movement had more than bored her, it had literally made her want to scream and tear her hair out. The slow classical music grated on her nerves; it was so excruciating that for a moment, she actually questioned her wisdom in being with Philip. But she reminded herself that this wasn't Philip's fault—he wasn't even here. He wisely—she realized—was at home.

"I liked it," Lola said cautiously.

They moved away from the stalls and sat at a small table on the side, sipping their champagne. "Did you?" Enid said. "There's a great debate over which ballet is better, 'Emeralds,' 'Rubies,' or 'Diamonds.' I personally prefer 'Diamonds,' but many people love the fire in 'Rubies.' You'll have to make your own decision."

"There's more?" Lola said.

"Hours and hours," Enid declared happily. "I've done quite a bit of thinking on the matter, and I've decided ballet is the very opposite of the Internet. Or those things you watch on your phone. What are they—podcasts? Ballet is the antidote to surfing the Web. It forces you to go deep. To think."

"Or fall asleep," Lola said, attempting a joke.

Enid ignored this. "Ideally, the ballet should put you into a transportive state. I've often said it's a version of meditation. You'll feel wonderful afterward."

Lola took another sip of champagne. It was slightly sour, and the tiny bubbles caught in her throat, but she was determined to keep her displeasure to herself. The evening was an opportunity to make Enid like her—or at the very least, to make Enid understand that she meant to marry Philip, and there was no use in Enid standing in the way. But still, Enid's invitation to the ballet had taken Lola by surprise. When she and Philip had returned from Mustique, she'd expected Enid would be furious about her moving in. Instead, Enid pretended to be overjoyed and immediately asked her to the ballet. "A girls' night," she'd called it, although Enid couldn't possibly believe she was still a girl, Lola thought. And then a more disturbing idea had crossed her mind: Perhaps Enid didn't object to her moving in with Philip at all, and planned to spend lots of time with them. Lola lowered her head over her glass and glanced up at Enid. If that were so, she thought, Enid would be in for a shock. Philip was hers now, and Enid would have to learn that when it came to relationships, three was a crowd.

"Did Philip tell you he danced ballet as a boy?" Enid asked. The thought of Philip in white tights startled Lola. Could this be true, she wondered, or was it merely a sign that Enid was becoming senile? Lola carefully took in Enid's appearance. Her blond hair was coiffed, and she was wearing a black-and-white plaid suit with a matching emerald necklace and earrings, which Lola coveted and wondered if there was some way she could get Enid to leave to her when she died. Enid did not look particularly crazy—and Lola had to concede that for an eighty-two-year-old woman, Enid looked pretty good.

"No, he didn't tell me," Lola said stiffly.

"You two have only just gotten to know each other, so naturally, he hasn't had time yet to tell you everything. But he was in *The Nutcracker* as a boy. He played the young prince. It was, and still is, a terribly chic thing to do. Ballet has always been a part of our lives. But you'll learn that soon enough."

"I can't wait," Lola said, forcing herself to smile.

The bells signaling the end of intermission began to chime, and Enid stood up. "Come along, dear," she said. "We don't want to miss the second act." Holding out her arm, she motioned for Lola to take it, and when she did, Enid leaned heavily on her, shuffling slowly toward the door to the theater and keeping up a relentless prattle. "I'm so happy you love the classic arts," she said. "The winter season of the ballet only lasts until the end of February, but then there's the Metropolitan Opera. And of course, there are always wonderful little piano concertos and even poetry readings. So one never need be deprived of culture. And now that you're living with Philip, it's so easy. You're right next door. You can accompany me to everything."

❖

Back at One Fifth, Philip was shaving for the second time that day. As he scraped the side of his cheek, he paused, holding up his razor. Something was missing. Noise, he thought. There was no noise. For the first time in months.

He went back to shaving. Splashing his face with water, he felt guilty about sneaking around behind Lola's back. Then he was irritated. He had every right to do as he pleased—after all, he wasn't married to the girl. He was only trying to help her by providing her with a roof over her head until she could figure out her situation.

Passing through the living room on his way out, he noticed that Lola had carelessly left her magazines strewn on the couch. He picked up *Brides*, then *Modern Bride* and *Elegant Bride*. This was too much. He would need to have a talk with her—one of these days—and make it clear where he stood in the relationship. He wasn't going to be backed into making promises he couldn't keep. And making his point, he took the magazines into the kitchen, where he pushed them down the incinerator chute, even though this was against the building's rules.

Then he took the elevator down to the ninth floor.

"Well, there. Look at you," Schiffer Diamond said, opening her door.

"Look at you," Philip replied.

She was dressed casually in jeans and a blue-and-white-striped French sailor's shirt, and she was barefoot. She still had that ability of making simple pieces of clothing look elegant, Philip noted, and unconsciously comparing her to Lola, found Lola lacking.

Schiffer put her hands on either side of his head and kissed him. "It's been too long, Oakland," she said.

"I know," he said, stepping in and looking around. "Wow," he remarked. "The apartment is exactly the same."

"I haven't done a thing to it. Haven't had time."

Philip went into the living room and sat down. He felt wonderfully at home, and strangely young, as if time hadn't passed at all. He picked up a photograph taken of the two of them in Aspen in the winter of 1991. "I can't believe you still have this," he said.

"The place is a time capsule. God, we were kids," she said, coming over to examine the photograph. "But we looked good together."

Philip agreed, struck by how happy they seemed. He hadn't felt that way in a long time. "Jesus," he said, replacing the photograph. "What happened?"

"We got old, schoolboy," she said, going into the kitchen. She was, as promised, making him dinner.

"Speak for yourself," he called back. "I'm not old."

She popped her head out the door. "Yes, you are. And it's about time you realized it."

"What about you?" he said. He joined her in the kitchen, where she was placing cut-up pieces of lemon and onion into the cavity of a chicken. He perched on the top of the stepstool where he'd sat many times before, drinking red wine and watching her prepare her famous roast chicken. She made other things as well, like chili and potato salad and, in the summer, steamed clams and lobsters, but her roast chicken was, to his mind, legendary. The very first Sunday they'd spent together, years and years ago, she'd insisted on cooking a chicken in the tiny oven in the kitchenette of her hotel room. When he teased her about it, pointing out that knowing how to cook wasn't very women's lib–ish, she'd replied, "Even a fool ought to know how to feed himself."

Now, putting the chicken in the oven, she said, "I've never lied about my age. The difference between us is that I'm not afraid of getting older."

"I'm not afraid, either," he said.

"Of course you are."

"Why? Because I'm with Lola?"

"It's not just that," she said. She went into the living room and put a log in the fireplace. She lit a long match and let it burn for a moment. "It's everything, Philip. Your whole demeanor."

"Maybe I wouldn't be like this if I had a hit TV show," he replied teasingly.

"Then why don't you do something about it? Why don't you go back to writing books? You haven't had a book out in six years."

He sighed. "Writer's block."

"Bullshit," she said, lighting the fire. "You're scared, schoolboy. You used to be different. Now you're reduced to writing these silly movies. *Bridesmaids Revisited*? What is that?"

"I've got the screenplay about Bloody Mary. It's going well," he said defensively.

"It's a soap, Philip. Another escape for you. It doesn't have anything to do with real life."

"What's wrong with escapism?"

She shook her head. "You've lived in the same apartment your entire life. You haven't moved an inch. And yet somehow you've managed to keep running away."

"I'm here, aren't I?" he said, echoing her line to him from the other day.

"You're here because you need a release from Lola. You need to pretend you have someplace else to go in case it doesn't work out. Which it won't. And then where will you be?"

"Is that what you really think?" he asked. "That I'm here to get away from Lola?"

"I don't know."

"I'm not," he said.

She walked past him and hit him playfully on the head. "Then why are you here?"

He grabbed her wrist, but she pulled away. "Don't bore me with that speech about how you can be in love with someone but can't be with them," she said.

"Well, it's true."

"It's utter crap," she replied. "It's for the weak and uninspired. What's happened to your passion, Oakland?"

He rolled his eyes. She always had that way of stirring him up, of making him feel potent and inadequate at the same time. But wasn't that what one wanted from a relationship? "It's not going to work," he said.

"Your penis?" she asked jokingly, going into the kitchen to check on the chicken.

"Us," he said, standing in the door. "We'll try it again, and it won't work. Again."

"So?" she said, opening the oven. She was as hesitant about it as he was, he thought.

"Do you really want to go there—again?" he asked.

"Christ, schoolboy," she said, holding up an oven mitt. "I've had it with convincing you. Can't you ever make an honest, decent decision on your own?"

"There it is," he said, coming up behind her. "You're always acting. Did you ever think about what it would be like if you weren't pretending to be in a scene?"

"I don't do that."

"You do. All the time."

She tossed the oven mitt on the counter and, closing the oven door, turned to face him. "You're right." She paused, holding his eyes with her stare. "I'm always acting. It's my defense. Most people have one. I, however, have changed."

"You're saying you've changed?" Philip said, with playful disbelief.

"Are you saying I haven't?"

"I don't know," Philip said. "Why don't we find out?" He lifted her hair and began kissing the back of her neck.

"Cut it out," she said, swatting at him.

"Why?" he asked.

"Okay, don't cut it out," she said. "Let's have sex and get it over with. Then we can go back to being as we were."

"I may not want to," he said warningly.

"You will. You always do."

She ran into the bedroom ahead of him and took off her shirt. She still had those small rounded breasts that always made him crazy. He stripped down to his boxer shorts and joined her. "Remember when we used to do that thing?" she asked.

"Which thing?"

"You know—that crazy thing where you lie on your back and put your feet up and I go on my stomach and pretend I'm flying."

"You want to do *that* thing?"

"Come on," she said, coaxing him onto his back.

For a moment, she balanced above him, putting her arms out to the sides, and then his legs began to buckle, and she collapsed on top of him, laughing. He was laughing, too, at the sheer silliness of it, realizing he hadn't laughed like this in a long time. It was so simple. He recalled how they would spend hours and hours together, doing nothing but playing on the bed, making up silly words and games. That was all they'd needed.

She sat up, brushing the hair out of her face. There it was, he thought. He was falling in love with her again. He pulled her down and rolled on top of her. "I may still love you."

"Aren't you supposed to say that after we have sex?" she murmured.

"I'm saying it before." In unison, they slipped off their underpants, and she held his penis as if weighing his hard-on.

"I want to feel you inside me," she said.

He slipped in, and for the first few seconds, they didn't move. She sighed, and her head fell back. "Just do it," she said.

He began moving, going in deeper and deeper, and it was one of those times when they were immediately in sync. She began to orgasm, screaming out freely, and he started to come himself, and when they were finished, fifteen minutes later, they looked at each other in awe. "That was amazing," he said.

She wriggled out from under him and sat on the edge of the bed, looking back at him. Then she lay back, resting her head on his chest. "Now what?"

"I don't know," he said.

"Maybe we shouldn't have done it."

"Why?" he asked. "Are you going to run away again?"

He got up and went into the bathroom. "No," she said, sitting up. She followed him and watched while he peed, crossing her arms. "But what *are* you going to do?"

"I don't know."

"You want to eat?"

"Yes," he said gratefully.

"Good. I've been dying to tell you about our new director. He doesn't speak. Only uses hand motions. So I've named him Béla Lugosi."

Philip opened a bottle of Shiraz, and seated himself on the stepstool, watching her while he sipped the wine. Once again, he was overwhelmed by a deep sense of contentment that seemed to make time stand still. There was only him and her in this kitchen at this moment. He'd always been here, he thought, and he always would be. He made a decision. "I'm going to tell Lola it's over," he said.

❦

The ballet didn't end until after eleven, so Lola and Enid got back to One Fifth close to midnight. Lola was exhausted, but Enid's energy hadn't flagged, despite her insistence on leaning on Lola for physical support. Halfway through the ballet, she'd asked Lola to take charge of her handbag, claiming it was too heavy—the ancient crocodile bag did weigh at least five pounds—and Lola was forced to spend the rest of the evening fishing out Enid's reading glasses, lipstick, and powder. The third time Enid asked for her compact, Lola had realized Enid was doing it on purpose to try to irritate her. Why else would the old woman be so insistent on continually touching up her makeup?

But then riding down Fifth Avenue in the taxi, they'd come upon the mighty glory of One Fifth, and Lola decided the evening had been worth all the trouble. Reaching the thirteenth floor, Lola found Enid's keys, opened her door, and handed Enid back her handbag. Enid rewarded her with a kiss on the cheek, something she'd never done. "Good night, dear," she said. "I had such a good time. I'll see you tomorrow."

"Do we have plans?" Lola asked.

"No. But now that you're living with Philip, we don't need plans. I'll knock on your door. Maybe we can go for a walk."

Great, Lola thought, going into Philip's apartment. Tomorrow was going to be about twenty degrees. "Philip?" she called.

When she didn't get an answer, she went through the apartment, looking for him. Philip wasn't home. This was perplexing. She called his cell phone and heard it ringing in his office. He'd probably gone to the deli and would be back in a minute. She sat down on the couch, took off her shoes, and kicked them under the coffee table. Then she noticed that her bridal magazines were missing.

She stood up, frowning, and began searching for them. There had been a dress in one of the magazines that was particularly fetching—it was beaded and strapless, with a long train that flowed out when you walked, and pooled elegantly around the feet when you stood still. If she couldn't find the magazine, she might never find that particular dress, because the bridal magazines didn't put all their pages on a website, so prospective brides actually had to buy the publication. She looked in the kitchen and then Philip's office, coming to the conclusion that he had accidentally thrown them out. She would have to scold him for it—he had to learn to respect her things. Going back into the kitchen, she poured the last of a bottle of white wine into a glass, then opened the garbage chute to dispose of the bottle. Philip had repeatedly told her not to put glass down the chute, but she refused to follow his orders. Recycling was such a pain, and besides, it was completely useless. The planet had already been ruined by previous generations.

And lo, stuck in the top of the narrow chute was one of her magazines. She pulled it out and, smacking it on the counter, glared. So Philip had thrown out her magazines on purpose. What did that mean?

Taking the glass of wine into the bathroom, she began running a bath. She assumed Philip wanted to marry her—why wouldn't he?—but that it would take some urging to pull it off. What she'd been telling James Gooch about Philip wasn't true at all. She was perfectly happy to force Philip down the aisle if she had to. Everyone knew that men needed to be marched to the church, but once they were, they were grateful. If necessary, she was even willing to get pregnant. Celebrities were always getting pregnant first and married later, and if she had a baby, it could be dressed up like a little bridesmaid and carried down the aisle in a basket by her mother.

She was stripped down to her bra and panties when she heard the key turn in the lock. Without covering up, she hurried into the foyer. Philip came in, unencumbered, she noted, by a deli bag, and wouldn't look her in the eye. Something was wrong.

"Where were you?" she asked, then adjusted her attitude to make it seem like she didn't care. "I had the best time with Enid at the ballet. It was so beautiful. I didn't know it would be like that. And 'Diamonds' was so cute. And Enid said you danced in *The Nutcracker* when you were a kid. Why didn't you tell me?"

He turned around and closed the door. When he turned back, he appeared to register the fact that she wasn't dressed. Usually, this excited him, and he'd put his hand on her breast. But now he shook his head. "Lola." He sighed.

"What is it? What's wrong?" she asked.

"Put on your clothes and let's talk."

"I can't," she said gaily, as if everything were fine. "I was just getting into a bath. You'll have to talk to me while I'm under bubbles." Before he could say more, she darted away.

Philip went into the kitchen and put his hands in his hair. Riding up in the elevator from Schiffer Diamond's apartment, he'd somehow imagined this would be easy, or at least straightforward. He would tell Lola the truth—that he didn't think it was a good idea if they lived together after all—and he would offer her money. She still had two weeks left on the lease of her old apartment, and he would take over the rent for six months until she found a regular job. He would even pay her cell phone bills and take her shopping on Madison Avenue if necessary. He considered telling her the whole truth—that he was in love with someone else—but decided that might be too cruel. Nevertheless, she was going to make this as difficult as possible. He was slightly drunk from having consumed nearly two bottles of wine with Schiffer, but feeling in need of an extra dose of Dutch courage, he poured himself a glass of vodka over ice. He took a swig and went into the bathroom.

Lola was soaping her breasts. He tried not to be distracted by her pink nipples, pert from their immersion in hot water. He flipped down the toilet seat and sat. "So where were you, anyway?" Lola asked playfully, flicking soap bubbles at his leg.

He took another sip of vodka. "I was with Schiffer Diamond. I had dinner with her in her apartment." This should have triggered the impending discussion about their own relationship, but instead, Lola barely reacted.

"That's nice," she said, drawing out the I in "nice." "Did you have a good time?"

He nodded, wondering why she wasn't more upset.

"You're old friends," she said and smiled. "Why shouldn't you have dinner? Even though you said you were going to work. I guess you got hungry."

"It wasn't exactly like that," Philip said ominously.

Lola suddenly understood that Philip was about to break up with her—probably over Schiffer Diamond. The thought made her insides twist in alarm, but she couldn't let Philip know. She ducked under the water for a second to get her bearings. If she could somehow prevent Philip from breaking up with her now, at this moment, his desire to be rid of her might pass, and they could go on as before. When she popped out of the water, she had a plan.

"I'm so glad you're home," she said, grabbing a pumice stone and briskly sanding her heels. "I've had some bad news. My mother just called, and she needs me to go to Atlanta for a few days. Or longer. Maybe a week. She's not doing very well. You know the bank took the house?"

"I know," Philip said. The financial woes of Lola's family terrified him, constantly pulling him back into this relationship and her dependency on him.

"So anyway," Lola continued, examining her feet as if trying to be brave about the situation, "I know you're leaving for L.A. in three days. I don't want to upset you, but I won't be able to come after all. It's too far away, and my mother might need me. But I'll be here when you get back," she promised, as if this were a consolation prize.

"About that—" Philip began.

She shook her head. "I know. It's kind of a bummer. But let's not talk about it, because it makes me sad. And I have to go to Atlanta first thing in the morning. And I need a really, really big favor. Do you mind if I borrow a thousand dollars for my plane ticket?"

"No." Philip sighed, resigning himself to the fact that he couldn't have the discussion now, but also somewhat relieved. She was leaving tomorrow anyway. Maybe she wouldn't come back, and there would be no need to break up with her after all. "It's no problem," he said. "I don't want you to worry. You help your mother—that's what's most important."

She stood up, and with water and soap sliding off her in a slurry mess, she embraced him. "Oh, Philip," she said. "I love you so much."

She moved her hands down his chest and started trying to unbutton his jeans. He put his hands on hers and pulled them away. "Not now, Kitty," he said. "You're upset. It wouldn't be fun for either of us."

"Okay, baby," she said, drying herself off. Playing to the moment, she went into the bedroom and began packing wearily, as if someone had died and she was going to a funeral. Then she went into Philip's office and wrote a note. "Could you give this to Enid?" she asked, handing it to him. "It's a thank-you for the ballet. I told Enid I would see her tomorrow, and I don't want her to think I forgot about her."

Early the next morning, Beetelle Fabrikant was surprised to get a phone call from Lola, who was at La Guardia airport, about to board a plane for Atlanta. "Is everything all right?" Beetelle asked, her voice rising in panic.

"It's fine, Mother," Lola replied impatiently. "I told Philip I was worried about you, and he gave me money to visit you for the weekend."

Lola hung up and paced the small waiting area. Now was the worst possible time to leave Philip alone, when he was all hopped up on Schiffer Diamond and separated from her by only four floors. But if Lola had stayed, he would have tried to break up with her. And then she would have had to cry and beg. Once you did that with a man, it was as good as over. The man might keep you around, but he would never respect you. It wasn't fair, she thought, scuffing her foot on the dirty airport carpet. She was young and beautiful, and she and Philip had great sex. What more did he want?

Her perambulations took her by a small newsstand, where Schiffer Diamond's face stared out at her from the cover of *Harper's Bazaar*. She was wearing a blue halter-necked dress and was in one of those model-y type poses with her back arched and her hand on her hip, her long dark hair glossy and straight. I hate her, Lola thought, having a visceral reaction to the photograph, but she bought the magazine anyway, and pored over the cover, looking for flaws in Schiffer's face. For a moment, Lola despaired. How could she compete with a movie star?

Her flight was called on the loudspeaker, and Lola went to stand in line at the gate. She glanced up at the TV monitor, which was broadcasting one of the morning shows, and there was Schiffer Diamond again. This time she was wearing a plain white shirt with the collar turned up, a profusion of turquoise necklaces, and slim black pants. As she stared at the monitor, Lola felt a vein in her throat thumping in anger.

"I came back to New York to start over," Schiffer was saying to the host. "New Yorkers are wonderful, and I'm having a great time."

"With my boyfriend!" Lola wanted to scream.

Someone bumped her. "Are you going to get on the plane?" the man behind her asked.

Jerking her Louis Vuitton rollerboard, Lola shuffled through first class to the back of the plane. If she were Schiffer Diamond, she'd be riding in the front, she thought bitterly, heaving her suitcase into the overhead compartment. She arranged herself in the tiny seat, smoothing down her jeans and kicking off her shoes. She examined the cover of *Harper's Bazaar* again and nearly wanted to cry. Why was Schiffer Diamond ruining her dream?

Lola leaned her head back against the seat and closed her eyes. She wasn't finished yet, she reminded herself. Philip hadn't broken up with her, and on Sunday, he was going to Los Angeles for two weeks.

He'd be busy with his movie—too busy, she hoped, to think about Schiffer Diamond. And while he was away, she would move the last of her things into his apartment. When he returned, there she'd be.

Arriving at the house in Windsor Pines, Lola saw that the situation had indeed taken a turn for the worse. Most of the furniture was gone, and all the precious artifacts from her childhood—her plastic ponies and Barbie Fun House and even her extensive collection of Beanie Babies—had been sold in a tag sale. All that remained was her bed, with its lacy white bedskirt and frilly pink comforter. This time around, Beetelle insisted on being determinedly cheerful. She dragged Lola to a barbecue at the neighbors', where she told everyone that she and Cem were so happy to be moving to a condo where they wouldn't have to worry about upkeep on a house. The neighbors tried not to acknowledge the Fabrikants' situation by showing off pictures of their new grandson. Not to be outdone, Beetelle exclaimed how Lola herself was almost engaged to the famous writer Philip Oakland. "Isn't he a bit old?" said one of the women with disapproval.

Lola gave her a dirty look, deciding the woman was jealous because her own daughter had only married a local boy who ran a landscaping business. "He's forty-five," Lola said. "And he knows movie stars."

"Everyone knows actresses are secretly whores," the woman remarked. "That's always what my mother said, anyway."

"Lola is very sophisticated," Beetelle jumped in. "She was always more advanced than the other girls." Then they all started talking about their little investments in the stock market and the falling prices of their homes. This was both depressing and boring. Glaring at the woman who'd made the remark about Philip, Lola realized that they were all just petty and narrow-minded. How had she ever lived here?

Later, lying in her bed in her barren room, Lola realized she would never have to sleep in this bed, in this room, in this house, ever again. And looking around the nearly empty space, she decided she wouldn't miss it one bit.

15

Connie Brewer promised Billy never to wear the Cross of Bloody Mary. She kept her promise, but as Billy hadn't said anything about framing it and putting it on the wall, two weeks after Sandy purchased it for her, she took the cross to a renowned framer on Madison Avenue. He was an elderly man of at least eighty, still elegant with slicked-back gray hair and a yellow cravat at his neck. He examined the cross in its soft suede wrapping and looked at her curiously. "Where did you get this?" he asked.

"It was a gift," Connie said. "From my husband."

"Where did he get it?"

"I have no idea," she said firmly. She wondered if she'd made a mistake by taking the cross out of the apartment, but then the framer said nothing more, and Connie forgot about it. The framer, however, didn't. He told a dealer, and the dealer told a client, and soon a rumor began to circulate in the art world that the Brewers now possessed the Cross of Bloody Mary.

Being a generous girl, Connie naturally wanted to share her treasure with her friends. On an afternoon in late February after a lunch at La Goulue, she invited Annalisa back to her apartment. The Brewers lived on Park Avenue in an apartment in which two classic-six units were combined into one sprawling apartment with five bedrooms, two nannies' rooms, and an enormous living room where the Brewers hosted a Christmas party every year, with Sandy dressed up as Santa and Connie as one of his elves, in a red velvet jumpsuit with white mink cuffs.

"I have to show you something, but you can't tell anyone," Connie said, leading Annalisa through the apartment to her sitting room, located off the master bedroom. In consideration of Billy Litchfield's insistence that the cross remain a secret, she had hung the framed artifact in this room, accessible only through the master bedroom, making it the most private room in the apartment. No one was allowed in except the maids. The room was Connie's fantasy, done up in pink and light blue silks, with gilt mirrors and a Venetian chaise, a window seat filled with pillows, and wallpaper with hand-painted butterflies. Annalisa had been in this room twice, and she could never decide if it was beautiful or hideous.

"Sandy bought it for me," Connie whispered, indicating the cross. Annalisa took a step closer, politely examining the piece, which was displayed against dark blue velvet. She didn't have Connie's interest in or appreciation for jewelry, but she said kindly, "It's gorgeous. What is it?"

"It belonged to Queen Mary. A gift from the pope for keeping England Catholic. It's invaluable."

"If it's real, it probably belongs in a museum."

"Well, it does," Connie admitted. "But so many antiquities are owned by private individuals these days. And I don't think it's wrong for the rich to guard the treasures of the past—I feel it's our duty. It's such an important piece. Historically, aesthetically . . ."

"More important than your crocodile Birkin bag?" Annalisa teased. She didn't for a moment think the cross was real. Billy had told her that Sandy had been buying Connie so much jewelry lately, he was developing a reputation as an easy mark. Knowing Sandy, he'd probably bought the piece from a shady dealer and had made the guy's day.

"Handbags are not important anymore," Connie admonished

her. "It said so in *Vogue*. Right now it's all about having something no one else possesses. It's about the one of a kind. The unique."

Annalisa lay down on the Venetian chaise and yawned. She'd had two glasses of champagne at lunch and was feeling sleepy. "I thought Queen Mary was evil. Didn't she have her sister killed? Or have I got the story wrong? You'd better be careful, Connie. The cross might bring you bad luck."

Meanwhile, a few blocks away in the basement offices of the Metropolitan Museum, David Porshie, Billy Litchfield's old friend, hung up the phone. He had just been informed about the rumor of the existence of the Cross of Bloody Mary, which was said to be in the hands of a couple named Sandy and Connie Brewer. He sat back in his swivel chair, folding his hands under his chin. Could it be true? he wondered.

David was well aware of the mysterious disappearance of the cross in the fifties. Every year it appeared on a list of items missing from the museum. The suspicion had always been that Mrs. Houghton purloined the cross herself, but as she was beyond reproach and, more importantly, donated two million dollars a year to the museum, the matter had never been thoroughly investigated.

But now that Mrs. Houghton was dead, perhaps it was time— especially as the cross had surfaced shortly after her death. Looking up Sandy and Connie Brewer on the Internet, David discovered exactly who they were. Sandy was a hedge-fund manager, of all things—typical that an arriviste should end up with such a rare and precious antiquity—and while he and his wife, Connie, deemed themselves "important collectors," David suspected they were of the new-money ilk who paid ridiculous prices for what David considered junk. People like the Brewers were not generally of interest to people like himself, a steward of the great Metropolitan Museum, except in how much money one might extract from them at the gala.

He couldn't, however, simply call up the Brewers and ask if they had the cross. Whoever sold it to them would have been smart enough to warn them of its provenance. Not that a shady past ever stopped a buyer. There was a certain psychology in the purchaser of such an item that wasn't dissimilar to the buyer of illegal drugs. There was the thrill of breaking the law and the high of getting away with it. Unlike the drug buyer, however, the illegal-antiquities purchaser had the continued elation of owning the piece, along with a feeling of immortality. It was as if mere proximity to such a piece might also convey everlasting life to its owner. And so, David Porshie knew, he was looking for a specific personality type along with the cross. The question was only how to make such a discovery.

David was prepared to be patient in his pursuit—after all, the cross had been missing for nearly sixty years—and what he needed was a mole. Immediately, he thought of Billy Litchfield. They'd been at Harvard together. Billy Litchfield knew quite a bit about art and even more about people.

He found Billy's cell number on a guest list from the events office and called him up the next morning. Billy was in a taxi, coincidentally on his way to Connie Brewer's to discuss the Basel art fair. When Billy heard David's voice on the phone, he felt his whole body redden in fear, but he managed to keep his voice steady. "How are you, David?" he asked.

"I'm well," David replied. "I was thinking about what you said at the ballet. About potential new patrons. We're looking for some fresh blood to donate money to a new wing. The names Sandy and Connie Brewer came up. I thought you might know them."

"I do indeed," Billy said evenly.

"That's wonderful," David said. "Could you arrange a small dinner? Nothing too fancy, maybe at Twenty-One. And Billy?" he added. "If you don't mind, could you keep the purpose of the dinner quiet? You know how people get if they suspect you're going to ask them for money."

"Of course," Billy said. "It's just between us." He hung up the phone in a panic. The taxi felt like a prison cell. He began hyperventilating. "Could you stop the cab, please?" he asked, tapping on the partition.

He stumbled out onto the sidewalk, looking for the nearest coffee shop. Finding one on the corner, he sat down at the counter, trying to catch his breath while ordering a ginger ale. How much did David Porshie know, and how had he found out? Billy swallowed a Xanax, and while he waited for the pill to take effect, tried to think logically. Was it possible David only wanted to meet the Brewers for the reason he'd stated? Billy thought not. The Metropolitan Museum was the last bastion of old money, although recently, they'd had to redefine "old" as meaning twenty years instead of a hundred.

"Connie, what have you done?" Billy asked when he got to the Brewers' apartment. "Where's the cross?"

Following her to the inner chamber, he regarded the framed cross with horror. "How many people have seen this?" he asked.

"Oh, Billy, don't worry," she said. "Only Sandy. And the maids. And Annalisa Rice."

"And the framer," Billy pointed out. "Whom did you take it to?" Connie named the man. "My God," Billy said, sitting on the edge of the chaise. "He'll tell everyone."

"But how does he even know what it is?" Connie asked. "I didn't tell him."

"Did you tell him how you came to have it?" Billy asked.

"Of course not," Connie assured him. "I haven't told anyone."

"Listen, Connie. You have to put it away. Take it off your wall and put it in a safe. I told you, if anyone finds out about this, we could all go to jail."

"People like us don't go to jail," Connie countered.

"Yes, we do. It happens all the time these days." Billy sighed.

Connie took the cross off the wall. "Look," she said, taking it to her closet, "I'm putting it away."

"Promise me you'll put it in a vault. It's too valuable to be left in a closet."

"It's too valuable to be hidden," Connie objected. "If I can't look at it, what's the point?"

"We'll discuss that later," Billy said. "After you put it away." It was possible, Billy thought with a glimmer of hope, that David Porshie didn't know about the cross—if he did, Billy reasoned, he'd be sending detectives, not arranging dinner parties. Nevertheless, Billy would have to make sure the dinner took place. If he didn't, it would further raise David's suspicions. "We're going to have dinner with David Porshie from the Met," Billy said. "And you're not to say a word about the cross—neither you nor Sandy. Even if he asks you point-blank."

"We've never heard of it," Connie said.

Billy passed his hand over the top of his bald head. Despite all his efforts to stay in New York, he saw his future. As soon as the three million dollars were available, he would have to leave the country. He'd be forced to settle in a place like Buenos Aires, where there were no extradition laws. Billy shuddered. Involuntarily, he said aloud, "I hate palm trees."

"What?" Connie said, thinking she'd missed a part of the conversation.

"Nothing, my dear," Billy said quickly. "I have a lot on my mind."

Coming out of Connie's building on Seventy-eighth Street, he got into a taxi and instructed the driver to take Fifth Avenue downtown. The traffic was backed up at Sixty-sixth Street, but Billy didn't mind. The taxi was one of the brand-new SUV types and smelled of fresh plastic; from the mouth of the driver came a musical patter as he conversed on his cell phone. If only, Billy thought, he could stay in this taxi forever, inching down Fifth Avenue past all the familiar landmarks: the castle in Central Park, the Sherry-Netherland, where he'd lunched at Cipriani nearly every day for fifteen years, the Plaza, Bergdorf Goodman, Saks, the New York Public Library. His nostalgia engulfed him in a haze of pleasure and sweet, aching bitterness. How could he ever leave his beloved Manhattan?

His phone rang. "You'll be there tonight, won't you, Billy boy?" Schiffer Diamond asked.

"Yes. Yes, of course," Billy said, although given the circumstances, it had crossed his mind that he should cancel all his events for the next week and lie low.

"Good, because I can't stand these things," Schiffer said. "I'm going to have to talk to a bunch of strangers and be nice to all of them. I hate being trotted out like a show pony."

"Then don't go," Billy said simply.

"Billy Bob, what's wrong with you? I have to go. If I cancel, they'll write about what a bitch I am. Maybe I should be a bitch from now on. The lonely diva. Ah, Billy," she said, sounding slightly bitter, which wasn't like her. "Where are all the men in this town?" She hung up.

Two hours later, Schiffer Diamond sat on a stool in her bathroom, having her hair and makeup done for the fourth or fifth time that day, while her publicist, Karen, sat out in the living room, reading magazines and talking on her cell phone while she waited for Schiffer to get ready. The hair and makeup people fluttered around the bathroom, wanting to make conversation, but Schiffer wasn't in the mood. She was feeling foul. Coming into One Fifth that very afternoon, she'd run into none other than Lola Fabrikant, who was scuttling into the building like a criminal.

Perhaps "scuttling" wasn't exactly the right word, as Lola hadn't scuttled but had walked in pulling her Louis Vuitton rollerboard behind her like she owned the place. Schiffer was momentarily shocked. Hadn't Philip broken up with her? Apparently, he hadn't had the guts. Damn Oakland, she thought. Why was he so weak?

Lola came in while Schiffer was waiting for the elevator; as a consequence, Schiffer was forced to ride up with her. Lola gushed over Schiffer as if they were best friends, asking how the TV show was going and saying how much she liked Schiffer's hair—although it was the same as always—and being careful to make no mention of Philip. So Schiffer brought him up. "Philip told me your parents are having some trouble," she said.

Lola sighed dramatically. "It's been awful," she said. "If it weren't for Philip, I don't know what we'd do."

"Philip's a peach," Schiffer remarked, and Lola agreed. Then, rubbing salt into the wound, Lola added, "I'm *so* lucky to have him."

Now, thinking about the encounter, Schiffer glared at herself in the mirror. "You're done," the makeup artist said, flicking Schiffer's nose with powder.

"Thank you," Schiffer said. She went into the bedroom, put on the borrowed dress and the borrowed jewelry, and called to her publicist to help zip her up. She put her hands on her waist and exhaled. "I'm thinking about moving out of this building," she said. "I need a bigger place."

"Why don't you get a bigger place here? It's such a great building," Karen said.

"I'm sick of it. All these new people. It's not like it used to be."

"Someone's in a mood," Karen said.

"Really? Who?" Schiffer asked.

Then Schiffer, the publicist, and the hair and makeup people went downstairs and got into the back of a waiting limousine. Karen opened her bag, took out several sheets of paper, and began consulting her notes. "*Letterman*'s confirmed for Tuesday, and Michael Kors is sending three dresses for you to try. Meryl Streep's people are wondering if you'll do a poetry reading on April twenty-second. I think it's a good idea because it's Meryl and it's classy. On Wednesday, your call time is one P.M., so I scheduled the *Marie Claire* photo shoot for six in the morning, to get that out of the way—the reporter will come to the set on Thursday to interview you. On Friday evening, the president of Boucheron is in town, and he's invited you to a private dinner for twenty. I think you should do that, too—it can't hurt, and they might want to use you in an advertising campaign. And on Saturday afternoon, the network wants to shoot promos. I'm trying to push the call time to the afternoon so you can get some rest in the morning."

"Thank you," Schiffer said.

"What do you think about Meryl?"

"It's so far away. I don't even know if I'll be alive on April twenty-second."

"I'll say yes," Karen said.

The makeup artist held up a tube of lip gloss, and Schiffer leaned forward so the woman could touch up her lips. She turned her head, and the stylist fluffed her hair and sprayed it. "What's the exact name of the organization again?" Schiffer said.

"The International Council of Shoe Designers. ICSD. The money is going to a retirement fund for shoe workers. You're giving the award to Christian Louboutin, and you'll be sitting at his table. Your remarks are on the teleprompter. Do you want to go over them beforehand?"

"No," Schiffer said.

The car turned onto Forty-second Street. "Schiffer Diamond is arriving," Karen said into her phone. "We're a minute away." She put down the phone and looked at the line of Town Cars and the photographers and the crowd of bystanders roped off from the entrance by police barricades. "Everyone loves shoes," she said, shaking her head.

"Is Billy Litchfield here?" Schiffer asked.

"I'll find out," Karen said. She talked into her cell phone like it was a walkie-talkie. "Has Billy Litchfield arrived? Well, can you find out?" She nodded and snapped the phone shut. "He's inside."

The car was waved forward by two security men, one of whom opened the door. Karen got out first and, after consulting briefly with two women dressed in black and wearing headsets, motioned for Schiffer to come out of the car. A ripple of excitement went through the crowd, and the blazing flashes began.

Schiffer found Billy Litchfield waiting just inside the door. "Another night in Manhattan, eh, Billy?" she said, taking his arm. Immediately, she was accosted by a young woman from *Women's Wear Daily* who asked if she could interview her, and then a young man from *New York* magazine, and it was another half hour before she and Billy were able to escape to their table. Making their way through the crowd, Schiffer said, "Philip is still seeing that Lola Fabrikant."

"Do you care?" Billy said.

"I shouldn't."

"Don't. Brumminger is at our table."

"He keeps turning up like a bad penny, doesn't he?"

"More like a million-dollar bill," Billy said. "You can have any man you want. You know that."

"Actually, I can't. There's only a certain kind of man who will deal with this," Schiffer said, indicating the event. "And he's not necessarily the kind of man one wants." At the table, she greeted Brumminger, who was seated opposite her on the other side of the centerpiece. "We missed you in Saint Barths," he said, taking her hands.

"I should have come," she said.

"We had a great group on the yacht. I'm determined to get you on it. I don't give up easily."

"Please don't," she said, and went to her seat. A plate of salad with a couple of pieces of lobster was already set at her place. She opened her napkin and picked up her fork, realizing she hadn't eaten all day, but the head of the ICSD came over, insisting on introducing her to a man whose name she didn't catch, and then a woman came over who claimed to have known her from twenty years ago, and then two young women rushed over and said they were fans and asked her to sign their programs. Then Karen arrived and informed her it was time to go backstage to get ready for her speech, and she got up and went behind the platform to wait with the other celebrities, who were being lined up by handlers and mostly ignoring each other. "Do you need anything?" Karen asked, fussing. "Water? I could bring you your wine from the table."

"I'm fine," Schiffer said. The program began, and she stood by herself, waiting to go on. She could see the crowd through a crack in the plasterboard, their eager and politely bored faces lifted in the semi-darkness. She felt a creeping loneliness.

Years and years ago, she and Philip would go to these kinds of events and have fun. But perhaps it was only because they were young and so wrapped up in each other that every moment had the vibrancy of a scene in a movie. She could see Philip in his tux, with the white silk scarf he always wore slung over his shoulders, and she remembered the feel of his hand around hers, muscular and firm, leading her out of the crowd and across the sidewalk to the waiting car. Somehow they would have gathered an entourage of half a dozen people, and they'd pile into the car, laughing and screaming, and go on to the next place, and the next place after that, finally heading home in the gray light of dawn with the birds singing. She would lie halfway across the seat with her head on Philip's shoulder, sleepily closing her eyes. "I'd like to shoot those birds," he'd say.

"Shut up, Oakland. I think they're sweet."

Peeking once more through the crack, she spotted Billy Litchfield at the front table. Billy looked weary, as if he'd tilted his head too many times at too many of these events over the years. He had recently pointed out that what was once fun had become institutionalized, and he was right, she realized. And then, hearing the MC announce her name, she stepped out into the lights, remembering that there was not even a warm hand to lead her away at the end of the evening.

When she was able to return to the table, the main course had been served and taken away, but Karen made sure the waiters had saved a plate for her. The filet mignon was cold. Schiffer ate two bites and tried to talk to Billy before she was interrupted again by the woman from the ICSD, who had more people Schiffer had to meet. This went on for another thirty minutes, and then Brumminger was by her side. "You look like you've had enough," he said. "Why don't I take you away?"

"Yes, please," she said gratefully. "Can we go someplace fun?"

"You have a seven A.M. call tomorrow," Karen reminded her.

Brumminger had a chauffeur-driven Escalade with two video screens and a small refrigerator. "Anyone for champagne?" he asked, extracting a half-bottle.

They went to the Box and sat upstairs in a curtained booth. Schiffer let Brumminger put his arm around her shoulder and lace his fingers through hers, and the next day, Page Six reported that they'd been spotted canoodling and were rumored to be seeing each other.

Returning to Philip's apartment on Tuesday, Lola dug out the old *Vogue* magazine with the photo spread of Philip and Schiffer (he hadn't, at least, tried to hide it, which was a good sign), and looking at the young, handsome Philip with the gorgeous young Schiffer made her want to march down to Schiffer's apartment and confront her. But she didn't quite have the guts—what if Schiffer didn't back down?—and then she thought she should simply throw out the magazine, the way Philip had thrown out hers. But if she did that, she wouldn't have the pleasure of staring at Schiffer's photographs and hating her. Then she decided to watch *Summer Morning*.

Viewing the DVD was a kind of divine torture. In *Summer Morning*, the ingenue saves the boy from himself, and when the boy finally realizes he's in love with her, he accidentally kills her in a car crash. The story was somehow supposed to be autobiographical, and while Philip wasn't actually in the movie, every line of dialogue delivered by the actor playing Philip reminded her of something Philip would say. Watching the love story unfold between Schiffer Diamond and the Philip character made Lola feel like the third wheel in a relationship where she didn't belong. It also made her more in love with Philip, and more determined to keep him.

The next day, she got to work and enlisted Thayer Core and his awful roommate, Josh, to help her officially move into Philip's apartment. The task required Thayer and Josh to pack up her things in boxes and plastic bags and, like Sherpas, carry it all to One Fifth.

Josh grumbled throughout the morning, complaining about his fingers, his back (he had a bad back, he claimed, just like his mother), and his feet, which were encased in thick white sports shoes that resembled two casts. Thayer, on the other hand, was surprisingly efficient. Naturally, there was an ulterior motive behind Thayer's efforts: He wanted to see the inside of One Fifth and, in particular, Philip Oakland's apartment. Therefore, he didn't object when Lola required him to make three trips, back and forth, dragging a garbage bag filled with Lola's shoes down Greenwich Avenue. In the past two days, Lola had sold off everything in her apartment, posting the details of the sale on Craigslist and Facebook, and presiding over the sale like a dealer of fine antiques. She took nothing less than top dollar for the furnishings her parents had purchased under a year ago, and consequently, she had eight thousand dollars in cash. But she refused to pay for a taxi to transport her belongings. If the last month of penury had taught her anything, it was this: It was one thing to lavishly spend someone else's money but quite another to shell out your own.

On the fourth trip, the trio ran into James Gooch in the lobby of One Fifth. James was pushing two boxes of hardcover copies of his book across the lobby with his foot. When he spotted Lola, he reddened. Her visits and text messages had stopped abruptly after his encounter with Philip, leaving James confused and hurt. Seeing Lola in the lobby with what appeared to be a young asshole and a young loser, James wondered if he should speak to her at all.

But in the next minute, she'd not only engaged him but convinced him to help her carry her things. So he found himself squeezed next to her in the elevator with the young asshole, who glared at him, and the young loser, who kept talking about his feet. It could have been his imagination, but holding a box of old shampoo bottles in his arms, James swore he felt waves of electricity coming from Lola and commingling with the electricity from his own body, and he imagined their electrons doing a little sex dance right there in the elevator in front of everyone.

Putting down the box in the foyer of Philip's apartment, Lola introduced James as "a writer who lives in the building," to the young asshole, who immediately began challenging James about the relevance of every successful living novelist. With Lola as his audience, James found himself easily rising to the occasion, putting the boy in his place by citing DeLillo and McEwan, whom the young asshole hadn't bothered to read. James's knowledge infuriated Thayer, but he reminded himself that this James person was insignificant, nothing more than a member of the hated boomer tribe who happened to live in this exclusive building. But then Lola began gushing about James's new book and his review in *The New York Times*, and Thayer figured out exactly who James was, sighting him in the crosshairs of his ire.

Later that evening, after Thayer had consumed two bottles of Philip Oakland's best red wine and was back in his dank hole of an apartment, he looked up James Gooch on Google, found he was married to Mindy Gooch, looked him up on Amazon, found that his yet unpublished novel was already ranked number eighty-two, and began constructing an elaborate and vicious blog entry about him in which he called James "a probable pedophile and word molester."

Lola, meanwhile, still awake and bored, sent James a text message warning him not to tell Philip he had been in the apartment because Philip was jealous. The message caused James's phone to bleat at one in the morning, and the uncharacteristic noise woke Mindy. For a moment, she wondered if James was having an affair, but dismissed it as impossible.

On most weekday mornings in One Fifth, Paul Rice was the earliest riser, waking at four A.M. to check the European markets, and to wheel and deal fish. His tank was completed and installed, running nearly the length of Mrs. Houghton's ballroom, and the interior was a model-maker's dream, a replica of Atlantis half buried under the sea, complete with old Roman roads leading out of sandy caves. The acquisition of his coveted fish was a cutthroat business and required viewing videos of hatchlings and then engaging in bidding wars in which the best fish went for a hundred thousand dollars or more. But every successful man needed a hobby, especially when most of his day entailed either making money or losing it.

On an unusually warm morning on a Tuesday at the end of February, however, James Gooch was also up early. At four-thirty A.M., James got out of bed with a stomach full of nerves. After a night of tossing and turning in anticipation, he had finally fallen asleep only to awaken an hour later, exhausted and hating himself for being exhausted on the most important day of his life.

The pub date for his book had finally arrived. That morning, he had an appearance on the *Today* show, followed by several radio interviews, and then a book signing in the evening at the Barnes & Noble on Union Square. Meanwhile, two hundred thousand copies would be released in bookstores all over the country, and two hundred thousand copies would be placed in iStores, and on Sunday, his book would be featured on the cover of *The New York Times Book Review*. The publication was going exactly according to plan, and since nothing in his life had ever gone according to plan, James was seized with an irrational sense of doom.

He showered and made coffee, and then, although he'd promised himself he wouldn't, he checked his Amazon rating. The number shocked him—twenty-two—and there were still five hours left until it was technically released. How did the world know about his book? he wondered, and decided it was a kind of mysterious miracle, proof that what happened in one's life was absolutely out of one's control.

Then, just for the hell of it, he Googled himself. On the bottom of the first page, he came across the following headline: GOOFY BOOMER HOPES TO PROVE LITERATURE IS ALIVE AND WELL. Clicking on it, he was taken to Snarker. Curious, he began reading Thayer Core's item about him. As he read on, his jaw dropped, and the blood began pounding in his head. Thayer had written about James's book and his marriage to Mindy, referring to her as "the navel-gazing schoolmarm," followed by a cruel physical description of James as resembling an extinct species of bird.

Gaping at the item, James was filled with rage. Was this what people really thought of him? "James Gooch is a probable pedophile and word molester," he read again. Wasn't this kind of statement illegal? Could he sue?

"Mindy!" he shouted. There was no response, and he went into the bedroom to find Mindy awake but pretending to sleep with a pillow over her head.

"What time is it?" she asked wearily.

"Five."

"Give me another hour."

"I need you," James said. "Now."

Mindy got out of bed and, following James, stared sleepily at the blog entry on his computer. "Typical," she said. "Just typical."

"We have to do something about it," James said.

"What?" she asked. "That's life these days. You can't do anything about anything. You just have to live with it." She read through the item again. "How'd they find out this stuff about you, anyway?" she asked. "How do they know we live in One Fifth?"

"I have no idea," James said nervously, realizing that the item could be traced back to him. If he hadn't run into Lola that day when she was moving, he would have never met Thayer Core.

"Forget about it," Mindy said. "Only ten thousand people read this stuff, anyway."

"Only ten thousand?" James said. Then his phone bleeped.

"What is that?" Mindy demanded in annoyance. She stared up at him with her pale, mostly unlined face, the result of years of avoiding the sun. "Why are you getting text messages in the middle of the night?"

"What do you mean?" James asked defensively. "It's probably the car service from the *Today* show." When Mindy left the room, James grabbed his phone and checked the message. As he'd hoped, it was from Lola. "Good luck today," she'd written. "I'll be watching!" followed by a smiley-face emoticon.

James left the apartment at six-fifteen. Mindy, unable to help herself, reread the blog item on her and James, and her mood became increasingly foul. Nowadays, anyone who committed the crime of trying to do something with her life became a victim of Internet bullying, and there was no retribution, no control, nothing one could do. In this frame of mind, she sat down at her computer and began a new blog entry, listing all the things in her life over which she had no control and had made her bitterly disappointed: her inability to get pregnant, her inability to live in a proper apartment, her inability to lead a life that didn't feel like she was always racing to catch up to an invisible finish line that moved farther away the closer she came. And now there was James's impending success—which, instead of relieving these feelings, was only bringing them into sharper focus.

When she heard the elevator ding at seven A.M., signaling Paul Rice's arrival in the lobby, she deliberately opened her door and let Skippy loose. Skippy, as usual, growled at Paul. Mindy, still in a lousy mood, didn't snatch Skippy away as quickly as she normally did, and Skippy attacked Paul's pant leg with a rabid viciousness that Mindy wished she herself could express. During the tussle, Skippy managed to rip a tiny hole in the fabric of Paul's pants before he was able to shake Skippy off. He bent down and examined the tear. Then he stood up, making an odd thrusting motion of pushing his tongue into his cheek. "I will sue you for this," he said coldly.

"Go ahead," Mindy said. "Make my day. It can't really get any worse."

"Oh, but it can," Paul said threateningly. "You'll see."

Paul went out, and upstairs, Lola Fabrikant got out of bed and turned on the TV. Eventually, James appeared on the screen. Perhaps it was the makeup, but James didn't look so bad. True, he appeared unnecessarily formal, but James was a little stiff in general. It would be interesting to loosen him up, Lola thought. And he was on TV! Anyone could be on YouTube. But real TV, and network TV at that, was a whole different level. "I watched you!" she texted. "You were great! xLola." Underneath, she included her new tagline, with which she signed off on all her e-mails and blog posts: *"The body dies, but the spirit lives forever."*

Up at Thirty Rock, the publicist, a lanky young woman with long blond hair and a bland prettiness, smiled at James. "That was good," she said.

"Was it?" James said. "I wasn't sure. I've never done TV before."

"No. You were good. Really," the publicist said unconvincingly. "We've got to hurry if we're going to make it to your interview at CBS radio."

James got into the Town Car. He briefly wondered if he would be famous now, recognized by strangers after appearing on the *Today* show. He didn't feel any different, and the driver took as little notice of him as he had before. Then he checked his e-mails and found the text from Lola. At least someone appreciated him. He opened his window, letting in a rush of damp air.

The day of Sam's father's book signing was strangely warm, leading to the inevitable discussion among his classmates about global warming. They agreed it was terrible to be born into a world where the adults had ruined the earth for their children, so that the children were forced to live under the shroud of impending Armageddon in which all living things might be wiped out. Sam knew his mother felt guilty about this—she was always telling him to recycle and turn off his light—but not every adult felt the same way. When he brought up the topic with Enid, she only laughed at him and said it had always been so: In the thirties, children had lived with food rationing and the threat of starvation (indeed, in the Great Depression, some people had starved); in the forties and fifties, it was air raids; and in the sixties and seventies, a nuclear bomb. And yet, she pointed out, people continued not only to survive but to flourish, given the fact that there were billions more people now than ever before. Sam didn't find this reassuring. It was the billions of people, he argued, that *were* the problem.

Marching through the West Village with his friends, Sam talked about how the earth was already two degrees cooler than suspected due to the proliferation of airplanes, which caused cloud cover and the dimming of the canopy, mitigating 5 percent of all sunlight. It was a scientific fact, he said, that during the two days following 9/11, when there were no flights and therefore less cloud cover, the temperature on earth had registered two degrees higher. The exhaust from airplanes caused a smaller particulate in the air and a greater reflection of light away from the earth's surface, he said.

Walking up Sixth Avenue, the group passed a basketball court with a game in progress. Sam forgot about climate change and peeled away to get in on the action. He'd been playing basketball on this particular litter-strewn, cracked asphalt court since he was two, when his father would bring him on spring and summer mornings to teach him how to dribble and throw. "Don't tell your mother, Sammy," his dad would say. "She'll think we were goofing off."

Today the pickup game was particularly vicious, due perhaps to the warm weather in which everyone had come outside with their pent-up winter energy. Sam was off his game, and after being elbowed in the throat and knocked against the chain-link fence, he called it quits. He picked up a bagel with cream cheese on his way home, then worked on his website, which he was upgrading to Virtual Flash. Then the buzzer rang, and the doorman said he had a visitor.

The man standing in the foyer had a distinct air about him— seedy, Sam thought. Looking Sam up and down, the man asked if his parents were home, and when Sam shook his head, he said, "You'll do. You know how to sign your name?" "Of course," Sam said, thinking he ought to close the door in the man's face and call the doorman to escort him out. But it all happened so quickly. The man handed him an envelope and a clipboard. "Sign here," he said. Unable to challenge grown-up authority, Sam signed. In a second, the man was gone, disappearing through the revolving doors of the lobby, and Sam was left holding the envelope in his hand.

The return address was for an attorney on Park Avenue. Knowing he shouldn't, Sam opened the envelope, figuring he could explain later that he'd opened it by mistake. Inside was a two-page letter.

The attorney was writing on behalf of his client, Mr. Paul Rice, who was being maliciously and systematically harassed by his mother, *without cause*, and if such actions did not cease immediately and reparations begin, a restraining order would be placed on his mother by Paul Rice and his attorneys, who were prepared to pursue this case as far as the law allowed.

In his bedroom, Sam read the letter again, feeling a white-hot adolescent rage engulf him. His mother was often annoying, but like most boys, he felt a fierce protectiveness toward her. She was smart, accomplished, and in his mind, beautiful; he placed her on a pedestal as the model to whom other girls must compare, although so far he had yet to meet another member of the female species who measured up. And now his mother was being attacked once again by Paul Rice. The thought infuriated him; looking around his room for something to break, and finding nothing of use, he changed his shoes and headed out of the building. He jogged down Ninth Street, past the porno shops and pet stores and fancy tea outlets. Sam meant to run along the Hudson River, but the entrance to the piers was blocked by several red and white barriers and a Con Edison truck. "Gas leak," a beefy man shouted as Sam approached. "Go around."

The utility vehicle gave Sam an idea, and he headed back to One Fifth. He suddenly saw how he might get even with Paul Rice and his threatening letter. It would inconvenience everyone in the building, but it would be temporary, and Paul Rice, with all his computer equipment, would be the most inconvenienced of all. He might even lose data. Sam smiled, thinking about how angry Paul Rice would be. Maybe it would make him want to leave the building.

At six-thirty in the evening, Sam headed over to the Barnes & Noble bookstore on Union Square with his parents. It was ten blocks from One Fifth, and the publicist wanted to send a car—no doubt, Mindy said, to make sure James would get there—but Mindy turned it down. They could walk, she declared. And reminding everyone of her recent vow to go green, she pointed out that there was no reason to waste gas and fill the air with carbon monoxide when God had given them perfectly good implements on which to get around. They were called feet. Ignoring his parents' banter, Sam walked a few feet ahead of them, still brooding about his day. He hadn't shown his mother the letter from Paul Rice's attorney. He wasn't going to allow Paul Rice to ruin his parents' big day. Sam wouldn't have been surprised if Paul had done it on purpose.

Outside the store, the Gooch family stopped to admire a small poster announcing James's reading, featuring the photograph of James taken at the shoot on the day he'd gotten the ride from Schiffer Diamond. James was pleased with the image: He looked appropriately brooding and intellectual, as if he alone were privy to some great universal secret. Stepping inside the store, he was greeted by the blasé publicist from that morning and two employees who escorted him up to the fifth floor. They sequestered him in a tiny office at the back of the store to wait while a cartload of books was brought in for him to sign. Holding a Sharpie, James paused, staring down at the title page and his name: James Gooch. This was, he thought, a historical moment in his life, and he wanted to remember his feelings.

What he felt, however, was a little disappointing. There was some elation, a bit of dread, and a lot of nothing. Then Mindy barked out, "What's wrong with you?" Startled, James quickly signed his name.

At five minutes to seven, Redmon Richardly came in to congratulate him and walked James toward the stage. James was astounded by the size of the audience. Every folding chair was filled, and the standing-room-only crowd swelled around the stacks. Even Redmon was shocked. "There must be five hundred people," he said, clapping James on the shoulder. "Good job."

James awkwardly made his way up to the podium. He could feel the crowd like one giant animal, anticipatory, eager, and curious. Again, he wondered how this had happened. How had these people even heard of him? And what could they possibly want—from him?

He opened his book to the page he'd selected and found his hand was trembling. Looking down at the words he'd struggled to write over so many years, he forced himself to concentrate. Opening his mouth and praying he could survive this ordeal, he began to read aloud.

♦

Later that same evening, Annalisa Rice greeted her husband at the door, dressed provocatively in a short Grecian column, her hair and makeup expertly applied so she appeared to have made hardly any effort at all. The look was slightly tousled and overwhelmingly sexy, but Paul barely noticed.

"Sorry," he mumbled, heading up the two flights of steps to his office, where he fiddled around with his computer for a moment and then gazed at his fish. Annalisa sighed and went into the kitchen, walking around Maria, the housekeeper, who was rearranging the condiments, and fixed herself a stiff drink. Carrying the vodka, she peeped into Paul's office. "Paul?" she said. "Are you getting ready? Connie said the dinner starts at eight. And it's eight now."

"It's my dinner," Paul said. "We'll get there when we get there." He went downstairs to change his suit, and Annalisa went into her pretty little office. She stared out the window at the monument in Washington Square Park. The perimeter of the park was encased in chain-link fencing and would be for at least the next year. The residents of the Village had been lobbying for years to have the fountain moved so it lined up perfectly with the monument, and they had finally won their battle. Sipping her cocktail, Annalisa understood the desire and pleasure in the attention to details. Thinking again about the time, she went into the bedroom to hurry Paul along. "Why are you hovering?" he asked. She shook her head and, once again finding communication difficult, decided to wait in the car.

Over at Union Square, James was still signing books. At eight o'clock, three hundred people were in line, eagerly clutching their copies, and as James felt obligated to speak to each and every one of them, it was likely he'd be there for at least another three hours. Mindy sent Sam back to One Fifth to do his homework. Walking down Fifth Avenue, Sam spotted Annalisa getting into the back of a green Bentley idling at the curb. Passing the car on the way into the building, Sam was strangely disappointed in her, and hurt. After helping her so often with her website, Sam had developed a little crush. He imagined Annalisa as a princess, a damsel in distress, and seeing her in the back of that fancy car with the chauffeur who was actually wearing a cap destroyed his fantasy. She wasn't a damsel in distress at all, he thought bitterly, but just another rich lady with too many privileges, married to a rich asshole. And he went inside.

Sam opened the refrigerator. As he seemed to be all the time now, he was ravenously hungry. His parents didn't understand how a growing boy needed to eat, and all he could find in the refrigerator were two containers of cut-up fruit, some leftover Indian food, and a quart of soy milk. Sam drank the soy milk straight from the carton, leaving a squirt for his mother's coffee in the morning, and decided he needed red meat. He would go to the Village restaurant on Ninth Street, sit at the bar, and eat a steak.

Stepping into the lobby, he came right up behind Paul Rice, who was heading out to the Bentley. Sam's heart began beating rapidly, and he was reminded of his scheme. Sam hadn't decided when he would execute his plan, but seeing Paul get into the backseat of the car, he decided he would do it tonight, while the Rices were out. Passing by the Bentley, he waved to Annalisa, who smiled at him and waved back.

"Sam Gooch is such a sweet boy," Annalisa said to Paul.

"His mother's a cunt," Paul said.

"I wish you would end this war with Mindy Gooch."

"Oh, I have," Paul said.

"Good," Annalisa said.

"Mindy Gooch and her stupid dog have harassed me one time too many."

"Her *dog*?" Annalisa said.

"I had my lawyer send her a letter this afternoon. I want that woman, that dog, and that family out of my building."

This was outrageous, even for Paul, and Annalisa laughed. "Your building, Paul?"

"That's right," he said, staring at the back of the driver's head. "The China deal went through today. In a matter of weeks, I'll be able to buy every apartment in One Fifth."

Annalisa gasped. "Why didn't you tell me?"

"I'm telling you now."

"When did it happen?"

Paul looked at his watch. "About forty minutes ago."

Annalisa sat back in the seat. "I'm astounded, Paul. But what does it mean?"

"It was my idea, but Sandy and I pulled it off together. We sold one of my algorithms to the Chinese government in exchange for a percentage of their stock market."

"Can you do that?"

"Of course I can do it," Paul said. "I just did." Without missing a beat, he addressed the driver. "Change of plans," he said. "We're going to the West Side heliport instead." He turned to his wife and patted her leg. "I thought we'd go to the Lodge for dinner to celebrate. I know how much you've always wanted to see it."

"Oh, Paul," she said. The Lodge was an exclusive resort in the Adirondacks that was rumored to be stunningly beautiful. Annalisa had read about it years ago and mentioned to Paul that she wished they could go there on their anniversary. But at three thousand dollars a night, it had been too expensive back then for them to even consider. But Paul had remembered. She smiled and shook her head, realizing that her slight dissatisfaction with Paul in the last couple of months was something she'd made up in her mind. Paul was still Paul—wonderful in his unique and unfathomable way—and Connie Brewer was right. Annalisa did love her husband.

Paul reached into the pocket of his pants and withdrew a small black velvet box. Inside was a large yellow diamond ring surrounded by pink stones. It was beautiful and gaudy, exactly the sort of thing Connie Brewer would love. Annalisa slipped it onto her right middle finger. "Do you like it?" Paul asked. "Sandy said Connie has one just like it. I thought you might want one, too."

"Oh, Paul." She put her hand on the side of his head and stroked his hair. "I love it. It's stunning."

Back in the Gooches' apartment, Sam rifled through his mother's underwear drawer and, finding a pair of old leather gloves, tucked them into the waistband of his jeans. From the tool-box in the cramped coat closet, he extracted a small screwdriver, a pair of pliers, an X-Acto knife, wire clippers, and a small spool of electrical tape. He stuck these items in the back pockets of his jeans, making sure the bulges were covered by his shirt. Then he rode the elevator up to Enid and Philip's floor and, slipping through the hallway, took the stairwell up to the first floor of the penthouse apartment.

The stairwell led to a small foyer outside a service entrance, and there, as Sam had known, was a metal plate. He put on his mother's gloves, took out the screwdriver, and unscrewed the plate from the wall. Inside was a compartment filled with cables. Every floor had a cable box, and the cables ran from one floor to another. Most boxes contained one or two cables, but on the Rices' floor, due to all of Paul's equipment, there were six. Sam tugged the cables out of a hole in the back and, using the X-Acto knife, cut away the white plastic casing. Then he clipped the wires and, mixing them up, spliced the wrong wires together using the pliers. Finally, he wrapped the newly configured wires in the electrical tape. Then he pushed the cables back into the wall. He wasn't sure what would happen, but it was guaranteed to be big.

16

Under regular circumstances, Paul Rice, the early riser, would have been the first to discover The Internet Debacle, as it would be later referred to by the residents of One Fifth. But on the following morning, James Gooch happened to be up first. Following his triumphant book reading the night before ("Four hundred twenty books sold, it's practically a record," Redmond had boasted), James was booked on the first flight from La Guardia to Boston at six A.M.; from Boston, he would go on to Philadelphia, Washington, St. Louis, Chicago, Cleveland, and then Houston, Dallas, Seattle, San Francisco, and Los Angeles. He would be away for two weeks. As a consequence, he had to get up at three A.M. to pack. James was a noisy, nervous packer, so Mindy was up as well. Mindy normally would have been testy about this disturbance to her sleep—considering sleep the most precious of all modern-day commodities—but on this day, she was forgiving. The evening before, James had made her proud. All the years of supporting him were paying off when they easily might not have, and Mindy found herself imagining enormous sums of money coming their way. If the book made a million dollars, they could send Sam to any university—Harvard, or perhaps Cambridge in

England, which was even more prestigious—without feeling a pinch. Two million dollars would mean university for Sam, and maybe the luxury of owning a car and housing it in a garage and paying off their mortgage. Three million dollars would get them all that plus a tiny getaway home in Montauk or Amagansett or Litchfield County in Connecticut. Beyond this, Mindy's imagination could go no further. She was so accustomed to living a life of relative deprivation, she couldn't picture herself needing or wanting more.

"Do you have toothpaste?" she asked, following James into his bathroom. "Don't forget your comb. And dental floss."

"I'm sure they have drugstores in Boston," James remarked.

Mindy closed the toilet seat and sat down, watching him go through his medicine cabinet. "I don't want you to have to worry about details," she said. "You're going to need all your concentration to handle the readings and interviews."

"Mindy," James said, putting a bottle of aspirin into a Ziploc bag. "You're making me nervous. Don't you have something to do?"

"At three in the morning?"

"I could use a cup of coffee."

"Sure," Mindy said. She went into the kitchen. She was feeling sentimental about James. In fourteen years of marriage, they'd never spent more than three nights apart, and now James would be away for two weeks. Would she miss him? What if she couldn't manage without him? But that, she reminded herself, was silly. She was a grown woman. She did practically everything herself anyway. Well, maybe not everything. James spent a lot of time looking after Sam. As much as she liked to complain about him, James wasn't all bad. Especially now, when he was finally making money.

"I'll get your socks," Mindy said, handing James his cup of coffee. "Do you think you'll miss me?" she asked, placing several pairs of worn socks into his suitcase and wondering how many pairs he would need for two weeks.

"I can do that," James said, annoyed by all the attention. Mindy came across a hole in the toe of one of his socks and stuck her finger through. "A lot of your socks have holes," she pointed out.

"It doesn't matter. No one is going to see my socks," James said.

"So *will* you miss me?" Mindy asked.

"I don't know," James said. "Maybe. Maybe not. I might be too busy."

In a last-minute panic, James left the apartment at four-fifteen A.M. Mindy considered going back to sleep but was too keyed up. She decided to check James's Amazon rating instead. Her computer came on, but there was no Internet service. This was strange. She checked the cables and turned the box on and off. Nothing. She tried the browser on her BlackBerry. Also nothing.

Paul Rice was now up as well. At five A.M. on the dot, he was to launch his algorithm in the Chinese stock market. At four-thirty A.M., he was seated behind his desk in his home office, a cup of café con leche sitting neatly on a coaster nearby, ready to begin. Out of habit, he plucked a pencil out of the silver holder and examined the tip for sharpness. Then he turned on his computer.

The screen flashed its familiar and comforting green—the color of money, Paul thought with satisfaction—and then . . . nothing. Paul jerked his head in surprise. Powering the computer should have kicked on the satellite system and Internet backup. He clicked on the Internet icon. The screen went blank. Finding a key, he unlocked the cabinet doors behind him and looked inside at the stacked metal hard drives. The power was on, but the array of lights indicating the exchange of signals was black. He hesitated for half a second and then ran downstairs to Annalisa's office. He tried her computer, which he'd always joked was like a Stone Age tool, but the Internet was out there as well.

"Holy fuck!" he screamed.

In the master bedroom next door, Annalisa stirred in her sleep. At the celebration dinner the night before, the Rices and Brewers had consumed over five thousand dollars' worth of rare wines before helicoptering back to the city at two A.M. She turned over, her head heavy, hoping Paul's voice had come from a dream. But there it was again: "Holy fuck!"

Now Paul was in the room, pulling on his pants from the night before. Annalisa sat up. "Paul?"

"There's no fucking Internet service."

"But I thought . . ." Annalisa mumbled, gesturing uselessly.

"Where's the car? I need the fucking car."

She leaned over the bed, picking up the handset on the landline. "It's in the garage. But the garage is probably closed."

In a frenzy, Paul buttoned his shirt while trying to hop into his shoes. "This is exactly why I wanted that parking spot in the Mews," he snapped. "For just this kind of emergency."

"What emergency?" Annalisa said, getting out of bed.

"There's no fucking Internet service. Which means I am fucked. The whole fucking China deal is fucked." He ran out of the room.

"Paul?" she said, following him and leaning over the banister. "Paul? What can I do?" But he was already in the hallway, punching the button for the elevator. It was all the way down in the lobby. Glancing at his watch, Paul decided he didn't have time to wait and began clattering down the steps. He burst into the lobby, waking the night doorman, who was dozing in a chair. "I need a taxi," Paul shouted breathlessly. "A fucking taxi!" He ran into the empty street, waving his arms.

When no taxis appeared, he started jogging up Fifth Avenue. At Twelfth Street, he finally saw a cab and fell into the backseat. "Park Avenue and Fifty-third Street," he screamed. Pounding on the divider, he shouted, "Go, go. *Go!*"

"I cannot run a red light, sir," the driver said, turning around.

"Shut up and drive," Paul screamed.

The journey to midtown was agony. Who would have thought there would be traffic before five A.M.? Paul rolled down his window and stuck his head out, waving and shouting at the other drivers. By the time the taxi pulled up in front of his office building, it was four-fifty-three A.M.

The building was locked, so it took another minute of kicking and screaming to arouse the night watchman. It was another couple of minutes to get upstairs and use his pass to unlock the glass doors of Brewer Securities, and a few more seconds to run down the hall to his office. When he got to his computer, it was five-oh-one and forty-three seconds. His fingers flew over the keyboard. When he was finished, it was five-oh-one and fifty-six seconds. He collapsed on his chair and leaned back, putting his hands over his face. In the two-minute delay, he had lost twenty-six million dollars.

Back at One Fifth, Mindy Gooch poked her head out the door. "Roberto," she said to the doorman, "there's no Internet service."

"I don't know anything about it," he said. "Ask your son, Sam."

At six-thirty, she woke Sam up. "There's no Internet service."

Sam smiled and yawned. "It's probably Paul Rice's fault. He's got all that equipment up there. It probably knocked out the service in the entire building."

"I hate that man," Mindy said.

"Me, too," Sam agreed.

Several floors above, Enid Merle was also trying to get online. She needed to read the column composed by her staff writer in the wee hours of the morning, to which she would add her trademark flourishes. But there was something wrong with her computer, and desperate to approve the column before eight A.M., when it would be syndicated online and then appear in the afternoon edition of the paper, she called Sam. In a few minutes, Sam and Mindy appeared at her door. Mindy had pulled on a pair of jeans below her flannel pajama top. "No one's computer is working," she informed Enid. "Sam says it has something to do with Paul Rice."

"Why would he be involved?" Enid asked.

"Apparently," Mindy said, glancing at Sam, "he's got all kinds of powerful and probably illegal computer equipment up there. In Mrs. Houghton's old ballroom."

When Enid looked doubtful, Mindy said, "Sam has seen it. When he went up to help Annalisa Rice with her computer."

Annalisa herself was nervously pacing the living room with her cell phone in hand when Maria came in. "Some people are here," Maria said.

"The police?"

"No. Some people from downstairs," Maria said.

Annalisa opened the front door a few inches. "Yes?" she asked impatiently.

Mindy Gooch, who still had smudges of mascara under her eyes from the night before, tried to push her way in. "The Internet service is out. We think the problem is coming from your apartment."

"We don't have Internet service, either," Annalisa snapped.

"May we come in?" Enid asked.

"Absolutely not," Annalisa said. "The police are on their way. No one is to touch anything."

"The police?" Mindy shrieked.

"That's right," Annalisa said. "We've been sabotaged. Go back to your apartments to wait." She closed the door.

Enid turned to Sam. "Sam?" she asked. Sam then looked at his mother, who put her arm around his head protectively. "Sam doesn't know anything about this," Mindy said firmly. "Everyone knows the Rices are paranoid."

"What is happening in this building?" Enid asked.

Then everyone went back to their respective apartments.

Back in the living room, Annalisa folded her arms, shook her head, and continued to pace. If no one in the building had Internet service, then perhaps Paul was wrong. He'd called her at five-thirty A.M., screaming about how he'd lost an enormous amount of money and claiming that someone had found out about the China deal and deliberately sabotaged his home computers. He insisted she call the police, which she had, but they only laughed and told her to call Time Warner. After ten minutes of begging, the representative agreed to send a repairman in the afternoon. Meanwhile, Paul was insisting that no one be allowed in the apartment until the police had dusted it for fingerprints and performed other forensic duties.

Downstairs at the Gooches', Mindy took a box of frozen waffles out of the freezer. "Sam?" she called out. "Do you want breakfast?"

Sam appeared in the doorway with his backpack. "I'm not hungry," he said.

Mindy put a waffle in the toaster. "Well, that's interesting," she said.

"What?" Sam asked nervously.

"The Rices. Calling the police. Over a little interruption of Internet service." The waffle popped out of the toaster, and she put it on a small plate, smeared it with butter, and handed it to Sam. "That's the way it is with out-of-towners. They just don't realize that in New York, these things *happen*."

Sam nodded. His mouth was dry.

"When are you getting home from school?" Mindy asked.

"The usual time, I guess," Sam said, looking down at the waffle.

Mindy picked up Sam's knife and fork and cut off a piece of his waffle, put it in her mouth, and chewed. She wiped the butter off her lips with the back of her hand. "Whenever you get home, I'll be here," she said. "I'm going to take the day off. As the head of the board, I need to deal with this situation."

Three blocks away, Billy Litchfield wasn't having any trouble with his Internet service. After a sleepless night of worry, he was up, checking the art blogs, *The New York Times*, and every other newspaper he could think of to see if there was any mention of the Cross of Bloody Mary. There wasn't, but Sandy Brewer was all over the financial pages with the announcement of his deal with the Chinese government to own a piece of their stock market, and already the outrage had begun. There were two editorials about the moral implications of such a deal, and how it might be a sign that high-earning individuals in the financial world could bond together to form their own kind of uber-government, with influence over the policies of other countries. It should be illegal, but at the moment, there were no laws in place to guard against such a possibility.

Sandy Brewer wasn't the only person in the blogs. James Gooch was as well. Someone had taken a cell-phone video of James during his reading at Barnes & Noble and posted it on Snarker and

YouTube. And now the hoi polloi were attacking James for his hair, his glasses, and his style of speaking. They were calling him a talking vegetable, a cucumber with specs. Poor James, Billy thought. He was so meek and mild-mannered, it was hard to understand why he could possibly be worth the negative attention. But he was successful now, and success was its own kind of crime, Billy supposed.

A few minutes later in midtown, Sandy Brewer, bloated and in a foul mood from the amount of alcohol he'd consumed the night before, strode into Brewer Securities, grabbed the soft basketball from the chair in his office, went into Paul Rice's office, and threw the basketball at Paul's head. Paul ducked. "What the fuck, Rice? What the fuck?" Sandy screamed. "Twenty-six million dollars?" The blood rushed to his face as he leaned across Paul's desk. "You'd better make that money back, or you're out of here."

❦

With Philip away in Los Angeles, Thayer Core was having a grand old time hanging out in Philip's apartment, drinking his coffee and red wine and occasionally having sex with his girlfriend. Thayer was far too self-centered to be particularly good at sex, but every now and then, when she let him, he would go through the motions with Lola. She made him wear a condom and sometimes two because she didn't trust him, which made it much less exciting but was made up for by the thrill of doing it in Philip's bed. "You know you don't love Philip," Thayer would say afterward. "Of course I do," she'd counter. "You lie," Thayer would say. "What kind of in-love woman has sex with another man in that man's bed?" "It's not really sex with you and me," Lola replied. "It's more something to do when I'm bored."

"Thanks a lot."

"You don't expect me to fall in love with you, do you?" Lola would ask, screwing up her face in distaste, as if she'd just eaten something unpleasant.

"Who's that young man I always see coming into the apartment?" Enid asked Lola one afternoon. She'd popped in to borrow a cartridge for her printer. She was always "borrowing" Philip's office supplies, and Lola couldn't understand why Enid didn't go to Staples, like everyone else. "You know, you can order supplies online," Lola said, crossing her arms.

"I know, dear. But this is much more fun," Enid said, pawing through Philip's stuff. "And you didn't answer my question. About the young man."

"Could be anyone," Lola said nonchalantly. "What does he look like?"

"Tall? Very attractive? Reddish-blond hair and a disdainful expression?"

"Ah." Lola nodded. "Thayer Core. He's a friend of mine."

"I assumed he was," Enid said. "Otherwise, I can't imagine why he'd be spending so much time in Philip's apartment. Who is he, and what does he do?"

"He's a gossip columnist. Just like you," Lola said.

"For whom?"

"Snarker," Lola said reluctantly. "But he's going to be a novelist. Or run a TV network someday. He's brilliant. Everyone says no matter what he does, he's going to be big."

"Ah, yes," Enid said, finding the cartridge. "I know exactly who he is. Really, Lola." She paused. "I'm a little worried about your judgment. You shouldn't be allowing that type of person into Philip's apartment. I'm not even sure you should be allowing him into the building."

"He's my friend," Lola said. "I'm allowed to have friends, aren't I?"

"I didn't mean to interfere," Enid said curtly. "I was only trying to give you some kind advice."

"Thank you," Lola said pointedly, following Enid to the door. When Enid had gone, Lola crept out into the hallway and examined the peephole in Enid's door. Was she standing on the other side, watching? How much could the old lady see out of that little hole, anyway? Apparently, too much. Returning to Philip's apartment—Philip's and her apartment, Lola reminded herself—she concocted a little story to explain Thayer's presence. Thayer was helping with her research for Philip. Meanwhile, she was helping Thayer with his novel. It was all perfectly innocent. Enid couldn't actually see into the apartment, so how could she know what was going on?

Lola hadn't meant to get so involved with Thayer Core. She knew it was dangerous but found she enjoyed the thrill of getting away with it. And being uncertain about her relationship with Philip, she justified her behavior by reminding herself that she needed a backup in case things with Philip didn't work out. Admittedly, Thayer Core wasn't much of a consolation prize, but he did know lots of people and claimed to have all kinds of connections.

But then Philip was coming home in a few days, and Lola warned Thayer that their time together had to end. Thayer was annoyed. Not because he wouldn't be seeing Lola but because he so enjoyed spending time in One Fifth. He liked everything about it, and simply entering the building on Fifth Avenue made him feel superior. Before going in, he often looked around the sidewalk to see if anyone was watching, envying him his position. Then he'd pass by the doormen with a wave. "Going up to Philip Oakland's," he'd say, making a jerking motion with his thumb. The doormen regarded him with suspicion—Thayer could tell they didn't like him and didn't approve—but they didn't stop him.

Dropping by Philip's apartment that morning, Thayer suggested he and Lola look at some Internet porn. Lola was eating potato chips, crunching them obnoxiously just for the hell of it, Thayer thought. "Can't," she said. "Why not? You a prude?" Thayer said. "Nope. No Internet service. It's all Paul Rice's fault. That's what everyone is saying, anyway. Enid says they're going to try to kick him out. Don't know if they can, but now everyone in the building hates him."

"Paul Rice?" Thayer asked casually. "*The* Paul Rice? Who's married to Annalisa? The society tartlet?"

Lola shrugged. "They're super-rich. She rides around in a Bentley and has designers send her clothes. I hate her."

"I hate them both," Thayer said, and smiled.

Heeding the call to action, Mindy and Enid had scheduled an emergency meeting of the board. On her way down to Mindy's, Enid paused outside Philip's door. Sure enough, she heard voices— Lola's and that of an unidentified man who, she assumed, was Thayer Core. Had Lola willfully misunderstood what she'd said? Or was she simply dumb? Enid knocked on the door.

Immediately, there was silence. Enid knocked again. "Lola?" she called out. "It's me. I need to talk to you." She heard hurried whispers, and then Lola opened the door. "Hi, Enid," she said with false cheer.

Enid pushed past her and found Thayer Core sitting on Philip's couch with a script in his hand. "Hello," Enid said. "And who might you be?"

Thayer suddenly became the proper prep-school boy whose image he'd been trying to shed for the past five years. He stood up and held out his hand. "Thayer Core, ma'am."

"Enid Merle. I'm Philip's aunt," Enid said dryly.

"Wow," Thayer said. "Lola didn't tell me you were Philip's aunt."

"Are you a friend of Philip's?"

"Yes, I am. And of Lola's. Lola and I were discussing my script. I was hoping Philip might be able to give me some pointers. But I can see you two have things to talk about," Thayer said, looking from Enid to Lola. "I need to get going." He jumped up and grabbed his coat.

"Don't forget your script," Enid said to him.

"Right," Thayer said. He exchanged a look with Lola, who smiled stiffly. Thayer picked up the script, and Enid followed him into the hall.

They rode down to the lobby without speaking, which was fine by Thayer. His head was full of ideas, and he didn't want to lose them by talking. In the past thirty minutes, he'd gleaned enough interesting material for several blog items. One Fifth was a hotbed of intrigue; perhaps he might create an entire series dedicated to the goings-on in the building. He could call it "The Co-op." Or perhaps "The Lives of the Rich and Privileged."

"Goodbye," Enid said firmly when the elevator doors opened into the lobby. Thayer nodded at her and hurried out. All he needed to continue his attack on the residents of One Fifth was a steady supply of information. He turned over the script in his hand and smiled. It was the first draft of a screenplay by Philip Oakland with a working title of "Bloody Mary." Philip Oakland would be furious if he discovered Lola had allowed an unfinished script to get out. And it wouldn't get out as long as Lola was a good girl and played along. From now on, Thayer decided, Lola could come to his apartment. She would keep him up to date on the goings-on in One Fifth, and when she was finished talking, she could give him a blow job.

Enid rang Mindy's bell. The door was opened by Sam, who had changed his mind about going to school, claiming he was sick. He led Enid into the tiny living room, where the three members of the board were engaged in a fierce discussion about Paul Rice.

"Can't we force him to allow Time Warner into his apartment?"

"Of course. It's the same as a handyman. And it's affecting the other residents. But if he refuses, we have to get a letter from the building's attorney."

"Has anyone tried to talk to him?"

"We all have," Enid said. "He's impossible."

"What about the wife? Maybe someone should talk to his wife."

"I'll try again," Enid said.

On the other side of the wall, Sam Gooch lay on his bed, pretending to read his mother's *New Yorker*. He'd left his door open so he could overhear the conversation. He looked up at the ceiling, feeling extremely pleased with himself. True, his actions had caused a great deal of trouble for everyone in the building, and he was scared to death of being found out, but it was worth it to get even with Paul. Sam guessed Paul would not be harassing anyone anymore, especially his mother. He would never say anything to Paul, but when they passed in the lobby, he would give Paul a certain look, and Paul would know Sam had been responsible. Hopefully, he'd never be able to prove it.

A few minutes later, Enid knocked on the Rices' door. Maria, the housekeeper, opened it a crack and said through the tiny slit, "No visitors."

Enid stuck her fingers in the crack. "Don't be silly. I need to see Mrs. Rice."

"Enid?" Annalisa called out. She stepped into the hallway, closing the door behind her. "This is not our fault."

"Of course it isn't," Enid said.

"It's because everyone hates Paul."

"A co-op is like a private club," Enid said. "Especially in a building like One Fifth. You may not necessarily like all the other members, but you do have to get along with them. Otherwise, it tears the whole building apart. Word gets out that it's not such a great building, and then everyone's real estate goes down. And no one likes that, my dear."

Annalisa looked down at her hands.

"There is an unspoken code of behavior. For instance, residents must strive to avoid unpleasant encounters. We can't have neighbors insulting each other. Yes, One Fifth is a fancy apartment building. But it's also people's homes. It's their sanctuary. And without the security of that sanctuary, people become angry. I'm afraid for you and Paul. Afraid of what will happen if you don't allow the repairman from Time Warner into your apartment."

"He's already here," Annalisa said.

"Ah," Enid replied, taken aback.

"He's by the service entrance. Perhaps you'd like to talk to him."

"Yes, I would," Enid said.

She followed Annalisa through the door that led to the stairwell. The repairman held several cables in his hand. "They've been cut," he said grimly.

"Hey, Roberto," Philip Oakland said, coming into One Fifth with his suitcase. "How's it going?"

"Been crazy around here," Roberto said, and laughed. "You missed a lot."

"Really?" Philip said. "Like what?"

"Big scandal. With the billionaire. Paul Rice. But your aunt took care of it."

"Ah, yes," Philip said, waiting for the elevator. "She always does."

"And then it turned out that someone cut the cables outside the billionaire's apartment. No one knows who did it. Then the billionaire called the police. Big scene between Mindy Gooch and Paul Rice. Those two really hate each other. So Paul Rice is making the co-op pay for cameras in the stairwells. And there was nothing Mrs. Gooch could do about it. Man, that lady was mad. And Mrs. Rice won't talk to anyone. The housekeeper calls ahead when she's coming down, and we have to motion to the driver to bring the car around. No one's mad at them, though, because someone did cut their wires, and Paul Rice gave the doormen a thousand bucks each to protect his wife. But now everyone who comes into the building, even the dry cleaner, has to register at the front desk and show ID. And if they don't have ID, the residents have to come down and get them. It's like a prison in here. Thing is, some people think it was your girlfriend's friend that did it."

"What?" Philip said. He jabbed the button for the elevator.

"That won't make it come any faster." Roberto laughed again.

Philip got into the elevator and punched the button for the thirteenth floor three times. What the hell was going on?

In Los Angeles, he'd gone right to work on the revisions for *Bridesmaids Revisited*. For the first couple of days, he'd put Lola out of his mind. She'd called him ten times, but he hadn't returned the calls. On his third evening in L.A., he'd phoned her back, thinking she would still be at her mother's house. She wasn't. She was in New York in his apartment. "Lola, we have to discuss this," he said.

"But I've already moved in. I thought that was the plan. I unpacked all my stuff. I only took a small corner of the closet in the bedroom, and I put some of your things in your storage locker in the basement. I hope you don't mind," she'd said, as if suddenly realizing he might.

"Lola, it's just not a good idea."

"What isn't? You asked me to move in with you, Philip. In Mustique. If you're saying you don't love me anymore . . ." She'd started crying.

Philip had buckled under her tears. "I didn't mean that. I do care for you, Lola. It's just that—"

"How can you say you care about me when you're trying to tell me you don't want me around? Fine. I'll leave. I'll go live on the street."

"Lola, you don't have to live on the street."

"I'm twenty-two years old," she'd said, sobbing. "You seduced me and made me fall in love with you. And now you're ruining my life."

"Lola, stop. Everything is going to be okay."

"So do you love me?"

"We'll discuss it when I get back," he'd said resignedly.

"I know you're not ready to say it yet. But you will," she chirped. "It's just an adjustment period. Oh, I almost forgot—your friend Schiffer Diamond is dating some guy named Derek Brumminger. It was in the *Post*. And then I saw them together, leaving the building in the morning. He's not very attractive. He's old and he's got bad skin. You'd think a movie star could do better, but maybe she can't. She's not so young anymore, either."

For a moment, Philip had been silent.

"Hello? Hello?" Lola had said. "Are you there?"

So she's gone back to Brumminger, he'd thought. After telling him to get rid of Lola. Why had he thought she'd changed?

"Lola," he said now, going into his apartment. "What's this business about your friend?"

He looked around. Lola wasn't home. He put his suitcase on the bed and knocked on his aunt's door.

Lola was with Enid. "Philip! You're home," Lola said, throwing her arms around him. He patted her on the back and looked at his aunt, who smiled and rolled her eyes. Lola went on, "Enid was showing me her gardening books. I'm going to fix up your terrace this spring. Enid says I can make tulip boxes. And then we can have cut flowers."

"Hello, Philip, dear," Enid said, slowly getting up from the couch. Not having seen her for two weeks, Philip realized she was getting old. Someday he would lose her, and then he'd truly be alone. The thought changed his mood: He was happy he still had his aunt, and that Lola was still living in his apartment, and that Enid and Lola were getting along. Perhaps it would work out after all.

"I want to show you what I did in the kitchen," Lola said eagerly.

"You were in the kitchen?" he asked in mock surprise. He followed her back to his apartment, where she showed off her handiwork. She had rearranged the contents of his kitchen cabinets so he no longer knew where anything was.

"Why did you do this?" he asked, opening the cabinet that had once held coffee and condiments but now contained a stack of plates.

She looked crushed. "I thought you'd like it."

"I do. It's better," he lied, looking carefully around the apartment and wondering what else she'd disturbed. In the bedroom, he cautiously opened the closet. Half his clothes—the jackets and shirts that had hung in an orderly fashion for years—were missing; in their place, Lola's clothing hung haphazardly, dangling from his hangers like Christmas ornaments.

"Have you forgotten about me?" she said, coming up behind him and slipping her hands into the front of his jeans. She scooted back onto the bed. With a hard-on that reminded him he hadn't had sex in two weeks, Philip put her ankles over his shoulders. For a second, he looked down at her bare, waxed pussy, remembering that this was not what he wanted. But it was there before him, and he dove in.

Afterward, searching through his kitchen for his misplaced

wineglasses, he said, "What's this story about your friend cutting the Internet cables to the Rices' apartment?"

"Oh. That." She sighed. "It was that horrible Mindy Gooch. She's jealous of me because her husband, James, is always trying to come on to me behind her back. She said Thayer Core did it. You remember, we went to his Halloween party. Thayer was only here like two times—he wants to write screenplays, and I was trying to help him—and Thayer keeps writing about Mindy and her husband on Snarker, so Mindy was trying to get even with him. And Thayer wasn't even in the building when it happened."

"How often has he been here?" Philip asked, his annoyance rising.

"I told you," she said. "Once or twice. Maybe three times. I can't remember."

In the apartment next door, Enid picked up her gardening books and shook her head in frustration. She'd tried everything she could think of to get rid of Lola—forcing her to go along to three upscale supermarkets on Sixth Avenue in search of canned flageolet beans, taking her to a Damien Hirst retrospective of dead cows and sharks, and even introducing her to Flossie—all to no avail. Lola claimed that she, too, had a love for flageolets, was grateful to Enid for introducing her to art, and was not even put off by Flossie. Begging Flossie to tell her about her old days as a showgirl, Lola sat rapt at the foot of the bed. Enid realized she'd underestimated Lola's tenacity. After the Internet Debacle, when Enid confronted Lola once again about her relationship with Thayer Core, all Lola did was look at her innocently and say, "Enid, you were right. He is a scumbag. And I'm never going to talk to him again."

Unlike Mindy Gooch, Enid did not believe Thayer Core had cut Paul Rice's cables. Thayer Core was a bully, and like most bullies, he lacked courage. He was far too fearful to take physical action, instead striking out at the world from behind the safety of his computer. Mindy's accusation was an attempt to divert attention from the real culprit, whom Enid suspected was Sam.

Luckily for Sam, the police made only a cursory investigation.

The incident was a prank, they said, due to animosity between residents. These pranks were becoming more and more common even in high-class apartment buildings. They received all kinds of complaints about neighbors now—from residents banging on ceilings with broomsticks, or ripping down each other's Christmas decorations, or insisting that a neighbor's cigarette smoke was drifting into their apartment and putting their children at risk for cancer. "I say live and let live," one of the officers said to Enid. "But you know what people are like these days. There's too much money and not enough space. And no manners. Makes people hate each other."

There had always been petty issues between residents at One Fifth, but until now, they had been countered by the collegial air of pride the residents took in living in the building. Perhaps the balance had been tipped by the Rices, who were so much wealthier than anyone else. Paul had threatened to sue, and Enid had to give Mindy a severe talking-to, reminding her that if Paul Rice went through with a lawsuit, the building would be forced to pay legal fees, which would be passed on to the residents in the form of an increase in monthly maintenance payments. After she saw the matter in financial terms that could directly affect her, Mindy agreed to back down and even wrote Paul and Annalisa Rice a note of apology. A tense truce was established, but then detailed items about these skirmishes began appearing in Snarker. Enid was sure the information was coming from Lola, but how could she prove it? As if Enid herself had something to do with it, Mindy took every opportunity to harass Enid about it, stopping her in the lobby to see if she'd read it and forwarding the blog to Enid's e-mail address.

"This can't go on. Something has to be done," Mindy exclaimed that morning.

Enid sighed. "If it bothers you so much, then hire the young man."

"What?" Mindy said, outraged.

"Hire him," Enid repeated. "He must be a hard worker if he puts so much effort into writing about One Fifth. He's at least halfway intelligent—I'm assuming he knows how to form a sentence, otherwise you wouldn't be so angry. Pay him a decent salary and work him hard. That way he won't have enough time to write anything on the side. But don't pay him so much that he can save up money to quit. Give him insurance and benefits. Turn him into a corporate drone, and you'll never have to worry about him again."

If only, Enid thought, all problems could be solved so easily. She went into the kitchen and made a cup of tea, sipping it carefully to avoid burning her mouth. She hesitated, then took her tea into the bedroom. She turned off the phones, pulled back the covers, and for the first time in years, got into bed during the day. She closed her eyes. She was finally getting too old for all this drama.

❦

The recent events in One Fifth had made Paul Rice more paranoid and secretive than normal, and he was continually losing his temper over things he might once have ignored. He screamed at Maria for folding his jeans the wrong way, and then one of his precious fish died and he accused Annalisa of killing it on purpose. Fed up, Annalisa went to a spa in Massachusetts with Connie Brewer for six days, and Paul was left facing a lonely weekend. He spent most weekends pursuing his own interests anyway, but he liked the comfort of having Annalisa around, and the fact that she'd left him, even temporarily, made him fear she might someday leave him permanently.

Apparently, Sandy Brewer didn't have the same concerns about his own wife. "Dude," he said, going into Paul's office, "the girls are away this weekend. Thought you might want to come to my house for dinner. There's someone I want you to meet."

"Who?" Paul asked. Ever since Sandy had flipped out about the two-minute delay in launching the algorithm, Paul had been watching Sandy closely, looking for evidence that Sandy was trying to replace him. Instead, Paul had found payments to an escort company that revealed Sandy had been paying prostitutes to service him during business trips. With Annalisa away, Paul wondered if Sandy would try to introduce him to a hooker.

"You'll see," Sandy said mysteriously. Paul agreed to go, thinking if Sandy had invited one of his prostitutes, Paul could leverage the information to his advantage.

Sandy loved to show off what his success and hard work had brought him, arranging for a formal dinner for three in his wood-paneled dining room, where two enormous David Salle paintings hung. The third dinner companion wasn't a prostitute after all, but a man named Craig Akio. Paul shook Craig's hand, noting only that Craig was younger than he and possessed sharp black eyes. They sat down to a glass of a rare white wine and a bowl of seafood bisque. "I'm a big admirer of your work, Paul," Craig Akio said from across the polished mahogany table. "Your work on the Samsun scale was genius."

"Thanks," Paul said curtly. He was used to being called a genius and took the compliment as a matter of course.

"I'm looking forward to working with you."

Paul paused with his spoon halfway to his mouth. This was unexpected. "Are you moving to New York?" he asked.

"I've already found an apartment. In the new Gwathmey building. A masterpiece of modern architecture."

"On the West Side Highway," Sandy joked.

"I'm used to cars," Craig said. "I grew up in L.A."

"Where'd you go to school?" Paul asked evenly. But he felt uneasy. It struck him that perhaps it would have been normal behavior for Sandy to have told him about this new associate before hiring him.

"MIT," Craig said. "You?"

"Georgetown," Paul replied. He looked past Craig's head to the David Salle paintings on the wall. Normally, he didn't notice such things, but the paintings were of two jesters with terrifying expressions—both jovial and cruel. Paul took a gulp of his wine, feeling inexplicably like the jesters were real and mocking him.

For the rest of the dinner, the talk was of the upcoming political election and its impact on business; then they moved into Sandy's study for cognac and cigars. Passing out cigars, Sandy began talking about art, boasting about his dinner with a man named David Porshie. "Billy Litchfield, he's a good friend of my wife's—when you get married, he'll be a good friend of your wife's as well," he explained to Craig Akio. "He set us up with the head of the Metropolitan Museum. Decent fellow. Knows everything about art, but I suppose that's not surprising. He got me thinking about improving my own collection. Going for the old masters instead of the new stuff. What do you think, Paul? Anyone can get the new stuff, right? It's only money. But no matter what they tell you, no one knows how much it'll be worth in five years or even two. Might not be worth anything at all."

Paul just stared, but Craig nodded enthusiastically. Sandy, sensing an audience for not only admiration but awe, opened the safe.

Connie had done what Billy had asked. She had put the cross away—into the safe in Sandy's study—so she could visit it anytime she liked. Nevertheless, she'd managed to keep the cross a secret. Sandy, however, was a different story. When Billy first came to him with the opportunity to buy the cross, Sandy hadn't thought much about it, considering it nothing more than another piece of old jewelry his wife wanted to acquire. Connie told him that the piece was important, a true antiquity, but Sandy hadn't paid attention until that evening with David Porshie. David approached art on a whole different level. After returning home that evening, Sandy had examined the cross again with Connie and began to understand its value, but was more taken by the coup he'd scored in obtaining it at all. It was something no one else had, and unable to keep this spectacular possession to himself, he had taken to bringing one or two select guests into his study after dinner to show it off.

Now, untying the black cords that bound the artifact in its soft suede wrappings, he said, "Here's something you won't see every day. In fact, it's so rare, you won't even find it in a museum." Holding up the cross, he allowed Craig and Paul to examine it.

"Where do you get a piece like that?" Craig Akio asked, his eyes glittering.

"You can't," Sandy Brewer said, wrapping up the cross and replacing it in the safe. He sucked on his cigar. "A piece like that finds you. Not unlike you finding us, Craig." Sandy turned to Paul, blowing smoke in his direction. "Paul, I'll expect you to teach Craig everything you know. You'll be working together closely. At least at first."

It was that last sentence that woke Paul up—"At least at first." And then what? He suddenly saw that Sandy meant for him to train Craig; once he'd accomplished this task, Sandy would fire him. There was no need for two men to do his job. Indeed, it was impossible, as the work was secretive, instinctive, and off-the-cuff. All at once he felt as if he were on fire and, standing up, asked for water.

"Water?" Sandy barked dismissively. "I hope you're not turning into a lightweight."

"I'm going home," Paul said.

He left Sandy's apartment, fuming. How long would it be before Sandy dismissed him from his job? Crossing the sidewalk, he got into the back of the chauffeured Bentley and slammed the door. Would he lose the car as well? Would he lose everything? At the moment, he couldn't keep up his lifestyle or even his apartment without his job. Yes, technically, he had plenty of money, but it fluctuated on a daily basis, flitting up and down and, like the pot of gold at the end of a rainbow, was impossible to pin down. He had to wait for exactly the right moment to make a killing, at which point he could cash out with what could be a billion dollars.

Unable to stop thinking about Sandy and how Sandy planned to ruin him, Paul spent the next thirty-six hours in his apartment in a panic. By Sunday morning, even his fish couldn't soothe him, and Paul decided to take a walk around the neighborhood. On the table in the foyer, he found *The New York Times*. Without thinking, he spread it open on the living room rug and began turning the pages. And then he found the answer to his problem with Sandy on the cover of the arts section.

It was a story—complete with photographs taken from a portrait of Queen Mary—about the unsolved mystery of the Cross of Bloody Mary. Having met the Brewers and suspecting that Sandy fit the profile of an art thief, David Porshie had arranged the story, thinking it might draw out someone who had information on the cross.

Now, reading the story while squatting on his haunches, Paul Rice put two and two together. He sat back, and as he explored the potential results of piecing together this information, the possibilities grew exponentially in his mind. With Sandy occupied in the legal entanglements of possessing a stolen artifact, he would be too busy to fire Paul. Indeed, Paul would go further—with Sandy gone, he could insert himself into Sandy's place, taking his position. Then he'd be running the fund, and Sandy, having garnered himself a criminal record, would be banned from trading. It would all be his, Paul thought. Then and only then would he be safe.

Taking the newspaper with him, he went out to the Internet café on Astor Place. He did some research and, finding the information he needed, constructed a fake e-mail account under the name Craig Akio. Then he composed an e-mail stating that he—Craig Akio—had seen the cross in the home of Sandy Brewer. Paul addressed the e-mail to the reporter who'd written the piece in the *Times*. Out of habit, Paul reread the e-mail, and, finding it satisfactory, hit "send."

Heading out into the weekend bustle of lower Broadway, Paul felt calm for the first time in weeks. As he entered One Fifth, he smiled, thinking about how no one was safe in the information age. But for the moment, at least, he was.

17

For Billy Litchfield, April brought not only spring showers but debilitating tooth pain. The miserable weather was exacerbated by what felt like one endless visit to the dentist's office. A dull pain that grew into a pounding percussion of agony finally drove him to the dentist, where an X-ray revealed that he had not one, but two decaying roots demanding immediate surgery. The situation required several appointments involving novocaine, gas, antibiotics, soft foods, and thankfully, Vicodin to ease the pain.

"I don't understand," Billy protested to the dentist. "I've never had even a cavity." This was a bit of an exaggeration, but nevertheless, Billy's teeth—which were naturally white and straight, requiring only two years of braces as a child—had always been a source of pride.

The dentist shrugged. "Get used to it," he said. "It's part of getting older. Circulation goes to hell, and the teeth are the first to go."

This made Billy more depressed than usual, and he upped his dosage of Prozac. He'd never been at the mercy of his body, and he found the experience not only humbling but capable of erasing every important achievement in his life. What the philosophers said was true: In the end, there was only decay and death, and in death, everyone was equal.

One afternoon while he was recovering from the latest injustice done to his jaw (a tooth had been removed and a metal screw inserted in its place—he was still waiting for the fake tooth to be constructed in the lab), there was a knock on his door.

The man who stood in the hallway was a stranger in a navy blue Ralph Lauren suit. Before Billy could respond, the man flashed a badge at him. "Detective Frank Sabatini," he said. "Can I come in?"

"Of course," Billy said, too shocked to refuse. As the detective followed him into his tiny living room, Billy realized he was still wearing his robe and had a vision of himself, hands cuffed, going to jail in the paisley silk number.

The detective flipped open a notebook. "Are you Billy Litchfield?" he asked.

For a second, Billy considered lying but decided it might only make things worse. "I am," he said. "Officer, what's wrong? Has someone died?"

"Detective," Frank Sabatini said. "Not Officer. I worked hard for the title. I like to use it."

"As well you should," Billy said. Explaining the robe, he added, "I'm recuperating from some dental work."

"That's tough. I hate the dentist myself," Detective Sabatini said pleasantly enough.

He didn't sound like he was ready to make an arrest, Billy thought. "Do you mind if I get changed?" Billy asked.

"Take your time."

Billy went into his bedroom and closed the door. His hands shook so fiercely, he had a hard time taking off the robe and putting on a pair of corduroy slacks and a red cashmere sweater. Then he went into his bathroom and gulped down a Vicodin, followed by two orange Xanaxes. If he was going to jail, he wanted to be as sedated as possible.

When he returned to the living room, the detective was standing by the side table, examining Billy's photographs. "You know a lot of important people," he remarked.

"Yes," Billy said. "I've lived in New York a long time. Nearly forty years. One accumulates friends."

The detective nodded and got right to it. "You're a sort of art dealer, aren't you?"

"Not really," Billy said. "I sometimes put people together with dealers. But I don't deal in art myself."

"Do you know Sandy and Connie Brewer?"

"Yes," Billy said softly.

"You were helping the Brewers with their art collection, right?"

"I have in the past," Billy admitted. "But they were mostly finished."

"Do you know about any recent purchases they might have made? Maybe not through a dealer?"

"Hmmm," Billy said, stalling. "What do you mean by 'recent'?"

"In the last year or so?"

"They did go to the art fair in Miami. They may have bought a painting. As I said, they're mostly finished with their collection. I'm actually working with someone else right now, quite intensely."

"Who would that be?"

Billy swallowed. "Annalisa Rice."

The detective wrote down the name and underlined it. "Thank you, Mr. Litchfield," he said, handing Billy his card. "If you hear anything else about the Brewers' collection, will you contact me?"

"Of course," Billy said. He paused. "Is that it?"

"What do you mean?" the detective asked, moving to the door.

"Are the Brewers in trouble? They're very nice people."

"I'm sure they are," the detective said. "Keep my card. We may be contacting you again soon. Good afternoon, Mr. Litchfield."

"Good afternoon, Detective," Billy said. He closed the door and collapsed onto his couch. Then he quickly got up and, sidling next to the curtain, peered out at Fifth Avenue. Every kind of cheap television crime scenario entered his mind. Was the detective gone? How much did he know? Or was he out there in an unmarked car, spying on Billy? Would Billy be tailed?

For the next two hours, Billy was too terrified to make a call or check his e-mail. Had he given himself away to the detective with his question about that being it? And why had he given the detective Annalisa Rice's name? Now the detective would get in touch with her. How much did she really know? Sick with fear, he went into the bathroom and took two more pills. Then he lay down on his bed. Mercifully, sleep came, a sleep from which he prayed he wouldn't have to wake.

He did, however—three hours later. His cell phone was ringing. It was Annalisa Rice. "Can I see you?" she asked.

"My God. Did the cop call you, too?"

"He just came by here. I wasn't home. He told Maria it had something to do with the Brewers and did I know them."

"What did she say?"

"She said she didn't know."

"Good for Maria."

"Billy, what's going on?"

"Are you alone?" Billy asked. "Can you come over here? I'd come to you, but I don't want the doormen seeing me going in and out of One Fifth. And make sure you aren't followed."

Half an hour later, Annalisa, seated in front of Billy, held up her hands. "Billy, stop," she said. "Don't tell me any more. You've already told me too much." She stood up. "You mustn't tell anyone anything. Not a word about this. Anything you say from now on can be used in a trial."

"Is it really that bad?" Billy said.

"You need to hire a lawyer. David Porshie will convince the police to get a search warrant—for all we know, the attorney general is already involved—and they'll search the Brewers' apartment and find the cross."

"They might not find anything," Billy said. "The cross isn't even in the apartment anymore. I told Connie to put it in a safety-deposit box."

"Eventually, they'll search that, too. It's only a matter of time."

"I could call Connie. And warn her. Tell her to take the cross away. Stash it in the Hamptons. Or Palm Beach. It was in One Fifth for sixty years, and no one knew a thing about it."

"Billy, you're not making sense," Annalisa said soothingly. "Don't make this worse for yourself than it already is. You're implicated, and if you contact the Brewers, you'll be charged with conspiracy as well."

"How long before they get me?" Billy asked.

"What do you mean?"

"Before I go to jail?"

"You won't necessarily go to jail. There are all kinds of things that can happen. You can plea-bargain or do a deal. If you went to the police right now, to the attorney general, and told him what you know, he'd probably agree to give you immunity."

"I should turn in the Brewers to save myself?" Billy said.

"That's what it amounts to."

"I couldn't," Billy said. "They're my friends."

"They're my friends, too," Annalisa said. "But Connie hasn't committed a crime by taking a gift from her husband. Don't be foolish," she added warningly. "Sandy Brewer won't think twice about doing the same thing to you."

Billy put his head in his hands. "This kind of thing, it just isn't done. Not in our set."

"It's not a child's tea party," Annalisa said sharply. "Billy, you've got to understand. All of the imagined traditions in the world won't help you. You've got to face the facts squarely and decide what to do. Meaning what's best for you."

"What happens to the Brewers?"

"Don't worry about the Brewers," Annalisa said. "Sandy is beyond rich. He'll buy his way out of this, you'll see. He'll claim he didn't know what he was buying. He'll claim he bought art from you all the time. You'll take the fall, not him. I was a lawyer for eight years. Trust me, it's always the little people who get thrown under the bus."

"The little people," Billy said, shaking his head. "So it's come to that. I'm one of the little people after all."

"Billy, please, let me help you," Annalisa said.

"I just need some time. To think," Billy said, showing her to the door.

❖

Two days later, Detective Frank Sabatini, accompanied by four police officers, arrived at the offices of Brewer Securities at three P.M. sharp. Detective Sabatini had found this hour most propitious for the arrest of white-collar criminals: They were back from their lunches by then and, with their bellies full, were much more compliant.

Frank Sabatini was very sure of his man. The day before, Craig Akio, having denied any knowledge of either the e-mail or the cross to Detective Sabatini, had mysteriously left for Japan, and citing the fact that his suspect might be given to run, like Mr. Akio, Detective Sabatini was able to obtain a search warrant for the Brewer abode. It happened to be the week of school vacation, and Connie had taken the whole brood, including the two nannies, to Mexico. The only ones home were the maids, who were helpless in the face of the law. It was, Sabatini thought, a very exciting morning, as the safe had to be opened by use of explosives. Nevertheless, his gunpowder man was very good, and nothing in the safe was damaged, including the cross. The confirmation that this was indeed the stolen item long missing was made by David Porshie, who'd been waiting for the detective's call.

Now, at Brewer Securities, hearing a commotion in the hallway, Paul Rice walked out of his spacious, entirely white office to join the few other partners and employees in watching Sandy Brewer being led out in handcuffs. "Jezzie," Sandy said to his assistant on his way out, "call my lawyer. There must be some mistake here." Expressionless, Paul observed the spectacle, and when Sandy was safely in the elevator, Paul went back to his desk. The office erupted in gossip and speculation: Everyone assumed Sandy had committed some kind of financial fraud, and they hurried back to their computers to clean up their accounts. Paul decided to take the afternoon off.

He found Annalisa in her prettily decorated office, researching something on the Web. When he appeared in the doorway, she jumped and quickly hit a button on her computer. "What are you doing home?" she asked in alarm. "Has something happened?"

"Nothing at all."

"Is everything okay?"

"Of course," Paul said. "Why shouldn't it be?"

"Considering what's gone wrong in this building in the past two months," she said with an edge of sarcasm, "I don't know."

"There's nothing to worry about now," Paul said, heading upstairs to visit his fish. "I've taken care of it. From now on, everything is going to be fine."

Billy Litchfield spent the two days leading up to Sandy Brewer's arrest in a haze of fear. He called no one, not trusting himself to behave normally, afraid, if asked, that he would inadvertently blurt out the story of his involvement with the cross. Four or five times, he considered leaving the country, but where would he go? He had a little bit of money, but not enough to stay away forever. Perhaps he could go to Switzerland, where he'd be able to collect some of his money. But the fear paralyzed him. Although he spent hours on the Internet Googling Sandy Brewer's name to see if anything had happened, the reality of booking a flight and packing a suitcase overwhelmed him. The very thought sent him to his bed, where he curled up in the fetal position under the covers. He had random, unhealthy, repetitive thoughts and kept thinking about a line from a ghost story that had terrified him as a kid—"I want my liver."

It also occurred to him that maybe Sandy Brewer wouldn't be caught, and they'd both go free. Who knew how much evidence the detective had? Perhaps it truly was nothing more than a rumor that might persist for a while and then go away. Mrs. Houghton had kept the cross on her bureau in her bedroom in One Fifth Avenue for years with no one the wiser. If he wasn't caught, Billy vowed he would somehow change his life. He had predicated his entire existence on social obligations, on the desire to be with the right people at the right time and in the right place. Now he saw all too clearly his mistake. He'd thought that this desire for the best in life was going to add up to something substantial and concrete. It hadn't.

Trapped in his apartment, he remembered the many times in his life when he had told himself, "Who needs money when one has rich friends?" He wondered how his rich friends could help him now.

Staring out his living room window at the same view he'd had for years—the Episcopal Church, the stones brown with grime—he saw that a scaffolding was being erected around his building. Of course. The owners were renovating to prepare for the conversion to co-op. He'd done nothing about his apartment situation, not knowing if he would be able to stay in New York City. Was it too late? Would it even matter? Taking himself back to bed, he turned on the television.

The story about Sandy Brewer's arrest was all over the evening news. The clip of Sandy being led out in handcuffs and then, with a policeman's hand on his head, pushed into the backseat of a squad car, played over and over. The newscasters claimed Sandy Brewer had been caught in possession of an invaluable English treasure believed to have come from the estate of one of the city's most important philanthropists, Mrs. Louise Houghton. There was no mention of Billy.

Immediately, Billy's house phone and cell phone began ringing incessantly. Friends or reporters? he wondered. He didn't answer either line. His apartment buzzer went off five or six times—apparently, whoever was trying to get in had made it up to his floor, because then there was a pounding at his door that eventually went away. Billy took refuge in his bathroom. It was only a matter of time before they came for him. He, too, would be all over the newspapers and the Internet, and there would be clips of him on the news and on YouTube, his head bowed in disgrace. His behavior was justifiable, perhaps, because he needed money, but no one would see it that way. Why hadn't he immediately turned the cross over to the Met? Because it would have besmirched Mrs. Houghton's name. But she was dead, and now her name was besmirched anyway, and he was probably going to jail. In despair, he even wondered why he had ever moved to New York in the first place. Why couldn't he have stayed in the Berkshires and been happy with what life had handed him in the beginning?

He opened his medicine cabinet and took out all his pills. He had several kinds now: two types of sleeping pills, Xanax, Prozac, and the Vicodin for his tooth pain. If he took all the pills and drank a bottle of vodka, he might be able to end it. But staring at the pills, he realized he didn't even have the courage to kill himself.

He could at least knock himself out. He took two Vicodins, two Xanaxes, and one of each kind of sleeping pill. Within minutes, he was asleep in a vibrant, multicolored dream that seemed to go on forever.

Enid Merle was one of the first people to hear about Sandy Brewer's arrest. A reporter from the paper who was on the scene called her immediately. As yet, all the facts weren't in, and the conclusion was that Sandy had somehow managed to buy the cross from Mrs. Houghton, who had stolen it from the Met. This allegation, Enid knew, was false. While it was true that Louise had possessed the cross, Enid guessed that she hadn't taken it from the Met but from Flossie Davis. Flossie had always been the obvious culprit, but what had never made sense to Enid was why Louise hadn't returned the cross to the Met in the first place. Instead, she'd kept both the cross and the secret, protecting Flossie from being punished for her criminal act. Louise was a devout Catholic; perhaps a moral imperative had prevented her from revealing Flossie's crime.

Or perhaps, Enid thought, there was another reason. Maybe Flossie had something on Louise. Enid should have gotten to the bottom of this mystery long ago, but she'd never considered it important enough. At the moment, there wasn't time. She had a column due, and since it concerned Louise Houghton, she would have to write it herself.

Enid looked through several printed pages of research on Sandy and Connie Brewer. The story wasn't of much importance in the larger world—certainly nowhere near the impact of a presidential election, or the innocent murder of civilians caught in a war, or all and any of the insults and indignities suffered by the common man. It was only about New York "society." And yet, she reminded herself, the desire for some kind of society was an innate human trait, for without it, there could be no hope of civilized man. Picking out a clip of an article from *Vanity Fair* written about Connie Brewer and her fabulous country house in the Hamptons, Enid wondered if it was possible to have a desire for too much society. The Brewers had everything in life—four children, a private plane, no worries. But it wasn't enough, and now the children's daddy might be going to jail. It was ironic that Sandy Brewer and Mrs. Enid Houghton should end up in the same sentence. If Mrs. Houghton had been alive, she never would have acknowledged an arriviste like Sandy. Enid sat back in her chair. There was a big chunk of the story missing, but her column was due in four hours. Positioning her hands above the keyboard, she wrote, "Louise Houghton was a good friend of mine."

♦

Eight hours later, Billy Litchfield woke up in his claw-footed bathtub. Checking his arms and legs, he was surprised to find himself still very much alive—and inexplicably exultant. It was the middle of the night; nevertheless, he felt an overwhelming desire to hear David Bowie. Sliding a CD into the machine, he thought, Why not? and decided to play the entire four hours of a two-CD set spanning Bowie's career from 1967 to 1993. As Billy listened, he walked around his apartment, dancing occasionally on the worn wooden floors in his bare feet, and flinging his paisley robe around his body like a cape. Then he started looking at photographs. He had hundreds of framed photographs in his apartment—hung on the walls, lined up on the mantelpiece, piled on top of books, and packed into drawers. While he was looking at his photographs, he thought he might as well play *all* his CDs. During the next twenty hours, he sensed that either his cell phone or land line was ringing again, but he didn't answer either one. He took more pills and at some point discovered that he'd consumed nearly a whole bottle of vodka. Then he found an old bottle of gin and, singing loudly along with the music, drank it down. He began to feel queasy, and wanting to maintain his dizzy feeling of pleasure in which nothing that had happened in the past seemed to matter, he took two more Vicodins. He felt a little better, and with his music still blaring—it was now Janet Eno—he passed out on top of his bed.

At one point, like a sleepwalker, he did get up and go to his closet. But then he collapsed again, and sometime in the middle of the night, his kidneys gave out, followed by his heart. Billy didn't feel a thing.

Act
Four

18

That evening, Schiffer Diamond ran into Paul and Annalisa Rice on the sidewalk in front of One Fifth. Schiffer was coming back from a long day of shooting, while Paul and Annalisa were dressed for dinner. Schiffer nodded at them on her way into the building, then she paused. "Excuse me," she said to Annalisa. "Aren't you a friend of Billy Litchfield's?"

Paul and Annalisa exchanged glances. "Yes," Annalisa said.

"Have you seen him?" Schiffer asked. "I've been trying to call him for two days."

"He doesn't seem to be answering his phone. I went by his apartment, but he wasn't home."

"Maybe he's gone away," Schiffer said. "I'm sure it's fine."

"If you talk to him, will you let me know?" Annalisa asked. "I'm worried."

Upstairs, Schiffer searched through a drawer in her kitchen, wondering if she still had the keys to Billy's apartment. Years ago—years and years now—when she and Billy had first become friends, they'd exchanged keys to each other's apartments in case of an emergency. She'd never cleaned out the drawer, so the keys should still be there, although there was a slim possibility that Billy had changed his lock. In the back of the drawer, she did find the keys. There was a blue plastic tag attached to the ring on which Billy had written LITCHFIELD ABODE, followed by an exclamation point, as if proclaiming their friendship.

Schiffer walked the three blocks to Billy's building, pausing under the scaffolding before trying the key in the front door. It still worked, and she passed a row of metal mailboxes. The door to Billy's mailbox was ajar, held open by several days' worth of envelopes. Perhaps Billy was away. Renovations had apparently begun in the building—the stairway leading to the fourth floor was covered with brown paper and secured with blue tape. Hearing music coming from inside Billy's apartment, she knocked loudly. At the other end of the hall, a door opened and a middle-aged woman, neatly groomed, stuck her head out. "Are you looking for Billy Litchfield?" she asked. "He's gone away. And he's left his music on. I don't know what to do. I've tried to call the super, but he doesn't answer. It's all because of the conversion. Billy and I were the last holdouts. They're trying to force us to move. The next thing you know, they'll probably turn off the electricity."

The thought of Billy being in this situation was depressing. "I hope not," Schiffer said.

"Are you going in?" the woman asked.

"Yes," Schiffer said. "Billy gave me his keys."

"Will you turn off the music? I'm just about going crazy here."

Schiffer nodded and went in. Billy's living room had always been overcrowded with stuff, but he'd kept it neat. Now it was a mess. His photographs were strewn on the floor, empty CD cases were scattered around the room, and on the sofa and two armchairs, several coffee-table books lay open to photographs of Jackie O. She found the stereo in an antique wooden cupboard and turned off the music. This wasn't like Billy at all. "Billy?" she called out.

She went down the short hallway to the bedroom, passing empty hooks on the walls where the photographs had been removed. The bedroom door was closed. Schiffer knocked and turned the handle.

Billy lay sprawled across his bed with his head hanging over the side. His eyes were closed, but the muscles under his pale, freckled face had stiffened, giving him a grim, foreign expression. The body on the bed was no longer Billy, Schiffer thought. The Billy Litchfield she'd known was gone.

"Oh, Billy," she said. Looped around Billy's neck was a long noose constructed of Hermès ties that trailed on the floor, as if Billy had been thinking of hanging himself but died before he could complete the act.

"Oh, Billy," Schiffer said again. She gently untied the loose knot around his neck and, separating the ties one from another, carefully hung them back up in Billy's closet, where they belonged.

Then she went into the bathroom. Billy was fastidious and had done his best with the space, placing thick white towels folded carefully on a shelf above the toilet. But the fixtures themselves were cheap and probably forty years old. She'd always assumed that Billy had money, but apparently, he had not, living exactly as he had when he'd first come to New York. The thought of Billy's secret penury added to her sadness. He was one of those New York types whom everyone knew but didn't know much about. She opened the medicine cabinet and was shocked by the row of prescription pills. Prozac, Xanax, Ambien, Vicodin—she'd had no idea Billy was so unhappy and stressed. She should have spent more time with him, she thought bitterly, but Billy had been like a New York institution. She'd always thought he'd be around.

Working quickly, she poured the contents of the prescription bottles into the toilet. As in most prewar buildings, there was an incinerator chute in the kitchen, where Schiffer disposed of the empty bottles. Billy wouldn't want people to think he'd tried to kill himself or that he was addicted to pills. Back in the bedroom, she spotted a crude wooden box on top of his bureau. It wasn't Billy's style, and curious, she opened it to find neat rows of what appeared to be costume jewelry folded in bubble wrap. Did Billy have a transvestite bent to his nature? If so, it was another aspect of his life that he wouldn't have wanted people to know about. Searching through his closet, she found a shoe box and shopping bag from Valentino. She put the wooden box into the shoe box and into the bag. Then she called 911.

Two police officers arrived within minutes, followed by EMS workers, who ripped open Billy's robe and tried to shock him back to life. Billy's body jumped several inches off the bed, and unable to bear it, Schiffer went into the living room. Eventually, a detective in a navy blue suit arrived. "Detective Sabatini," he said, holding out his hand.

"Schiffer Diamond," she said.

"The actress," he said, perking up.

"That's right."

"You found the body. Why?"

"Billy was a good friend. I hadn't heard from him in a couple of days. I came by to see if he was okay. Obviously, he wasn't."

"Did you know he was under investigation?"

"Billy?" she said in disbelief. "For what?"

"Art theft," the detective said.

"That's impossible," Schiffer said, folding her arms.

"It's not only possible, but true. Did he have any enemies?"

"Everyone loved him."

"Did he need money?"

"I don't know anything about his financial affairs. Billy didn't talk about it. He was very . . . discreet."

"So he knew things about people?"

"He knew a lot of people."

"Anyone who might want him dead? Like Sandy Brewer?"

"I don't know who that is."

"I thought you were good friends."

"We were," Schiffer said. "But I hadn't seen Billy in years. Not until I moved back to New York nine months ago."

"I'm going to need you to come to the station for questioning."

"I need to call my publicist first," she said firmly. The reality of Billy's death hadn't hit her yet, but this was going to be a mess. She and Billy would likely end up on the front page of *The New York Post* tomorrow.

Early the next morning, Paul Rice was trawling through the Internet when he came across the first item about Billy Litchfield's death. He didn't connect Billy to the Brewer scandal, so the news didn't have a big impact. But then he saw several small pieces from *The New York Times* to *The Boston Globe*, stating that Billy Litchfield, fifty-four, a sometime journalist, art dealer, and society walker, had been discovered dead in his apartment the evening before. The coverage in the *Daily News* and the *Post* was much more extensive. On the covers of both newspapers were glamour shots of Schiffer Diamond, who had discovered the body, and a photograph of Billy in a tux. There were other photographs as well, mostly of Billy with various socialites and one of him arm in arm with Mrs. Louise Houghton. The police were investigating, suspecting foul play.

Paul turned off his computer. He considered waking his wife and giving her the news, but realized she might start crying. Then he would be stuck in an emotional scene not of his own making and therefore of an unpredictable length. He decided to tell her later instead.

Hurrying through the lobby, he spotted several photographers just outside the door. "What's going on?" he demanded of Roberto.

"Someone died, and Schiffer Diamond found the body."

Billy Litchfield, Paul thought. "But why are they here? Outside One Fifth?" Roberto shrugged. "Never mind," Paul barked, and knocked on Mindy's door. She opened it a crack, trying to keep Skippy, who was barking and jumping on her leg, inside and away from Paul. For the moment, Paul had gained the upper hand in the building; Mindy had to agree to keep Skippy out of the lobby in the morning and evening when Paul would be passing through. "What is it now?" she said, glaring at him with hatred.

"That," Paul said, motioning to the paparazzi outside.

Mindy came out without the dog, closing the door behind her. She was still in her cotton pajamas but had thrown on a chenille robe and flip-flops. "Roberto," she said. "What is this?"

"You know I can't keep them away. The sidewalk is public property, and they're entitled to be there."

"Call the police," Paul said. "Have them arrested."

"Someone died, and Schiffer Diamond found the body," Roberto repeated.

"Billy Litchfield," Paul said.

Mindy gasped. "Billy?"

"I want something done about this," Paul said, continuing his rant. "Those photographers are blocking my point of egress, and I can't get to my office. I don't care how famous someone is, they have no right to disturb the regular workings of a building. I want Schiffer Diamond out. And while we're at it, we should remove Enid Merle. And Philip Oakland. And your husband. And you, too," he said to Mindy.

Mindy's face turned red. Her head felt like a rotten tomato that was about to explode. "Why don't *you* move?" she screamed. "Ever since you moved into this building, there's been nothing but trouble. I've had it with you. If I get one more complaint from you or your wife about this building, I don't care what it costs, I don't care if our maintenance goes up five thousand dollars a month, we will sue you and we will win. No one wants you here. I should have listened to Enid and broken up the apartment. It wouldn't have made any difference—you've ruined the apartment with your stupid fish and your stupid computer equipment, and the only reason you've gotten away with it is because there aren't any bylaws about goddamn fish."

Paul turned to Roberto. "Did you hear that?" he said. "She's threatening me." He snapped his fingers. "I want you to write down what happened. I want her on notice."

"I'm not involved," Roberto said, backing away while gleefully noting that it wasn't yet seven A.M., and already he had a bonanza of gossip. It was going to be a very interesting day.

"Fuck you," Mindy said, jutting her head forward in rage. Instead of reacting to this insult, Paul Rice merely stood there, shaking his head at her as if she were utterly pathetic. This further fueled her anger. "Get out!" she screamed. "You and your wife. Pack your bags and leave this building." Taking a breath, she added, "Immediately!"

"Mrs. Gooch," Roberto said soothingly. "Maybe you should go back inside."

"I will," Mindy said, pointing her finger at Paul. "And I'm going to get a restraining order against you. You won't be allowed to come within fifty feet of me. Try going in and out of the building when you can't go through the lobby."

"Go ahead," Paul said with a taunting smile. "There's nothing I'd like better. Then I can sue you personally. By the way, lawyers' fees add up quickly, so you'd better plan on selling your apartment to cover them." He would have continued, but Mindy went inside and slammed the door.

"Nice," Roberto said.

Paul couldn't tell if the doorman was kidding or genuinely on his side. Either way, it was irrelevant. If need be, he could have Roberto fired. Indeed, he could have all the doormen fired—and the super as well. Putting his hands over his face, he ran through the paparazzi and got into his car.

Safely seated in the backseat of the Bentley, Paul took a deep breath and began texting instructions to his secretary. The confrontation with Mindy Gooch hadn't disturbed him; having brilliantly arranged for Sandy's arrest without implicating himself, Paul was feeling confident and in control. Sandy was back in the office, having been released on bail, but his concentration was shot. Eventually, Paul figured, there would be a trial, and Sandy might go to jail. When he did, the business would be all Paul's, and this was only the beginning. The China deal was working brilliantly, and eventually, other countries might be forced to buy the algorithm as well. He could make a trillion dollars. It wasn't so much these days. Most countries had deficits that size.

As the car headed up Park Avenue to his midtown office, Paul checked the numbers of various stock markets around the world and received a Google alert. Both he and his wife had been mentioned in an item about Billy Litchfield on some society website.

Paul wondered again if he should have woken his wife to tell her—given all the fuss about Billy's death, he may have miscalculated the importance of the information. But it was too late to go back to the building and too early for a phone call. He decided to send her a text.

He wrote: "Check the papers. Your friend Billy Litchfield is dead." Out of habit, he quickly scanned the message, and then, deciding that it might be interpreted as too cold, he added, "Love, Paul."

In a fury, Mindy went to her computer and wrote, "I HATE THAT MAN. I HATE HIM. I WILL KILL HIM." Then she remembered about Billy and, Googling his name, saw that his death was all over the papers. Billy was only fifty-four. She was overcome with shock, followed by grief, and despite reminding herself that for years, she hadn't liked Billy so much, considering him a snob, she began sobbing. Mindy was one of those women who took pride in the fact that she almost never cried, partly because when she did, it wasn't a pretty sight. Her nose and eyes swelled up, and then her mouth opened and hung askew as clear snot dripped out of her nostrils.

Mindy's horrendous, high-pitched wailing woke Sam. His chest squeezed with fear, as he assumed his mother had somehow found out that he'd cut the cables outside the Rices' apartment and was about to be arrested. The caper hadn't yielded the hoped-for response, although Paul Rice had certainly been angry. For the past two weeks, Sam had been living in fear that he might get caught, but the police hadn't really bothered to investigate, only questioning the doormen and Enid and a few other residents the next morning. But then they'd gone away and hadn't returned. His mother insisted the culprit was the blogger Thayer Core, who was always writing terrible stories about One Fifth. But Sam guessed Enid suspected him. "Retribution is tricky, Sam," she'd said one afternoon when he'd run into her on the sidewalk near the park. "The insult isn't usually worth the risk of punishment. And eventually one learns that karma has a surprising way of taking care of these situations. All you have to do is sit back and watch."

Now, bracing himself for the inevitable, Sam entered his mother's office. "What's the matter?"

She shook her head and opened her arms, pulling him awkwardly onto her lap. "A friend of ours died."

"Oh," Sam said, relieved. "Who?"

"Billy Litchfield. He knew Mrs. Houghton."

"The bald guy," Sam said. "The one who was always around Annalisa Rice."

"That's right," Mindy said. Recalling the scene she'd just had with Paul in the lobby, she was furious again. I'm going to tell Annalisa Rice the news about Billy myself, Mindy thought. Kissing Sam and shooing him away, she went into the lobby filled with cruel determination.

As she rode up in the elevator, she realized that since Paul knew about Billy's death, Annalisa likely did as well. Nevertheless, Mindy wanted to see how she was taking the news—she hoped Annalisa felt horrible—and now, with Billy gone, maybe the Rices would leave New York and return to Washington, where they belonged. Or perhaps they would move farther away, to another country. If they left, she wouldn't make the same mistake twice with the apartment. This time, she and Enid and Philip would split it up, and with James making money at last, they might even be able to afford it.

Maria opened the door. Mindy glared at her. These rich people, Mindy thought, shaking her head. They couldn't even be bothered to open their own doors. "Is Mrs. Rice here?" she asked.

Maria held her finger up to her lips. "She's sleeping."

"Wake her up. I have something important to tell her."

"I don't like to do that, ma'am."

"Do it!" Mindy snapped. "I'm the head of the board."

Maria backed away in fright, and while she scurried up the

stairs, Mindy strolled into the apartment. It had changed drastically since she'd snooped around at Christmas, and no longer bore any resemblance to a hotel. Although Mindy knew nothing about decorating, being one of those people who became unaware of an environment after five minutes, even she could appreciate the beauty of what Annalisa had done. The floor in the second foyer was now lapis lazuli, and in the center was a round table inlaid with marble on which sat a huge spray of pink apple blossoms. For a moment, Mindy waited in the second foyer, but when she didn't hear any noise from upstairs, she went into the living room. Here was a series of inviting couches and divans done in soft blue and yellow velvets, and an enormous silk rug with a swirly design in delicious oranges, pinks, creams, and blues.

Annalisa Rice was certainly taking her time getting up, Mindy thought in annoyance, and sat down on a plush couch. It was stuffed with down, and Mindy sank into the cushions. Striped silk curtains hanging from the French windows pooled elegantly on the floor, and scattered around the room were little tables and more flower arrangements. Mindy sighed. If only she'd known James's book would be a success, she scolded herself. Then she might have had this room for herself.

Upstairs, Maria was knocking on Annalisa's bedroom door. Annalisa rubbed her forehead, wishing Maria would go away, but the knocks were growing more insistent. Resigned, she got out of the four-poster bed. She'd been hoping to finally get some rest— since Sandy Brewer's arrest, she'd hardly slept at all. Billy was sure to be arrested as well, but after her conversation with him, he hadn't taken her calls. Annalisa had gone by his apartment at least five times, but he wouldn't answer his buzzer. Even Connie wasn't talking to her—or to anyone, for that matter. "I don't know who my friends are anymore," Connie had said. "Someone ratted us out. For all I know, it might have been you. Or Paul."

"Connie, don't be ridiculous. Neither Paul nor I have any interest in hurting you or Sandy. Of course you're scared. But I'm not your enemy." Her entreaties made no difference, and Connie hung up, telling her not to bother to call again, as their lawyer had forbidden them to talk to anyone. Paul was the only one who seemed mysteriously unaffected—or rather, Annalisa corrected, positively affected. He'd become less brooding and secretive and had finally agreed to allow the apartment to be photographed for the cover of *Architectural Digest*. The only snag was that she'd need to get permission from the building for the photography equipment to be brought up in the service elevator.

Putting on a pair of velvet slippers and a heavy silk robe, she opened her bedroom door. "There's a lady downstairs," Maria said, looking over her shoulder nervously.

"Who?" Annalisa said.

"That lady. From the building."

"Enid Merle?"

"The other one. The mean one."

"Ah, Mindy Gooch." What did Mindy want now? She probably had some fresh complaint about Paul. Which was nervy of her, considering Paul believed Sam had cut the wires. Annalisa herself was skeptical. "A thirteen-year-old boy getting the better of you, Paul?" she'd scoffed. "I don't think so." Now she said to Maria, "Make some coffee, please. And put out a few of those nice croissants."

"Yes, missus," Maria said.

Annalisa took her time brushing her teeth and carefully cleansing her face. She put on a flowing white blouse and a pair of navy blue slacks and slipped the yellow diamond ring from Paul onto her middle right finger. She went downstairs and was irritated to find Mindy sitting comfortably in the living room, examining a Victorian silver card case. "Hello," Annalisa said formally. "Maria is serving coffee in the breakfast room. Come with me, please."

Mindy stood up, replacing the object on the side table. Well!, she thought, following Annalisa through the apartment. Annalisa had certainly become grand, but that was typical of people with money—eventually, they always believed they were better than everyone else. Motioning for Mindy to sit, Annalisa poured coffee into two china cups with enameled rims. "Sugar?" she asked. "Or are you a sugar-substitute girl?"

"Sugar," Mindy muttered, frowning. She picked up the tiny silver spoon and shoveled several spoonfuls into her coffee. "You've done a lot of work in here. The apartment is beautiful," she said reluctantly.

"Thank you," Annalisa said. "It's going to be photographed for the cover of *Architectural Digest*. They'll need to use the service elevator. I'll let the super know the date beforehand." She looked Mindy in the eye. "I'm assuming I can count on you not to make any trouble."

"I guess it's fine," Mindy said, unable to come up with a reasonable objection.

Annalisa nodded and took a sip of her coffee. "Now, what can I do for you?" she asked.

"So you haven't heard," Mindy said. She narrowed her eyes in anticipation of delivering her blow. "Billy Litchfield is dead."

Annalisa's hand froze, but then she calmly took another sip of coffee. She dabbed her lips with a small linen napkin. "I'm sorry to hear that," she said. "What happened?"

"No one knows. Schiffer Diamond found him dead in his apartment last night." Mindy glanced at Annalisa, surprised by her lack of reaction. There were bluish shadows under her eyes, but the slate-gray irises were staring back coldly, almost challengingly, Mindy thought. "There are photographers outside," she said. "It's common knowledge that you and Billy were good friends. And you're always in the society columns. So you might want to lie low for a few days."

"Thank you," Annalisa said. She put her cup back onto the saucer. "Anything else?" she asked.

"I guess not," Mindy said, suddenly not having the nerve to bring up Paul's attack on her that morning, or the fact that Mindy wanted them out of the building.

"Well, then," Annalisa said, standing up. The interview was clearly over, and Mindy was forced to stand as well. At the door, she turned back, once again wanting to bring up Paul and his behavior, but Annalisa's face was impassive.

"About Paul," Mindy began.

"Not today," Annalisa said. "Nor any other day as well. Thank you for coming by." And she firmly closed the door. Outside in the small hallway, Mindy heard her turn the lock.

When Mindy had gone, Annalisa rushed upstairs and grabbed her BlackBerry. She was about to call Paul when she saw his text. So he knew already. Going back downstairs, she went into the living room and sank into an armchair. She had an urgent desire to call someone—anyone—to lament Billy's death, but she realized there was no one to whom she might speak. All the people she knew in this world were Billy and Connie's friends and were relative strangers. Billy had been more than a best friend, though. He'd been her guide and adviser; he'd made this world entertaining and fun. Without him, she didn't know what she was going to do. What was the point of all this now? She slumped forward, putting her head in her hands.

Maria came into the room. "Mrs. Rice?" she asked.

Annalisa immediately sat up and smoothed the skin under her eyes. "I'm fine," she said. "I just need a moment to myself."

One floor below, Enid Merle pushed through the little gate that separated her terrace from Philip's, and knocked on his French door. Philip opened it looking, as he had ever since he'd returned from Los Angeles, miserable. Enid wasn't sure if his relationship with Lola was making him depressed, or the fact that Schiffer Diamond had been seen all over town with Derek Brumminger.

"Have you heard?" Enid asked.

"What now?" Philip said.

"Billy Litchfield is dead."

Philip put his hands in his hair.

Lola came out of the bedroom wearing a T-shirt and a pair of Philip's boxer shorts. "Who's dead?" she asked with interest.

"Billy Litchfield," Philip muttered.

"Do I know him?" Lola asked.

"No," Philip said sharply.

"Okay," Lola grumbled. "You don't need to yell."

"Schiffer found the body," Enid said, addressing Philip. "One can only imagine. You must give her a call."

"Schiffer Diamond found the body?" Lola exclaimed with enthusiasm. Rushing past Enid and Philip, she went out to the terrace and looked over the edge. There was a throng of photographers and reporters outside the entrance, and she recognized the top of Thayer Core's head. Damn, she thought. Thayer would probably be calling her any minute requesting information, and she would have to give it to him. If she didn't, he would once again threaten to post Philip's unfinished script, and Philip would be furious.

She went back inside. "Are you calling her?" she asked Philip.

"Yes," Philip said. He went into his office and closed the door.

Enid looked at Lola and shook her head. "What's wrong now?" Lola demanded. Enid only shook her head again and went back to her own apartment. Lola sat down on the couch in a huff. Philip had just gotten over having his things rearranged and no longer banged the cabinet doors every time he was in the kitchen. But now this Billy Litchfield person had died, and Philip would go back to being in a bad mood again. It was all somehow Schiffer Diamond's fault. Philip would have to pay attention to her, and Lola would have to fight her off again. Lola lay back on the couch, absentmindedly rubbing her stomach. Aha, she thought. There was the answer: She would get pregnant.

Philip came out of his office, went into the bedroom, and began getting dressed. Lola followed him. "Did you talk to her?" she asked.

"Yes," Philip said, taking a shirt out of the closet.

"And? How is she?"

"How do you think?" Philip said.

"Where are you going now?" Lola said.

"To see her."

"Can I come?" Lola asked.

"No," Philip said.

"Why not?"

"She's working. On location. It's not appropriate."

"But what about me?" Lola said. "I'm upset, too. Look." She held out her hands. "I'm shaking."

"Not now, Lola, please." He pushed past her and went out the door.

Sure enough, her phone began bleeping moments later, announcing a text from Thayer Core. "Just saw Oakland leave the building. What's up?"

Lola thought for a moment and, realizing she had an opportunity to cause trouble for Schiffer, wrote, "Going to see Schiffer Diamond. She's on location somewhere in the city."

Next door, Enid was also getting ready to go out. Her sources told her that Billy was suspected of selling Sandy Brewer the cross, although Billy Litchfield's involvement wasn't the only thing that perplexed her.

She went down to the lobby, passing by the Gooches' apartment. Inside, Mindy was on the phone with her office. "I'm not coming in today," she said. "A very good friend of mine passed away unexpectedly, and I'm too upset to leave my house." She hung up and opened a new file for her blog, already having decided to use Billy's death as a topic. "Today, I officially became middle-aged," she wrote. "I'm not going to hide from the truth. Instead, I'm going to scream it from the rooftops: I am a middle-aged woman. The recent and untimely death of one of my most beloved friends has pointed up the inevitable. I have finally reached the age when friends start dying. Not parents—we all expect that. But friends. Our peers. My generation. And it's made me wonder how much time I have left myself, and what I'm going to do with that time."

Crossing the street, Enid knocked on Flossie Davis's door, then let herself in with the key. She was surprised to find Flossie out of bed and sitting in the living room, looking out the window at the commotion in front of One Fifth. "I was wondering how long it would take you to get here," Flossie said. "You see? I was right all along. The cross was in Louise Houghton's apartment. And no one believed me. You don't know what it's been like all these years, knowing the truth, and no one listened. You don't know—"

"Stop," Enid said, cutting her off. "We both know you took the cross. And Louise found out and made you give it to her. Why didn't she turn you in? What did you have on her?"

"And you call yourself a gossip columnist," Flossie said, clicking her tongue. "It sure took you long enough to figure it out."

"Why did you take it?"

Flossie snorted. "Because I wanted it. It was so pretty. And it was right there. And it was only going to be locked up in that stupid museum along with every other dead thing. And Louise saw me take it. I didn't know she saw me until I went to the Pauline Trigère fashion show. Louise sat next to me, and she'd never done that before. 'I know what you have in your bag,' she whispered. Louise was scary even then. She had those strange blue eyes—almost gray. 'I don't know what you're talking about,' I said. The next morning, Louise came down to my apartment. I was living in Philip's apartment then. Philip wasn't born yet. And you were working at the newspaper and not paying attention to anyone except yourself."

Enid nodded, remembering. How different life had been in those days. Entire families often lived in a two-bedroom apartment, sharing one bathroom, but they'd been lucky. Her father had bought the two apartments side by side and was going to turn them into one large apartment when he'd suddenly died of a heart attack, leaving Enid with one apartment and Flossie and her little daughter with the other. "Louise accused me of taking the cross," Flossie said, continuing her story. "She threatened to turn me in to the authorities. She said I would go to jail. She knew I was a widow, trying to take care of my child. She said she would take pity on me if I gave her the cross. Then she was going to slip it back into the museum and no one would be the wiser."

"But she didn't give it back," Enid said.

"That's right," Flossie said. "Because she wanted it for herself. She wanted it all along. She was greedy. And besides, if she'd given it back to the museum, she wouldn't have been able to hold it over my head."

"You had something on her," Enid said. "But what?"

Flossie looked around the room as if to make sure no one could overhear them. She shrugged, then leaned forward in her chair. "Now that she's dead, she can't do anything to me. So why not? Why not let the world know? Louise was a murderer."

"Oh, Flossie." Enid shook her head mournfully.

"You don't believe me?" Flossie said. "Well, it's true. She killed her husband."

"Everyone knows he died from a staph infection."

"That's what Louise made people think. And no one ever questioned her. Because she was Louise Houghton." Flossie began to wheeze with excitement. "And everyone forgot—all that time she spent in China before she came to New York? She knew all about diseases. How to cure them and how to make them worse. Did anyone ever think about what she was growing on that terrace? About what was in her greenhouse? I did. And one day, I found out. 'Belladonna,' I said. 'If you turn me in, I'll turn you in,' I said. She didn't dare return the cross then. Without it, she would have had nothing on me."

"It doesn't make sense," Enid said.

"Who said it had to make sense?" Flossie said. "You know perfectly well what it was about. Louise didn't want to leave that apartment. It was her pride and joy. And then, after she'd spent a million dollars to do it all up the way she liked, and everyone was calling her the queen of society, her husband wanted to sell it. And there wasn't a thing she could do about it. He had all the money, and the apartment was in his name. He was always smart that way. He probably guessed what Louise was really like. And sure enough, she sent him on that trip, and two weeks later, he was dead."

"You know you're still not safe," Enid said. "Now that the cross has been discovered, they'll reopen the case. Someone may have seen you take it. A guard, perhaps, who's still alive. You could go to jail."

"You never had any common sense!" Flossie snapped. "Louise paid off the guards. So who's going to tell them—you? You would turn in your own stepmother? If you do, you'll have to tell the whole story. About how Louise was a murderer. You'll never do it. You wouldn't dare. You'll do anything to preserve the reputation of that building. I wouldn't be surprised if you'd commit murder yourself." Flossie took a deep breath, gearing up for another attack. "I've never understood you or people like you. It's only a stupid building. There are millions of them in New York City. Now get out." Flossie started wheezing. After Enid fetched a glass of water and made sure the attack had passed, she left.

Outside, Enid stood on the sidewalk across the street from One Fifth, gazing at the building. She tried to see the building the way Flossie saw it—as just another building—but couldn't. One Fifth was like a piece of living art, unique and beautifully executed, perfectly positioned at the end of Fifth Avenue, in close—but not too close—proximity to Washington Square Park. And there was the address itself. "One Fifth." Clean and authoritative and imply-ing so many things—class and money and prestige and even, Enid thought, a bit of magic, the kind of real-life magic that made life so endlessly interesting. Flossie was wrong, Enid decided. Everyone wanted to live in One Fifth, and if they didn't, it was only because they lacked imagination. She raised her hand to hail a cab and, get-ting into the backseat, gave the driver the address of the New York Public Library.

❦

Alan, the PA, rapped on the door of Schiffer Diamond's location trailer. The door was opened a crack by the publicist, Karen. "Philip Oakland's here," Alan said, standing aside to let Philip pass. Behind him was a band of paparazzi and two news crews, having discov-ered the location of the day's shooting at the Ukrainian Institute on Fifth Avenue and then finding Schiffer's trailer on a side street. Billy Litchfield wasn't of particular interest to them, but Schiffer

Diamond was. She had found the body. It was possible she'd had something to do with his death or knew something about it or had given him drugs or taken drugs herself. In the trailer was a leather couch, a small table, a makeup area, a bathroom with a shower, and a tiny bedroom with a single bed and chair. The lawyer, Johnnie Toochin, who had been called in to help with damage control, now sat on the leather couch, talking on his phone. "Hey, Philip," Johnnie said, greeting him with a raised hand. "What a mess."

"Where is she?" Philip asked Karen, who motioned to the bedroom. Philip opened the narrow door. Schiffer was sitting on the bed wearing a terry-cloth robe, her legs crossed beneath her. She was staring blankly at a script but looked up when Philip came in.

"I don't know if I can do this today," she said.

"Of course you can. You're a great actress," Philip said. He sat down in the chair across from her.

"That was one of the last things Billy said to me." She pulled the robe across her body as if she were cold. "You know, if it weren't for Billy, we might never have met."

"Yes, we would have. Somehow."

"No." She shook her head. "I wouldn't have become an actress, and I wouldn't have done *Summer Morning*. I keep thinking about how a chance meeting with one person can change your life. Is it fate or coincidence?"

"But you had the opportunity. And you made it work."

"That's right, Philip," she said. She looked at him, her expression vulnerable. She had yet to have her makeup done. Her face was clean, and there were little lines around her eyes. "I keep wondering why we can't do that. Make it work."

"I fucked up again, didn't I?" Philip said.

"Yeah." She nodded. "And I guess I did, too. All those years, I kept thinking, What if? What if I hadn't gone to Europe. Or what if I'd seen you that time when you came to L.A."

"Or what if I'd managed to break up with Lola?" Philip asked. "Would you still being seeing Brumminger?"

"You have to ask?" Schiffer said.

"Yeah," Philip said. "I guess I've never managed to ask the right question."

"Will you ever manage it, Philip? If not, we should end this right now. I need to know. I want to move on one way or another. I want it to be clean."

Philip leaned back in the chair and put his hands in his hair. Then he started laughing.

"What's so damn funny?" she asked.

"This," he said. "This situation. Look," he said, sitting next to her on the bed and taking her hand. "This is probably the worst time to ask you this, but do you really want to marry me?"

She looked down at his hand and shook her head. "What do you think, schoolboy?"

19

A couple of hours later, Schiffer Diamond, made up and wearing a long gown for the scene at the Ukrainian Institute, came out of her trailer. Philip was still holding her hand, as if he didn't dare let go of her, and after he helped her down the steps, the photographers closed in with their cameras. Philip and Schiffer exchanged a look and began running down the sidewalk to a waiting van. The paparazzi were taken by surprise, and there was a jostling in the crowd, and two photographers were knocked down. Nevertheless, Thayer Core managed to hold up his iPhone and snap a picture of the happy couple, which he then e-mailed to Lola. "I think your BF is cheating on you," he wrote.

Lola got the e-mail immediately and tried to call Philip. She'd suspected something like this would happen, but now that it had, she couldn't believe it. Philip didn't answer his phone, of course, so she texted Thayer Core to find out where he was. Then she opened the closet to get dressed, her hands trembling so violently with frustration and anger that she knocked several tops off their hangers. This gave her a wicked idea, and she went into the kitchen, found the scissors, and pulling several pairs of jeans from the shelf on Philip's side of the closet, cut the legs off. She refolded the tops of the mangled jeans and replaced them on the shelf. Then she kicked the cutoff legs under the bed, put on her makeup, and went out.

She found Thayer standing behind a police barricade on Seventy-ninth Street. There was a carnival atmosphere, with the presence of the paparazzi drawing the attention of passersby who kept stopping to find out what was going on. "I'm going in," Lola announced grimly, stepping around the barricade. Four beefy Teamsters were blocking the entrance. "I'm Philip Oakland's girl-friend," she said, attempting to explain why she must be allowed to pass.

"Sorry," one of the Teamsters said, impassive.

"I know he's in there. And I have to see him," she wailed.

A young woman sidled up next to her. "Did you say you were Philip Oakland's girlfriend?" she asked.

"That's right," Lola said.

"He just went in with Schiffer Diamond. We thought *they* were together."

"I'm his girlfriend," Lola said. "I *live* with him."

"You're kidding," the girl said, and put her cell phone in Lola's face to record her remarks. "What's your name?"

"Lola Fabrikant. Philip and I have been together for months."

"And Schiffer Diamond stole him from you?"

"Yes," Lola said, realizing she had an opportunity to play a sig-nificant part in this drama. Rising to the occasion, she summoned her most confused tone of voice and said, "I woke up this morning, and everything was fine. Then two hours ago, someone texted me a photograph of the two of them holding hands."

The girl gasped in horror. "You just found out?"

"That's right. And I might even be pregnant with his baby."

"What a scumbag!" the girl declared in female solidarity.

Hearing this pronouncement on Philip's character, Lola was momentarily worried that she'd gone too far. She hadn't meant to say she was pregnant, but she'd gotten caught up in the moment, and it had just slipped out. But she couldn't take it back now—and besides, Philip *had* wronged her. And it certainly was possible that she could be pregnant.

"Brandon!" the girl shouted, waving at one of the photographers and pointing at Lola. "She says she's Philip Oakland's girlfriend. And she's having his baby. We need a photograph." The photographer leaned across the barricade and snapped Lola's picture. Within seconds, the rest of the pack followed suit, aiming their cameras at her and clicking off shots. Lola put her hand on her hip and posed prettily, glad that she'd had the foresight to dress in high heels and a trench coat. At last, she thought. This was the moment she'd been waiting for her entire life. She smiled, knowing it was crucial she look stunning in the photographs that would undoubtedly be all over the Internet in a matter of hours.

Billy's death was not ruled a suicide but an accidental overdose. He hadn't taken as many pills as suspected; rather, it was the combination of four different kinds of prescription medication that did him in. Two weeks after his death, a service was held for him at St. Ambrose Church, where Billy had mourned the death of Mrs. Louise Houghton just nine months earlier.

It turned out that Billy had recently made a will, leaving all his worldly belongings to his niece and requesting that a service be held in the church patronized by his idol, Mrs. Louise Houghton. Many of the hundreds of people who knew Billy came, and although the Brewers claimed Billy had sold them the Cross of Bloody Mary, there was, people agreed, no way to prove it, especially when Johnnie Toochin revealed that Mrs. Houghton had left Billy a wooden box filled only with costume jewelry. However, the box was never discovered, and so the provenance of the cross remained a mystery, and Billy's reputation stayed intact.

During his memorial service, several people gave eulogies about how wonderful Billy was, and how he represented a certain era in New York, and how, with his passing, that era was finished.

"New York isn't New York anymore without Billy Litchfield," declared an old-monied banker who was the husband of a famous socialite.

Perhaps it wasn't, Mindy thought, but it still went on, the same as always. As if in confirmation of this fact, Lola Fabrikant flounced in halfway through the service, causing a stir in the back of the church. She was wearing a short black low-cut dress and, inexplicably, a small black hat with a veil that just covered her eyes. Lola thought the hat made her look mysterious and alluring, in keeping with her new role as the slighted young woman. The day after Schiffer and Philip were photographed together, Lola's picture had appeared in three newspapers, and there were discussions about her on six blogs, in which the general consensus was that she was a babe and could do better than Philip. But after that, the interest in her had quickly waned. Now, although it would mean seeing Philip and Schiffer and Enid, she and Thayer had decided she ought to attend Billy's service, if only to remind people of her existence.

Lola had agreed reluctantly. She could face Philip and Schiffer if she had to, but she was terrified of Enid. The day she'd gone to confront Philip on the set at the Ukrainian Institute, she'd returned to One Fifth after being "assaulted"—her words—by the paparazzi, realizing if she hung around any longer, she would lose her mystique. Safely inside Philip's apartment, she waited for him all afternoon, going over the situation again and again in her mind and wishing she could take it all back. She reminded herself that she didn't know for a fact that Philip and Schiffer were really together; he might have only been comforting her after all. She would have to figure out a way to exonerate herself. But at about five, Enid appeared in Philip's apartment, coming up silently behind Lola, who was in the kitchen, pouring herself yet another vodka. Lola was so startled she nearly dropped the bottle.

"Oh, good, dear," Enid said. "You're here."

"Where else would I be?" Lola asked nervously, taking a gulp of her drink.

"The question is, where should you be?" Enid said. She smiled broadly and sat down on the couch, patting the place next to her. "Come here, dear," she said, giving Lola a frightening smile. "I want to talk to you."

"Where's Philip?" Lola demanded.

"I imagine he's still with Schiffer."

"Why?"

"Don't you know, dear? He's in love with her. He always has been, and I'm afraid for your sake, he always will be."

"Did Philip ask you to tell me this, or are you doing it on your own?"

"I haven't talked to Philip since this morning. I have, however, talked to quite a few other people who have informed me that you're going to be in the papers tomorrow. Don't look so surprised, dear," Enid said. "I work for a newspaper. I have many, many contacts. That's one of the advantages of being old. One collects lots of friends. Are you sure you don't want to sit down?"

Lola tried to beg for mercy. "Oh, Enid," she cried out, and kneeling down, she buried her head in the couch in shame. "It wasn't my fault. This girl came up to me, and I didn't know what to say. She somehow got it out of me."

"There, there," Enid said, patting Lola's head. "It happens to everyone once. You were just like a snake about to be attacked by a mongoose."

"That's right," Lola said, although she had no idea what a mongoose was.

"I can fix everything. I only need to know if you're pregnant, dear."

Lola sat up and felt around for her drink. "I could be," she said, becoming defiant.

Enid crossed one aged leg over the other. "If you are carrying Philip's child, I suggest you pour that glass of vodka down the sink. Immediately."

"I told you," Lola said. "I don't know if I'm pregnant or not."

"Why don't we find out?" Enid said. She reached into a paper bag and took out a pregnancy test.

"You can't make me do that," Lola shrieked, jumping back in horror.

Enid held out the kit. When Lola shook her head, Enid placed it on the coffee table between them.

"Where's Philip?" Lola said. "If Philip knew what you were doing—"

"Philip is a man, my dear. And, unfortunately, slightly weak. Especially in the face of female hysteria. Men just can't bear it, you know? They tune it out." Enid crossed her arms and, looking Lola up and down, said soothingly, "I only have your best interests at heart. If you are pregnant, you'll need looking after. Of course, you will have the baby. It would be so lovely if Philip had a child. And we'll make sure you're taken care of for life. I have an extra bedroom, and you can live with me." She paused. "On the other hand, if you do take the test and you're not pregnant, I'll make sure the story goes away quickly. With very little harm to you." Enid gave Lola another terrifying smile. "But as you said, I can't make you take the test. If you don't take it, however, I'm going to assume you're not pregnant. And if you're not pregnant and you continue to lie about it, I'll make your life a living hell."

"Don't threaten me, Enid," Lola said warningly. "No one threatens me and gets away with it."

Enid laughed. "Don't be silly, my dear. Threats are only meaningful if you have the power to execute them. And you, my dear, do not." She stood up. "I've tolerated your antics for quite a while. But today you've made me very, very angry." She nodded at the coffee table. "Take the test."

Lola grabbed the box. Enid was old, but she was still the meanest mean girl Lola had ever encountered, and Lola was afraid of her. So afraid, in fact, that she actually peed on the plastic indicator and handed it over to Enid, who examined it with grim satisfaction. "Now, that's lucky, my dear," she said. "It seems you're not pregnant after all. If you were, it might have been complicated. We wouldn't have known who the father was. Not until the baby was born. It could have been Philip's—or Thayer Core's. And that's no way to bring a child into the world, now, is it?"

Lola had come up with a hundred responses—after the fact. In the actual moment, facing Enid, she wasn't able to think of what to say.

"Consider this an opportunity, dear," Enid said. "You're only twenty-two. You have a chance to start over. I had a long conversation with your mother this afternoon, and she's on her way to pick you up and take you back to Atlanta. She's a lovely woman, your mother. She should be here in an hour. I've booked a room for you at the Four Seasons hotel so you can enjoy your last night in New York in style."

"Oh no," Lola said, finding her voice. She looked around in a panic, spotted her handbag next to the door, and grabbed it. "I'm not leaving New York."

"Be sensible, dear," Enid said.

"You can't make me," Lola shouted. She opened the door, knowing only that she had to get away. She frantically pressed the button for the elevator as Enid followed her into the hallway.

"Where are you going? There's no place to go, Lola."

Lola turned her back and pressed the button again. Where was the elevator? "You haven't any money," Enid said. "You don't have an apartment. Or a job. You have no choice."

Lola turned. "I don't care." The elevator came at last, and she stepped in.

"You'll be sorry," Enid said. As the doors were closing, Enid made one last attempt to dissuade her. "You'll see," she called out, adding fiercely, "You don't belong in New York."

Now, in the church, Lola remembered with glee how Enid's plan had backfired. Her admonishment that Lola didn't belong in New York had only made her more determined. In the past two weeks, she'd put up with quite a bit of hardship, returning home with her mother—who had begged Lola to stay in Windsor Pines and even tried to fix her up with the son of one of her friends who was getting a business degree—but Lola wouldn't hear of it. She sold several pairs of shoes and two handbags on eBay, scraping together enough money to return to New York. She forced Thayer to take her in, and for the time being, she was living with Thayer and Josh in their little hellhole, sharing Thayer's tiny bed. On the third day there, she'd broken down and actually cleaned the bathroom and the kitchen sink. And then that disgusting Josh, thinking she was free bait, had tried to kiss her, and she'd had to fight him off. She couldn't bunk with Thayer much longer. She had to find her own place—but how?

She tried to peer around the many heads in front of her, looking for Philip and Enid. She spotted the back of Enid's coiffed head first. What would Enid do when she found out she was back in New York? Sitting next to Enid was Philip. Seeing the back of his head, with that too familiar longish dark hair, brought back all the fresh hurts and indignities she'd suffered at his hands as well.

After rushing out of his apartment on what would turn out to be her final evening in One Fifth, she'd wandered around the West Village, weighing her options. But after two hours, her feet began to throb, and she'd realized Enid was right—she had no money and no place to go. She'd returned to One Fifth to find her mother and Philip and Enid waiting. They were calm, treating her with kid gloves as if she were a mental patient who'd had a breakdown, and Lola realized she had no choice but to comply with their plan. Then she'd had to endure the disgrace of allowing her mother to help her pack up her things. Philip was disturbingly distant throughout the process, as if he had become a completely different person. He'd behaved as if he hardly knew her and they hadn't had sex a hundred times—and this, to Lola, was the most unfathomable of all. How could a man who had put his head between your legs and his penis inside your vagina and mouth, and kissed you and held you and tickled your stomach, suddenly act as if none of it had happened? Riding uptown in the taxi with her mother, she had burst into tears and cried and cried and cried. "Philip Oakland is a fool," Beetelle declared fiercely. "And his aunt is even worse. I've never met such an awful woman." She put her arms around Lola's head and stroked her hair. "It's a good thing you got away from those terrible people," she said, but this only made Lola cry harder.

Beetelle's heart broke for her daughter, reminding her of her own heartbreaking incident in New York with the doctor. She would have been about Lola's age then. Pulling her daughter closer, Beetelle felt helpless in the face of Lola's distress. It was the first time, she realized, that Lola was discovering the terrible truth about life: It wasn't what it seemed, and fairy tales did not necessarily come true. Nor could men be relied upon to love you.

The next morning, Philip came to the hotel to see Lola. For a moment, she'd held out hope that he would tell her it was all a mistake, and he loved her after all. But when she opened the door, his expression revealed that he hadn't changed his mind; indeed, as if to make a point, under his arm were the *Post* and the *Daily News*. They went downstairs to the restaurant, and Philip put the papers on the table. "Do you want to see them?" he asked. She did, of course, but didn't want to give him more ammunition. "No," she replied haughtily, as if she were above such things.

"Listen, Lola," he began.

"Why are you here?" she asked.

"I owe you an apology."

"I don't want to hear it."

"I made a mistake with you. And I'm sorry. You're young, and I should have known better. I never should have allowed our relationship to continue. I should have ended it before Christmas."

Lola's stomach dropped. The waiter brought her food—eggs Benedict—and Lola looked at her plate, wondering if she'd ever be able to eat again. Had her whole relationship with Philip been a lie? Then she understood. "You used me," she accused him.

"Oh, Lola." Philip sighed. "We used each other."

"I loved you," Lola said fiercely.

"No, you didn't," Philip said. "You loved the idea of me. There's a big difference."

Lola threw her napkin onto her plate of eggs. "Let me tell you one thing, Philip Oakland. I hate you. And I will always hate you. For the rest of my life. Don't you come near me, ever again."

Holding her head high, she got up and walked out of the restaurant, leaving Philip sitting there, embarrassed.

A little later, leaving the hotel with her mother, Lola wondered how she would ever recover. When they got to the airport, however, she bought the papers; and seeing her photograph on the third page of the *Post*, and reading the brief story about how Philip had dumped her for Schiffer Diamond, she began to feel better. She wasn't some little nobody. She was Lola Fabrikant, and someday she would show Philip and Enid what a mistake they'd made in underestimating her.

Now, scanning the pew containing Philip and Enid, she saw Schiffer Diamond sitting next to Philip, followed by auburn-haired Annalisa Rice. A few pews behind them was that awful Mindy Gooch, with her rigid blond bob, and next to her was James Gooch, with that familiar sweet bald spot on the top of his head. Ah, James Gooch, Lola thought. She'd forgotten about James, who was apparently back from his book tour. Now he sat before her, like Providence. She took out her iPhone. "I'm behind you in the church," she texted.

It took a minute for her text to reach him. Hearing the bleat, he turned his head slightly and felt in his pocket for his phone. Mindy glared at him. James gave a guilty shrug, took out his phone, and surreptitiously checked the message. The skin on the back of his neck reddened, and he turned the phone off.

"I miss you," Lola had texted. "Meet me in the Mews at three o'clock."

❦

An hour later, James Gooch stood in a corner of the overcrowded living room in the Rices' apartment and, looking around to make sure Mindy wasn't somewhere in the room watching him, reread Lola's text, his stomach thumping with excitement and curiosity.

Leaving the church, he'd looked for her, but she was already outside, posing for the photographers. He considered speaking to her, but Mindy quickly pulled him away. Now, checking his watch, he saw that it was nearly three. Weaving through the crowd, he scanned the room for Mindy. A waiter passed by with a tray of caviar piled on top of tiny blintzes, and James popped two into his mouth. Another waiter freshened his glass of champagne with a bottle of Dom Perignon. Annalisa Rice had gone all out in Billy's honor, inviting at least two hundred people back to her apartment to further mourn his loss. Billy's sudden death had shocked James, and coming back on the plane from Houston, he had even read Mindy's blog about it; for once, he had to agree that she was right. The death of a friend did make you realize that life was finite, and there was only so much time left in which to be young—or youngish, anyway.

But Billy's death was only one in a bizarre series of events that had plagued One Fifth while he'd been away. There was the Internet Debacle, and the discovery of the Cross of Bloody Mary, which people postulated had been hidden in Mrs. Houghton's apartment. Then Billy's overdose. And Lola's assertion that she was pregnant by Philip Oakland, who had dumped her for Schiffer Diamond. This was to be followed—according to Mindy—by an impending announcement that Philip Oakland and Schiffer Diamond were to be married after an appropriate period of mourning. It was all slightly outrageous, James thought—and what about poor Lola Fabrikant? Did anyone care what had happened to her? He wondered but he didn't dare ask.

Now he would find out. Discovering Mindy in the dining room talking to Enid—they were friends again, it seemed, and appeared to be in a deep discussion about their favorite topic, One Fifth—he nodded at her, trying to catch her attention. "Yes?" she said curtly.

"I'm going to walk Skippy," he said over the noise of the chattering crowd.

"Why?" she said.

"Because he needs to go out."

"Whatever." She rolled her eyes and went back to her conversation. James tried to slip out the door but was waylaid by Redmon Richardly, who was talking to Diane Sawyer. Redmon grasped him by the shoulder. "Do you know James Gooch?" he said. "His book's been number one on *The New York Times* best-seller list for five weeks now." James nodded and moved away but was stopped by the editor in chief of *Vanity Fair*, who wanted to talk to him about writing a piece about Billy's death. When James was finally able to get down to his apartment, it was three-ten. He grabbed Skippy and hurried around the corner to the Mews.

Walking slowly on the tiny cobblestoned street, he didn't see her at first. Then he heard his name called, and she stepped out from the shadows of a doorway covered with vines. For a second, James was startled by her appearance. After the funeral, she must have gone home and changed, for she now had on dirty jeans and an old red ski parka. But she wore the same sweet, fawning expression that always made him feel admired and protective of her. Skippy jumped on her leg and she laughed, leaning over to pet the little dog. "I've been wondering what happened to you," James said. "Are you all right?"

"Oh, James," she said. "I'm so happy to see you. I was afraid you wouldn't come. Everyone's taken Philip's side, and I've lost all my friends. I don't even have a place to live."

"You're not sleeping on the street?" James asked, horrified, once again taking in her appearance.

"I've been sleeping on a friend's couch," she said. "But you know how it is. I can't stay there forever. And I can't go home to Atlanta. I don't have a home to go back to even if I wanted to. My parents went bankrupt."

"Good God," James said. "How could Oakland do this to you?"

"He doesn't care about me. He never did. He used me for sex, and when he'd had his fill, he went back to Schiffer Diamond. I'm really alone, James," she said, grabbing on to his sleeve as if she were afraid he might try to get away. "I'm scared. I don't know what to do."

"The first thing you need to do is to get an apartment. Or a job. Or both," James stated with authority, as if such things were easily accomplished. He shook his head in disbelief. "I still can't believe Oakland kicked you out and didn't at least give you some money."

"He didn't," Lola said. She was lying; Philip had sent a check for ten thousand dollars to her parents' condo, and Beetelle had FedExed it to her at Thayer's address. But James didn't need to know this. "Philip Oakland is not what people think he is," she said.

"He's exactly what I always thought he was," James said.

Lola looked up at him and took a step closer, then glanced away, as if she were ashamed. "I know we hardly know each other," she said in a small voice, "but I was hoping you might be able to help me. There's no one else I can ask."

"You poor thing," James said, adding boldly, "tell me what I can do and I'll do it."

"Can I borrow twenty thousand dollars?"

James blanched at the sum. "That's a lot of money," he said carefully.

"I'm sorry." She took a step backward. "I shouldn't have bothered you. I'll figure something out. It was nice knowing you, James. You were the only person who was nice to me in One Fifth. Congratulations on all your success. I always knew you were a star." And she began to walk away.

"Lola, stop," James called.

She turned and, giving him a brave smile, shook her head. "I'll be okay. I'll survive somehow."

He caught up with her. "I do want to help you," he said. "I'll figure something out." They arranged to meet up under the arch in Washington Park the next afternoon.

James then returned to the party, where he immediately bumped into the devil himself—Philip Oakland. "Excuse me," James said.

"Heard your book is number one on the list," Philip said. "Congratulations."

"Thanks," James said curtly. For once, he noted, Philip Oakland didn't seem to be in a rush to move away. James decided to make Philip uncomfortable. Considering Lola's situation it was the least he could do. "I just saw your girlfriend," he said accusingly.

"Really?" Philip looked confused. "Who?"

"Lola Fabrikant."

Now Philip looked embarrassed. "We're not together anymore," he said. He took a sip of champagne. "I'm sorry—did I hear you correctly? Did you say you'd just seen her?"

"That's right. In the Mews," James said. "She has no place to live."

"She was supposed to be back in Atlanta. With her parents."

"Well, she's not," James said. "She's in New York." He would have said more, but Schiffer Diamond came over and took Philip's hand. "Hello, James," she said, leaning forward to kiss him on the cheek as if they were old friends. Death, James supposed, made everyone old friends. "Did you know Billy, too?" he asked. He suddenly remembered that she had found the body, and immediately felt like an idiot. "I'm sorry," he said.

"It's okay," Schiffer said.

Philip jiggled her hand. "James said he just saw Lola Fabrikant. In the Mews."

"She was at the funeral," James said, trying to explain.

"I'm afraid we missed her." Schiffer and Philip exchanged a glance. "Excuse me," Schiffer said, and moved away.

"Nice to see you," Philip said to James, and followed her.

James took a fresh glass of champagne from a tray and stepped into the crowd. Schiffer and Philip were standing a few feet away, holding hands, nodding as they spoke to another couple. Apparently, Philip Oakland didn't even feel guilty about what he'd done to Lola, James thought with disgust. He moved into the living room and sat down on a plushy love seat and scanned the room. It was filled with bold-faced names—the art folk and media types and socialites and fashionistas who comprised the chattering classes and had defined his and Mindy's world in New York City for the last twenty years. Now, having been away for a month, he had a different perspective. How silly they all seemed. Half the people in the room had had some kind of "work" done, including the men. Billy's death was just another excuse for a party, where they could drink champagne and eat caviar and talk about their latest projects. Meanwhile, out on the street, homeless and probably hungry, was an innocent young woman—Lola Fabrikant—who'd been taken up by this crowd and summarily spit out when she didn't meet the exact requirements.

A man and a woman passed behind him, whispering, "I heard the Rices have a Renoir."

"It's in the dining room. And it's tiny." There was a pause followed by high-pitched laughter. "And it cost ten million dollars. But it's a *Renoir*. So who cares?"

Perhaps he should ask Annalisa Rice for the twenty thousand dollars for Lola, James thought. She apparently had so much money, she didn't know what to do with it.

But hold on, James thought. He had money now, too, and more than he'd expected. Two weeks ago, his agent had informed him that if the sales of his book continued at the same rate—and there was no reason to think they wouldn't—he would earn at least two million dollars in royalties. Despite this astonishing news, when James returned to New York and his daily routine, he saw that his circumstances hadn't changed at all. He still awoke every morning as James Gooch, married to Mindy Gooch, living his odd little life in his odd little apartment. The only difference being that right now, during this two-week break from his book tour, he had nothing to do.

James stood up and crossed the living room, stepping out onto the lowest of the Rices' three terraces. He leaned over the edge, looking up and down Fifth Avenue. It, too, was exactly the same. He finished his champagne and, looking into the bottom of the glass, felt empty. For once in his life, there was no sword of doom hanging over his head; he had nothing to complain about and nothing about which to hang his head. And yet he didn't feel content. Stepping back through the French doors, he looked at the crowd and wished he were still in the Mews with Lola.

The next afternoon, James met Lola under the arch in Washington Park. Determined to be a hero, James had spent the morning trying to find Lola an apartment. Mindy would have been shocked at his industriousness, he thought wryly, but Mindy never needed his help, and Lola did. After making several calls, Redmon Richardly's assistant told him about an apartment that might be available in her building on Eighteenth Street and Tenth Avenue. The rent was fourteen hundred dollars a month for a studio, and after tracking down the owner, who had not only heard of his book but had read it and loved it, James made an arrangement to see the apartment at three. Then he'd gone to the bank and, feeling like a criminal, withdrew five thousand dollars in cash. Strolling toward the park, he found Lola already waiting. She had mascara under her eyes as if she'd been crying and hadn't bothered to wash it away. "Are you all right?" he asked.

"What do you think?" she said bitterly. "I feel like a homeless person. Everything I own is in storage—and it's costing me a hundred and fifty a month. I have no place to sleep. And the bathroom in that place I'm staying is disgusting. I'm afraid to take a shower. Were you able to . . . figure something out?"

"I brought you some money," James said. "And something else— something that should really make you happy." He paused for effect, then said proudly, "I think I may have found you an apartment."

"Oh, James," she exclaimed.

"It's only fourteen hundred a month. If you like it, we can use the cash to pay your first month's rent and a deposit."

"Where is it?" she asked cautiously. When he told her, she looked disappointed. "It's so far west," she said. "It's practically on the river."

"It's within walking distance of One Fifth," James assured her. "So we can visit each other all the time."

Nevertheless, Lola insisted on taking a taxi. The cab pulled up to a small redbrick building that James suspected, given the location, had probably once been a flophouse. On the street level was an Irish bar. He and Lola walked up a narrow staircase to a short hall-way with a linoleum floor. The apartment was 3C, and after trying the handle, James found the door open and he and Lola went in. It was a tiny space, no bigger than three hundred square feet—a room, really, in a normal person's house—with a tiny closet, a tiny bathroom with a shower, and two cupboard doors that opened to reveal a minuscule kitchen. But it was clean and bright and located on a corner, so it had two windows.

"Not bad," James said.

Lola's heart sank. Had she really fallen so low in the short nine months she'd been in New York?

The landlady was a salt-of-the-earth type with a pile of bleached hair and a New York accent. Her family had owned the building for a hundred years; her biggest requirement, after an ability to pay, was "nice" people. Was Lola perhaps James's daugh-ter? No, James explained, she was a friend who'd had a rough time with an ex-boyfriend who'd dumped her. The perfidy of men was one of the landlady's favorite topics; she was always happy to help out a fellow female sufferer. James proclaimed the arrangement a done deal. The apartment, he declared, reminded him of his first apartment in Manhattan and how thrilled he'd been to have his own space and to be making his way in New York. "The good old days," he said to the landlady, peeling off three thousand dollars in hundreds. The extra two hundred would be used to cover Lola's utilities.

"Now all you need is a bed," James said when the deal was com-pleted. "Why don't we get you a foldout couch? There's a Door Store on Sixth Avenue." Walking east, James noticed her glum expression. "What's the matter?" he asked. "You don't look happy. Aren't you relieved to have your own apartment?"

Lola was in a panic. She hadn't planned on getting an apartment at all, and especially such a shabby, depressing little place. She'd meant to take the money from Philip and James—thirty thousand in total—and install herself in Soho House, from where she would relaunch herself into New York society in style. How had her plan gone awry so quickly? And now three thousand dollars were gone. "I didn't expect it to happen this suddenly," she said.

"Ah," James said, holding up a finger. "That's New York real estate. If we hadn't taken the apartment, it would have been gone in an hour. You've got to act fast." At the Door Store, James purchased a couch with a queen-size foldout bed in a sensible navy blue fabric that wouldn't show stains, the feel of which made Lola shudder. It was the floor model, James exclaimed, saying it was a great deal. And another fifteen hundred dollars was gone.

James finally escorted her back to the empty apartment, where she was to wait for the bed to be delivered. "I don't know how you managed to do all this," Lola said weakly. "Thank you." She kissed James on the cheek.

"I'll come by tomorrow and see how you're settling in," he said.

"I can't wait," Lola said. There was still the remainder of the fifteen thousand dollars James might give her, but she didn't dare ask for it now. She would have to talk to him about it tomorrow, though.

When James left, she immediately went to Thayer Core's apartment. "I got my own place," she said.

"How'd you manage that?" Thayer said, looking up from his computer.

"James Gooch found it," Lola said, taking off her coat. "He paid for it, too."

"He's an idiot."

"He's in love with me." Lola was suddenly thrilled to be getting out of Thayer and Josh's apartment. Thayer was becoming unreasonable, asking her for oral sex and pouting when he didn't get it, saying he had something on her and would use it if he had to. "What?" she'd scoff. "You'll see," he'd say vaguely.

"Shut up, Thayer. You're a douchebag," she reminded him now.

"I thought you were trying to get back into One Fifth. I need information."

"I'll get it from James."

"What if he requires sex in exchange?"

"I have sex with *you*, so what's the difference?" Lola replied. "At least he doesn't have diseases."

"How do you know?"

"I know," she said. "He's only been with one woman for the past twenty years. His wife."

"Maybe he sleeps with hookers on the side."

Lola rolled her eyes. "Not every man is like you, Thayer. Decent men do exist."

"Uh-huh," Thayer said, nodding. "Like James Gooch. A man who's an inch away from cheating on his wife. Although if I were married to Mindy Gooch, I'd cheat, too."

The next day, knocking on the door of her new apartment, James found Lola sitting on the bare mattress of the foldout couch, crying. "What's wrong now?" James said, edging next to her.

"Look around," Lola said. "I don't even have a pillow."

"I'll bring you one from home. My wife won't notice."

"I don't want some old pillow from your house," Lola said, wondering how she'd managed to pick the cheapest man in Manhattan as her savior. "Do you think you could give me some money? Maybe the fifteen thousand dollars?"

"I can't give it to you all at once," James said. "My wife will get suspicious." Having given the matter a great deal of thought, James had settled on a plan to pay Lola's rent for six months while giving her two thousand dollars a month in spending money. "And when you get a job," he said, "you'll be fine. You'll have much more money than I did at your age."

From then on, James went by the apartment every afternoon, often taking Lola to lunch at the Irish pub downstairs—to make sure she had one decent meal a day, he said—and then hung around her apartment afterward. He liked the uncluttered space and the afternoon sunlight that poured through the windows, noting that Lola's apartment got more light than his own. "James," she said. "I need a TV."

"You have your computer," James said. "Can't you watch TV shows on that? Isn't that what everybody does these days?"

"Everybody has a computer. And a TV."

"You could read a book," James said. "Have you read *Anna Karenina*? Or *Madame Bovary*?"

"I have, and they're boring. Besides, I don't have room for books," she complained, gesturing at the tiny space.

James bought her a TV—a sixteen-inch Panasonic—that they placed on the windowsill.

On the day before James was to go back out on book tour, he turned up at her apartment earlier than usual. It was eleven o'clock, but she was still sleeping, her head resting on the down pillow she'd bought from ABC Carpet, along with a down comforter that James suspected cost over a thousand dollars. When he questioned her about it, however, she said she'd bought it on sale for a hundred. He didn't expect her to sleep without covers, did he? No, he did not, he agreed, and let it go.

"What time is it?" she asked now, rolling over in her bed.

"It's almost noon," he said. He found the fact that she was still in bed slightly annoying, and wondered what she'd been up to the night before that would cause her to sleep till midday. Or perhaps she was depressed. "I'm leaving tomorrow morning. First thing," he explained. "I wanted to say goodbye. And to make sure you were okay."

"When will I see you again?" She stretched, extending her arms up to the ceiling. She was wearing an orange tank top with nothing underneath.

"Not for a month."

"Where are you going?" she asked in alarm.

"England, Scotland, Ireland, Paris, Germany, Australia, and New Zealand."

"That's terrible."

"Terrible for us but good for the book," James said.

She threw back the comforter and patted the mattress. "Snuggle me," she said. "I'm going to miss you."

"I don't think . . ." James said cautiously, despite his beating heart.

"It's only a hug, James," she pointed out. "No one can object to that."

He got into bed next to her, awkwardly arranging his long body so several inches of space remained between them. She turned to face him, curling up her knees into his groin. Her breath was pungent with the lingering smell of vodka and cigarettes, and he wondered once again where she'd been the night before. Had she had sex with someone?

"You're funny," she said.

"Am I?"

"Look at you." She giggled. "You're so stiff."

"I'm not sure we should be doing this," he said.

"We're not doing anything," she countered. "But you want to, don't you?"

"I'm married," he whispered.

"Your wife never has to know." She trailed her hand down his chest and touched his penis. "You're hard," she said.

She started kissing him on the mouth, thrusting her fat tongue between his teeth. James was too startled to resist. This was so different from Mindy's kisses, which were dry little pecks. He couldn't recall the last time he'd kissed someone like this, marveling that people still did this—that he could still do this—this making-out thing. And Lola's skin was so soft, like a baby's, he thought, touching her arms. Her neck was smooth and unwrinkled. He tentatively touched her breasts through the fabric of her shirt, feeling her nipples erect. He rolled on top of her, pushing himself up on his arms to stare down at her face. Should he go further? He hadn't made love in so long, he wondered if he would remember the moves.

"I want you inside me," she said, touching the mound of his penis. "I want your fat cock in my wet pussy."

The mere suggestion of this sex act was too much, and as he was trying to unzip his jeans, the inevitable happened. He came. "Damn," he said.

"What's wrong?" She sat up.

"I just . . . you know." He slid his hand into his jeans and felt the telltale wetness. "Fuck!"

She got onto her knees behind him and rubbed his shoulders. "It doesn't matter. It's only the first time."

He took her hand and brought it to his lips. "You are so sweet," he said. "You're the sweetest girl I've ever known."

"Am I?" she said, jumping off the bed. She pulled on a pair of cashmere sweatpants. "James?" she asked in a syrupy voice. "Since you're leaving and I won't see you for a month . . ."

"Do you need some money?" he said. He reached into his pants pocket. "I've only got sixty dollars."

"There's an ATM in the deli around the corner. Do you mind? I owe the landlady two hundred dollars. For utilities. And you don't want me to starve while you're away."

"I certainly don't," James said. "But you should try to get a job."

"I will," she reassured him. "But it's hard."

"I can't support you forever," he said, thinking about his aborted attempt at sex.

"I'm not asking you to," she said. On the sidewalk, she took his hand. "I don't know what I'd do without you."

He extracted five hundred dollars from the ATM and handed it to her. "I'll miss you," she said, flinging her arms around him. "Call me the minute you get back. We'll get together. And next time it will work," she called over her shoulder.

James stared after her, then set off down Ninth Avenue. Had he just been taken for a ride? No, he assured himself. Lola wasn't like that. And she'd said she wanted to do it again. He strolled down Fifth Avenue full of confidence. By the time he reached One Fifth, he'd convinced himself it was a good thing he'd ejaculated prematurely. No fluids were exchanged, so it couldn't really be called cheating.

20

Early that evening, on her way to Thayer Core's place, Lola paused across the street from One Fifth and stared at the entrance. She often did this, hoping to run into Philip or Schiffer. The week before, they'd announced their engagement, and the news was all over the tabloids and on the entertainment programs, as if the union of two middle-aged people was not only a big deal but an inspiration for all lonely, still-single middle-aged women everywhere. Schiffer had gone on *Oprah* to promote *Lady Superior*, but really, Lola thought, to boast about her upcoming nuptials. Their marriage was part of a hot new trend, Oprah said, in which women and men were finding first loves from the past and realizing they were meant for each other all along. "But this time around, one is older and wiser—I hope!" Schiffer remarked, which drew knowing laughter from the audience. They had yet to set a date or a place but wanted to do something small and non-traditional. Schiffer had already picked out a dress—a short white sheath covered in silver bugle beads—which Oprah held up for the cameras. While the audience oohed and ahhed, Lola felt sick. It should have been her wedding Oprah was blathering on about, not Schiffer's. And she would have chosen a better dress—something traditional, with lace and a train. Lola couldn't stop thinking about the wedding; filled with envy and anger, she possessed a pernicious fantasy of confronting either Philip or Schiffer. Hence her occasional stakeouts of One Fifth. And yet she didn't dare linger too long—she might encounter Philip or Schiffer but might as easily run into Enid.

Three days after Billy Litchfield's memorial service, Enid called her, and Lola, not recognizing the number, took the call. "I hear you're back in New York, dear," Enid said.

"That's right," Lola said.

"I wish you hadn't come back," Enid said with a disappointed sigh. "How do you plan to survive?"

"Frankly, Enid, it's none of your business," Lola said, and hung up. But now she was on Enid's radar, and she had to be careful. She wasn't sure what Enid might do.

That evening, however, standing across from the building, she saw only Mindy Gooch going in, pulling a little cart filled with groceries behind her.

"I need a job," Lola said to Thayer a few minutes later, plopping onto the pile of dirty clothes that Josh called his bed.

"Why?" Thayer asked.

"Don't be an idiot. I need money," Lola said.

"You and everyone else in New York under the age of thirty. The baby boomers took all the money. There ain't any left for us young'uns."

"Don't joke," Lola said. "I'm serious. James Gooch has gone away again. And I only got five hundred dollars out of him. He's so cheap. His book has been on the best-seller list for two months. And he gets five thousand dollars for every week he's on the list. As a bonus." She crossed her arms and narrowed her eyes. "I told him he should give me the money."

"What'd he say?" Thayer asked. "You've had sex with him, right? So he owes you. Because there's really no reason for you to have sex with him other than money."

"I'm not a whore," Lola grumbled.

Thayer laughed. "Speaking of which, I might have a job for you. Someone e-mailed us a request today. They're looking for writers. Female writers. For a new website. It pays a thousand dollars a post. That made me suspicious. But you might check it out."

Lola took down the information. Doing nothing in New York City was much more expensive than she'd imagined. If she spent too much time in her tiny studio apartment, she began to go crazy. By the time nine P.M. rolled around, she had to get out and took sanctuary at one or two of several nightclubs in the Meatpacking District. The doormen knew her and usually let her in for free— pretty, unattached young women were considered an asset. And she rarely paid for a drink. But she still had to eat, and she had to buy clothes so she would look good to get the free drinks. It was a vicious cycle. To maintain even this lifestyle, she needed cash.

The next day, Lola went to the address on the e-mail. The building wasn't far from her own: It was one of the grand new structures that had popped up around the High Line, overlooking the Hudson River. She was going to Apartment 16C, and rather than calling up, as they would have done at One Fifth, the doorman merely asked her to sign in on a time sheet, as if she were going to an office. Knocking on the door, she was greeted by a youngish man with an alarming tattoo around his neck; upon closer inspection, she saw that not just his neck was tattooed but his entire right arm. He was also wearing a ring in his left nostril. "You must be Lola," he said. "I'm Marquee." He didn't bother to shake her hand.

"Marquee?" she asked, following him into a sparsely furnished living room with an unobstructed view of the West Side Highway, the brown waters of the Hudson, and the New Jersey skyline. "Your name is Marquee?" she asked again.

"That's right," Marquee said coolly. "You got a problem with it? You're not one of those people who has a problem with names, are you?"

"No," Lola said with a scoff, letting Marquee know right away that he wasn't going to intimidate her. "I've just never heard of anyone with that particular name."

"That's because I made it up," Marquee said. "There's only one Marquee, and I want people to remember it. So, what's your experience?" he asked.

Lola looked around the living room. The furnishings consisted of two small couches, which at first glance appeared to be covered in white fabric. On closer inspection, Lola saw they were covered in bare white muslin, as if they were wearing only their undergarments. "What's yours?" she said.

"I've made some money. But you can see that," he said, indicating the apartment. "You know how much a place like this costs?"

"I wouldn't want to guess," Lola replied.

"Two million. For a one-bedroom."

"Wow," Lola said, pretending to be impressed. She stood up and walked to the window. "So what's this job?"

"Sex columnist," Marquee said.

"That's original."

"It is," Marquee said without irony. "See, the problem with most sex columns is—there's no sex in them. It's all that relationship bullshit. Nobody wants to read that. My idea is brand-new. No one's ever done it before. A sex column that's really about sex."

"Isn't that called porn?" Lola asked.

"If you're going to call yourself a sex columnist, I say, show me the sex."

"If you're going to hire me to have sex, I suggest you show me the money," Lola replied.

"You want cash?" Marquee said. "I've got cash, and plenty of it." He pulled a wad of bills out of his pocket and waved it in front of her. "Here's the deal. A thousand dollars a pop."

"I'll need half up front," Lola said.

"Fine," Marquee said, peeling off five one-hundred-dollar bills. "And I'm going to need details. Length and width. Distinguishing characteristics. What went where and when."

That evening, instead of going to a club, Lola stayed home and wrote about sex with Philip. She found it surprisingly easy, cathartic, even, working herself up into a froth about the cruelty he'd exhibited in dumping her for Schiffer Diamond. "He had a fat penis with swinging balls in a sack of prickly skin. And he had wrinkles on the back of his neck. And little hairs beginning to sprout from his earlobes. At first I thought those little hairs were cute." Finishing the entry and reading it over, she found herself longing to do it again and decided Philip deserved more than one measly post. By changing his name and profession, she ought to be able to get at least three more entries out of him. And then thinking about the best way to spend the money, she paged through one of the tabloid magazines and found a bandage-wrap Hervé Léger dress that would look amazing on her.

A few days later, Enid Merle was cleaning out her kitchen cabinets. She did it every year, not wanting to become one of those old women who accumulated dust and junk. Enid had just taken down a metal box filled with old silver when her buzzer rang. She opened the door to find Mindy Gooch standing in the hallway in a huff. "Have you seen it?" Mindy asked.

"What?" Enid asked, slightly annoyed. Now that she and Mindy were friendly again, Mindy wouldn't leave her alone.

"Snarker. You're not going to like it," Mindy said. She strode through Enid's living room to her computer and brought up the website. "I've been complaining about these posts by this Thayer Core for months," she scolded, as if the posts were somehow Enid's fault. "And no one took them seriously. Perhaps someone will, now that there's one about Philip."

Enid adjusted her glasses and peered over Mindy's shoulder. "The Rich and the Restless" was written in small red block letters, and underneath, in large black type, "Hell Hath No Fury" next to a photograph of Lola taken outside the church at Billy's memorial service. Enid pushed Mindy aside and began reading.

"Lovely Lola Fabrikant, spurned lover of seedy screenwriter Philip Oakland, gets even with him this week by penning her own brilliant version of sex with a man who bears a satisfying resemblance to the aging bachelor." The words "brilliant version" were highlighted in red, and clicking on them, Enid was taken to another website called The Peephole, featuring yet another photograph of Lola, followed by a graphic description of a young woman having intercourse with a middle-aged man. The description of the man's teeth, hands, and the little hairs on his earlobes was unmistakably of Philip, although Enid couldn't bear to read the details about his penis.

"Well?" Mindy demanded. "Aren't you going to do something?"

Enid looked up at Mindy wearily. "I told you to hire him—this Thayer Core—months ago. If you had, this would have ended."

"Why should I be the one to hire him? Why can't you?"

"Because if he works for me, he'll only continue to do the same thing. He'll go to parties and make things up and write unpleasant things about people. If you hire him, he'll be working for a corporation. He'll be stuck in an office building, taking the subway like every other working stiff, and eating a sandwich at his desk. It'll give him a new perspective on life."

"What about Lola Fabrikant?"

"Don't worry about her, my dear." Enid smiled. "I'll take care of it. I'll give her exactly what she wants—publicity."

Two days later, the "true" story of Lola Fabrikant appeared in Enid Merle's syndicated column. It was all there: how Lola had tried to fake a pregnancy to get a man, how she was obsessed with clothes and status, how she never gave a thought to being responsible for her own actions, or even what she might do for anyone else—making her the ultimate example of all that was wrong and misguided about young women today. Portrayed in Enid's best schoolmarmish tone, Lola came off as the poster child for bad values.

On the afternoon the piece came out, Lola sat on the bed in her tiny apartment, reading all about herself on the Internet. The newspaper lay beside her computer, folded open to Enid's column. The first time Lola read it, she burst into tears. How could Enid be so cruel? But the column wasn't the end of it, having ignited a firestorm of negative comments about Lola on the Internet. She was being called a slut and a whore, and her physical features had been dissected and found somewhat lacking—several people had hypothesized, correctly, that she'd had a nose job and breast implants—and hundreds of men had left messages on her Facebook page, describing what they'd like to do to her sexually. Their suggestions weren't pleasant. One man wrote that he would "shove his balls down her throat until she choked and her eyes bulged out of her head." Until that morning, Lola had always enjoyed the Internet's unfettered viciousness, assuming that the people who were written about somehow deserved it, but now that the negativity was directed at her, it was a different story. It hurt. She felt like a wounded animal, trailing blood. After reading another post about herself in which someone wrote that the Lola Fabrikants of the world deserved to die alone in a flophouse, Lola once again burst into tears.

It wasn't fair, she thought, holding herself while she rocked on the thin mattress. She had naturally assumed that when she did become famous, everyone would love her. Desperate, she texted Thayer Core again. "Where are you????????!!!!!!!!" She waited a few minutes, and when there was again no response, she sent another text. "I can't leave my house. I'm hungry. I need food," she wrote. She sent the text, followed immediately by another: "And bring alcohol." Finally, an hour later, Thayer responded with one word: "Busy."

Thayer eventually turned up, bearing a bag of cheese doodles. "This is all your fault," Lola screamed.

"Mine?" he asked, surprised. "I thought this was what you always wanted."

"I did. But not like this."

"You shouldn't have done it, then." He shrugged. "You ever hear of 'free will'?"

"You have to fix this," Lola said.

"Can't," he said. He opened the bag of cheese doodles and

stuffed four into his mouth. "Got a job today. Working for Mindy Gooch."

"What?" Lola exclaimed in shock. "I thought you hated her."

"I do. But I don't have to hate her money. I'm getting paid a hundred thousand dollars a year. Working in the new-media department. In six months, I'll probably be running it. Those people don't know squat."

"And what am I supposed to do?" Lola demanded.

Thayer looked at her, unmoved. "How should I know?" he said. "But if you can't make something out of all this publicity I got you, you're a bigger loser than I thought."

June arrived, and with it, unseasonably warm weather. The temperature had been over eighty degrees for three days; already the Gooches' apartment was too warm, and James was forced to turn on the sputtering air conditioner. Sitting beneath it one morning, perched over his computer and thinking about starting another book, he listened to the sounds of his wife and son packing in Sam's bedroom next door. He checked the time. Sam's bus left in forty minutes. Mindy and Sam would be leaving any minute—as soon as they did, he would read Lola's sex column. When he'd returned from the final leg of his book tour, exhausted and jet-lagged, he'd claimed he was too tired to even think about writing but had managed to get over to Lola's apartment six times in ten days and, on each visit, had made fantastic love to her. One afternoon, she had stood above him while he spread open her labia and licked her firm little clit; on another occasion, she'd fucked him while he lay on his back, positioning her bottom in front of his face, and he had slid his middle finger in and out of her puckered asshole. In the evenings after these encounters, Mindy would come home and remark that he appeared to be in a good mood. He would reply that yes, he was, and after all his hard labor, didn't he have a right to be? Then Mindy would bring up the country house. They couldn't, she conceded, afford a house in the

Hamptons, but they could find something in Litchfield County, which was just as beautiful, and maybe even better than the Hamptons because it was still filled with artists and not yet overrun with finance types. In her usual pushy way, Mindy had convinced him to drive up to Litchfield County for the weekend; they'd stayed at the Mayflower Inn to the tune of two thousand dollars for two nights while they looked at houses during the day. Mindy was, James knew, trying to be reasonable, limiting their choices to houses under one point three million dollars. James found something wrong with every one, but in an act of defiance, perhaps, Mindy had signed Sam up for a month of tennis camp in the tony little town of Washington, Connecticut, where Sam would be residing in the dorm of a private school.

Now, while Mindy was packing Sam's things, James was wondering if he dared take a quick peek at Lola's column. In her last installment, she had written about the time James had alternated between penetrating her with a vibrator and his own penis. Unlike Mindy, Lola had the good sense to change his name—calling him "The Terminator," because he caused orgasms that were so strong, they could be terminal—and James was so chuffed, he couldn't be angry. He had even bought her an enameled Hermés bracelet, which she'd been desperate for, saying all the women on the Upper East Side had one, cleverly paying cash so Mindy couldn't trace the purchase. He looked longingly at his computer, anxious to know if Lola had written about him again, and if so, what she'd said. But with Mindy in the apartment, he decided it was too risky. What if she caught him? Valiantly resisting temptation, he got up and went into Sam's room.

"Four weeks of tennis," James said to his son. "Do you think you'll get bored?"

Mindy was placing packages of white cotton athletic socks into Sam's bag. "No, he will not," she said.

"I hate this business of taking on the customs of the upper classes," James said. "What's wrong with basketball? It was good enough for me."

Mindy snorted. "Your son is not you, James. As a fairly intelligent adult male, you should have figured that out by now."

"Hmph," James said. Mindy had been a bit curt with him lately, and since he feared her shortness might be due to a suspicion about his affair with Lola, he didn't push it.

"Besides," Mindy said. "I want Sam to feel comfortable in the area. We'll have a house there soon, and I want him to have lots of new friends."

"We will?" James said.

Mindy gave him a terse smile. "Yes, James, we will."

James was suddenly nervous and went into the kitchen to pour himself another cup of coffee. A few minutes later, Mindy and Sam kissed him goodbye and went off to the bus station; Mindy would go on from there to her office. The second the door closed, James rushed to his computer, typed in the requisite address, and read, "The Terminator strikes again. Wrapping my hot, wet pussy around his cock, he did another one of his dastardly deeds and tickled my asshole while I pumped him for juice."

"Lola," James had said after reading the first installment about his sexual exploits. "How can you do this? Don't you worry about your reputation? What if you want to get a real job someday and your employer reads this?"

Lola only looked at him like he was once again hopelessly out of touch. "It's no different from all those other celebrities with sex tapes. It hasn't hurt them. Just the opposite—it's *made* their careers."

Now, continuing to read Lola's blog, James felt himself getting a hard-on that pushed against his leg, demanding immediate attention. He went into the bathroom and jerked off, hiding the evidence in a tissue that he flushed down the toilet. He looked into the mirror and nodded. The next time he saw Lola, he decided, he would definitely try for anal sex.

▼

Mindy watched Sam get on the bus for Southbury, Connecticut, waving at his window until the bus pulled out of the underground garage. Hurrying through Port Authority, she was relieved to have gotten Sam safely away, where Paul Rice couldn't hurt him. She flagged a taxi, slid onto the backseat, and fished the folded piece of notepaper out of her bag. "Sam did it" was written in pencil, in Paul Rice's tiny block lettering. The paper bore the logo of the Four Seasons Hotel in Bangkok. Apparently, Paul Rice had quite a few of these pads.

She refolded the note and put it back in her purse. She'd found the tightly folded paper in her mailbox just the other day, and while James was convinced she wanted a country house for her own self-aggrandizement, she'd begun pursuing it as a way to get herself and Sam out of Paul's way, without raising suspicion. A man who could take over an entire country's stock market was probably capable of anything, including persecuting a little boy. While everyone else in One Fifth had been diverted by Billy's death, Paul hadn't attended either his memorial service or Annalisa's party. For all Mindy knew, Paul might still be investigating who cut his Internet wires, and eventually, he might be able to prove it was Sam.

Like Paul Rice, Mindy knew Sam had done it. She would never tell anyone, of course, including James. But it wasn't the only secret she was keeping. Striding into her office, she passed Thayer Core, sitting in his cubicle like a caged animal, scrolling through a long list of e-mails. Mindy stopped and stuck her head over the edge of the cubicle, looking down at Thayer as a reminder of her authority over him.

"Have you printed out the notes from yesterday's meeting?" she asked.

Thayer pushed back his chair and, as if to thwart her authority, put his feet up on his desk and crossed his arms. "Which meeting?" he said.

"All of them." She moved away, then stopped, as if remembering something. "And I also need a hard copy of Lola Fabrikant's sex column."

When Mindy was safely in her office, Thayer muttered, "Can't you read it on your computer? Like everyone else?" He got up and strolled through the maze of cubicles to the printer, where he retrieved Lola's column. He read it briefly and shook his head. Lola was fucking James Gooch again. Could Mindy really be so dense that she didn't know Lola was writing about her own husband? Ugh. It meant he and James Gooch now had one degree of separation. But James gave Lola money, and since Thayer enjoyed the same privileges as James for free, he couldn't really object.

"Here you go," Thayer said with a flourish, placing the printout on Mindy's desk.

"Thank you," she said, continuing to stare at her computer.

Thayer stood for a moment, watching her. "Can I have a raise?" he asked.

This got her attention. Putting on her reading glasses, she picked up the printout and glanced at it, and then him. "How long have you been here?" she asked.

"A month."

"I'm already paying you a hundred thousand dollars a year."

"It's not enough."

"Check back with me in five months, and I'll see what I can do."

Fucking old bag, Thayer thought, returning to his cubicle. But surprisingly, Mindy wasn't that bad, not as bad as he'd thought she'd be. She had even taken him out for a beer and asked him all kinds of uncomfortable questions about where he lived and how he was surviving. When he told her he lived on Avenue C, she grimaced. "That's not good enough for you," she said. "I see you in a better place—like a walk-up in the West Village." She'd given him advice about getting ahead, suggesting he attempt to appear "more corporate" by wearing a tie.

For some reason, he had taken her advice. The woman was right, he'd thought, upon returning to his disgusting apartment. It wasn't good enough for him. He was twenty-five years old. There were men his age who were billionaires, but he was making a hundred thousand a year, an enormous sum compared to that of his friends. After scouring Craigslist, he'd found an apartment on Christopher Street, a walk-up with a bedroom that was barely large enough to contain a queen-size bed. It was twenty-eight hundred a month, which ate up three quarters of his monthly salary, but it was worth it. He was moving up in the world.

Seated behind her desk with her reading glasses perched on her nose, Mindy carefully read the latest installment of Lola's sex column. Lola had quite a way with the description of the sex act and, not content to limit it to plumbing, also provided a detailed account of her partner's physical characteristics. The first four columns had featured Philip Oakland as her lover, but this column and the previous one were most definitely about James. Although Lola called the man the Terminator, which made Mindy laugh out loud, the description of his penis, with its "constellation of tiny moles on the shaft, forming, perhaps, Osiris," was James. Nor was it only the comments about his penis that gave him away. "I want to know every part of you. Including the dirty place," the Terminator had said. It was exactly the same argument James had used on Mindy in the early years of their marriage when he'd wanted to try anal sex.

Putting the column aside, Mindy went back to her computer and, typing in the address of the Litchfield County real estate agency, scrolled down and found the photographs and description of a house. The past weekend, looking at real estate, the agent had explained that there was very little in their price range—there was hardly anything on the market for under a million three. She did have the perfect house for them, but it was a little more expensive. Did they want to look at it anyway? Yes, they did, Mindy said.

The house was a bit of a wreck, having only been recently vacated by an aged farmer. But these kinds of houses almost never came up. It still had twelve original acres, and the house, built in the late seventeen hundreds, had three fireplaces. There was an old apple orchard and a red barn (falling down, but barns were very inexpensive to restore), and it was located on what was considered one of the best streets in one of Litchfield County's most exclusive towns—Roxbury, Connecticut. Population twenty-three hundred. But what a population. Arthur Miller and Alexander Calder had lived nearby, as well as Walter Matthau. Philip Roth was only miles away. And the house was a steal—only one point nine million.

"It's too much," James protested in the rental car on the way back to the city.

"It's perfect," Mindy said. "And you heard what the real estate agent said. Houses like this one never come up."

"It makes me nervous, spending all that money. On a house. And it needs lots of restoration. Do you know how much that costs? Hundreds of thousands of dollars. Yes, we have the money today. But who knows what will happen in the future?"

Indeed, Mindy thought now, pressing the intercom button on her phone. Who knew? "Thayer," she said, "could you come into my office, please?"

"What now?" Thayer asked.

Mindy smiled. She'd been pleasantly surprised by Mr. Thayer Core, having discovered that he was not only a crackerjack assistant but a fellow trafficker in evil, paranoia, and bad thoughts. He reminded her of her very own self at twenty-five, and found his candor refreshing.

"I need another hard copy," she said. "In color."

In a few minutes, Thayer returned with a printout of the brochure for the house. Mindy clipped the brochure to Lola's two sex columns about James and placed a Post-it note on top on which she'd written, "FYI." She handed the stapled pages to Thayer. "Could you messenger this to my husband, please?"

Thayer flipped through the pages and, nodding in admiration, said, "That ought to do it."

"Thank you," Mindy said, shooing him away.

Thayer called the messenger service to pick up the package. He slipped the papers into a manila envelope and, as he did so, emitted a little laugh. He'd ridiculed Mindy Gooch for months, and while he still found her slightly ridiculous, he had to give the woman credit. She had balls.

A couple of hours later, Mindy called James. "Did you get my package?" she asked.

James murmured a terrified assent. "Well, I've been thinking about it," she continued. "And I want to buy that house. Immediately. I don't want to wait another day. I'm going to call the real estate agent now and make an offer."

"Great," James said, too scared to sound enthusiastic.

Mindy leaned back in her chair, curling the phone cord around her finger. "I can't wait to get started on the renovations. I've got all kinds of ideas. How's the new book coming, by the way? Are you making progress?"

In the penthouse apartment in One Fifth, Annalisa Rice studied the seating chart for the King David event, writing the numbers of various tables next to each name on the twenty-page guest list. It was, as usual, a tedious process, but someone had to do it, and now that she had replaced Connie Brewer as the chairman of the event, the duty fell to her. She suspected Connie hadn't wanted to give up her position, but with Sandy's trial coming up, the other members of the committee didn't think Connie's involvement was a good idea. Connie's presence would remind people of the scandal involving the Cross of Bloody Mary, and instead of covering the event, reporters would write about the Brewers instead.

The gala was in four days and was expected to be even more spectacular than the year before. Rod Stewart was performing, and Schiffer Diamond had agreed to host the event. After Billy's death, Annalisa and Schiffer had become close, at first finding solace in each other's company and then seeing their mutual sorrow blossom into an actual friendship. Being public figures, they found they had some things in common. Schiffer suggested Annalisa hire her publicist, Karen; meanwhile, Annalisa had introduced Schiffer to her crazy stylist, Norine. *Lady Superior* was on hiatus, and Schiffer would often pop upstairs in the late morning for coffee, which they'd take on Annalisa's terrace; sometimes Enid would join as well. Annalisa relished these moments. Enid was right—a co-op was like a family, and the antics of the other residents were always a source of gentle amusement. "Mindy Gooch finally took my advice and hired Thayer Core," Enid reported one morning. "So we won't have to worry about him anymore. James, meanwhile, is having an affair with Lola Fabrikant."

"That poor girl," Schiffer said.

"Mindy or Lola?" Annalisa asked.

"Both," Schiffer said.

"Poor Lola, nothing," Enid exclaimed. "That girl was a gold digger. Worse than Flossie Davis. All she wanted was to live in One Fifth and spend Philip's money."

"Don't you think you were a little cruel to her, Enid?" Schiffer asked.

"Absolutely not. One has to be firm with that kind of girl. She was sleeping with Thayer Core behind Philip's back and in Philip's bed. I suppose she's like a virus—she keeps coming back," Enid said.

"Why did she come back?" Annalisa asked.

"Sheer, misguided determination. But she won't get far. You'll see," Enid said.

Now, recalling this conversation, Annalisa found she couldn't blame Lola for wanting to live in One Fifth. She, like Enid and Schiffer, loved the building. The only problem was Paul. Having heard about Schiffer and Philip's engagement, he kept insisting she use her influence to get Philip and Enid to sell him their apartments, pointing out that Philip and Schiffer would need a bigger apartment, and wouldn't Enid want to move as well? No, Annalisa replied. The plan was that Schiffer and Enid were going to trade apartments, then Philip and Schiffer would combine the two thirteenth-floor apartments into one. Then Paul suggested *they* move to a bigger apartment, to something in the price range of forty million dollars. To this, she'd also objected. "It's too much, Paul," she said, wondering where his rabid desire for the bigger and better would end. They'd put the discussion aside when Paul briefly became obsessed with buying a plane—the new G6, which wouldn't be delivered for two years. Paul had put down a deposit of twenty million dollars but complained bitterly about the unfairness of life, because he was number fifteen on the list and not number one. His obsessions, Annalisa noted, were getting more and more out of control, and just the other day, he'd thrown a crystal vase at Maria because she'd failed to immediately inform him of the arrival of two fish. Each fish cost over a hundred thousand dollars, and had been specially shipped from Japan. But Maria hadn't known and had left the fish sitting in their containers for five critical hours, during which time they might have died. Maria quit, and Annalisa paid her two hundred thousand dollars—a year's salary—not to press charges against Paul. Annalisa hired two new housekeepers instead of one, which seemed to mollify Paul, who insisted the second housekeeper be on fish duty twenty-four hours a day. This was disturbing but paled in comparison to Paul's attitude toward Sam.

"He did it," Paul said one evening at dinner. "That little bastard. Sam Gooch."

"Don't be crazy," Annalisa said.

"I know he did it," Paul said.

"How?"

"He gave me a look. In the elevator."

"A thirteen-year-old boy gave you a look. And you know he did it," Annalisa said, exasperated.

"I'm having him followed."

Annalisa put down her fork. "Let it go," she said firmly.

"He cost me twenty-six million dollars."

"You ended up making a hundred million dollars that day anyway. What's twenty-six million compared to that?"

"Twenty-six percent," Paul replied.

Annalisa assumed Paul was exaggerating when he said he was having Sam followed, but a few nights later, as she was preparing for bed, she discovered Paul reading a detailed document that didn't appear to be the charts and graphs he normally perused before going to sleep. "What's that?" she demanded.

Paul looked up. "It's the report on Sam Gooch. From the private detective."

Annalisa snatched it out of his hands and began reading aloud. "'The suspect was at the basketball court on Sixth Avenue . . . Suspect attended field trip to the Museum of Science and Technology . . . Suspect went into 742 Park and remained inside for three hours, at which time suspect exited, taking the Lexington Avenue subway to Fourteenth Street . . .' Oh, Paul," she said. Disgusted, she ripped the report into pieces and threw it away.

"I wish you hadn't done that," Paul said when she returned to bed.

"I wish you hadn't, either," she said, and turned off the light.

Now, every time she thought about Paul, a knot formed in her stomach. There appeared to be an inverse relationship between the amount of money he made and his mental stability. The more money he made, the more unstable he became, and with Sandy Brewer absorbed in the preparations for his trial, there was no one to keep Paul in check.

Putting aside the seating chart, Annalisa went upstairs to change. The depositions for Sandy's upcoming trial had begun, and being among several people who had seen the cross, Annalisa and Paul were on the list. Paul had done his deposition the day before and, following the advice of his lawyer, claimed to have no recollection of seeing the cross, or of any discussions about it, or of Billy Litchfield's potential involvement. Indeed, he claimed to have no recollection of Billy Litchfield at all, other than a belief that Billy might have been an acquaintance of his wife's. Sandy Brewer had been at the deposition and was relieved by Paul's faulty memory. But Paul didn't know as much as Annalisa did, and to make matters worse, the lawyer had informed her that Connie Brewer would be at her deposition that afternoon. It would be the first time she'd seen Connie in months.

Annalisa selected a white gabardine pantsuit of which Billy would have approved. When she thought of him now, it was always with a slight bitterness. His death had been both pointless and unnecessary.

The deposition was held in a conference room in the offices of the Brewers' law firm. Sandy wasn't there, but Connie was sitting between two members of the Brewers' legal team. At the head of the table was the counsel for the state. Connie looked frightened and wan.

"Let's begin, Mrs. Rice," said the state counsel. He wore a misshapen suit and had boils on his skin. "Did you ever see the Cross of Bloody Mary?"

Annalisa looked over at Connie, who was staring down at her hands. "I don't know," Annalisa replied.

"What do you mean, you don't know?"

"Connie showed me a cross, yes. But I can't say if it was the Cross of Bloody Mary or not."

"How did she describe it?"

"She said it belonged to a queen. But it might have come from anywhere. I thought it was costume jewelry."

"Did you ever have a discussion with Billy Litchfield about the cross?"

"No, I did not," Annalisa said firmly, lying. Billy had died for the stupid cross. Wasn't that enough?

The questioning continued for another hour, and then Annalisa was dismissed. Connie walked with her to the elevator. "Thank you for doing this," Connie murmured.

"Oh, Connie," Annalisa said, and hugged her. "It's the least I can do. How are you? Can't we have lunch?"

"Maybe," Connie said hesitantly. "When all this is over."

"It'll be over soon. And everything will be okay."

"I don't know about that," Connie said. "The FCC has barred Sandy from trading because he's under investigation, so we have no money coming in. I've put our apartment on the market. The lawyers' fees are huge. Even if Sandy does get off, I'm not sure I want to live in New York anymore."

"I'm sorry," Annalisa said.

Connie shrugged. "It's just a place. I'm thinking we should move to a state where no one knows us. Like Montana."

That evening when Paul got home, Annalisa tried to tell him about her day. Going into his office, she found him standing before his giant aquarium, staring at his fish. "Connie says they're going to have to sell their apartment," she said.

"Really?" Paul said. "What do they want for it?"

She looked at him in astonishment. "I didn't ask. For some reason, it didn't seem appropriate."

"Maybe we could buy it," Paul said. "It's bigger than this place. And they're desperate, so we could probably get it for a good price. Real estate is going down. They'll have to sell quickly."

Annalisa stared at Paul, the knot in her stomach tightening in fear. "Paul," she said cautiously. "I don't want to move."

"Maybe not," Paul said, keeping his eyes on his fish. "But I'm the one with the money. Ultimately, it's my decision."

Annalisa stiffened. Moving slowly, as if Paul were unbalanced and could no longer be trusted to react like a normal person, she edged toward the door. She paused and said softly, "Whatever you say, Paul," quietly closing the heavy double doors behind her.

❖

The next morning, Lola Fabrikant woke at noon, groggy and slightly hungover. She wrenched herself out of bed, took a painkiller, then went into the tiny bathroom to examine her face. Despite the amount of alcohol she'd consumed the night before at a birthday party for a famous rapper, her skin looked as fresh as if she'd just returned from a spa. In the last couple of months, she'd learned that no matter what she put in her body, or what she subjected it to, the effects never showed on her face.

Unfortunately, the same couldn't be said of her apartment. The tiny bathroom was grimy, scattered with makeup and various creams and potions; a bra and panty set from La Perla was crumpled on the floor next to the toilet, where she'd tossed them as a reminder to hand-wash. But she never seemed to get around to domestic chores these days, and so her apartment was becoming, as

James Gooch said, a pigsty. "Find me a cleaning woman, then," she'd retorted, adding that the condition of her apartment didn't seem to prevent him from wanting to be there.

She stepped into the plastic-molded shower, which was so small she banged her elbow reaching up to shampoo her hair, reminding her again of how much she hated the place. Even Thayer Core had managed to get a bigger apartment in a better location, which he never ceased to point out. Ever since he'd taken the job with Mindy Gooch, Thayer had become a bore and was obsessed with getting ahead, even though he was only, as Lola pointed out, a glorified assistant, despite the fact that he had a business card claiming he was an associate. She still saw him but only late at night. After a long evening of clubbing, she'd realize she was going home to an empty apartment and, feeling unbearably lonely, would call him, insisting that he let her spend the night. He usually did but made her leave with him at eight-thirty in the morning, claiming he no longer trusted her alone in his apartment, and now that he had a decent place, he wanted to keep it that way.

Running conditioner through her hair, she bolstered herself with the thought that soon she, too, would have a larger apartment. That afternoon, she had an audition for a reality show. The *Sex and the City* movie had been a huge success, and now some producers wanted to do a reality-show version. They'd read her sex column and, contacting her through her Facebook page, asked her to audition, saying she'd be a perfect real-life Samantha. Lola agreed and couldn't imagine how she wouldn't get the part. For the past week, she'd been envisioning herself on the cover of *Star* magazine, like one of those girls from *The Hills*. She'd be more famous than Schiffer Diamond—and wouldn't that show Philip and Enid Merle? The first thing she'd do with her money would be to buy an apartment in One Fifth. Even if it was a tiny one-bedroom, it wouldn't matter. She'd haunt Philip and Enid and Schiffer Diamond for the rest of their lives.

The audition was at two, giving her plenty of time to buy a new outfit and get ready. Wrapping herself in a towel, she extracted a shoe box from under the bed and counted up her cash. It had taken her a couple of days to recover from Enid's attack on her in the newspaper, but she *had* recovered, and when she did, she'd pointed out to Marquee that she was now genuinely famous and he needed to pay her more money. She asked for five thousand dollars, which sent him into hysterics, but he agreed to up her payment to two thousand. So far, that had added up to eight thousand dollars; then there was the ten thousand Philip Oakland had given her and the two thousand dollars she got regularly from James Gooch. With James paying her rent and utilities, she'd been able to save twelve thousand dollars. Now she extracted three thousand dollars in hundred-dollar bills, which she planned to spend on something outrageous at Alexander McQueen.

Going into the boutique on Fourteenth Street, she immediately spotted a pair of suede over-the-thigh boots with buckles up the sides. As she tried them on, the saleswoman cooed about how only she could wear them, which was all Lola needed to make up her mind. She purchased the boots, which were two thousand dollars, and carried them home in an enormous box. She zipped up the boots and pulled on the Hervé Léger bandage dress she had, in fact, bought a few weeks ago. The effect was startling. "Gorgeous," Lola said aloud.

Full of brio, she cabbed it to the audition, although it was only seven blocks away in the offices of a well-known casting director. Going into the building, Lola found herself riding up in the elevator with a pack of eight other girls, who were obviously also going to audition. Lola assessed them and decided she was prettier and had nothing to worry about. When the elevator doors opened on the fifteenth floor, there were even more young women, in every shape and size, lined up along the wall in the hallway.

This had to be a mistake. The line snaked through a doorway and into a small waiting room. A girl walked by with a clipboard. Lola stopped her. "Excuse me," she said. "I'm Lola Fabrikant. I have an appointment for an audition at two."

"Sorry," the young woman said. "It's an open call. You have to wait in line."

"I don't wait in lines," Lola said. "I write a sex column. The producers contacted me personally."

"If you don't wait in line, you won't get to audition."

Lola huffed and puffed but went to the end of the line.

She was stuck on the line for two hours. Finally, after she inched through the hallway and into the waiting room, it was her turn. She went into a rehearsal room, where four people sat behind a long table. "Name?" one of them asked.

"Lola Fabrikant," she said, tossing her head.

"Do you have a photo and résumé?"

"I don't need one," Lola scoffed, surprised that they didn't seem to know who she was. "I have my own column online. My picture is on it every week."

She was asked to sit in a small chair. A man aimed a video camera at her while the producers began asking questions.

"Why did you come to New York?"

"I . . ." Lola opened her mouth and froze.

"Let's start again. Why did you come to New York?"

"Because . . ." Lola tried to continue but was stifled by all the possible explanations. Should she tell them about Windsor Pines and how she'd always thought she was destined for bigger things? Or was that too arrogant? Maybe she should start with Philip. Or how she had always seen herself as a character in *Sex and the City*. But that wasn't exactly true. Those women were old and she was young.

"Er . . . Lola?" someone asked.

"Yes?" she said.

"Can you answer the question?"

Lola reddened. "I came to New York," she began again stiffly, and then her mind went blank.

"Thank you," one of the producers said.

"What?" she asked, startled.

"You can go."

"Am I done?"

"Yes."

Lola stood up. "Is that it?"

"Yes, Lola. You're not what we're looking for, but thank you for coming in."

"But . . ."

"*Thank you.*"

Opening the door, she heard one of them call out, "Next."

In a state of confusion, Lola stepped into the elevator. What had just happened? Had she blown it? Wandering down Ninth Avenue toward her apartment, she felt numb, then angry, then full of grief, as if someone had just died. Climbing the worn steps to her apartment, she wondered if the person who had just died was her.

She flopped onto the unmade bed, staring at a large brown-rimmed water stain on the ceiling. She'd pinned her whole future on that audition—on getting the part. And now, two hours later, it was over. What was she supposed to do with her life now? Rolling over, she checked her e-mails. There was one from her mother, wishing her luck on the audition, and a text from James. James, she thought. At least she still had James. "Call me," he'd written.

She punched in his number. It was nearly five o'clock, meaning it was a little late to be calling, as his wife sometimes came home early, but Lola didn't care. "Hello?" James asked in a stage whisper.

"It's me. Lola."

"Can I call you right back?"

"Sure," Lola said. She hung up, rolled her eyes, and tossed the phone onto the bed. Then she began pacing, walking back and forth before the cheap full-length mirror she'd placed against one of the bare walls. She looked damn good—so what was wrong with those producers? Why hadn't they seen what she saw? She closed her eyes and shook her head, trying not to cry. New York wasn't fair. It just wasn't fair. She'd been in New York an entire year, and not one thing had worked out properly. Not Philip, or her "career," or even Thayer Core. Her phone rang—James. "What?" she said in annoyance. And then, remembering that James was one of her last meal tickets left at the moment, she lightened her tone. "Do you want to come over?" she asked.

James was outside in the Mews with Skippy, not daring to make this call in his own apartment. "I need to talk to you about that," he said tensely.

"So come over," Lola replied.

"I can't," he hissed, looking around to make sure he wasn't being overheard. "My wife found out. About us."

"What?" Lola shrieked.

"Take it easy," James said. "She found your sex column. And apparently, she read it."

"What's she going to do?" Lola asked with interest. If Mindy divorced James, it opened up new possibilities.

"I don't know," James whispered. "She hasn't said anything yet. But she will."

"What *did* she say?" Lola asked, growing irritated.

"She says we have to buy a house. In the country."

"So?" Lola shrugged. "You'll get divorced and she'll live in the country and you'll be in the city." And I will move in with you, she thought.

James hesitated. "It's not that simple. Mindy and I . . . we've been married for fifteen years. We have a son. If we got divorced, I'd have to give her half. Of everything. And I don't exactly want to do that. I've got another book to write, and I don't want to leave my son."

Lola cut him off. In a steely voice, she said, "What are you trying to say, James?"

"I don't think we can see each other anymore," James said in a rush.

Suddenly, Lola had had enough. "You and Philip Oakland," she screamed. "You're all the same. You're all a bunch of wimps. You *disgust* me, James. You *all* do."

Act
Five

In anticipation of the date for Sandy Brewer's trial, *The New York Times* did a series of stories about the Cross of Bloody Mary. A famous historian claimed the cross was the cause of not just one crime but, over the last four hundred years, several, including murder. A priest, guarding the treasure in eighteenth-century France, was bludgeoned to death in a routine robbery of the sacristy. The list of stolen items included four francs and a bedpan, as well as the cross. The robbers likely hadn't known what they had, and it was speculated that they sold it to a junk dealer. Nevertheless, from there the cross appeared to have ended up as part of the property of an ancient dowager duchess named Hermione Belvoir. When she died, the cross once again disappeared.

Now it was back, and Sandy Brewer was to be tried for art theft. If Billy had lived, Annalisa reminded herself, he probably would have taken the fall for the crime. But dead men couldn't talk, and the defense had never been able to find the mysterious wooden box left to Billy by Mrs. Houghton—or, for that matter, anything else connecting him to the crime. So the prosecution opened its jaws on Sandy Brewer. He tried to plea-bargain, offering to pay a huge fine of over ten million dollars, but in the months since the discovery of the cross, the stock market had dipped precipitously, the price of oil had surged, and regular people were losing their houses and retirement savings. A recession was just around the corner, if not already in the backyard. The people, claimed the DA's office, demanded the head of the grotesquely rich hedge-fund manager, who had not only made more than his share of money off the little people but had stolen another country's national treasure as well.

As a corollary, there was renewed interest in Mrs. Houghton. Her good works, personality, and motivations were examined in another big piece in the *Times*. In the seventies, when the Metropolitan Museum was nearly broke, Mrs. Houghton had single-handedly saved the venerable institution with a donation of ten million dollars. Nevertheless, the rumor that she had taken the Cross of Bloody Mary resurfaced. Several old coots who had known her were interviewed, including Enid, all of whom insisted that Mrs. Houghton was incapable of such an act. Someone remembered that the rumor was started by Flossie Davis, and the reporter tried to interview Flossie, but Enid intervened. Flossie was a very old lady with dementia, she said, and was easily agitated. An interview might literally kill her.

Taking advantage of the moment, Sotheby's held an auction of Mrs. Houghton's jewelry. Now deeply curious about the apartment's previous owner, Annalisa Rice attended the preview. She wasn't a great lover of jewelry, but as she stared down into the cases that contained Mrs. Houghton's extensive collection, she was overcome with emotion. A sentiment, perhaps, about the connective thread of tradition and how one woman's life might lead into another's. It was why mothers passed things on to their daughters, she supposed. There was a transfer of power in the transference of possessions. But mostly, Annalisa decided, it was about belonging, and about things being in their rightful place. Mrs. Houghton's jewelry belonged where it always had been, in the penthouse apartment in One Fifth. Bidding fiercely at the auction, she was able to buy twelve pieces. When she brought the jewelry home and placed it in the large velvet jewelry box on her bureau, she experienced an odd sensation, as if the apartment were nearly complete.

Now, on the evening of the King David gala, Annalisa Rice planned to wear Mrs. Houghton's jewels for the first time. Leaning in to the mirror in the vast marble bathroom, she clipped on a pair of diamond and pearl earrings and stood back to study the effect. The large pearls were a natural yellow, which complemented her auburn hair and gray eyes. This reminded her once again of Billy and how pleased he would have been with the apartment and with her. Adjusting the earrings, she was startled by Paul's voice.

"What are you thinking about?" he asked.

She looked up and found him standing in the doorway, staring at her. "Nothing," she replied quickly, then added, "What are you doing home? I thought you were going to meet me at the gala."

"I changed my mind," he said. "It's our big night. I thought we should go together."

"How nice."

"You don't sound happy."

"I am, Paul. I was just thinking about Billy Litchfield. That's all."

"Again?" Paul said.

"Yes, again," she repeated. "He was my friend. I'll probably always think about him."

"Why?" Paul said. "He's dead."

"Yes, he is," she replied sarcastically, walking past him into the master bedroom. "But if Sandy hadn't been caught, he would still be alive." She opened her closet. "Shouldn't you start getting ready?"

"What did Billy have to do with it?" Paul said. He took off his shoes and began removing his tie. "I want you to stop thinking about Billy Litchfield."

"Are you the thought police now, too?"

"It's time to move on," Paul said, unbuttoning his shirt.

"Billy sold Sandy the cross," Annalisa said. "Sandy must have told you."

Paul shrugged. "He didn't. But in every business maneuver, there's usually a random element that you don't foresee. I suppose Billy Litchfield was that element."

"What are you talking about now, Paul?" Annalisa said, coming out of the closet with a pair of strappy gold high-heeled shoes. "What business maneuver?" She opened the jewelry box and took out a platinum-and-diamond art deco bracelet that had also belonged to Mrs. Houghton.

"Sandy Brewer," Paul said. "If I hadn't taken him out, you wouldn't be standing here putting on Louise Houghton's jewelry."

Annalisa froze. "What do you mean?" she said, fumbling with the bracelet.

"Come on," Paul said. "You knew Sandy was probably going to fire me. Over that glitch. On the China deal. How was I supposed to know Billy Litchfield was involved with Sandy and the cross? But if you trace it back to the source, it's really Sam Gooch's fault. If Sam hadn't cut the wires, I wouldn't have had to do what I did."

"What did you do, Paul?" Annalisa asked softly.

"Sent that e-mail to the *Times* about the cross," Paul said, stretching his neck as he placed his bow tie around his collar. "Kids' stuff," he said, jerking the ends of the tie. "A simple game of dominoes. Knock one down and they all fall over."

"I thought Craig Akio sent the e-mail," Annalisa said, being careful to keep her tone even.

"Also kids' stuff," Paul said. "A fake e-mail account—anyone can do it." He slipped on his tuxedo jacket. "That was a stroke of brilliance—and luck. Best way to get rid of two people at once. Get them to take each other out."

"Goodness, Paul," Annalisa said, her voice trembling slightly. "Is no one safe around you?"

"Not in this building," he said, going into his closet. "I still need to figure out how to get Mindy Gooch and that bastard son of hers out of One Fifth. When they're gone, I plan to restore their apartment to its original glory—luggage space."

He slipped on his patent-leather dress shoes and held out his arm. "Are you ready?" he demanded, seeing her still standing there, fumbling with the bracelet. "Let me help you."

"No," she snapped, and took a step back from him. At that moment, the tab slipped into the hasp, and recovering herself, she held up her wrist. With a nervous little laugh, she said, "It's okay. I got it myself."

The first thing Annalisa did when taking over as head of the committee for the King David gala was to move the event to the newly refurbished Plaza. Getting out of the Town Car Annalisa had sent for her, Enid nodded in approval. With the restoration of the great hotel, perhaps New York was back, she thought, slowly walking up the red carpet that led to the grand entrance. There were paparazzi on either side, and hearing them call out her name, Enid paused briefly and nodded her coiffed head, getting a kick out of the fact that the paparazzi still wanted to take her picture. Just inside was a line of bagpipers. A young man in a black suit appeared and took her arm. "There you are, Ms. Merle," he said. "Annalisa Rice asked me to escort you."

"Thank you," Enid said. Philip had wanted to come with her, just like old times, but Enid had refused. She could make it perfectly well on her own, and besides, now that Philip was engaged, he should go with his fiancée. It was time to move on, she'd insisted. And so Philip and Schiffer had gone ahead to do press, which was as it should be.

The event was being held in the gold-and-white ballroom and was three flights up. Enid had always taken the stairs, which were marble and felt like part of a movie set, but the kindly young man led her to the elevator. Enid looked around the metal box and shook her head. "Somehow it doesn't have quite the same effect," she remarked.

"Excuse me?" the young man said.

"Never mind. It doesn't matter."

The elevator doors opened into the large foyer where the cocktail portion of these evenings was always held, and Enid felt better again, seeing that nothing had really changed. Then Annalisa Rice came forward and, kissing her on both cheeks, said, "I'm so glad you made it."

"I wouldn't have missed it, my dear," Enid said. "Your first big charity event. And the head of the committee. Are you giving a speech? The head of the committee always gives a speech."

"Yes. I wrote something this afternoon."

"Good girl," Enid said. "Are you nervous? You shouldn't be. You've met the president, remember?"

Annalisa took Enid's arm and walked her to the edge of the room. "Paul did something terrible. He just told me. It slipped out while we were getting dressed—"

Enid cut her off. "Whatever it is, you must forget it. Put it out of your mind. You must behave as if everything is wonderful, no matter what you're feeling. People expect it of you now."

"But—"

"Billy Litchfield would have told you the same thing," Enid said. Seeing the look of terror on Annalisa's face, Enid patted her arm reassuringly. "Rearrange your expression, my dear. That's better. Now go on. You have a roomful of people wanting to talk to you."

"Thank you, Enid," Annalisa said. She walked off, and Enid moved into the room. Several long tables covered in white cloth were set up along the walls, displaying the wares of a silent auction. Enid stopped in front of a large color photograph of an enormous yacht. Below was a description of the yacht, and a sign-up sheet on which bidders could write down their offer. "*The Impressor*," it read. "Two-hundred-and-fifty-foot super-yacht. Four master staterooms with king-size beds. Twelve staff members, including yoga and scuba-diving instructors. Available in July. Bidding starts at two hundred and fifty thousand a week."

Enid looked up and found Paul Rice by her side. "You should bid on this," Enid said.

Paul, for some reason, glared at her, although Enid thought this was probably his usual reaction to being greeted by relative strangers. "Really?" Paul said. "Why?"

"We all know about your aquarium, dear," Enid said. "You obviously like fish. There's a scuba-diving instructor on board. The ocean is like a giant aquarium, I suppose. Have you ever scuba-dived?"

"No," Paul said.

"I've heard it's very easy to learn," Enid said, and moved away.

The gong sounded for dinner. "Nini!" Philip exclaimed, having just found her in the crowd. "I've been looking for you all night. Where were you?"

"I was having a little chat with Paul Rice."

"Why on earth would you do that? Especially after all the trouble he's caused in the building."

"I like his wife," Enid declared. "Wouldn't it be lovely if something happened to Paul, and Annalisa ended up in the apartment without him?"

"Plotting a murder?" Philip asked, and laughed.

"Of course not, dear," Enid replied. "But it's happened before."

"Murder?" Philip said, shaking his head.

"No, dear," Enid replied. "Accidents."

Philip rolled his eyes and led her to the head table. They were seated with Annalisa and Paul, and Schiffer, of course, and a few other people whom Enid didn't know, but who appeared to be business associates of Paul's. Schiffer was seated next to Paul with Philip next to her, followed by Enid. "This is a wonderful event," Schiffer said to Paul, trying to make conversation.

"It's good for business. That's all," Paul replied.

Philip put his arm across Schiffer's back, touching the nape of her neck. Schiffer leaned toward him, and they kissed briefly. On the other side of the table, Annalisa watched with a pang of envy. She and Paul would never have that now, she thought. Standing up to give her speech, she wondered what they *would* have.

She made her way to the podium. On a monitor in front of her was a copy of her speech. Annalisa looked out at the sea of faces. Some people looked expectant, while others sat back in their chairs, looking smug. Well, why shouldn't they be smug? she thought. They were all rich. They had helicopters and planes and country houses. And art. Lots and lots of art. Just like her and Paul. She glanced over at him. He was drumming his fingers on the table as if he couldn't wait for the evening to be over.

She took a breath and, veering from her prepared remarks, said, "I'd like to dedicate this evening to Billy Litchfield."

Paul jerked his head up, but Annalisa went on, "Billy lived his life in the pursuit of art as opposed to money, which probably sounds like a horrifying idea to those of you in the financial world. But Billy knew the real value of art—that it wasn't in the price of a painting but in what art gave to the soul. Tonight all of your donations go to children who don't have the privilege of having art in their lives. But with the King David Foundation, we can change that."

Annalisa smiled, took a breath, and continued, "Last year we raised over twenty million dollars in pledges. Tonight we want to raise more. Who's willing to stand up and make the first pledge?"

"I will," said a man in the front. "Half a million dollars."

"A half million over here," said another.

"A million dollars," someone shouted.

"Two mil."

Not to be outdone, Paul stood up. "Five million dollars," he said.

Annalisa stared at him, her face impassive. Then she nodded, feeling a rush of excitement. The pledges continued. "Five million here, too!" exclaimed another man. In ten minutes, it was over. She'd raised thirty million dollars. Ah, she thought. So this was what it was all about.

Afterward, as she returned to her seat, Enid reached out and grabbed her wrist. Annalisa bent down to hear what she was saying. "Well done, my dear," Enid whispered. "Mrs. Houghton couldn't have done it better herself." Then she glanced over at Paul and, pulling Annalisa closer, said, "You're very much like her, my dear. But you must remember not to go too far."

Six weeks later, Annalisa Rice leaned over the railing of the super-yacht and watched as Paul and the onboard scuba instructor disappeared beneath the surface of the waters in the Great Barrier Reef. She turned around, and almost immediately, one of the twelve crew members was by her side. "Can I get you anything, Mrs. Rice? Iced tea, perhaps?"

"Iced tea would be lovely."

"What time would you like lunch?" the young woman asked.

"When Mr. Rice gets back. Around one."

"Will he be diving again this afternoon?"

"I hope not," Annalisa said. "He's not supposed to."

"No, ma'am." The girl nodded and went into the galley to get the tea.

Annalisa climbed the two flights of stairs to the top deck, where eight lounge chairs were arranged around a small pool. At one end was a covered cabana with more deck chairs; at the other end was a bar. Annalisa lay down on one of the deck chairs in the sun, tapping her fingers on the teak frame. She was bored. This was a terrible thought, especially for someone who was on a two-hundred-and-fifty-foot super-yacht. On the deck above, on the very top of the ship, was a helicopter, a speedboat, and an assortment of Jet Skis and other water toys, all of which she might employ for her pleasure. But she wasn't interested. She and Paul had been on the yacht for two weeks, and she was ready to get back to One Fifth, where she could at least be away from Paul during the day. Paul wouldn't consider it, though. He'd fallen in love with his new hobby—scuba diving—and refused to cut his vacation short. He'd spent two million dollars to get the yacht, he pointed out, outbidding another guest at the King David gala by a hundred thousand dollars, and he planned to get his money's worth. She couldn't argue with him about that, could she? Besides, he added, it was the old lady downstairs—what was her name? Enid something—who'd suggested that he bid on the yacht in the first place.

Annalisa found this strange, along with Enid's remark about going too far. Annalisa couldn't understand what Enid had meant, but she didn't doubt that Enid wanted Paul out of the building. Perhaps she figured a month without Paul Rice was better than nothing. But she needn't have worried. She would probably get her wish, since Paul kept talking about how he wanted to sell One Fifth as soon as they returned.

"The place is too small for us," he complained.

"We're only two people," Annalisa countered. "How much space do you need to take up in the world?"

"A lot," Paul said, not catching her sarcasm.

She'd smiled but, as was often her habit now, didn't respond. Ever since Paul had told her how he'd engineered Sandy Brewer's downfall and, consequently, Billy Litchfield's death, Annalisa had moved through her days on autopilot while trying to figure out what to do about Paul. She didn't know who he was anymore— and he was dangerous. And when she'd brought up the topic of divorce, Paul wouldn't hear of it.

"If you really want to move," she'd ventured one evening as he was feeding his fish, "perhaps you should. I could keep the apartment . . ."

"You mean like in a divorce?" Paul had asked softly.

"Well, yes, Paul. It happens these days."

"What makes you think I'd give you the apartment?" he'd said.

"I've done all the work on it."

"With my money," he'd scoffed.

"I did give up my career for you. I moved to New York."

"And it hasn't exactly been a hardship for you, has it?" Paul had replied. "I thought you loved it here. I thought you loved One Fifth. Although I don't understand why."

"That's not the point."

"You're right," Paul had said, turning away from his fish and going to stand by his desk. "It's not the point. What *is* the point is that divorce is out of the question. I've had some meetings with the Indian government. They may be interested in doing the same kind of deal as the Chinese. A divorce would be inconvenient right now."

"When would it be convenient?" she'd asked.

"I don't know." He hit a button on his computer. "On the other hand, as you've learned from the Billy Litchfield situation, death can be a much more practical solution. If Billy hadn't died, he'd probably be in jail. That would have been terrible. Who knows what happens to people like him in prison?"

So she had her answer. And since then she kept wondering if it was only a matter of time before Paul did her in as well. What imaginary slight would set him off? If she stayed with him, she'd be in a prison herself, always watching him, trying to gauge his mood, living in fear of the day when she couldn't mollify him.

Paul returned from scuba diving half an hour later, full of information about the various sea life he'd seen. At one o'clock, they sat down at opposite ends of a long table covered in crisp white linen and ate lobster and a citrus salad. "Are you going to dive this afternoon?" she asked.

"I'm thinking about it. There's an old wreck near here that I want to explore."

Two servers came in wearing gray uniforms and white gloves. They removed the plates and carefully laid out the silver for dessert. "Would you like more wine, ma'am?"

"No, thank you," Annalisa said. "I have a bit of a headache."

"It's the barometric pressure. It's changing. We may have some bad weather tomorrow."

"I'll have more wine," Paul said.

As the server filled his glass, Annalisa said, "I really wish you wouldn't dive this afternoon. You know it's dangerous to do more than two dives a day. Especially after you've been drinking."

"I've had less than two glasses," Paul said.

"It's enough," she protested.

Paul ignored her and defiantly took another sip of wine. "It's my vacation. I'll do as I please."

After lunch, Annalisa went to the stateroom to take a nap. While she was lying on the king-size bed, Paul came in to get changed. "I don't know," he said, yawning. "I might not dive after all."

"I'm glad you're being sensible," Annalisa said. "And you heard what the server said. The pressure's changing. You don't want to get caught in bad weather."

Paul looked out the stateroom window. "It's perfectly sunny," he said in his usual contrarian style. "If I don't go, it could be days before I have another chance."

As Paul was suiting up, the captain of the yacht came out, holding a dive table. "Mr. Rice," he said. "I need to remind you that this is your third deep dive today. You can't stay down for longer than thirty minutes total, and you'll need to include ten minutes to surface."

"I'm well aware of the time/nitrogen/oxygen ratio," Paul said. "I've been doing math since I was three." Holding the regulator over his face, he jumped in.

As Paul descended, weightless and with the familiar childlike joy he'd recently discovered in being unfettered by gravity, he was joined by the yacht's scuba instructor. The water was particularly clear in the Great Barrier Reef, even at eighty feet, and Paul had no trouble finding the wreck. The old ship was fascinating, and as Paul swam in and out of the hull, he was overcome by a feeling of pure happiness. This was why he couldn't stop diving, he told himself. Then Paul recalled something from the diving manual and tried to remind himself that the giddy feeling could be a sign of impending nitrogen narcosis, but he quickly dismissed it. Surely he had another five or ten minutes. The giddy feeling increased, and when Paul saw the scuba instructor motioning for him to go up, instead of following his instructions, Paul swam away. For the first time in his life, he thought irrationally, he was denying the rigid rules of the monstrous numbers that had dominated his life. He was free.

The scuba instructor swam after him, and what ensued next was an underwater tussle worthy of a James Bond movie. Eventually, the instructor won, twisting himself behind Paul's back and putting him in a choke hold. Slowly, they ascended to the surface, but it was too late. An air bubble had formed and lodged itself in Paul's spine; as he rose, the air bubble expanded rapidly. When Paul reached the surface, it exploded, ripping apart the nerves in his spine.

▼

"Yoo-hoo," Enid Merle said, shouting up to Annalisa Rice. Annalisa looked over the side of the terrace, where she was overseeing the erection of a large white tent, and spotted Enid waving in excitement. "A reporter at the paper just called me—Sandy Brewer has been convicted. He's going to jail."

"Come upstairs and tell me about it," Annalisa called to her below.

In a few minutes, Enid arrived on the terrace, panting slightly as she fanned the air in front of her face. "It's so hot. I can't believe how hot it is for September. They say it's going to be ninety degrees on Saturday. And we'll probably have a thunderstorm."

"We'll be fine," Annalisa said. "We have the tent and the whole apartment. I've cleared out most of Paul's things from the ballroom, so we'll have that space as well."

"How is Paul?" Enid asked, by rote.

"Exactly the same," Annalisa said. As she always did when she spoke about Paul, she lowered her voice and solemnly shook her head. "I saw him this morning."

"My dear, I don't know how you can bear it," Enid said.

"There's always the slight chance that he'll recover. They say miracles do occur."

"Then he could end up being another Stephen Hawking," Enid said reassuringly, patting Annalisa on the arm.

"I've decided to donate money to the facility for a wing in Paul's name. Even if Paul never comes out of the coma, it's possible, in ten years, someone with similar injuries will."

"It's the right thing to do, my dear," Enid said, nodding approvingly. "And you still go to see him every day. It's so admirable."

"It's only thirty minutes by helicopter," Annalisa said, moving into the cool of the apartment. "But tell me all about Sandy."

"Well," Enid said, taking a large breath equal to the importance of her news. "He's been sentenced to five years."

"That's terrible."

"The prosecutor wanted to make an example of him. He'll serve less time, I'm sure. Maybe two and a half years. Then he'll get out, and everyone will forget about it. They always do. What I don't understand is how Sandy Brewer got the cross in the first place."

"Don't you know?" Annalisa asked.

"No, my dear. I don't."

"Come with me," Annalisa said. "I have something to show you."

She led Enid upstairs to the master bedroom. There, on the top of her bureau, was the crude wooden box Mrs. Houghton had left Billy. "Do you recognize this?" Annalisa asked, opening the lid. She took out the jewelry she'd bought from Mrs. Houghton's estate and, pointing to the hinge at the back, held out the box to Enid. "It has a false bottom," she said.

"Oh my goodness," Enid said, taking the box and examining it. "So that's where she kept it." She handed the box back to Annalisa. "That would be very Louise. Hiding it in plain sight. How did you get the box, dear?"

"Schiffer gave it to me. After the King David gala. She was moved by what I said about Billy, and she insisted I take it."

"But how did she get it?"

Annalisa smiled. "You don't know that, either? She took it from Billy's apartment on the day she found him."

"Clever girl," Enid said. "I'm so happy she and Philip are marrying at last."

"Let's go upstairs," Annalisa said. "I want you to see the ballroom."

"Oh my dear, it's marvelous," Enid exclaimed, passing through the large double doors. The floor had been restored to its original black-and-white marble checkerboard, the aquarium was gone, and the marble mantelpiece was newly polished, revealing the intricate carvings telling the story of the goddess Athena. Luckily, Paul had never touched the ceiling, so the painting of sky and cherubs still remained. Scattered around the room were little tables and chairs and vases filled with sprays of white lilies and lilacs. The room smelled heavenly, and strolling to the fireplace, Enid examined the detailed carvings. "Wonderful," she said, nodding in approval. "You've done so much in such a short period of time."

"I'm very efficient," Annalisa replied. "And of course, I needed something to keep me busy. After Paul's accident. It still isn't appropriate to be seen out in public."

"Oh no, my dear," Enid said. "Not for another six months, at least. But a private affair in your own apartment is a different story. And it's only seventy-five people."

"I did invite Mindy and James Gooch. And Sam," Annalisa said. "I've decided that Mindy is like one of those old hags in a Grimms' fairy tale. If you don't invite her, she wreaks havoc."

"How true," Enid said in agreement. "And it's always wonderful to have children at a wedding." She looked around the room with pleasure. "Ah, the times we used to have in this ballroom. When Louise was alive and still young. Everyone wanted to be invited to those parties, and everyone came. From Jackie O to Nureyev. Princess Grace when she was still Grace Kelly. Even Queen Elizabeth came once. She had her own security detail. Handsome young men in bespoke suits."

"But now it turns out that Mrs. Houghton was a thief," Annalisa said, looking directly at Enid. "Or so it seems."

Enid stumbled a little, and Annalisa took her arm to steady her. "Are you okay?" she asked, leading Enid to a chair.

Enid patted her heart. "Yes, dear. It's the heat. Old people don't do well in the heat. That's why one is always hearing those terrible stories about old people who die in heat waves. Could I have some water, please?"

"Of course," Annalisa said. She pressed the button for the intercom. "Gerda? Could you please bring up some ice water for Ms. Merle?"

The water arrived right away, and Enid took a large gulp. "That's better. Now what were we talking about, dear?"

"The cross. And Mrs. Houghton."

Enid looked away. "You're so very much like her, dear. I saw it that night at the gala."

Annalisa laughed. "Are you saying I've got a precious antiquity hidden in the apartment?"

"No, dear," Enid said. "Mrs. Houghton wasn't a thief. She was other things, but pilfering antiquities from a museum was not her style."

Annalisa sat on the small gold ballroom chair next to Enid. "How did she get it, then?"

"You're awfully curious," Enid said.

"I'm interested."

"Some secrets are best left at that—as secrets."

"Billy Litchfield died because of it."

"Yes, my dear," Enid said, patting her hand. "And until just now, when you showed me the box, I never imagined that Billy Litchfield would have been involved in selling the cross. It wasn't in his character."

"He was desperate," Annalisa said. "His building was going co-op, and he didn't have the money to buy it. He was convinced he would have to leave New York."

"Ah, New York," Enid said, taking another sip of water. "New York has always been a difficult place. Ultimately, the city is bigger than all of us. I've lived here for over seventy years, and I've seen it happen again and again. The city moves on, but somehow the person does not, and they get run over in the process. That, I'm afraid, is what must have happened to Billy." Enid leaned back in her chair. "I'm tired, my dear," she said. "I'm getting old myself."

"No," Annalisa said. "It wasn't New York. Paul was responsible. Sandy Brewer showed him the cross one evening. Paul thought Sandy was going to fire him because he lost twenty-six million dollars on the morning of the Internet Debacle. So Paul sent an e-mail to the *Times*."

"Aha," Enid said. And then, with a wave, as if she wished to sweep it all away, added, "There you go. Everything always works out for the best."

"Does it?" Annalisa said. "I still need to know how Mrs. Houghton got the cross." She looked directly into Enid's eyes, her gaze not wavering. Louise, Enid remembered, could do that, too—stare a person down until she got exactly what she wanted. "Enid," she said softly. "You owe me."

"Do I?" Enid gave a little laugh. "I suppose I do. Otherwise, who knows what would have happened to the apartment? Very well, my dear. If you want the truth so much, you'll have it. Louise didn't take the cross from the Met. She took it from my step-mother, Flossie Davis. Flossie took the cross because she was silly and stupid and thought it was pretty. Louise saw her take it and made Flossie give it to her. Louise, I'm sure, intended to return it to the museum, but Flossie had a bit of dirt on Louise. She was quite sure that Louise killed her husband."

Annalisa stood up. "I thought you said he'd died from a staph infection."

Enid sighed. "That was how I remembered it. But after Billy died, I had a chat with Flossie. And then I went to the library. There's no doubt Randolf Houghton did return to One Fifth with some kind of infection. But the next day, he rapidly went downhill and died twelve hours later. The cause of death was never deter-mined conclusively—but that wasn't unusual in those days. They didn't have all the tests and medical equipment they do now. The assumption was that the infection had killed him. But Flossie never believed it. Apparently, one of the maids told Flossie that right before Randolf died, he lost his voice and couldn't speak. It's one of the symptoms of belladonna poisoning. Very old-fashioned."

"So Louise was a murderer?" Annalisa said.

"Mostly, Louise was a passionate gardener," Enid replied care-fully. "She once had a greenhouse on her terrace but took it down after Randolf died. Flossie insists she was growing belladonna. If she were, she would have needed a greenhouse to do it in. The plant can't survive in direct sunlight."

"Ah," Annalisa said, nodding. "And I suppose you wanted me to do the same thing to Paul."

"Absolutely not," Enid said. "Although it's crossed my mind that ultimately Randolf's death was for a good cause. Louise did so much for the city. But she never would have gotten away with it today. And of course, your husband is still alive. I know you wouldn't do anything to hurt him."

"No, I wouldn't," Annalisa said. "Paul is quite harmless now."

"That's good, dear," Enid said, standing up. "And now that you know everything, I really must run. Schiffer and I are going to switch apartments this week, and I must start packing."

"Of course," Annalisa said. She took Enid's arm and escorted her down the two flights of steps. At the front door, she paused. "There is still one thing you haven't told me," she said. "Why did Mrs. Houghton do it?"

Enid emitted a cackle. "Why do you think? Her husband wanted to sell the apartment." She paused. "Now you must tell me something as well. How did you do it?"

"I didn't," Annalisa said. "I only begged Paul not to go."

"Of course," Enid said. "And isn't that a typical man? They never listen."

An hour later, Philip found his aunt in her kitchen, precariously balanced on top of a stepstool, taking things out of the top shelf of a cabinet. "Nini," Philip said sharply, "what are you doing? The movers will pack everything up." He took her hand and helped her down. "It's the day before my wedding. What if you fell? What if you broke your hip?"

"What if I did?" she asked, affectionately patting his cheek. Thinking of Annalisa, she said, "It would all continue. It always does, one way or another."

⬥

The morning of Philip and Schiffer's wedding day was hazy and hot. The clouds were expected to burn off, but there might be thunderstorms later in the day. In the overheated kitchen of the Gooches' apartment, Mindy Gooch was going over a catalog for

Sub-Zero refrigerators with James. "I know it's only a country house, but we might as well get the best. We can afford it. And then we won't have to worry about replacing it for at least twenty years." She looked up at James and smiled. "In twenty years, we'll be in our mid-sixties. We'll have been married for almost forty years. Won't that be amazing?"

"Yes," James said with what had become a nearly permanent jumpiness. Mindy had yet to say a word about Lola, but she didn't have to. The fact that she'd messengered those columns was enough. They would never talk about it, James thought, the way they never talked about anything that was wrong in their marriage. Of course, Mindy didn't have to do that, either, not when she wrote about their marriage in her blog.

"What do you think?" Mindy asked now. "The forty- or the sixty-inch? I say sixty, even though it's three thousand dollars more. Sam will be having friends up to the country, and we'll need lots of room for food."

"Sounds great," James said.

"And did you get the toilet paper and paper towels?" Mindy asked.

"I did it yesterday. Didn't you notice?" James asked.

"Well, really, James," Mindy said, "I'm a little busy here. Renovating the house and turning my blog into a book. That reminds me, Sam is bringing his little girlfriend to the wedding. I've asked Thayer Core to come by here at two o'clock to pick Sam up, then they'll meet Dominique at Penn Station. She's coming in from Springfield, Massachusetts. You can thank me for that—I thought you'd probably want to spend the day undisturbed, so you can work on your new book."

"Thanks," James muttered.

"And one more thing," Mindy continued. "Dominique is Billy Litchfield's niece. Ironic, isn't it? But I suppose life is like that—it's a small world. Sam met her at tennis camp, and she's going to Miss Porter's in the fall. So don't say anything negative about Billy. She's very sensitive, I think. But we don't have to feel too sorry for her. Sam says she inherited three million dollars from Billy's estate. It was in a Swiss bank account. Who would have thought Billy had so much money?"

Later that day, around midafternoon, Lola Fabrikant awoke in Thayer Core's bed, exhausted. Thayer was out—probably running errands for that awful Mindy Gooch, she thought—and out of habit, Lola immediately turned her phone on. She was supposed to have Saturdays off, but her new boss, the crazy director Harold Dimmick, had already sent her six frantic e-mails, demanding that she come by his apartment so she could advise him on what to wear to Schiffer and Philip's wedding. For a moment, Lola considered ignoring the e-mails but thought better of it. Harold Dimmick had bizarre habits and barely spoke, but he was so crazy he had to pay his assistants a salary of eighty thousand dollars a year to get anyone to work for him. Lola needed both the job and the money, so she put up with Harold and the long hours. Harold had just started shooting an independent film and was working round the clock; consequently, she was as well.

She got up and went into the small bathroom, splashing water on her face. Looking in the mirror, she wondered once again what had happened to her life. After James had refused to see her, her fortunes had quickly taken another turn for the worse. Marquee had disappeared, along with his website, The Peephole, and while Lola was furious because he still owed her two thousand dollars, there wasn't a thing she could do. She'd tried living on her own for a bit, but her money had begun to run out quickly, and she'd had to beg Thayer to let her move in with him. She'd even tried looking for a regular job, but it turned out James had been right about the effects of writing a graphic sex column. Every potential employer seemed to know about it, and she couldn't even get an interview for an interview. Then she'd run into Schiffer Diamond during one of her stakeouts of One Fifth. Schiffer had spotted her standing by the bushes in front of Flossie Davis's building, and had crossed over to greet her. "Hey, kiddo," she said, as if they were actual friends and she hadn't stolen Philip away from her. "I've been wondering what happened to you. Enid said you were back in town."

Lola tried to remind herself of her hatred of Schiffer Diamond but was overwhelmed by Schiffer's persona—she was a movie star, after all, and if someone had to take Philip away, wasn't it better that it was Schiffer Diamond and not some other twenty-two-year-old like herself? So Lola found herself pouring out all her troubles, and Schiffer agreed to help her, saying it was the least she could do. Schiffer had arranged for her to meet Harold Dimmick, one of the directors on *Lady Superior*. Due to Schiffer's recommendation, Harold had hired her, but Lola no longer believed Schiffer had anything to do with it. Harold was such a freak, only someone as desperate as Lola would even consider the job.

"So you're finally up," Thayer said, coming into the apartment.

"I worked last night until three A.M., if you recall," Lola snapped. "Not everyone has a cushy nine-to-five job."

"Try nine-to-seven," Thayer said. "And the Gooch is making me work today. Have to take her kid to the train station to meet his girlfriend."

"Ugh," Lola said. "Why can't she go herself? It's her kid."

"She's working," Thayer said. "On her book."

"It's going to be horrible. I hope it's a flop."

"It'll probably be huge. She gets over a hundred thousand views on her blog."

"She could have at least gotten us invited to the wedding."

"You still don't get it, do you?" Thayer scoffed. "We're considered the help."

"Well," Lola said, insulted. "If you want to think about yourself that way, go ahead. I never will."

"What do you plan to do about it?" Thayer asked.

"I'm not going to just sit around and let things happen to me. And neither should you. Listen, Thayer," Lola said, going into the tiny kitchen and taking a bottle of VitaWater out of the mini refrigerator, "I'm not going to continue to live like this. I've been looking at ads for real estate. There's a tiny apartment in the basement of a building on Fifth Avenue, between Eleventh and Twelfth Streets, for four hundred thousand dollars. The building just went co-op."

"Ah," Thayer said. "Billy Litchfield's old building."

"With your hundred thousand a year and my eighty, that's ninety thousand a year after taxes. That's almost eight thousand a month. We ought to be able to afford a mortgage on that."

"Right," Thayer said. "And the apartment is probably the size of a shoe box."

"It was a storage room. But so what? It's on Fifth Avenue."

"And the next thing you know, you'll be wanting to get married," Thayer said.

"And?" Lola said. "It's not like you'll ever find anyone better than me."

"I'll think about it," he said. The skies outside the window were darkening, and there was a clap of thunder. "Storm's coming," Thayer said. "I'd better get moving."

While he was waiting in Penn Station with Sam, the clouds passed over without producing rain. Coming out of the station on Seventh Avenue with Dominique in tow—she was a scrawny kid with limp blond hair, Thayer noted—the air was so still and hot, it was almost nauseating. Thayer flagged down a taxi and urged his charges into the backseat. "I've never been to New York before. It's so crowded. And ugly," Dominique exclaimed.

"You haven't seen the good part yet. Don't worry, kid, it gets better," Thayer said. As the taxi edged down Fifth Avenue, another bank of thunderclouds rolled across lower Manhattan. The skies opened just as the taxi pulled up in front of One Fifth, pelting Thayer and Sam and Dominique with drops of rain the size of pennies.

"I'm soaked!" Dominique screamed, running into the building.

Roberto came forward with an umbrella—too late—and shook his head, laughing. "Bad weather out there, eh, Sam?"

Sam wiped the water off his face. "They said it was supposed to clear up later."

"I'm sure it will. Just in time for the wedding. Mrs. Rice always gets what she wants," Roberto said, and winked.

In honor of the occasion, the lobby was festooned with hundreds of fragrant white roses. Dominique looked around in wonder, taking in the uniformed doormen, the paneled walls, and the riot of flowers. "I can't believe you live here," she said, turning to Sam. "When I grow up, I'm going to live here, too."

Thayer smirked. "Good luck."

The scent of the flowers drifted into the Gooches' apartment, assaulting Mindy's nose as she sat poised in front of her computer. Inhaling deeply, she closed her eyes for a moment and sat back in her chair. When had it begun, she wondered, this mysterious and unfamiliar feeling of contentment? Was it when Annalisa Rice had returned to One Fifth without Paul? Or had it actually begun earlier, when she'd started writing her blog? Or had it perhaps sneaked up on her when she discovered James was having sex with Lola? God bless that little slut, Mindy thought. Thanks to Lola, she and James now had the perfect marriage. James didn't dare cross her. And she no longer had to worry about providing him with sex. Let him have his occasional tartlet on the side, she thought. She had everything she wanted.

Positioning her fingers above the keyboard, she typed: "The Joys of Not Having It All." She paused for a moment and, gathering her thoughts, began:

"Why shouldn't life be easier if it can be? Accept good fortune and damn the rest."

Acknowledgments

My thanks to Ellen Archer, Pamela Dorman, Sarah Landis, and Beth Gebhard at Voice; and to Charles Askegard, Calvin Bushnell, Sara Colleton, Duff, and Anne Hearst McInerney.